Barbara Morris

THE PROMISED JOURNEY

CACTUS RAIN
PUBLISHING

Arizona USA

The Promised Journey

Published by Cactus Rain Publishing, LLC
San Tan Valley, Arizona, USA
www.CactusRainPublishing.com

ISBN 978-1-947646-03-2

Cover Design by Cactus Rain Publishing, LLC
Photo Credit: Barbara Morris; Skye, Scotland, 2013

Published June 1, 2018
Published in the United States of America

Barbara Morris

THE PROMISED JOURNEY

To Brenda
My definitive Rose!
(Have I said that before?
Must be right, then!)
Lots of love
Barbara
xxx

DEDICATION

Dedicated to all of my family and friends in Langholm, Wooler, Skye and Canada. This one is for you!

ACKNOWLEDGMENTS

Apparently, writing is a lonely business, but stories do not get written without the help of some genuine and generous people. Thank you to the "usual crew" of trusted and willing friends for their thoughts, opinions, proofreading skills and time. It makes me less nervous to know you are covering my back.

Thank you to Joanne Wright at Canadian Surrogacy Options for sharing her knowledge and keeping me within the constraints of the timeline. It was a pleasure corresponding with you.

To Morag Kimm, ex-neighbour and long-time friend, thank you for translating my English into your first language, the beautiful Scots Gaelic. Long may it be spoken and sung!

A big shout-out to Canadian musicians, The Fugitives. Amazingly talented storytellers in melodic form who helped me focus and get this tale onto paper. Thank you.

To Nadine Laman and her wonderful team at Cactus Rain Publishing, thank you for the pointers, the suggestions and the polish. It is a joy being a part of this family.

Finally, to the incredible individuals from every aspect of my life who have, in recent years, shown me what real strength of character and real love is all about. It is greater than any fiction. Thank you.

《•》《•》《•》

OTHER WORKS BY BARBARA MORRIS

One Missed Step
Road Without Signposts

《•》《•》《•》

PART I
September 2003

August 2003

Northumberland, England

It was a pile of stones: red, misshapen and formed into a bowl which three or four adults could occupy cosily. Cosy in terms of proximity to each other, as it could rarely, even on the warmest summer's day, be described as a sun-trap. There was a perpetual wind, which sometimes dropped nicely to a breeze, but normally hovered around gusting level. However, this rarely detracted from the view, which made even the most irregular of walkers gaze out from under their gale-whipped hats and stand in awe, taking in the panorama. Winnie intended to sit in that very bowl, once she had recovered from the steep ascent.

To the north of the bowl lay the border with Scotland, the three peaks of the Eildon hills desperate to be recognised in the already undulating landscape. To the east the sea was a blue-grey horizon, broken up here and there by the distant hills; and to the southwest sat the leaden lump of Cheviot, which enticed all with promises of unparalleled views from its peak, but which squeezed every last ounce of energy from those who took on its flanks.

At just before seven on a dry August morning, Winnie took one more careful breath in, her gaze scanning the remainder of the skyline where Cheviot gave way to its curvier sister, Hedgehope. Winnie settled herself onto the side of the bowl, not trusting her new trainers to guide her safely over the rim. It was the freshest morning of the month so far, and the sun on the pan tiles of her own roof, yards and yards below her, only added to the warmth her aerobic efforts had produced. As far as she could see, green blended with yellow and beige vegetation, which in turn sat nicely with the powder blue sky. It was glorious and Winnie was content. Although it had not always been the case, this particular date in late August did not cause tears of regret, nor did it bring any sort of fear or grief into her heart. It was the only day of the year when she quietly allowed her mind to wander across the ocean, and she had learned to appreciate rather than dread it.

Winnie was sixty-two, but had never been fitter. She was a rambler and liked to golf and swim, but no amount of physical exercise could cure the crow's feet at her eyes or prevent her hair from shining silver. She ignored it all. Acknowledging the aging process was not advisable, for in Winnie's case it did not mean the loss of figure or faculties, but rather that the odds of her dream being realised were becoming longer and longer.

As the sheep below her greeted the morning with a chorus of appreciation, Winnie tutted at her use of the word dream. It implied that her wishes were permanently on her mind and, truthfully, this was not the case. A retired teacher, she counted many of her ex-pupils, who lived locally, as her friends and was rarely lonely. She also had a gentleman caller, who wanted nothing more than an intelligent conversation about gardening or the odd political debate, and which allowed her a certain jaunty reputation in town. She had no family nearby, but her house was to her satisfaction and her pension would "see her out." In the last year she even had a small tattoo positioned on her wrist so that it sat beneath her watch face and was noticed every morning and night as she rose or retired. She was more or less satisfied and did not dwell particularly on her dream.

Winnie scratched her wrist and removed the watch to gaze at the six figures inked there, plain black as if done with a calligraphy pen: 24.08.56. Forty-seven years ago to the day. Once, after a particularly animated discussion with Charlie on the virtues of hedge trimmers, her watch had flown from her wrist, and she had told him the date marked the day she had first set foot on British soil. It was only the tiniest of misdirection on her part and she felt no guilt.

The air tickled her nose as she took another breath. She was almost certain it was the pollen in the air which made it prickle and cause her eyes to drown in liquid. What else could it be on this day, when the sun warmed her bones and the sheep waited to greet her descent with their usual suspicion? She traced her thumb slowly over the figures, closed her eyes for a moment until she saw the wide streets and overhead wires of a different town, surrounded by different mountains. She smiled to herself, *one day*.

Hauling herself to her feet and shaking out her jogging trousers until they felt comfortable again, Winnie took one more circular scan of her familiar environment before turning her body back towards home. She had the whole of this day ahead of her, and she could indulge in as many memories as she felt happy with. It was a pleasant feeling, and as she headed downhill, she did not even feel the need to shade the sun from her grey eyes.

CHAPTER 1

Vancouver Island

Alasdair Wilder was what his mother termed "snotted under," and, as well as the permanent crust around the base of his nose, his six-year-old body was experiencing its first headache. He was not at all impressed by the heavy dullness which pressed its fists between his eyes and punched him every time he coughed. Colds were not funny, whether they were common or otherwise. He shifted beneath his duvet and lay flat on his back, groaning as the pressure in his head also shifted and settled. Even two days off school was too high a price to pay, and, at this rate, he would also be spending the weekend in bed. He was not happy.

As the sun began to give shape to his furniture and pictures, he could hear his dad moving across the floor above. It was definitely his dad; his stride was long and with a purpose. His mum tended to wander from corner to corner, with slower, indecisive steps, and Alasdair had often wondered what her morning routine must be which involved her covering every inch of the floor. Now his dad was running the shower to the heat he needed, and his parents were having a conversation that he could not hear. He closed his eyes against the murmurings and must have drifted off again, because when he next opened them, his room was brighter and his dad was standing, fully dressed, in the doorway.

"Hey, Al," grinned David Wilder, moving towards his son. "How's it going this morning?"

Alasdair swallowed before answering and instantly screwed up his face. "It hurts."

"What hurts, bud?" asked David, touching the patient's brow and lowering himself onto the bed.

"Everything."

"Everything?" David nodded his head. "Well, I know that feeling. Hey, did I ever tell you about the time I got this scar?"

Immediately Alasdair swiped at the one tear which had run under his chin and looked up at his father's face. David leaned closer and traced his finger across his upper cheek. There, beneath his green eyes and just above the area of grey-brown hair which permanently graced his jaw, was a line of paler, more prominent skin. The lines around David's eyes creased further as he watched his son's imagination begin to spark.

"Did you fall out of a tree? Oh, did somebody throw a snowball with a stone in it? That's a dangerous game," Alasdair announced, using his mother's words. Then his eyes opened wider still. "Did Uncle Neil punch you in the face?"

"Not on that occasion," stated David, holding up his hands and fearing that the actual cause was about to prove much less entertaining. "No, I fell down the riverbank at the back of the house. There was no fence there then and something must have cut me on the way down. Had to have stitches, the lot."

"And it hurt," nodded Alasdair, completely understanding.

"It did, but then so did the three breaks in my leg and then the pneumonia. Boy, that makes your chest so tight it hurts just to breathe. So, buddy, I know how you're feeling. But here's the good news: I got better and so will you. Mom will be here in a minute with some medicine."

As David rose, stretching his long body and reaching his hands towards the ceiling, Alasdair sat up.

"Can I see it again?"

David offered his face for inspection without protest and smiled as he watched the boy's serious investigation of a long-acknowledged flaw in the skin. Alasdair's miniature fingers touched the scar lightly, as if he feared there might still be pain to it. His blue eyes, exactly the same shape if not the same shade as his mother's, seemed to brighten in that moment. As always, when he studied any aspect of his son, David's utter pride contained a thin vein of anxiety. So far, their family unit had been blessed with unquestioning acceptance. Father, mother, son. At forty-nine years the boy's senior, David knew that the day was coming when this astonishing, innocent being would begin to frown and want to know more. Why were his friends' dads so much younger than his? Why did his dad look much older than his mum, when most parents looked about the same age? Why was his dad's hair starting to lose its original colour? Kate Wilder was forever reminding her husband that he must cease to visit these worries or risk giving birth to them prematurely, when there was plenty enough time for that.

Alasdair lay back, a frown appearing as if David had indeed summoned it.

"What does youth mean?" he asked, his eyes wandering over David's full head of greying hair.

"Youth?" David swallowed, his eyebrows lifting, "Erm, a young man, person, I suppose."

Alasdair's face remained puzzled. "When I asked Mom about your scar, she said you must have got it when you were a wild youth. I thought it might mean like the Scouts or something."

"She said that, did she?" responded David, smiling in spite of his surprise at Kate's unusual avoidance of the truth; he had a fleeting picture of a small group of boys in caps, comparing catapults and sporting "Wild Youth" sweatshirts.

"Yes," sniffed Alasdair, closing his eyes. "She must have been thinking of a different scar. Or somebody else."

"I guess so," David touched his son's head lightly. "I'll go chase up that medicine."

The mid-September sun still had the power to illuminate the kitchen without the need for electric light, and as David padded barefoot into the peaceful space, he could hear Kate moving around the pantry, her low humming the only sound on the air.

"How's he doing?" she cried, sensing David's presence before she emerged carrying the laundry basket. She threw a balled-up pair of socks in his general direction, but it banked hugely to his left and landed in the log basket by the range. At her husband's incredulous face, she sniggered and handed over another pair personally. "Well, it was my left hand, and, I am extremely handicapped at this moment in time."

As Kate moved from behind the basket, she automatically cradled her belly in her hands, then patted it affectionately. She was enormous. With just under a month left to carry, the child was already low in her pelvis. Kate looked almost comical as she moved awkwardly back to the sink to pick up the junior paracetamol.

"I do not waddle, and pity help anyone who uses that word a second time."

"He's still hot," David finally answered her question. "Like his mother."

"I'm not ..." began Kate, before rolling her eyes and halting on her way out of the door. She put her free hand against her side as her hip bone was no longer accessible and opened her eyes wide. "How can you sit there and say that with a straight face, when I look like a Weeble? When I've got so much excess ... everything ... that I accidentally knock things off surfaces as I pass? Dave, there are bits of me that might never see the light of day again, and you still think I'm hot? If I didn't know you better, I might think you were deranged."

David could no longer hold in his laughter, and, his feet finally clothed, he stood and held up his arms in an "I-don't-know-what-you-mean" gesture. But he knew exactly what he was doing. He knew that when he stood tall in front of her, his arms unfolded to expose his chest, Kate found it incredibly difficult to walk away from him. This was not arrogance on his part, but rather experience; invariably, she would end up tucked under his chin, even if it was for the shortest time, and it had been this way in all of the nine years they had been married. For some continually unfathomable yet heart-warming reason, Kate found contact with his body a physical necessity. It could be a hug or a hand on his face or something much more fundamental. Whatever shape it took, Kate's needs made each day worthwhile, and as she tried to accommodate her "handicap" against him, she sighed, vexed.

"Do you remember how I used to look?" she pouted, "like, when my face wasn't blown up like a beach ball and you could actually find my ribs? Do you think we'll ever visit that place again, you and I?"

David moved his chin over her scalp, his hands massaging her shoulders, testifying to them both that he was unable to fold his arms across her back, and felt her sigh again. Yet he was smiling-grinning, in fact– because he remembered her at this very stage when carrying Alasdair. In spite of the doubts and fears she had brought to the table daily, she had lost most of the weight within six months and had finally accepted that she was still worth his time. It had been so unlike her, the brutal self-criticism, but it had lasted only as long as the baby blues; and by the time Ally had started to sleep through the night, she was once again happy for David to lay his eyes on her without her cringing or covering the scar on her lower abdomen. They would surely visit that place again.

"Hey, Kit," he began, pushing her far enough away from him to fix her with his eyes, "do you remember how I used to look? Like, when my hair wasn't the colour of dirty silver and you could actually–"

"Oh, you can mock all you want." Kate screwed up her face, disengaging her bulk from him. "But you've never carried an extra ounce in your life, and believe me, it's going to take real effort this time to get half as flat a stomach as yours. I'm not as young as I was."

"That is true," allowed David, raising his voice to combat the increased volume of the kettle and to make sure Kate's ears heard his agreement as she began her laboured ascent to her son's room. "But you'll always be younger than me."

He was almost sure there was some mumbled retort, but was content to remain ignorant of it and instead tried to work out which stage of breakfast preparation Kate had reached. There were eggs cracked into a bowl that had yet to be beaten, and a loaf lay waiting to be sliced near the toaster. It was a start, and if it meant she spent more time with Ally, where she assumed nobody was assessing her body, he was happy enough to carry on with the chore. But there was more than his son's cold or his wife's anxieties on his mind as he switched on the radio.

Two days previously they had acknowledged the anniversary of the death of Kate's mother, Fiona. It had been ten years exactly since her passing, and it was easy to imagine that it was a much longer period, so much had changed and touched them all since then. But ten years it had been, and, within those ten years, David had regained his life. Fiona had never been a stranger in their house. She may not have visited them physically, but she had been spoken of and referred to on many ordinary days, and her name rarely caused anything but gentle smiles from the adults present. She was, after all, Alasdair's mysteriously beautiful, untouchable grandmother, and he had loved to hear tales of his mum's childhood on the Isle of Skye, where she had been raised by that particular lady and her sister Beth. The boy had visited the tiny bay Kate had called home only once as a sleeping infant, and so had yet to experience the sheep and seaweed and rock pools. One day, they would take him there and show him off to everyone who had ever been considered a friend.

But it was not the only anniversary which needed commemorating this month, for the following day was Kate's birthday, and David had the smallest kernel of an idea forming for the perfect gift. He had only a limited number of hours at his disposal, however, to organise it, and he needed to get to work where his telephone conversations would not be overheard by his wife.

On her eventual return downstairs, Kate found David already booted and under his hat, shoving a final piece of toast into his mouth. He shrugged on a padded jacket and pointed at the range. "Eggs in the warmer," he mumbled. "Ally okay?"

"He's asleep again. Sorry I missed breakfast," her face was melancholy, her eyes downcast. She seemed permanently out of sorts, the most ridiculously unimportant situations bringing frustration or sadness upon her.

"Hey, Kit, cheer up, honey," David flicked on the kettle as he laid his dirty plate by the sink. "You know I can't leave you when you look like that, and I really need to get going."

"But I'm fine," she assured, opening her eyes wide. "I just wanted to have breakfast with you. These mornings won't last much longer. Soon I'll either be sleeping or crying or leaking everywhere. I'll be a moody, dripping bag of blubber who won't be out of the house for ... well, I don't know."

David had folded his arms, without actually sighing, and stood waiting to see if she needed to add more words to her speech. Kate looked as if she might, but then sat down at the table instead and cupped her chin in her hands. She stared out at the sunlit trees, lost for a moment or two, and then hoisted herself back onto her feet and patted her belly.

"You still here?" she frowned at David, but with bright eyes, showing gratitude for his eternal patience.

"On my way."

"Oh!" Kate continued as she walked David to the door. "Ally is desperate to get back to school to tell his friends about your broken leg and pneumonia. He's very impressed. He's probably going to want to inspect the scene of the devastation, so we'd best get the fence lined with chicken wire, I think."

"For sure," he agreed, then turned. "Okay, I'll be in the office this morning. The rest of the time I'll have the mobile with me. Is yours fully charged?"

"Charging."

"Right, my love," he hooked his arm around her neck and kissed her as she liked to be kissed. "Have an easy day. Call me anytime– and do not get maudlin. It's your birthday tomorrow, and Al and I are looking forward to it. Be great if you could do the same."

As Kate closed the door, she moved to the window where she could watch his departure. Hormones. They were the most useless and damaging of all unseen entities. They caused nothing but problems. Indeed, each time Kate allowed herself to acknowledge them, they were always angry and were undoubtedly the cause of her unrest. What else did she have to be agitated or unsettled about? She was married to a man she could not physically be without; and, as busy as he was, there he stood, taking the time to appreciate the blue above the trees and to breathe in the freshest air. Her son was on the mend, would hopefully be up and about and looking for trouble within the next day or so, and she was only a month from greeting another tiny being. Yes, hormones had to be the problem. Hormones, or the fact that Skye was haunting her as it always did at this time of year.

"Do not get maudlin," she warned, repeating David's phrase, and making her way instead to the back door. The sun blinded her for a second, but was so welcome on her face that she did not falter in its glare and instead watched David reverse his truck past the house. She waved at him, and in turn, he raised his hand, his signature open-palmed salute to her. The least she could do for this man was to send him out on his daily grind with a smile. He wound down his window.

"Nice day for a walk if he fancies some air," he shouted above the engine, his eyes hidden by sunglasses. "Just be careful with my family."

"As ever," she cried back and disappeared indoors.

So, where to begin? Kate needed a challenge for the day, one which would occupy her mind so completely that she would forget the anxiety attached to Alasdair's high temperature and prevent her from sinking onto the window seat and pretending that the greens, blues and golds on view were Scottish and not Canadian. Such moments were dangerous, yet oddly appealing, which in turn made Kate doubt her own mind. Why did she assume that wallowing in nostalgia was a worthwhile pastime? It was not the giggly, wine-drenched recollections of friends which had the potential to crescendo into shouts of recognition and laughter. Kate's wistfulness was visited when she was alone, the type which made her heart shimmer and quake; and her memories of the first seventeen years of her life, both good and bad, were at their most cutting when the sun was shining and the air was sweet. Why should this be the way of it? The following day she would celebrate her twenty-seventh birthday with the people she needed and loved, and in the place she wanted to be. Kate shook herself one last time and turned towards the warming oven, just as the first long ring of the telephone interrupted her day.

《 • 》《 • 》《 • 》

By the time David had reached the timber yard, the sun seemed to have temporarily worn itself out and retired behind a bank of low clouds. As he jumped down from the truck, his sunglasses carelessly shoved back into the glove compartment, he was struck immediately by the silence. In all of the years he had worked here, as a young cutter through to owner/manager, he had never known it this quiet on a weekday. David stood, mesmerised, his keys cold in his fist. The skidder stood looking positively desolate, although the forwarders had obviously already left the site and there were four trucks by the shed. Men had clocked in and departed for their particular worksites, but still there should have been more movement, more activity in the air; the office windows were blank, no light shining from within. At that very moment, his foreman Rob appeared in the doorway, and David immediately raised his eyebrows in a frown.

"Am I really early or really late?"

Rob's face was pale and shiny as he pulled his raincoat onto his back. "I tried to catch you at home. There's been a crash on the highway. We think it might be Mike and Jay."

David took a step back. "No. How do you—"

"They haven't turned up yet," Rob replied hopelessly, as he climbed into the passenger seat of David's truck. "And Joe saw the accident. It was a red Nissan and ... the school bus."

"Ah, shit," cursed David, hustling himself behind the wheel once more. "How bad?"

"He said the Nissan was a mess, the side of the bus opened up."

David blanched. "No, no, no! Have you rung Charlotte?"

Rob rubbed his scalp as he leaned forward and clipped home his seatbelt. He nodded for David to do the same and instantly the man followed suit. "I was waiting to see what the state of play was."

"Okay," agreed David, swallowing a sudden bout of nausea. "Yes. There's no point in having half a story. Had the medics arrived when Joe saw it?"

"Just, and the highway patrol."

David pulled his truck up to the yard's exit and halted, just as Kate, behind the wheel of the family SUV, sped past.

"What the hell?" shouted David and hesitated for only a second before sounding the horn in one long, desperate blare of noise. "Shit, Kate, what are you doing?"

It took no longer than thirty seconds for the truck to cover the distance between it and the SUV, in spite of the maniacal speed at which Kate was driving. David continued to flash his lights at the vehicle in front of him, but could not bring himself to sound the horn again in case it spooked his wife into swerving.

"Easy, Dave. She's braking!"

David had already registered the red lights and switched his foot from accelerator to brake in as smooth a movement as his racing heart allowed. He was aware of sweat on his forehead and under his arms as he watched Kate ease the vehicle onto the verge; but now, ahead of them, just before the road bent away from their vision, all three of them were also aware of flashing lights and dust.

The scene seemed to check David's panic, and by the time he had run to the SUV and opened the door, his face showed more disbelief than exasperation. His chosen words were jettisoned immediately, however, when he saw the smears of dirt and tears on Kate's face. Her breathing was heavy as her hands remained clamped to the steering wheel and she did not move her face away from the horrific scene in front of her until he physically pried her hands open. She was shaking.

"Where do you think you're going?" David purposely kept his voice steady, as he pulled her around to face him. Her lip trembled, allowing a tiny moan to escape.

"It's the school bus, Dave."

"I know, honey. I know. Can you climb down?"

Kate was incapable of any movement whatsoever, and he was mystified as to how she had made it so far. The thought of her driving in this state brought a fresh film of sweat to his upper lip. He took her by her elbows and eased her awkward body down onto the grass. Immediately, her arms were around his neck and she was huddled against him as much as she was able. David closed his eyes for a moment or two, trying to remember how he had felt an hour earlier in their house in the woods when they had been hidden from the everyday world and its indiscriminate cruelty. Rob appeared at his side.

"Should I– ?" Rob began.

David nodded. "Take the truck and find out what you can. I need to get her home. Let me know, Rob. I want to see Charlotte either way."

"I'll call you," confirmed Rob and left them alone.

David looked around him. The SUV was more or less off the highway, but there was sure to be traffic of all sorts heading their way; and, indeed, Rob and the truck were flagged down a mere three hundred metres or so farther down the road. He could hear the wail of a second fire engine; this was not a good place to be. Kate slumped against him.

"Okay, Kit," he slid his arms around her and held her upright. She may have considered herself a bag of blubber, but at five foot six she was still a whole twelve inches shorter than him, and he was more than capable of lifting and carrying her over to where the tree-covered bank met the verge. "So who's with Al?"

"He was asleep," she snuffled into David's neck, offering nothing further.

David muttered under his breath before placing his wife gently on the wiry verge. "Just have a seat for a minute, until you feel a bit better, okay sweetheart?"

The needled soil was damp but not unpleasantly so, and Kate sat with her hands loose in her lap, her eyes gradually coming back into focus. David took the opportunity to call Rose, issue some semi-explanatory order regarding their son, and as he ended the call, found a more sheepish Kate looking up at him. It was as if she had only just realised he was there, and he was struck by a memory so clear that he started back from her face, surprising her. She misread his expression completely.

"When Rob said it might be Mike, I wanted to make sure you were okay," she croaked. "Then when he said it was the school bus ..."

"It's okay, Kitty," he sat and pulled her against his shoulder, still shaken by the recollection. "I'll take you home in a minute, before the road seizes up. Just take another few moments. Breathe, honey."

As Kate began to settle, the thump of her heart growing gentler against his side, David thought again of what he had seen. It was sheer horror and panic on a damp, grey face, and he had witnessed it only once before with Kate, ten years previously. He could see it all clearly, even whilst sitting on the edge of a busy road, amongst noise and chaos. The smell of distress in a dim room, the way the teenage Kate had viewed him as he had tried to reach out to her tortured mind. She had stood in front of him, wrapped in a blanket, her face the same pale mask of anxiety as she had finally accepted that he was not, as she had thought for the first seventeen years of her life, the father she had never met, and that her mother was not the innocent, wronged party she had assumed her to be. After those particular fear-drenched few days, Kate had begun to change and, in all the time they had spent together since, he had never witnessed that level of dread again until today.

《•》《•》《•》

Fiona had been David's reason to breathe, from the moment she had arrived from Scotland to work as a nanny until the day she had fled, disgraced and pregnant, taking his precious daughter Hazel away from him. It amazed him still that the human framework could be presented with a life worth living and somehow then survive the desolation of when that particular life was brutally removed without choice. Yet he had survived for more than seventeen years with no sight or sound of his wife, daughter or the "other" child; had trudged through years of work and occasional periods of incredulity, and had ended up asked to guide both Hazel and Kate through Fiona's painfully premature passing, which he had approached with equal amounts of gratitude and intrigue.

More to the point, Fiona had been everything to Kate– mother, father, friend– and for her to be presented with the knowledge of her mother's error, the knowledge that her conception had broken more than one life, without that precious person being there to explain it to her, had shown the world Kate's true character.

She had panicked, faltered, but eventually accepted, and perhaps that was because of her youth and upbringing, not in spite of it. She had consumed the whole situation and, somehow, spat out the irrelevancies and bitterness and finally, unbelievably even now, had taken him by the heart and forced him to believe in them as a viable prospect.

She had wanted him, she had fought her family for him, she had married him and given him a child. He owed her his life. He felt her take in a deep breath, and knew that it was time to take her home. As he shifted slightly, he found her looking straight at him, her face still pale but dry to the touch.

"I don't know why," she shook her head as she spoke. "I wasn't thinking. But Dave, any other day Al would have been on that bus and then ... I knew you would be on the scene. I needed you. You're the only one–"

"Come on. Let's get you back. I want to see the boy. I want you both safe."

CHAPTER 2

Vancouver Island

Had the school bus driver not ridden the verge after the front tyre blew, the vehicle would have avoided making contact with the concrete barrier lining the route. As it was, he merely clipped it with the wheel rims, but it was enough to deflect the vehicle onto the middle of the highway. There Mike and Jay, travelling to work on an ordinary Friday morning after picking up a set of windshield blades for the skidder, saw the shower of sparks as the connection was made, but did not have time to frown before the impact. Mike, fifty-eight years old and father of three, was crushed by the bus radiator grill before it pushed the Nissan against the barrier on their side of the road. From there, the car was sandwiched between bus and barrier and dragged by the momentum, which also cut open the side of the bus like a can of ham.

Nobody saw the actual destruction. The bus driver was out of his seat, struggling with the steering wheel, willing the weight of his charge to slow down and stop so that he could catch the red raw breath in his lungs. He saw only the road meandering wildly in his vision before dust and debris isolated him from even this.

Mike was dead, Jay unconscious and oblivious beside him. The seven young passengers heading to school hid themselves, huddled and screaming, while cold air rushed into their haven from the gash in the vehicle's metal skin. William Jeffrey was lucky. He had been thrown sideways across the aisle, in spite of his seatbelt, and only his school-bag, rather than his calf, was sliced in two. Through the screaming brakes and smoke that assaulted his senses in the next few seconds, William sat up and stared in awe at the fluttering explosion of paper and leather coming from where his bag had been. In the next moment he was knocked senseless by the seat in front of him. His friends merely howled and shouted, seeing nothing but the darkness behind their tightly shut eyelids.

The first witnesses came across the scene within two minutes of the collaboration of twisted metal sliding to a halt. Through the smoke, dust and violent colours it seemed as if the entire world was holding its breath, not daring to acknowledge what had taken place. But there was work to be done. The area needed to be isolated, protected, and tape and cones, flags and flares appeared from the inside of vehicles as if those involved had rehearsed this on a regular basis. Some drivers slowed to help; some knew they would be nothing but superfluous to the horrific situation and moved on to a place where they could nurse their shock and tell the tale to others. Joe Flanagan, running as close to late as was still excusable, had recognised the cherry red Nissan in spite of its injuries and, sickened to the stomach, had sped the remainder of the way to the timber yard. From there Rob had sent the men out as normal, unable to accept what was happening on the word of Joe alone. But there was no doubt left to entertain. Mike had been killed, his son Jay lay broken and bleeding in the back of an ambulance, and, with a pained heart, Rob had driven slowly back up to "The Edge." David had needed to be told.

The Edge had been named for obvious reasons. The river Cowichan cut a ravine through the family's woodland estate, and the house, which had stood for over eighty years, sat near to the edge of the steep bank for easy access to the water. It was a white clapboard house with obligatory verandah comprising three storeys and had been gradually updated since the time Kate had become the second Mrs David Wilder. There was a lawn to the front, its borders shrubbed and bushed, and outbuildings to the rear, which acted as a windshield in winter and a shade in the summer. It had always been viewed, happily by its occupants, as isolated, but in the last ten years David had put up five large chalets a few hundred yards through the woods from them. Peter's Lane, named after David's late father, had developed into a pleasant little community, the families who lived there all young and thriving, with the exception of Rose. Rose Wilder– mother to David, grandmother to Hazel and Alasdair and matriarch to all who lived in the woods. On an ordinary day she could be found sitting in contented comfort on the window seat of No. 3 Peter's Lane. But today she was sitting beside her son at the same kitchen table she had favoured her entire married life.

As she stared at her own hands, wondering how the arthritic fingers could possibly belong to someone who still considered themselves to be reasonably in their prime, David shifted his feet under the table and rubbed both eyes simultaneously. Today he looked older than he had any right to, and Rose touched his shoulder as she finally moved over to the range.

"I should go and see Charlotte," David's voice was so defeated it was barely audible.

"You know what, Davey boy? I think you'd be better off here. I can go. I want to see her and she'll appreciate the gesture. Let me go?"

David shrugged his shoulders, cracking his knuckles as if he needed the discomfort to remind him that he was still present. His jaw was set in a stiff line, his eyes blank, and honestly the last thing he wanted to do was to move from his seat. But his left leg was sleeping and he had a duty to make sure that Mike's wife was coping with the worst possible news. Still his body did not lever itself off the chair, and his leg tingled and ached.

"Mom?" The call came from the floor above him, a faint question, thick with cold. Finally, David scraped back his chair and ran his hand over his scalp.

"You're right, I guess," admitted David, then hesitated. "They were picking up blades, Rose, for me. I need to tell her ..."

"There will be plenty of time for that, son. I'll take my car."

David found Alasdair awake and collapsed against his pillow, but with considerably more colour in his cheeks. He managed a slight wave as his father sloped into the room, then hauled himself up the bed.

"Where's Mom? And why aren't you at work?"

David wandered over to the window, massaging his aching fingers. "She's having a nap. What's up?"

"It was quiet and I wondered what she was doing."

When David was forthcoming with no further information, Alasdair leaned over on his elbow and occupied himself with trying to work out if his dad was worried, sad or just "busy in his head." On rainy non-school days he had once or twice studied the man from the beanbag in the corner of his office. When his dad was busy in his head he would become totally silent, not even moving his lips while he concentrated. Then, immediately on completion of the task, he would lean back in his chair and snap his fingers, declaring to his son and the world in general that the crisis had passed. But today he did not have papers or maps in front of him, and Ally could think of no reason for him to be sad, so he must be worried.

"Why are you worried?"

"I'm not worried, Al. I'm a bit sad, is all."

Alasdair frowned. He was not usually wrong where his dad was concerned, and it wasn't like the man to keep his explanations to himself. Maybe it was something really, really bad.

"Is the baby okay?" the boy's voice seemed overly emphatic and David immediately felt guilty as well as sad and out of his depth. He nodded his head slowly, but seated himself near to his son's head immediately.

"Your mom is fine and so is the baby. Don't worry about them, Al, they're absolutely fine."

When David once more fell silent and looked down at his feet, Alasdair made use of the pause and announced his intention to use the bathroom. He climbed past his father's shoulder unchallenged, but as he stood upright for the first time in two full days, Alasdair's eyes rolled back in his head, and suddenly he was tottering to his left, completely unaware of the reasons behind this. Before David could do a thing, he had tipped forward and banged his head against the chest of drawers, sending his collection of ceramic dogs and a pile of inherited ancient comics spilling onto the floor.

"Whoa, son," cried David, grabbing him around the waist and lifting him up into his arms before he fell full length onto the floor. Technically, Alasdair was "too big to be carried;" he was all long limbs and bony torso. But on this occasion he was quite happy to lean his bruised forehead against his dad's shoulder until the pain eased and the room came back into focus.

"Owww," he moaned into David's shirt, more embarrassed than hurt. "Ow."

"Hey, take it easy there. Let me see?"

There was a tiny red mark above his left eyebrow, and that was all. He allowed David a total of three seconds of scrutiny before he began to squirm. "I need to go."

"Okay, bud, just take it a bit slower."

On the floor above, Kate was not napping. She was sitting on the edge of her still-pristinely made bed, perfectly calm and motionless. There had been more than one moment like this in her relatively young life when Kate had retreated inside her body, allowing it to freeze and to let her concentrate, concentrate on not thinking, on not imagining nor accepting the latest developments taking place around her. She was in no danger, her blood pressure was normal and her eyes clear, but she had not moved for over half an hour; her wrists ached from supporting her and her feet felt swollen as they dangled above the wooden floor. When eventually her brain insisted she come back into the room and acknowledge her stiff limbs, she also heard a bump and moan come from Ally's bedroom. Her eyes moved to the top of the stairs which lead from the open-plan bedroom down to the next floor, and finally she unlocked her joints and hobbled towards them. David was already on his way up, his brow furrowing as soon as he saw her face.

"Did we wake you?" he enquired, rubbing his jaw.

"Nope."

He gently stroked her face as he passed her by, heading towards his wardrobe, where he fished out a thin fleece and pulled it over his head. Kate watched his expression throughout this, marvelling at how one shocking incident could alter his appearance so completely. The lines around his eyes were more apparent, he continually chewed his bottom lip, giving him an unusually anxious look, and his shoulders were slumped. Immediately Kate straightened her own shoulders and cleared her throat.

"Is that Al up and about?" her voice was as cheerful as she could manage, for this was how they worked. They never sank to the bottom of the ocean at the same time, and whoever floundered first relied on the other to buoy them back to the surface. So far in their lives together they had managed it, and Kate was determined that this would not be the day the system failed. She could do it. She merely had her overactive imagination concerning her son and the school bus to contend with, but David had lost a friend. He nodded his answer, making his way back to the stairs. Kate reached out and took his elbow, guiding him back to her side. His eyes were painfully bleak. "Davey," Kate held his chin in her hands, "he can find his own way back to bed, I think."

David tried to lift his face and appear pragmatic, but instantly shook his head instead and allowed himself to look down at her with an honest expression. "Jay has to make it, Kit. He has to."

"There's hope, right? That's the main thing. Dave, remember that it was a chance thing. Are you going to agree with me on that?"

"But that's what is ripping my guts out. I didn't need those blades urgently, it just seemed an opportunity, when they live practically next door ..."

Kate let her hands slip from his chin down to his shoulders and pressed her forehead against his, but he was not ready to pardon himself so soon into the disaster. In spite of the burden of her shape, she could feel the man tense and unyielding, and it confused her. He never held back from her, ever. She had witnessed him upset, angry and weary countless times; and once, not so long ago, she had thrown a log at him, narrowly missing his head, when he had lost his temper at her refusal to stop splitting firewood. But following each of these occasions, he had allowed her to bring him out of it. Now she felt cold and unsure. Putting her arms around him had never seemed patronising before, but today it was beyond her courage. Biting her lip, Kate took a step away from him and watched as he walked towards the stairs.

"I need to see Charlotte," his voice was gruff and Kate could think of no reply. She did not even ask him to take care because, in the light of the day's events, she risked him frowning at her insensitivity. Instead, Kate followed him onto the staircase, her eyes fixed on his hair as he took the stairs two at a time, moving at a pace she could not match. He was actually running from her, and, in awe of this, she sat on top step and held her arms across her belly. The child inside her was beyond precious, but it had never felt more of a hindrance. David had not touched her intimately for what seemed an eternity, and in her present frame of mind, she wanted nothing more than to be tasting his warm skin, the two of them isolated from every other being. She sat motionless as she heard the door close and the truck pull away, but was finally forced to move again when the telephone rang.

21

"Hello?"

"Kate Wilder! How's the mother of my grandson this morning?"

"Oh hi, Neil. I'm ..." Kate paused, massaging her belly with her left hand. "Well, it's been a bit ... there was an accident this morning."

"What and who?" Neil Wilder's voice had suitably altered.

"Mom?" Alasdair had obviously heard her voice.

Kate suddenly felt overwhelmed and she lowered herself onto the bed, untwisting the cord of the phone as she did so. She felt it brush her bare shin and it caused a shudder. There was too much to contemplate, and so she simply pushed the words out of her mouth.

"Mike Forsyth was killed in a car crash with the school bus. Jay is in hospital."

As Neil conveyed his shocked dismay and Alasdair called out to her once more, Kate finally burst into tears. She did not wail or sob, she simply keened, not breathing until Neil's distraught voice from across the miles cut through her own misery. She heaved in air, simultaneously shaking the tears from her face in tiny diamond drops.

"Neil. Can you come over? Please? I can't ... I'm so fat and useless and I don't think I can help him. He won't let me near him and if I can't help, then—"

"Mo-om!"

"Oh, shit. Please, Dad, can you come?"

Neil replaced the phone on the wall of his workshop and stood completely motionless for a second, staring at the oily prints visible on the plastic of the receiver. It was one year and ninety-seven days since he had an alcoholic drink of any kind. He knew this because it was one year and eighty-seven days since Sophie and Abbie had moved in with them, ten days after he had downed half a bottle of Jack Daniels at the wake of their parents. It had been so easy to sip and then neck the burning bourbon, even after years of almost complete abstinence, because shock and grief had given him the excuse. But, although the taste and smell of the liquid did nothing for him, he recognised the dull hollowness which accompanied the self-imposed denial, and felt the need to tackle it in the usual way, with positive physical action. But Kate's words had arrested his limbs, and instead, he continued to stare at the loops and ridges of his own fingerprints. Never before, during the ten years he had known her, had Kate called him "Dad." Not once, and somehow he had managed to brush aside the astounding declaration in favour of trying to calm her down. But it had been a plea and he had recognised it. He was needed and he needed to act accordingly.

As he climbed the wooden external staircase which led from the workshop to the living space, Neil wiped his hands on an old rag and tucked it into the back pocket of his jeans. Before he had crossed the threshold, he was aware of a familiar tune being hammered out on Sophie's toy xylophone, and there she was, sitting cross-legged on the hearth rug, failing to impress the two Labradors with her musical prowess. Andie was nowhere in sight, and Abbie was all but dozing, in spite of the commotion, in the swing suspended from the main ceiling beam. At his appearance her thumb flew from her mouth, and instantly she began to bounce.

"Dad-dy! Coffee?"

In spite of his anxiety, Neil could not help but grin. The first time the three-year-old had imitated Andie's regular enquiry, they had laughed so loudly and made such a fuss that it was now how she habitually greeted his tall frame. She was struggling inside her contraption of straps and wooden bars, her arms alternating between reaching for help and trying to ease her body upwards unaided; but before he was halfway towards her, Neil was intercepted by Sophie. There was only thirteen months between the sisters, but Sophie with her long blonde hair tied loosely with a ribbon was infinitely less childish in body and soul than her sibling. Now she smiled and waved her hammer up at him.

"Hey, Dad?" she said, taking his hand. "I'm having a concert. Will you sing?"

Neil blew air out of his mouth and scratched at his jaw, edging his way past her to reach Abbie, whose restlessness was peaking in front of him. "A concert? Are people coming to watch?"

Sophie pondered this question. Abbie, finally released from her prison, crawled her way around Neil's flannel shirt until she was clamped to his back, giggling and grabbing his hair to steady herself. Sophie's face became decisive.

"Maybe Grandma Iris. Mom and Abbie. Maybe Ally and that lot from down there."

"Maybe," agreed Neil. "Where's Mom?"

"I think it's her needle time."

In their bedroom, Andie was sitting bare-legged on top of the duvet, her face as free from grief as Neil could remember it, and it sparked a flame of comfort inside him on this otherwise odd day. The empty insulin syringe lay on the bedside cabinet, and as she rubbed her thigh, Andie rearranged her long skirt so that it fell easily around her ankles.

Her diabetes, diagnosed only six years earlier, had brought them, unusually, nothing but hope and a dazzling horizon, where there had barely been a horizon before. For the subsequent tests had also cleared her of a possible hereditary affliction, one which had tainted her past and present, and this release had allowed them both to consider an alternative future: the adoption of Sophie and Abbie and the realisation that both Neil and she could finally appreciate, without guilt, the joy of sharing their lives with the next generation.

It had seemed even more appropriate, since Neil himself was an adoptee who had been brought into the fold of a warm, loving, and grateful family as a two-week-old infant. Without ever having considered the possibility of such an opportunity, he knew without a doubt that he wanted to balance the books and give back what had been given to him.

Andie smiled in his direction, but his strained features brought her instantly to her feet. "What is it? Who was on the phone?"

"Kate. How do you feel about me going over there?"

Andie picked up the syringe and dropped it into the bin. "If it's the baby, we'll all go. Do you really think those pair will let you go without them?"

Neil grabbed Andie's hand as she passed him. "It's not," he frowned. "Dave lost one of his team in a car accident this morning, and Kate is struggling."

"Oh ... no," Andie's eyes suddenly hooded with shock, her free hand flying to her mouth. Neil cringed against her reaction. "Who was it?"

"Mike Forsyth. He's worked there since Pete ... hell, he was there when I started as a cutter."

Andie moved away, releasing his hand, her inbuilt clock telling her that it was approaching the optimum length of time the girls could be out of her sight. At that very moment Abbie wandered in, her thumb back in her mouth. She was dragging the commandeered xylophone behind her, its metallic tinkle sounding each time it grazed the lip of a floorboard. It was like a slow drill in Neil's head, but he did nothing to stop her journey. As soon as she had both of their eyes on her, she settled herself on the floor and raised the hammer. Neil rubbed his chin.

"Okay," breathed Andie, looking at his face. It seemed inexplicable to her that the man was three years short of his fiftieth birthday, with only a few lines on his face to betray this fact. He dressed as he had always done, with no real regard for anything but comfort, and his hair had lost some of its brightness, settling instead on a dull, wheat colour. Yet he was still the same tall, blue-eyed loner who had claimed her heart on their second date, when they had sat next to each other on a bench by the sparkling water of the Lost Lagoon and had told each other their darkest secrets and fears. Twenty-two years later, those same secrets and fears were in the public domain, but the pair of them remained content to contain themselves within their closed unit, stretching it only in the last few years to include the members of his immediate family and two orphaned toddlers. But today, a crucial member of their group was floundering, and Neil was standing taller already.

"Okay," repeated Andie. "So what is Kate saying?"

Neil frowned and finally picked up Abbie from the floor, settling her in Andie's arms before she could begin to protest too much. "I'm pretty sure she's just tired, with a bit of panic thrown in maybe. She says she can't help him."

"And Rose isn't around?"

Neil shook his head. "She's gone to sit with Charlotte. Mike's wife. And ... Kate asked me to go."

Andie nodded her understanding as Abbie laid her forehead against her cheek.

"See what you can do. I've only the one appointment today. I'll take the girls over to Mom's. You can ring me if you're not coming home tonight."

Neil took a breath in and shook his head, tickling Abbie's chin until she could hardly breathe for laughing and squirming. "Oh, I'll be home, babe. As soon as Dave sees me there, he'll make it all right between them. To be fair, he'll be in a state. It's crap timing, is all."

Abbie squealed. "Daddy said a rude word!"

Andie placed her palm over Neil's mouth. "You weren't meant to hear it, so let's pretend it never happened, okay, Abbs?"

Abbie's eyes were huge, but she reached out and pulled Andie's hand away, forgiving Neil with her smile. "Okay."

Neil winked at her, marvelling again that he was being permitted to connect with and raise this beautiful child, when his only biological offspring had been removed and kept from him for so long. As he kissed both of them and turned to leave, Sophie was standing in the doorway, her arms folded, eyes creased.

"What word was it?" she enquired, sternly.

Andie clamped Abbie's mouth.

"Nothing that need concern you, miss."

"Agreed," answered Neil, moving her stubborn body aside as he left the room. "All you need to concern yourself with is taking care of that poisoned toe so the nursery is willing to take you back. The sooner the better."

Sophie followed his retreating figure, frowning. She watched him hunt through the biscuit barrel, shove a piece of flapjack into his mouth and throw his padded jacket around his shoulders. He was showing all the signs of leaving, and as far as she was concerned, this was not the plan for the coming day. He was supposed to be in charge when Andie went to her work appointment, and they had a concert to rehearse. But he was hunting for the keys to the truck and had not even offered her a piece of flapjack. Something was up.

"Where are you going? Can I come? I'll wrap up ..."

"You're going to Iris' for the day," said Neil, going through the pockets of his thicker coat. "Which, trust me, Soph, will be much better fun than where I'm going. Andie! Seen my keys?"

Sophie had seen his keys. They had at some point over the course of the previous evening slipped down the side of the sofa and were dangling between the wooden slats and the floor. She had seen them when her xylophone hammer had flown from her hand and rolled beneath the trailing tartan throw, so she knew exactly where they were. While Andie joined in the hunt, Sophie sank onto her knees and pushed her hand very slowly out of sight until her fingers closed around the heavy bunch. One firm tug and they were free in her small palm, but still she said nothing and shoved them beneath her crossed legs, watching her parents work as a team to solve the problem. Maybe if she sat there for long enough, the keys digging into her thigh, her dad would give up on his plan and stay here with them. Safe. Sound.

She watched as Neil retreated back into the bedroom and Andie checked all the key hooks, of which there were many. Even Abbie joined in, diving under the kitchen table and announcing that there were no keys to be found, in an annoyingly helpful voice. Sophie began to feel a sudden burden in her heart. She had the power to make everyone a little more contented in an instant, which was without a doubt the right thing to do, but they would be grateful for the shortest of times and the outcome would still be the same. Neil would hurry out of the door on some mission and they would be left behind, forgotten. She sat more firmly than ever, accepting the pressure of the unyielding objects as her penance. When Neil moved into her sight again, Sophie saw the frustration paining his face.

"How can they have disappeared?" he spat, running his fingers through his hair and pulling open drawers on the bureau.

Andie, without even raising her head from her search, soothed him with two words. "Easy, babe."

As he slammed home a drawer, he turned to her and fixed Andie with an expression Sophie had never witnessed before. His voice was low, "Kate called me Dad."

Andie froze instantly but there was no horror on her face, simply a wide-eyed surprise, and Sophie was immediately on her feet, the keys no longer a priority. What was this? She wandered over to where her parents were assessing each other and stood looking up at them until they were forced to be aware of her.

"What did Kate call you?"

"A bad word?" piped up Abbie, grinning as she grappled to her feet, suddenly interested.

Neil and Andie regarded each other for one more semi-private second, before he turned his body to Sophie. However, any words he may have been trying to form disappeared along with his frown as the bunch of keys came into his sight. Instead he spared his daughter one patient look and moved past her to retrieve them. Instantly, Sophie's eyes filled with tears.

"Daddy? What did she call you?"

The words did seem to make him hesitate, but Sophie needed him to stop. She watched as he moved around the room. He rubbed Abbie's hair and kissed Andie, but when he turned back to where she stood, one tear already burning her cheek, he took Sophie's hand and led her out onto the external landing, closing the door behind them.

There was a remnant of summer breeze at the top of the stairs, which caught Sophie's hair and threw it in her face. She picked up a strand and shoved it in her mouth, still clinging to Neil's hand as he squatted in front of her. She watched him from behind her veil of blonde, grateful that his face was still kind.

"Sophie, don't hide the keys, sweetheart. You know I'll be absolutely fine, right? I drive the truck all the time, all over the place."

"But," Sophie touched his rough chin, "you're supposed to look after us today, not drive anywhere."

Neil sighed and pulled her little body into his arms. "I know. It's unexpected and … well, these things happen sometimes, but I promise you I will be careful. I'll drive slowly and I'll be back tonight. How's that?"

He could feel her inhaling, could almost hear her trying to rationalise the situation in her own head, but this was not a new occurrence and, as ever, had to be faced by both of them. Neil felt her fingers twiddle with the hair at the back of his neck.

"There's no flood, is there?" her voice was a whisper in his ear.

"The road is bone dry."

"Okay," she consented at last, and kissed his cheek. "But, Dad, what did Kate call you?"

Neil straightened his spine in his usual awkward way and towered over her. For a further thoughtful moment he looked out over the woodshed roof, the scrub track and out into the dark green of the conifer plantation, before turning back to the still-curious face. Time was moving on, and this was a conversation for another time, another year.

"Hey. How old are you?"

"Four. And a bit."

"Right," agreed Neil, finally gathering all of her hair up and trying to tighten the ribbon around it. "When you are exactly eight years old, in fact on your eighth birthday, I'll tell you all about Kate and what she said. I'll tell you on that day and only on that day."

"But–"

"Nope, sweetheart. I have to go now. I'll tell you when you're eight, and I'll be back before you're asleep."

Sophie watched as he descended the stairs. She had played the only card she possessed, the honest fear card, and she had lost. Really, there was nothing else to do but to go back inside and wait for her dad to return.

Chapter 3

Vancouver Island

It was after three on that awful afternoon when David finally drove the truck back up the driveway to The Edge. Although he kept his speed reasonable to accommodate the camber of the road, gravel and dust still gave up the fight against the heavy vehicle and pelted the paintwork mercilessly. David felt his frown deepen even further as his eyes fell on the '98 GMC Sierra parked in front of the verandah steps; Neil had made an appearance, and David guessed that it was no coincidence that he had turned up on such a day. It was more than likely that Kate or indeed Rose had decided that this crisis was too much for David to carry alone, but this brought no gratitude from him. He fought down his resentment at the interference as he halted his truck behind Neil's.

He did not immediately exit his seat. Instead, David leaned his head forward against the steering wheel and closed his eyes. Two hours in the company of Charlotte as she had held the hand of her grown son, followed by thirty minutes or so of supporting his shocked workforce before letting them go early, had taken its toll. Only during the last five minutes of that stilted, disbelieving conference amongst his stricken crew had he allowed Kate to creep back into his mind.

He had perfected the ability to compartmentalise. It had been a necessity, a tool to keep him sane. He had loved Fiona, he had watched out for his younger brother from the moment he had been brought into their home, he had been astounded by the level of pride he had for his daughter, and he merely existed when Kate and Al were not by his side. Each of these people were kept in separate boxes in his heart, because allowing them to spill over into each other was confusing and diluted the feelings he had for each. It was not an ideal way to live, and family gatherings still had the potential to be awkward. But he never quite let the walls of these boxes cave in, preferring to live as much as possible within the confines belonging to Kate, Alasdair and him. He had been concentrating on how best to appease and comfort his wife for the whole of the journey home, yet here was Neil invading his space, no doubt providing a shoulder for Kate when he should have been the one to do just that. Well, who else was she going to call? And here was the man himself walking towards him. David set his jaw and climbed down from the truck. To his credit, Neil looked a little sheepish.

"So, Kate called you," stated David.

"Actually, Dave, I called her, just to see how she was getting on, and it all came spilling out. I couldn't just sit back ..."

"Is she okay?" interrupted David, leaning against the side of the vehicle.

"Well," Neil forced his voice to be patient, "she panicked, but she seems to have come round. She'll be glad you're home. What's the latest?"

David twisted his mouth to one side and shook his head. "Who knows? There may be spinal damage; Charlotte is possibly the strongest woman I've seen, but she ... she was grey. Shit, Neil, it was Mike. Mike."

Neil stood next to the man, replicating his stance, and staring across the lawn to the woods beyond. There was very little anybody could say in times like this, certainly nothing which made the situation more comprehensible. From nowhere on a sunny fall day, metal had connected with bone and tissue at speed, and metal had emerged the victor. The consequences were hideous.

The dead man's youngest was heading into the tenth grade, his daughter was on the point of travelling up to Whistler for the winter, and Jay was unconscious, oblivious to the passing of his own father. In what way would their lives differ from this moment on? How Charlotte was coping was beyond his imagination, and in response to all of this, David had merely spoken quietly to all concerned and offered to do what he could. It was nothing. It meant nothing, words strung together in sentences which had fallen on stunned, unresponsive ears; but it had passed the appropriate amount of time before everyone could go home and nurse their own private grief. And, here in his own home, David's only achievable goal had been postponed by the arrival of yet another unexpected complication in the shape of Kate's father.

Neil, in turn, had sat facing Kate as she slumped on the sofa, nursing the child moving inside her, and had listened as every doubt she had ever entertained about her age, her strength, her ability to support her husband had risen to the surface. He had barely recognised the girl who had adamantly announced to the world that she could support "her love" through any crisis.

It was the only time Neil had witnessed such faltering self-doubt from Kate, and it made her seem more like her mother than ever. Not for the first time did he thank God that he saw his own features in her face for, even this far down the road, he knew he would not have had the strength to sit beside her if she had been the image of Fiona.

All he had been able to do was to let her speak and to attempt to assure her that she was overreacting. David was in shock, he had a right to be, and his only crime had been to put a grieving family's needs before her sensitivities. It was not a reflection on their relationship and Kate had finally begun to accept this when the sound of David's truck had put an end to the conversation. Neil had left her lying there, and she had yet to make an appearance outside. David seemed in no rush to move to check on her.

"How are your lot?" the man finally asked, rubbing his left eye which was already bloodshot from previous abuse.

Neil stared at his boots. "Oh, they're doing fine. Sophie didn't want me to drive over, of course, thought I was going to spend the day safely by her side."

"Hmm," David shrugged. He felt unable to comment further on the child's continual fear of road travel, because it was totally rational, today as much as any other, for someone whose birth parents had gone on an ordinary car journey in heavy rain and never come home again.

"She wanted to know why Kate called me Dad," Neil added. "I told her I'd explain it when she was older. I guess there are a few unusual conversations ahead of us."

As Neil raised his head again he found David looking straight at him. He held his gaze and waited for his statement to cause a reaction.

The two men were almost the same height, Neil a couple of inches shorter, but today they were on a level with each other in all aspects. He may have been eight years younger than the tired, drained man before him, but they were equals, each with their own strengths and weaknesses; and these days, Neil was no longer frightened of the man.

"I didn't ... well ..." breathed David.

"She's never called me Dad before this morning," clarified Neil. "Took me by surprise, but I don't think she even realised she'd said it. She was desperate."

David closed his eyes. "Why? Why was she desperate? I needed to see Charlotte and that was all."

"Don't ask me what makes pregnant women act the way they do," Neil held up his hands. "But I'm not staying away if she needs–"

"Fair enough," interrupted David already heading towards the back door. "You coming back in for a while?"

Neil did not answer but followed his older brother, accepting that this was one of those days when they would merely tolerate each other's company rather than enjoy it. Glancing at his watch, he cringed at the passage of time, trying not to allow the image of Sophie's tiny frown take him over completely. But this was family life, right? Taking part, getting involved, helping whoever needed you at the most appropriate time.

As Neil watched David's boots scale the steps to the door, he caught himself remembering all the previous years when he and Andie had locked their doors on the world and sustained only themselves and their dogs. No absentee, illegitimate daughter, no wronged brother or neglected parents who had only ever offered him sanctuary, and no precious, abandoned youngsters who merely wanted him safe.

It had not been a better life, but it had been an infinitely simpler one. However, he had to get back to those innocents who needed him the most and let his brother and Kate remind each other that they were alive and together.

"I'd better go," he shouted, turning back towards his vehicle. "I don't want her worried for any longer than necessary."

He had reached the door of the Sierra before David answered him. "Be careful, then. Are you still coming over tomorrow night?"

"I wasn't sure there would be–"

"Davey, is that you?" the voice was Kate's, stronger and loaded with genuine hope; and Neil watched as the man visibly relaxed in front of him, allowing a more positive light into his green eyes. David shrugged at the man's words and leaned his arm on the door jamb, but in the next second had straightened his spine and looked once more in Neil's direction.

"Come over unless you hear different. We could all do with a distraction. And thanks."

Neil waved away his appreciation and climbed behind the wheel, mentally placing a tick in the Kate and David box. Within a good hour and a half, if traffic was accommodating, he would be able to tick the Sophie box and unwind in time for the evening routine of baths, stories and collapsing onto the sofa with Andie. It was an attractive enough prospect, and by the time he was halfway down the driveway, his mind was fully occupied with his own little family.

David found Kate sitting upright on the sofa. She had kicked off her sandals earlier, and they lay, pointing away from her, as if she had taken two steps and simply left them in her wake. Her feet were bare and her hands were hidden beneath her thighs. She followed his every move as he made his way past her footwear and knelt in front of her.

All he did was remove her hands from their hiding place and grip them in his. That was all it took for the tears to come again, and she had been so determined to be strong and capable in front of him.

"For God's sake," she wailed. "What is wrong with me? I've been waiting for you all afternoon, to show you how indispensable I am, and all I manage to do is blub like a child. You're here now and you don't need this."

"Kit," his voice was low, "what I need is you, whether you're crying or moaning or throwing pieces of split wood at my head. That's all I need and surely you know that."

Kate squeezed another tear onto her cheek, but could not prevent a smile from making an appearance. She shook her head at the memory. "God, Dave, have you any idea how close I came to braining you with that log? Thank God my aim is as appalling as it always was. Why do you put up with my carry on?"

"Because you're worth it, carry on and all," David said, hoping that those words would prove enough.

"Snap," replied Kate and wrapped the man's head in her arms. This time David's arms made sure that he cradled her as tightly as he could, and he remained there until the light-headedness and pure shock of the day had subsided. At one point he felt the unborn child move against his chest, and only then did he pull away and allow her to cup his rough chin in her hands and kiss him. "Now," she whispered, "are you okay? And what's the news from the hospital?"

《•》《•》《•》

For the first time in three days Alasdair had been allowed downstairs to eat dinner. He was under the impression that he had earned this privilege by following every order he had been issued with and had subsequently "recovered," but the truth was that both Kate and David had wanted his chatter at the table. It had been a reasonably cheery meal, with the boy only enquiring once if his dad was still sad, the remainder of the time being devoted to retelling the tale of David's freak accident years and years before. Alasdair's eyes had grown wider and his questions more complex as his dad fuelled his imagination. Even Kate had listened intently, although she had heard two or three versions of the event before. By eight o'clock he had exhausted both his list of questions and himself and had to be hoisted upstairs on David's back. Kate allowed a sigh of remembrance for a time when she had been light enough to be carried upstairs by the man, before waddling through to the sitting room and closing the curtains. By the time David joined her, there was a crystal glass glinting with a dark peaty liquid waiting for him.

"Hey, Dave?"

"He's sleeping, honey."

Kate propped herself onto one elbow from her position on the sofa and watched as he sank into his chair and cradled the heavy glass against his chest.

"Great. But that wasn't my question."

She waited until he took his eyes from the flames in the hearth and settled them on her own instead. He looked wiped out and she almost changed her mind, but his raised eyebrows meant that it was too late to fudge her way out of it.

"Something has always bugged me about your accident, and in all the times I've heard the story told, you've never really made it clear."

David's patient face took on an intrigued look. "You think about it often, then?"

"No, not that often, but you know, without the accident we wouldn't be here together. Hell, I wouldn't be here at all."

Kate stopped herself and swallowed, this concept completely astounding her as always. She shook her head against the wonder of it. "Back when this started, I used to think about it all the time, what Mum did, but I couldn't decide whether to hate her or thank God for her. I still have moments when I sweat it out, missing her, not believing she could do that to you or Neil. Sometimes I just want to blether away to her, to look into her eyes and find out exactly what was going on in her head. Most days I just sit back and content myself that I've got all this life."

As her words filled the space between them, David's features began to soften, and when she at last looked at him, he was smiling slightly. "So, what's preying on your mind? There was never a great deal to tell, really. The whole thing was down to my stupidity, anyway, nothing much to add to that."

Kate manoeuvred herself upright in one surprisingly fluid movement and tried to rearrange her not-so-loose top around her bump. She pushed her fringe out of her eyes and ran her tongue over her bottom lip.

"What on earth is it?" grinned David, recognising the amount of thought she had given this.

"Okay, here's the thing," Kate always used her hands when speaking, and David sipped his whisky as he watched her arms begin to conduct her words. "You've lost your footing on those rotten steps, but you've managed to dig your hands into the soil and you're more or less steady. I've seen the bank, it's not completely vertical; and, okay, there was a lot of ice and not many footholds, but you were stable and safe enough. So what made the difference? How did you go from that to falling thirty feet all of a sudden?"

"I guess ... I just slipped," shrugged David. "I should never have been anywhere near–"

"Do you remember the moment you knew you were going to fall? Was it terrifying?"

David frowned, genuinely surprised at the level of serious interest being shown at this particular time. "Kit, it was nearly twenty-eight years ago."

"And?"

"And ... I," he made a big play of searching the room for an answer, which Kate declined to help him find.

"You know, the longer you take," she pointed out, "the more I know you're keeping something back. Do you think that I haven't watched you for ten years, David Wilder? And yes, it could be because you're very easy on the eye, but mostly it's so that I can try to work out what's going on in that brain when you're being evasive. What amazes me is that you don't realise that I've got you sussed, matey, even if I do let you get away with it most of the time."

"Well, you're way off the mark, sweetheart. There's no mystery. The handrail couldn't take my weight, and naturally–"

"What handrail?"

"The steps had a handrail and I ended up hanging from it. Look, if I was sketchy on the details before, it's because I'm not so keen on admitting it was an idiotic thing to do. And then, of course, Fiona turned up and there I was, helpless and embarrassed. She did her usual "the-world-is-ending" routine, and Pete and Neil couldn't quite reach me in time. I tried to speak to her, to calm her down, and ended up losing my grip. Not my finest hour."

Kate's face took on an air of superiority. "Well, you see, in all the times I've heard about it, you've never once mentioned Mum. Didn't even know she was on the scene, and it looks like she was the cause of it all. Again."

David closed his eyes momentarily and then sat forward in his seat, holding his glass in both hands. He sighed and took a sip. "I didn't intentionally exclude her part in it," his voice bordered on the apologetic, and Kate began to regret her flippancy. "I guess it was always easier not to mention her name. Not everybody is as comfortable as we are with her, and it would make no sense to Al."

Kate felt her nose prickle, and if she had not been so burdened by bulk, she would have climbed onto the chair beside him and shown her complete understanding. Instead she merely sat slightly ashamed and tried to think of a retort to get the conversation back onto a lighter note.

"Sorry," she said quietly, "I'm an arse. For somebody who continually tries to guess the whole world's motives, I'm surprisingly rubbish at it."

"So maybe it's time to give up trying?" he suggested.

Kate nodded and sank back down into her supine position, staring first at the ceiling and then over at the fire, enjoying the heat on her face. It had been a day and a half, and not one that she wished to visit again in a hurry. But, her son was safe, her father had made her feel better in her own skin, and her husband was sitting here with her, breathing the same air and content to be doing just that. Perhaps it was indeed time to sit back and simply let the past rest easier in its grave.

The following day she would be another year older, and she should only think of her mother kindly on that particular day. The woman may have betrayed David, turning to his naive sibling for comfort on an incredibly significant night; but she had also brought a needy, vulnerable being into a world not altogether pleased to see it, and she had loved her just as much as she had her first child.

For a last few minutes, Kate allowed herself to marvel at her own existence. The unarguable truth was that if David had not been holed up in hospital, if Fiona had not been missing him so much that a night out with Neil had appeared attractive, and if their misdirected feelings had not gotten the better of the pair, then she would not be walking this earth, and the precious boy sleeping on the floor above her would never have called her "Mom."

《•》《•》《•》

When Kate next opened her eyes, the fire was low and the late-night news was barely keeping David awake. She stretched out her feet and wet her lips, watching his head nod every three or four seconds, but as she shifted to check on the actual time, her stomach gave a painful spasm and she grabbed the back of the sofa with her right hand.

"Kit?"

The room spun wildly before David's face appeared above hers. "Ooo Dave. It hurts."

"What is it? Is it—"

Kate did not hear the rest of the enquiry as she vomited onto her own chest and began to choke. She knew David was still speaking to her as he tried to sit her upright, but the sounds made no sense and her grip on the back of the sofa did nothing to aid her. She could not take a breath in quickly enough before she retched again, this time sideways onto the floor, and her feet slid from under her, connecting with the sofa's armrest. She began to panic, her eyes black and wide as she fought her own body for the right to move and breathe.

"Okay, okay," David's voice at last cut through her fear. "Easy. Easy, Kitty. I'm here, it's fine."

She felt his hands pull her forward quite forcefully and allow her feet at last to swing forward onto the rug. But there was a sticky mess beneath her bare soles ,and, as he hauled her up to stand, she knew it was not merely the contents of her stomach, but also the hot, thick liquid running from between her legs.

"Dave," she croaked. "What the hell?"

"First things first," he took her face between his palms and made her focus on him. "Listen. There's nothing to panic about. Let's just get rid of this mess and see what's happening."

Kate stood trembling as he removed her soiled top, wrapped it in a ball and dropped it away from them. Her legs were quaking and her teeth began to chatter as she wiped her face with the back of her hand and took hold of David's upper arm. He steadied her.

"Dave," her voice was slightly stronger, "it wasn't like this with Ally. Nothing like this. What if I've hurt her? What if this morning ..."

"Kate, you're not a doctor. Neither am I. So, I'm going to phone one. They'll tell us what to do, okay?"

"Okay." For once, Kate had no argument whatsoever at her disposal. "But I can't sit down, look at the mess I've made already."

"Hey, we were due a new sofa anyway. Just, please, stay calm. Take it easy."

As David left the room Kate tried to ignore the foul-smelling mush between her toes and instead concentrated on wrapping her arms around her extended stomach as she lowered herself back onto her seat. Her skin felt tighter than ever, and somewhere below the curve of her belly, something was cutting through flesh and leaving a burning trail behind it. Every movement it made found her biting her lip and screwing up her eyes.

With Alasdair, her waters had broken, and she had experienced a few medium contractions before they had decided that the safest course was a caesarean. It had been uncomfortable and worrying, but she had been in a hospital bed, hooked up to monitors with surgeons debating the best way forward. Here she was sitting in an ordinary room, leaking onto her own sofa, trying to come up with perfectly sensible reasons why this could hurt quite so much and why it was happening so soon. And the ache was ascending again. It was climbing over the top of the mountain of dense pain and descending instead as some sort of molten lava inside her.

Kate gasped as she desperately tried to knead away the agony with her hands.

"Da-vey!" she howled, completely devoid of control, "Come and stop this, please. Stop it hurting!"

She was aware of his silhouette against the bright hall light as he talked to whoever had answered the phone before another wave of nausea caused her eyes to close and her head to burrow itself into her knees. There were acres of dark red velvet behind her eyelids, and it would have been so easy to slide her whole body amongst its folds and surrender her soul, but there was another body running towards her.

"Mom?"

Kate snapped open her eyes and tried to look at her son from her crouched position.

"Alasdair!" she heard David cry out. "Leave her, son. Come away."

"But Dad, she ..."

So this is how I'm going to die, mused Kate, huddled in a ball, life draining away from me and I can't even kiss my son goodbye. What an uninspiring anti-climax to it all.

CHAPTER 4
Isle of Skye

"Stuart! Did you take your phone out of your overalls?"

"Hey Haze? That was Beth across the bay saying she couldn't make out the whole of that sentence and could you please shout it a bit louder!"

When her husband trailed his way through from their sitting room to the utility "cupboard" of their farm cottage, it was to find Hazel MacIntyre staring at the revolving drum of the washing machine, her hands resting on the worktop above it. She turned her head slowly at Stuart's approach and watched as he rolled the half-eaten sandwich into his other cheek and stopped in his tracks.

"You know," he pointed out, "you wouldn't need to ask that if you had checked the pockets yourself."

"Every single time!" Hazel threw her arms in the air. "It's the easiest thing in the world! When you put your overalls in the laundry, you put your phone on the dresser. That's three phones now, Stu. How many more?"

"So, if it's every single time, how come it's only three phones? Okay, okay, Haze. But you said you would check them as a backup, remember?"

"I know, I forgot," cried Hazel, storming past him, "and that's why I'm so bloody mad!"

As Stuart scratched his head of dark curls and watched Hazel take out her frustration on the dishes piled in the sink, he could feel the phone in his back pocket. It was on vibrate so as not to unduly disturb their day, but with his brother on holiday and only his dad at the farm, he liked to keep it to hand. As he took another bite into the thick bread he smiled at the way her ponytail swatted the air as she flounced and pondered the best time to put her mind at rest. It was just past twelve-thirty on Saturday, the 20th September, and Hazel, who had been patiently waiting until a decent hour to call her sister and wish her a happy birthday, was in a bad mood of her own creation. Not for the first time did Stuart commend himself for his patience as he watched her mutter and shake her head, but the sun was shining on the bay, he had nothing to do until the stock that evening, and his phone was not in the washing machine. Three positives made this a good day.

Stuart swallowed his food and pushed his hand into his back pocket as unobtrusively as he could manage. Hazel's frantic movements had begun to slow, her mutterings were becoming even less audible, and the slight shift to relative peace was like a green light in his brain. She had suffered enough, time to ease her pain and slot him straight back into her good books. There were only a couple of inches between them in height, and he rested his chin on her shoulder comfortably and looked at their shared view from the kitchen window, awaiting some sort of reaction. Thankfully she didn't actually squirm away from him.

"You hadn't even taken the plastic film off the screen," she sighed. "This has got to be the shortest lifespan yet."

"Hey Haze," he replied, "look at this day. We could bike to Sligachan, have a pint and be back in time for you to call Kate. How does that sound? You could lead the way, if you wanted to. See if we could make the whole journey this time without breaking any bones."

As Hazel stacked the last dish and emptied the bowl, she looked out at the brightness. Her habit of automatically coming up with an objection to any idea of Stuart's was beaten into the background by the thought of cycling in the sun, the waters of Loch Sligachan twinkling beside them as they passed their time together. Top that off with a glass of lager, watching walkers hoisting rucksacks onto their backs to take advantage of the weather, whilst smugly acknowledging that you would be resident on every sunny day, and you had your bonus. Plus, she needed the exercise and liked to see Stuart's legs in shorts. She turned to face him, and her husband mirrored the beginnings of the smile at the edges of her mouth. But as she spoke, her shoulders had already begun to sag.

"How's your dad going to get in touch? We said we'd be around as long as Bruce was away, and now, no mobile."

"And that's your only objection?"

Hazel pouted. "Well, it's a pretty reasonable one."

With a magician's sleight of hand, Stuart produced his mobile and grinned as she shrieked, first in glee and then at him for being "possibly the most God-forsakenly annoying man that walked the earth." He took it as a compliment and slid the phone into the pocket of her jeans.

"Tell you what, you look after it for the day," he stated. "Too much responsibility to lay at my door."

"Okay, I'll take the phone, you take your wallet. What a team. Are you ready to go now?" Hazel was hunting the dry laundry for her cycling shorts and her gloves. Even on a sunny day her fingers tended to be white and lifeless by the time they had gripped handlebars for more than a mile, and gloves were as essential to her as her helmet.

"I'll check the tyres first," Stuart called and exited the door.

As Hazel clipped her helmet straps neatly under her chin, she allowed herself a tiny moment of assessment in the mirror. Her face was tanned and her eyes brown, a reasonably attractive combination; and with the addition of the sky-blue headgear, she thought she could probably pass for someone still in their mid-twenties. Today she and Stuart might even appear like athletic tourists to the general public. She wondered what the chances were of her persuading him to speak with an Italian accent for the duration of the cycle.

He looked swarthy enough and she knew the odd word, courtesy of *Gregory's Girl*; but it was almost bound to end in tears, and Hazel could almost guarantee that the first people they met would want to know which part of Italia they were from. Best just to be Hazel and Stuart from Camastianavaig, married and in their thirties. "Only just in their thirties," she reminded the face in front of her and moved away, "Bella, bella."

It was turning into a remarkable day, the kind where every detail remained ultra-defined on recollection. The Braes road took a little longer to cover than usual due to a flock of sheep in no particular hurry, followed by a protracted chat with some cyclists heading back to Portree. But by Peinchorran, Hazel was nicely geared up for the almost impassable areas of path along Loch Sligachan, and there were the Black Cuillins nestling just behind Glamaig.

The mountains were indeed black in the glare of the afternoon and made the hills in the foreground a deep blue near their summits, descending through to an olive green. The row of houses at Sconser made a nice neat border at the base of these hills, but she could barely look at them as the first section of path seemed designed to kill rather than to encourage.

In spite of the amount of concentration required, Hazel could not stop marvelling at the sights and declared that she had not experienced clarity like this for years. The loch showed barely a ripple until it lapped the shore and the sky was producing only tiny wisps of white safely to the south of them. She dared not even look back to gauge Stuart's reaction, as it surely would have resulted in her being catapulted from her cycle and deposited in a winded, skinned pile amid the sheep droppings and rocks. Instead she slowed down even more and held her head firmly against the breeze which definitely held the first fragrance of the season's turn. Still she grinned.

Her sister Kate had spent most of her life adoring September, the month of her birth. She had always seemed to measure each new year from then rather than January, stating that the air always smelled brand-new, and that the light sparkled clearer and brighter than at any other time. Hazel had reacted to these thoughts as she did to most of Kate's odd musings, by filing them away and embarrassing her with the recollections at a later date.

Today Kate would have loved the perfumes of the water, the colours of the peaks and the fear of the unknown terrain her bike wheels juddered over. It would have been a perfect Skye birthday. But she was far away, probably sound asleep in her big bed as the Canadian dawn began to consider waking itself and stretching around her.

Kate had yet to acknowledge her big day, and Hazel's smile faltered slightly. She missed her, just as she missed their mum; but at the merest hint that the moment's pure joy might turn into a nugget of sadness, she strangled those feelings and forced herself to think of Kate's other peculiar theories: theories which made Hazel look at her through incredulous eyes and which Kate seemed incapable of keeping to herself.

"What d'you mean, they're male?"

"Of course they're male– and most of them are as arrogant as sin."

"Mum? Kate reckons all even numbers are male and odd numbers are female. Have you any idea what she's actually trying to say?"

"I'm saying, even numbers are hard, obnoxious, a bit full of themselves. Especially ten. I mean, what's so great about being ten? Okay, you're at the end of a sequence, but so what? Eight, too, really high-handed. Odd numbers are lovely. Round and soft and quite shy, so female obviously. Except five. I'm not sure which side of the fence five is on."

"Mum! You've got to hear this complete insanity ..."

Stuart, as easygoing and gorgeous as he was, had no opinion whatsoever on the personality of numbers. He did not view the colour red as annoying, blue as unconventional, or yellow as insipid, and ginger biscuits were not the "product of a twisted mind."

Stuart did, however, bring her a cup of tea in bed every single morning in life before he headed out onto the hill and shouted hello each time he crossed the threshold of their home. He didn't have to nip her brain or tickle her thoughts to make her feel she was part of something special, he just needed to keep coming home and loving her company.

That was more than enough for Hazel; and today, as the first few tents appeared and the ground became flatter ahead of them, he was beginning to creep up on her, whooping as three gulls squawked up in front of them. They had negotiated the water pouring from the mountainside by dismounting, but as they pulled away from it, Stuart's front wheel sat dangerously close to her right leg.

"It's a race then?" shouted Hazel.

"If that's what you—"

Hazel knew better than to wait for confirmation. If she had any chance of staying ahead of her husband, she needed to take him by surprise, and she had changed gears and was bouncing her mountain bike through the gravel and grass before he had a chance to finish his sentence. Danger was forgotten by both of them in the quest to be first to the campsite, as were all other thoughts of Hazel's. There would be time later, when she had spoken to both Kate and David, to wonder for the millionth time if she truly accepted that particular relationship.

By the time the bikes were stacked against the back of the hotel and cold glasses were resting in front of them on the picnic table, Hazel's face was fading from magenta to a delicate coral pink in shade. They sat and smirked at the flattened state of each other's hair, but both were enjoying the act of breathing steadily too much to actually speak. Instead, Hazel undid her ponytail and shook her head violently until most of her hair had fluffed up. As she reached forward to her glass for a second time, Stuart pointed to her skinny forearm, frowning.

"You're bleeding there, Haze."

There was indeed a deep scratch from just above her tiny wrist as far as her elbow.

"Wow," she grimaced. "Don't know how. It doesn't hurt."

Stuart looked around him. "Well, if that's the only injury, I think we can chalk this up as our first true Loch Sligachan success. It's been a long time coming."

"I'll drink to that."

Stuart nodded, sipping his lager, and watched as Hazel dampened her glove-clad index finger and rubbed at the narrow streak of scarlet on her arm. The sun had dried the blood, and by the time she had succeeded in cleaning the worst of it from her tanned skin, she had created instead an area of pink irritation. Without saying a word, she moved her cold glass up and down her arm to combat the ache. Stuart made a point of focussing on the people at the adjacent picnic table while she did this, and she appreciated the gesture; Hazel hated a fuss, even if the person fussing was her husband.

"Man, that's a warm sun," stated Stuart, rubbing his shoulders, and in response, Hazel stretched her arms out in front of her and laid her head on the table. "Maybe we should head back by the main road. Or we could have more than one pint and get Kenny to pick us up later?"

"Not a bad idea," she declared and let out a contented sigh. The rough, wooden slats smelled faintly of vinegar and the very early stages of decay; but from her position, head on its side, Hazel was enjoying the sun illuminating the grass and the sound of the river beyond. To complement this, she suddenly remembered that she did not have to cook later, there being plenty leftover casserole from the night before, and immediately she felt her smile widen. She was almost sleepy from satisfaction, and Stuart rubbed her hair as she let her eyes close, but another second and Hazel felt the phone buzzing in the side pocket of her shorts. She looked at Stuart in mild despair.

"Aw shit, Stuey– hang on, it's not your dad." As Hazel tried to press the receive button through the material of her gloves, she accidentally pressed the disconnect button and in her awkwardness, dropped the phone onto the grass into the bargain. "Bugger it! Here," she handed it over. "Looks like it's safer with you after all."

"They'll ring back," he replied.

"Hope so," Hazel rolled her eyes at her own inadequacy and finally threw off her gloves. "Because I'm pretty sure it was an international number, and there's only about fifty pence credit on that phone."

Quiet descended for a moment or two between them, but it was an agitated silence and by no means peaceful. Hazel glanced at her watch and bit her lip before speaking.

"It'll be about seven in the morning over there. You never know," her voice was a mixture of hope and doubt, "Alasdair might have got them up early and they got tired of waiting for us to phone."

"Sounds ... fair enough." He looked at her through questioning eyes.

Immediately, Hazel was on her feet, feeling the muscles in her recently worked thighs stretch and burn. "You're right. Something's up. Have you any change at all? I'll use the phone inside."

There followed a joint and not altogether successful rummage for coins amongst pockets and the debris on the table, before Hazel grabbed a note from the open wallet and announced that she would acquire the money necessary for the pay phone from the barman. She had not moved three yards towards the door, however, when the mobile started to buzz and ring once more. This time, Stuart hoisted it to his ear and effortlessly pressed the connect button simultaneously, looking straight at Hazel as he did so.

"Hello? Hi, David, how's it going with you?"

Hazel had never really been known for her patience, and it took all of her willpower not to stand in front of Stuart and shove her hand four inches from his face. But she did not, and listened quietly as he took his turn to speak. Yes, the phone had rung but Hazel had dropped it. No, they were not at home but at Sligachan, making the most of the weather. Sure, Hazel was available. Throughout the entire exchange, Stuart had not smiled, although neither had he looked particularly concerned. Hazel grinned as he passed her the mobile, but when he merely shrugged, she felt herself shiver in the sunlight.

"Hi, Dad. You're up early."

"Hazel," David's words were not diminished by the thousands of miles of air, sea and mountains between them. "It's really great to hear your voice."

"Same here. I was going to call later. Kate up and about yet?"

As Hazel began to wander around in a loop, her finger pressed into her free ear, Stuart drained his glass. The tone of David's voice had been unusual, although he had given very little away, but Stuart had not been around his wife for a dozen or so years without knowing that their summer's day jaunt was drawing to a close. They had enjoyed a few moments out of time, taken in masses of fresh air and shining views and relaxed into their holiday selves. No work, no others to consider, nothing to fret over. But whether there was a drama unfolding or not, Hazel would find it almost impossible to sit back down and regain the precious peace of the previous few minutes. He began to gather together their gear, watching Hazel's body language. She was on the third lap of her own personal circle when she stopped dead and sat on the grass. Stuart dropped his helmet and was at her side as the colour began to drain from her face. Yet she was smiling, grinning, laughing. Then she was reaching wildly for his arm, and holding the mobile out to him.

"Here, Stuey," she gasped, tears squeezing their way out into the sunlight. "Take it. Speak to him. Kate's had the baby. The baby, she's arrived."

As he took the mobile from her hand, he sat beside her on the grass and kissed her. "I'm guessing that Kenny will be picking us up then," he laughed, and then "David! Tell me everything so I can tell her again when she stops blubbing."

《•》《•》《•》

When Alasdair had been born, it had taken Kate at least a day to recover completely from the anaesthetic, and both she and her son had been inordinately sleepy. At the time, Kate had been under the illusion that her perfect specimen of infant had been born quiet and amenable. It had become plain on the third day, when he had decided that he had slept long enough, that he was perhaps not the "most mature baby that ever lived." Today, she had never felt more awake in her life, and she wondered if her heightened state had been caused by the entirely unexpected intensity of pain she had encountered. Her flesh was torn, she felt as if a medicine ball had been removed from her without the aid of surgery, and still she could not rest her eyes. They were wide, gummed open and staring. She must look hideous.

A caesarean section had not been necessary this second time, and Kate desperately tried to remind herself that this was a good thing in spite of the throbbing, tattered parts of her body. Her biggest fear had always been that she might have to stop Ally from sitting on her lap, which he tended to do when he was tired. Now, she could cuddle him close without fear. She squirmed, testing her ability to cope with different levels of pain, and thought of the last nine or so hours with the incredulity of someone who had survived a train wreck. She was alive. The child was being taken care of in another room, was apparently also unscathed by her early arrival, and slowly, slowly Kate began to allow herself to think about what she had just done. By the time David walked back into the room, she had given in to the emotions tugging at her heart, but she halted her tears as soon as he looked at her.

"What did she say? Was she worried? Did you tell her the baby's going to be okay? Oh, Dave, I still can't believe it. Not really ready for this ..."

Instead of sitting on the edge of the bed and taking her hand, David stood a couple of feet away and studied every aspect of her. The hairs stood to attention on Kate's arms in an instant at the depth of his gaze.

"Well?" this time Kate's voice was barely above a whisper. "Was she really disappointed not to be–"

"Hey, Kit, slow down," his voice was like warm honey to a sore throat. "Hazel is nothing but delighted. Excited beyond even her usual level."

Kate let out a breath. "So, why are your eyes so worried?"

Still he remained a short distance away, but he shook his head slightly and smiled his typical smile; one side of his mouth slightly higher than the other, no teeth on show, but so much feeling behind it all. She smiled tentatively in return, hoping that whatever sentiment he was about to announce did not have a "but" at the end of it. He had time only to take her hand, however, before Alasdair's face appeared in the doorway and the words were postponed.

"Dad? Is it too soon?"

"Is that Alasdair Wilder still in his pyjamas?" cried Kate, throwing her hands up. "Well, it's high time I was back at home then. Get yourself in here, Squirtle."

For the first time in his life, Alasdair moved at a sedate, adult pace and eyed his mother from slightly behind David's right arm.

"Have you stopped being sick?"

"I have indeed," replied Kate, folding her arms, "and I've had a bath. Even cleaned my teeth, so I'm expecting a really big hug. Right now, please."

Alasdair's arms felt thin but welcome as they stayed around her neck for too short a time. She also felt him exhale against her cheek and hoped that it meant he felt better. The air in the room seemed to ache with unasked questions, and Kate tried to pull herself farther up the bed to assure everybody that she was not broken, just a little bruised. She held onto her son's hand as he sat near her shoulder. Rose took a seat and scanned the room.

"Right," began Kate, holding Alasdair's hand in the air and then wrapping it around her neck. "I suppose Granma Rose told you what's happened, Al?"

Alasdair nodded then frowned, twiddling her ear as he spoke. "But, you're still fat. How come?"

Kate watched David back away, giving them space and trying not to smirk.

"You're right," Kate sighed. "And I'm going to be like this for a week or two, but I think it's a wee bit flatter. Not as big a bump as it was."

"I guess," he replied, scanning the room as Rose had done. "Where is it?"

"The nurses are making sure she's completely okay. You can see her through the glass as soon as she's ready, but you won't be allowed in the same room, not with that snotty nose."

Alasdair sat facing her suddenly and kissed her on the cheek. "Happy birthday, Mom!"

"Thanks, Ally."

He wrinkled his nose, which desperately needed to be wiped, and lay back against her pillow. "You and the baby will have the same birthday. Every year."

"Yip," Kate smiled, "Every single year I'll get to say happy birthday to her and she'll get to say it to me. Fancy that."

It took Kate a couple of moments to realise that she was staring at the small fingers still entwined in hers. As soon as she became aware of it, the prickles in her nose were so violent that they threatened to make her sneeze. She looked at Rose in desperation, her bottom lip clamped in her teeth, and the woman came to her rescue as she had done many times in the past.

"Hey, Ally, I'm starving. You want to come with me and see if we can get some breakfast?"

He was off the bed in a second, Kate releasing his hand at the last minute, and she watched him bound after his grandmother, only looking back as he reached the door. "Have you opened your presents yet, Mom?"

"Not yet," Kate pointed at him as if he was the only one who could be given credit for remembering such an important detail. "I won't open any unless you're with me."

When they were alone again, Kate closed her eyes and held open her arms to the man in the room. As her face touched his throat, breathing in the scent of him, she felt a little quiver in her heart and her hands clasped themselves behind his head. How had all of this taken place? As recently as the previous morning, they had little more to think about than their son's gradually reducing temperature. A mere twenty-four hours later, Mike was dead, and Kate had delivered a tiny female infant into a shocked and ill-prepared household. The speed of said delivery had placed everybody in a semi-stupor. All Kate could really remember was the blood, the incredible roughness of the carpet as she had crawled on her hands and knees, and her terror that her son would be scarred for life by the experience. Rose's face had appeared, and the next thing the carpet beneath her had been replaced with blissfully cold cotton sheets. The practicalities of cleaning up after the baby had finally made her appearance were a lost experience, as was the ambulance journey; but the examination, stitches and bath were clear in her mind. And all of it was incredible.

"Let it out, sweetheart," David spoke into her still damp hair. "I'm here and you are the most amazing woman."

"Don't be too impressed, Dave," she spoke against his skin, "I haven't managed everything yet."

David could have reassured her that she would manage and she may even have believed him, but he did not wish to stop her thinking of and acknowledging the situation. It was way too dangerous and too soon to try to minimise what was going on, and so instead he held her until he felt her sag against him. He placed her gently back against the pillow and pulled up a chair instead.

"Are you sure you don't need to sleep? I can go—"

"Don't you dare leave me, Dave."

David stayed put. He looked as wiped out as she felt, but she needed his face in her sight, even when he continued to look preoccupied and concerned. Kate raised her eyebrows, trying to get him to share. When he narrowed his eyes once again, she braced herself for whatever was coming next.

CHAPTER 5

Vancouver Island

It was also a day of firsts for Alasdair Wilder. For the first time ever in his life, he had a chocolate-covered doughnut for his breakfast. He was very fond of doughnuts, was always willing to try any new combination of filling and coating, but had never ever been allowed to have one as his first meal of the day. Still, he was sitting in a hospital café in his pyjamas, so it really wasn't that remarkable in the scheme of things. He didn't particularly like his glass of milk, it was nowhere near cold enough and tepid milk made him want to gag, so he sipped instead at Rose's tea while she was speaking to the man selling comics. On her return, empty-handed, she turned her eagle eye on him, the one which made him wonder if she really did know absolutely everything that happened in the world.

"Would a cup of tea suit you better, Al?" Rose enquired. When he nodded sheepishly, she sat beside him and put his jacket back around his shoulders. "Well, I can get you one of your own, or we could share this one."

"Sharing is fine," Alasdair replied, then, "I wonder if Mom has had breakfast yet. She must be starving. It looked like she lost her whole dinner."

Rose cupped her chin in her hand and watched the boy continue to nibble away at the chocolate, exposing the dough beneath. He did not seem in any way upset by his statement, but looked up at her when she did not reply immediately.

"Was it a bit scary?" asked Rose.

"It was a bit messy, but she's been sick before," Alasdair answered, his nose wrinkling at the memory. "Not on the carpet, though."

Rose tried to recall how much the boy had actually seen before Jessie Morgan had persuaded him to come and spend the night with her. He had witnessed the vomiting, the blood and his mother wailing like some ghost in eternal turmoil, but she was almost positive he had seen none of the actual birth. She sipped her tea and pushed the cup his way, wishing that her half contained a drop of brandy to steady her own fluttering insides. But, this was only the beginning, and at least there was no physical damage to any human, although the rug was most definitely bound for the garbage tip.

"I wonder who she'll look like." Alasdair swallowed the last piece of bald doughnut and wiped his hands on the front of his pyjamas. "Do babies have faces this early? I mean, I know she belongs to Hazel and Stu, but if she's been inside my mom, then maybe a little bit of her has rubbed off too. Maybe she'll look a bit like me?"

"Well," grinned Rose, "you can judge that for yourself. Let's go back and see if you're allowed to see her."

Even to Rose, the boy looked a bit ridiculous. He was decked out in a pair of yellow pyjamas, chosen for the cartoon character rather than the colour, around which was draped a dark blue parka. On his feet were his winter boots, even though the country was barely out of summer, but at least he had tied his laces. He was about six inches past her hip bone in height already but weighed less than fifty pounds. Rose felt as if she was accompanying a very brightly coloured stick insect. Thankfully, Alasdair had as yet no concept of either his unusual height or appearance, and it did mean that they maintained the same pace when walking along the hospital corridor. They met David coming out of Kate's room. His bleak face lit up as soon as he saw his son.

"Wow, Al," he laughed. "Are you not stewing in that coat?"

Alasdair shook his head, his thoughts clearly focussed on his latest mission. "When can I see her?"

David took his hand in his. "I'm going to check on what's happening. You want to come?"

Rose found Kate lying back, eyes staring through the window at the grey morning light, not a hint of movement on her face. Her hands were clasped across her belly, the habit of cradling her burden obviously still with her, but she placed them firmly by her sides when she became aware of Rose. She smiled and shook her head in wonder.

"That's that, then, Rose."

"Yes," said the older woman quietly. She wandered slowly round to the head of the bed. "Well, now, David has taken Al along to see what's going on. So, I would say, that means you can sleep for a bit longer, if you'd rather. Apart from the sore bits, how are you feeling?"

"I'm going to be okay. I think. I don't know," Kate's brow was suddenly a series of folds. "I'm not going to feed her, Rose. I'm not even going to be the first person to give her a bottle when she's off the tube, because if everything had gone to plan, that would have been Hazel's job. I'm just her auntie, I have to be just her auntie from today onwards. Will you be on my side about this?"

"Are there likely to be different sides?" Rose asked surprised.

Kate leaned forward as far as was comfortable, her voice that of a conspirator. "I think those nurses are going to start on me as soon as you lot have gone."

Rose patted Kate's hand. "Hey, most of them know the situation. I can go and have a word if you like."

"You could do that," agreed Kate, "but not yet. Stay for a wee while. Oh Rose, what a bloody night."

Rose could only agree as she tried to pour some insipid-looking liquid into a beaker without dislodging the plastic lid from the jug. Kate took it gratefully, wondering how the two men in her life were coping at that very moment. Her nose grew dense as she admitted to herself that she felt left out. They were together nearby, watching, and no doubt discussing, the miracle in front of them, and she wanted more than anything else to be the third limb again. Then she thought of Hazel and allowed herself a tiny little commendation. She had just given her sister the chance to become part of her own triangular unit.

Not just a bloody night, thought Kate, what a bloody year.

Kate thought of the day she had presented David with an idea. An idea which was not unheard of in similar circumstances, but one which had the potential to cause countless raised eyebrows for those who were aware of the atypical and frankly extraordinary dynamics of their particular family; an idea which had in fact caused their first serious disagreement. She had been sitting in the window seat of the sitting room, her knees tucked under her chin, one sock dangerously close to unrolling and dropping to the floor, as she went over Hazel's latest letter for a second time. David had been chopping wood outside, the splitter making three or four regular sounds before breaking to allow Alasdair to collect and stack, and her face had begun to flush as her heart grew along with the idea.

Hazel's words had been upbeat in a way. She and Stuart had made a decision, and they were relieved to have finally brought the whole thing to a conclusion. Children were not going to come to them, it was a fact, and they had decided to accept it.

"At some point you've just got to give in and accept, right? Maybe not accept but agree, at least. I mean, the stitch was more or less the last resort, and the worst thing, the really crappy thing, was that we got to the point of hoping. That was cruel, right? This pregnancy lasted a week and a half longer than the other three, and I fell for it. Fell right into the trap. Stuart was so mad. Not at me, just at whoever is apparently controlling this thing. I think we decided at the same time that we'd had enough. So, there it is. The MacIntyre dynasty is now in the hands of Bruce and Catriona. Poor buggers, that's pressure! And the Wilders stop with your Alasdair, unless you feel like going through it all again?"

Of course, Hazel had merely meant that David and she could add to their own household, but the words had jumped out at her from the page; and that night, when Alasdair had fallen asleep on the sofa, Kate had extricated him from her arms and sat on the floor at David's feet instead.

"Hello, you," he had murmured, finally moving his eyes from the TV when she had begun to grin. "What?"

"Now then," she said, loving the way he looked straight at her. "Here's the thing. I could sit here and spin you a yarn which would probably take the whole night, and in the end, because you were really irritated or worn out by the constant jabbering, it would result in me rushing to get the gist of the story out into the air, and you would end up just sitting staring at me. So, I'm just going to … hey, don't switch off yet, I'm coming to the point, honest."

"And I'm sitting here, ready," David had stated, rubbing his chin, a sure sign that he had to call on his reserves of patience.

"Right. Okay, so I can't stand what Hazel has been through, is still going through. All that hope and worry, then disappointment, but I think I could change that. I think maybe I could offer to carry their baby for them. Their baby, you know, their bits and pieces of DNA and stuff, and I'd just be the oven it was cooking in. Hah! I haven't seen that level of interest in my blether for years!"

David had indeed stared at her for the duration of the punctuated discussion which had followed. His voice had started off at a reasonable enough pitch, when there had still been the possibility she was jesting; and they had managed to keep it to a quiet exchange of opinions until Alasdair had been deposited upstairs, and he had not raised his voice at all until she had announced her intention to Google flight details. That was when he had grabbed her departing wrist and looked down at her with truly wide eyes.

"Hold it!"

CHAPTER 6

August 2002 • Vancouver Island

"Hold it!"

The socks on Kate's feet allowed her to skid a little as David's grip on her wrist halted her progress. His eyes said exactly what she had thought they would, which was the very reason she had been avoiding his gaze for the past half hour. When he did not begin his list of objections there and then, however, she twisted her wrist slightly and entwined her fingers in his.

"I get it," she smiled at him. "I understand that this is completely—"

"Well, I'm glad you understand," he said evenly. "But trying to sell it to me is different than actually checking travel information. Checking travel information is making it more like a decision than a discussion, and there's no way I've finished discussing this."

Kate took half a step backwards and planted both of her feet firmly on the floor. "Well, maybe if you hadn't interrupted, you'd know that I haven't made any decision at all. I was just going to see what we were up against … logistically. And for that, I need to find out how much everything is going to cost."

"And 'everything' means?"

"Procedures, travel costs, getting Hazel over"

"Procedures? Is today really Day One of this? Be honest."

"Absolutely! Hazel's letter got me thinking; in fact, if you look closely at what she wrote, she's practically suggesting it. Well, not really, but it just seemed to make a sort of sense. People do it all the time."

David folded his arms, expecting her to move off and continue with her quest, allowing him extra time to gather more arguments in his head. But Kate did not move, fixing her grey eyes on his and inviting his further opinion. This proved one thing. It proved that she had put a monumental amount of thought into it, had a stack of her own arguments at the ready. David sighed, almost accepting defeat. Almost. This was far too serious to allow her to bulldoze him, but if he knew anything about his wife, it was that she would take this as far as possible. He creased his eyes, unsure if he wanted to subject Alasdair to days of adult conversations and mere token responses to his son's daily news. But there would be no shelving anything, not while Kate's present attitude remained.

"Okay, Kate," David shook his head. "I know you're not going to let this drop, but I'm asking you to please, please take this seriously. Look into it all if you have to, but promise me you're not halfway down that road already."

"I'm not!"

"And no flippant, off-the-cuff statements, not in front of Al and definitely not where Hazel is concerned."

Kate watched him walk away, running one hand through his short hair, wondering how she was supposed to promise him anything when he had left the room. She followed him through to the kitchen. His flannel shirt had worked itself free from the waistband of his jeans at the back, and on any other day she would have made a huge fuss of tucking it back in for him, making sure her fingertips grazed his skin until she had his full attention. But right at that moment she was too irritated by his assumptions to touch him at all. He paused by the sink to fill the kettle and she positioned herself against the unit, noticing that his jaw seemed locked tight.

"So if you're okay for me to look into it, what's that face for?" Kate asked, jabbing her finger vaguely in his direction.

He gave her a dubious look. "You know full well what it's for. This is the face I make when we both know I have a point, but you're not willing to accept it. You're incapable of just saying 'fine, you might be right, tell me what you really think before I go any further.' Your only goal is to win me over, and sometimes, Kate, the need to win becomes more important to you than the idea itself."

"Bloody hell!" Kate cried, her eyebrows knitted in pain as his voice grew firmer and he continued to use her actual name. She hated that and he knew it. She was also almost positive she did not deserve it, and unfairness in any form drove her insane. But David was shaking his head slightly, apparently trying to organise some sort of grand declaration in his head, whilst reaching for two mugs. As if she was going to accept a cup of tea from him after this betrayal. "Anything else in there needing to make itself heard?"

"Plenty, but I doubt you'll listen."

"What the hell is this?" Kate shouted. "Why are you being so shitty?"

For an instant she saw irony swim in his eyes; but as her own gaze felt like ice even to her, he did not smile, and put the mugs down. "Because this is serious and dangerous. So. Tell me I'm wrong. Tell me I haven't just pointed out the truth. Say that to me and I'll apologise."

"What truth?" Kate's face was red, and scarlet fingers were creeping onto her neck and throat as the man ceased all other activity and looked down at her. His eyes were intense, and Kate took an actual step away from him.

"That the winning sometimes takes over from the actual idea."

Kate's lips were clamped so tightly they almost hurt. She drew in a breath. "You are completely wrong."

David waited, finally raising his eyebrows doubtfully when she said nothing else. He could not have annoyed her more if he had laughed in her face.

"Right, so now I'm a liar?"

"I didn't say that," David's voice had taken on a patient tone; and in spite of the fact that his jaw was covered in her favourite amount of rough greying hair, she felt like punching it, just to see if his face could take on a completely original expression and she could change his tone to something more stimulating. She resisted the temptation. Instead, she scratched at the inside of her wrist and dared him to antagonise her even further. He managed to do just that by not uttering a word. So she exerted the only control she felt she had; she held his gaze and tried to stare him out. Mature, thought Kate, and continued to do it anyway.

David deliberately made a point of turning his back on her as he reached for the teapot, but he could feel her bristling behind him. He had made some mistakes in his life, the kind that could still make him sweat in the black of the night. But he had vowed long ago never to subject Hazel to even one more of his making, and Kate's enthusiastic self-confidence could not simply be embraced and encouraged. It had to be talked about for more than three hours at least. He turned and faced her.

"It worries me, you know," his voice had dropped slightly, as if he might be willing to entertain her thoughts at last. "It scares me the way you think you are capable of everything. You're capable of a hell of a lot, we both know that, but just slow down here."

"But it makes so much sense," cried Kate, desperately latching onto his reasonable tone. "She can get pregnant at the drop of a hat, but can't carry. I can carry. All they have to do is give me the fertilised egg, and I'll grow it for them."

"Jeez, Kate, listen to yourself," his eyes were black with incredulity. "We're talking about something which has probably been Hazel's only focus since they married, which may have caused any number of problems between Stuart and her, and you're about to go marching in there with what you think is the solution."

"But it might be the solution!" Even Kate recognised with a wince how childish her voice sounded.

"It might be," he agreed, but his words were becoming harder and louder, "but you can't even hint at this to them without much, much more thought! This is not the same as us redecorating the house or you working for Andie. This could be life changing if it's successful, but it could be just as life changing if it fails. Think about it properly!"

Kate felt the blotches on her neck suddenly intensify in heat as she stared at him, waiting for him to apologise for raising his voice. Instead he stared silently back at her.

"I don't know how we got to this stage," Kate said, suddenly throwing her hands up. "I just wanted to check the costs involved and suddenly we're in the middle of this ... well, whatever this is. Is it a fight?"

"Depends what you call a fight."

"Well, it's the first time you–" Kate stopped mid-sentence and felt her face flush hotter still. She actually bit her tongue to stop the words, but she heard them in her head anyway and found herself embarrassed. She looked down at her feet, her mouth twisting with vexation.

"It's the first time I've argued with you for this length of time?" David asked, "the first time I haven't let you have your own way immediately?"

As Kate looked up at his face, a shiver rolled across her shoulders and the blood began to pound in her ears. Somehow, unbelievably, David was making her wary of her next words. This was new. She was used to saying her piece freely, confident that there would always be a back and forth which she could more or less steer any way she liked. But his face was businesslike, and suddenly she noticed every twelve inches of their height difference and felt the years between them stretch farther than they ever had to date. Although their eyes were once again connecting, she had lost all sense of control over the situation and felt truly confused. She moved deliberately towards the door, aware that he did not try to stop her.

"I didn't mean ... I don't think I was going to say that," she almost whispered, then, "and stop calling me Kate."

By the time she had reached the first-floor bathroom, Kate was aware that the pressure initially confined to her frontal lobe was graciously attempting to share itself equally with the rest of her brain. She was sure that in spite of feeling anger and surprise in fairly equal amounts, embarrassment had beaten them all to the top of the tree. He had known exactly what she had thought and almost said, and had even called her on it. She stood by the sink, questioning her own reflection.

The Canucks sweatshirt, inherited from her husband after it had accidentally gone in the hot wash, was no longer keeping her cosy, and she didn't particularly like the way the orca logo was gnashing its teeth at her. Or was it grinning? She was, after all, a fool and deserved to be laughed at. Kate ran her fingers over the logo's stitching, wondering if the man she loved had been humouring her since their union. Maybe in all that time she had never managed to influence him and had never made so much sense that he had marvelled at her ideas and solutions. Maybe he had simply not wanted to argue. She was a fool indeed.

Kate lowered the lid on the toilet seat and slumped onto it, baffled; five minutes of honest words and she was completely deflated. Who knew that David had so much clout? From mid-morning, she had been formulating and enjoying her thoughts, trying to imagine Hazel's reaction to them, completely sure that David would be not only impressed but in awe of her. Now she felt ridiculous. Granted, they were an incredibly serious set of suggestions and needed a lot of investigation, but they were also unbelievably positive and would make such a fantastic difference to her sister's entire outlook on life. David would do anything for Hazel. He still felt he owed her years of attention, so what was his problem?

More importantly, how long had he viewed herself as someone to be patronised? She was his wife, his partner, his equal, or at least that had been her impression. But perhaps she was over-thinking the whole blessed thing. She sighed, annoyed that she was so completely transparent to him when she had always thought herself unpredictable, clever and influential. "You bloody moron."

Kate could hear no sound from any floor as she crept along the corridor to Alasdair's room, and this was a relief. Her son's dark space, lit only by the pale blue disc of night-light above his bed, was where she wanted to remain undetected for as long as possible. The place where she could once again feel like a responsible adult and not some misguided child with impossibly wild notions. The boy's hairline was the only uncovered part of Alasdair's body, and she smiled at how fair it was. She remembered how his initial baldness had produced fine hair slowly and in uneven bursts, but by the time he was into his second year, his head was covered in white-blonde waves. It had darkened only slightly since that time, and it looked like it might settle on his grandfather's rather than his father's shade.

She hovered by his headboard, allowing her eyes to adjust to the blue of the light, and stroked a few straying strands from his fringe. "You still think I'm smart, don't you, son?"

Kate was surprised at the hollowness inside her and tried to give it a name. Shock, maybe. Shock that David had felt like her elder for the first time. Foolishness certainly, and she supposed a little bit of disappointment. It had been a really optimistic day until the moment she had involved someone else, and she had imagined their evening would be made up of a small celebration and much excited planning. Perhaps it was the absence of this potential enjoyment which was making her feel empty.

When Alasdair failed to stir, sit up or put his arms around her neck in appreciation of her, Kate wandered to the window and tried to find the stars. The sky was navy blue, the tall conifers black against it, and she wondered if the frost was already beginning to coat the windows of their vehicles. Below and to the right of the windowsill, a tell-tale shaft of light made the grass a green-brown; and as she watched, there was a movement from near the woodpile, and then David was illuminated, most of his face hidden behind the armful of logs. He was walking with a purpose, the cold air probably tickling his nose and quickening his step, and she wondered if he would look up if she knocked on the window. She hesitated, her hand raised, then dropped it, imagining how truly hollow she would feel if he completely ignored her. This was not how she had envisaged her Saturday night, and suddenly colder than ever, she lay beside Alasdair and let his little body share its warmth.

In the sitting room, David finally turned his face away from the blaze in the hearth and leaned back in his chair. He had stacked most of the gathered logs onto the fire without thinking, and the air was noisy with the roar of the bone-dry wood. His eyes wandered around the room. The temperature was cosy, the lamps sympathetic and the whisky bottle peeking at him from behind the glass-fronted cabinet promised comfort of its own, but the place felt off-kilter; there was no other human in his eye-line or within earshot. In spite of the shadows flickering on the walls, the whole room was too static and it made his stomach roll a little. Still, he did not move. Instead, he closed his eyes and replayed all the expressions he had seen on Kate's face. The worst had been the hurt surprise, and he felt his nostrils flare in frustration. She had to appreciate what he was saying. She had to see his point. She wasn't stupid or selfish, so surely she recognised this as the most potentially damaging idea she had in a long time. Slowly, David opened his eyes and let them focus.

This was possibly the most hazardous proposal since she had told him that she loved him, that she would love nobody but him, and that she would wait until he was ready. Possibly, it was the most dangerous idea since she had suggested that late forties was plenty young enough to bring another child into the world and that she would give him what he had missed when Hazel had been taken from him. David's eyes began to ache in his head and he sat forward quickly.

"But this is different," he mumbled out loud. "Too much hope involved. Too much."

As David poured himself a small drink at last and wandered over to the window, he caught sight of Hazel's discarded letter. He had read it at the lunch table and had felt vexed at her situation, but also relieved that she and Stuart were still supporting each other and were together in their acceptance of it all. He wondered what Kate had seen that he had not, how the initial idea had gripped her to the extent it had, and picked up the cold sheaves of paper. He could hear his daughter's voice as he read, and by the time he had digested her words properly, his drink sat untouched on the floor at his feet. He thought again of the range of Kate's expressions and creased his eyes at the possibility that he had handled the whole thing pretty shabbily. But sometimes she just needed to be stopped in her tracks. That was all he was truly guilty of doing, and it had been necessary.

"Ah, shit," he said to the still room, and thought of her completely deflated exit. He had caused that, and he had caused her to hide her embarrassment away somewhere else in the house. He could picture her defeat and imagined how she would be lying beside him that night, her beautiful body somehow turned away from him and inaccessible, a wall as solid as it was imaginary built between them beneath the sheets. He should make amends sooner rather than later. But not yet.

The window seat was, in fact, a storage unit of sorts, and by removing the cushion, the wooden lid lifted easily. David had to resort to switching on the overhead light to find what he was looking for, which transformed the room from snug ally to austere prosecutor in an instant, and he switched it off again as soon as he had the photo album under his arm. The album had a tough card exterior which had only slightly curled at the edges, and it smelled only of the lavender sachets Rose had stored beside it, but it spoke entirely of abandonment.

Amongst its pages, however, David found enough to bring a smile to his face. Unlike these days, when Kate took photos of absolutely everything and plastered most of the images randomly in her sewing room, these photographs were of special family events. All had a white border and were fitted into adhesive corners to hold them in place. The first few were in black and white; but by the time Fiona and Hazel featured, the images were in colour, and he smiled at the first one of Hazel. She had so much dark brown hair. Fiona had initially been concerned at the amount, but had been unable to stop smiling nevertheless. That tiny, breathing miracle had caused them both to temporarily lose their wits, and they had grinned for days. There was one of him, remarkably clean shaven, holding the newborn's perfect face against his, and he marvelled that he had ever looked so young. And contented. And fulfilled.

He moved his eyes from his own to those of his perfect child and caught the emotion in his throat. His daughter had a right to feel as he had felt, and Kate had made a suggestion to that effect, which he had halted and decried. They needed to talk about it further, he was adamant about that, but perhaps there was something to be heard as well as to be said. He closed the album and stood. The room was too damned quiet and still.

Lying motionless beside Alasdair, Kate was more or less meditating. Her eyes were fixed on the night-light, and all she was really aware of was that the boy's heat was welcome against her. Eventually, however, she was aware of a muffled beat, regular and in addition to her heart. She sat up and listened intently. There was definitely a movement on the air which had not been there before, and she thought she even recognised the pattern. As she eased open the bedroom door, she smiled in full recognition, not just at the words and melody of the song being played, but that David had taken the time to hunt through their CDs and choose this particular song to end the impasse.

She wandered slowly to the top of the stairs, relief gradually allowing her to sing along, and she believed every word as it came out of her mouth. This was their time and nothing could break them. Not stress, not disappointment, not heartache and certainly not a spat involving hypothetical ideas. Not when she knew that the flame was still burning between them.

As Kate put her head around the doorway of the sitting room, she found him hunkered by the fire, his back to her, settling the disintegrating logs to his satisfaction. His shirt remained partially un-tucked, and there were twin dimples at the base of his spine where the skin was forever taut and smooth. She stopped singing and padded across the miles between them. He only had time to turn his head before she had wrapped her arms around him and was fastened against his long back.

"You're right," she sighed against the nape of his neck, "sometimes I lose sight. Sometimes I don't let you talk. In fact, there's a chance I'm the biggest pain in this strong neck you've ever had to contend with. Sorry."

In spite of the body clamped to him, David managed to stand; and by the time she had slid to the floor, he had turned and taken both of her hands in his. His eyes had returned to green from angry black, and she was grateful.

"We're going to talk about this. I'm not–" he twisted his mouth as he hesitated. "It might be a great idea. I'm not sure, is all. I got scared for Hazel. And for you, if it doesn't work."

Kate nodded her resignation. "I know."

David hooked her hands around his neck and let out a relieved breath as she lifted her face to be kissed. Her lips were cold and he pulled her onto his lap as he sat, rubbing her white hands back to life. "God, Kit, you're freezing. And I hate fighting."

"So that was definitely a fight then? I had sort of dialled it back to a mild disagreement in my head. Still, at least it was an important enough subject. Be worse if our first one had been over ... sport or something."

"Well, that'll never happen," he spoke with a serious tone, "we both know that hockey trumps rugby every time. There isn't even one doubt–"

David's words were transformed from English into a hissed curse as Kate slid her bloodless hand beneath his shirt and spread her fingers wide across his back for maximum effect. He could barely even squirm as she sat solidly on his lap, watching his reaction with a smile.

"What's up, Davey?" she asked. "I'm not allowed to touch you now?"

"Jeez, get that hand out of there!"

"Och, you're a big baby. Tuck yourself in then, you know I'm wanton. Tea?"

David watched her hurry away, sliding as she held onto the door frame and then disappearing before he had a chance to retaliate. For a moment, he contented himself that the crisis seemed to have passed and looked forward to sharing a hot drink with her. But in the next second, he was on his feet, pulling his shirt free from his jeans. He found her, singing once more, by the still-unused teapot and mugs. When she smiled in his general direction, he took great satisfaction in watching her face stay on his, catching his mood as he reached his hands up to the top of the door frame.

She moved her eyes to his flat exposed stomach where they stayed for another two seconds, her head tilted slightly.

She glanced at the boiling kettle. "No tea, then?"

David shrugged his shoulders, leaving the decision to her. He watched her look him over, and in the interim, scratched absently at his rough chin. Slowly she moved past the sink, letting her hand trail along the worktop as if she had yet to make up her mind. He could not stop the grin breaking out into the room at her pretence. As soon as she heard him laugh, she joined in and jumped into his arms. He had already braced himself for the eventuality, which meant he turned without effort as her legs wrapped around his waist and carried her through to the hallway. She laid her head against his, kissing his shoulder through the fabric of his shirt until this became not nearly good enough.

Before he had walked another two strides, she had yanked the checked flannel away from his skin and was kissing his collarbone without hindrance. His legs quivered in response and he slid both hands down her back, before allowing the wall to prop them both up. With his hands hooked into the back of her jeans, he felt her tense against him. It was the most beautiful reaction, and when he found her mouth already open against his own, he guessed they would make it no farther than the sofa.

CHAPTER 7

January 2003 • Vancouver Island

Hazel could barely stand upright, and she knew that if she had even one more sip of wine, she would keel over completely. Her stomach muscles hurt, and she wrapped one arm around herself as she tried desperately to laugh out loud. If only she could force out the sound, then her aching abdomen would release its grip and she would be able to relax again. But how was she supposed to do this when her little sister was herself rolling about on the floor, cackling like a demented goose? Kate had been sitting on the sofa like a regular person until a few minutes ago, when the combination of nerves, excitement and the little wine they had allowed themselves had caused the current mayhem on a late January Sunday. Hazel had set them off by announcing that if Stuart ever fled the scene, she would definitely set up home with Sawney Bean.

"Sawney Bean?" Kate asked, her eyes wide. "Is that so?"

"Well, yes. Come on, that accent, those eyes, brawny arms. Why would you even hesitate?"

"So, you'd join forces with one of Scotland's most vicious cave dwellers," stated Kate, impressed.

"What?" Hazel had turned her head lazily.

Kate had begun to snigger and as her words had flowed, she had slid from the sofa to the floor. "You'd be a cannibal's wife? You can't even eat a chicken leg."

Hazel had shrugged and waved her glass in the air. "It's possible that I've got the wrong Bean."

"No, don't say that," Kate had snorted. "This Bean is much more interesting. I'm seeing you throwing limbs into a big pot. Eating men for supper."

"Wouldn't be the first time."

"Ain't that the truth."

It had gone downhill from there. Sean Bean's attributes had eventually been assessed and applauded, although Kate had declared him not tall enough for her; and by the time Hazel had spilled some white wine down her front and tripped over the hearth rug, they were well on their way to madness. What finally pushed them over the line was when Hazel used the word "malarkey" to describe their current state. Kate ended up crying into her glass, before curling up on the floor.

"Oh, Lordy," Hazel finally breathed. "Oh, that hurt. A lot."

"Agreed," replied Kate, her head resting on her arm in her semi-foetal position. She used her shirtsleeves to wipe her eyes and eventually sat upright. As she did so, the back door of The Edge slammed, and she heard Alasdair running through from the kitchen.

"Boots!"

The word came from both his mother and father as he appeared in the doorway, and it caused his immediate U-turn, which almost set Hazel off again; but she quashed it and put her empty glass on the mantelpiece. Holding out her hand, she hauled Kate to her feet, and when the men entered, it was to find the pair of them standing calmly by the fire. David grinned as soon as he saw them, which had Kate smirking once more with the last few remnants of hysteria.

"What?" he asked.

"Nothing," replied Hazel. "Nothing that the men of this house need know, at any rate."

"This makes me very nervous," sighed Stuart, who glanced at the empty wine bottle and at the easy way his wife and sister-in-law stood, arms linked, soaking up the warmth from the fire. "Here, let me near those flames."

Finally unbooted, Alasdair appeared again, and Kate grabbed him around the waist before he was halfway across the room. He squealed in protest but she carried on, throwing him over her shoulder and marching towards the stairs. The debate about whether his jeans were indeed "soaked and dirty" continued upstairs until the words were lost to the others. David slumped into his chair and stretched out his legs so that his toes at least had a chance of sharing the hijacked heat. Absently, he cracked his knuckles. The action finally saw Hazel blow the last of her laughter out of her mouth, and she sat opposite him on the sofa, grimacing slightly at how hot her jeans had become. She leaned her head back.

"Here, Dad," her voice was curious. "What happened to the shelf for the paperweights? Or the paperweights, for that matter?"

Stuart followed the line of her gaze, which landed on a spot about a foot below the ceiling, not recalling any such shelf from his previous visit.

"Paperweights went with Rose," smiled David. "The shelf was never replaced after we re-wired."

Hazel nodded as if this made perfect sense. "Kate was never much of a collector."

Stuart continued to survey the room as the blood came back into his fingers. His only recollection of the room, pre-Kate and pre-refurbishment project, was that it had been unremarkable; flock wallpaper, dark brown sofa, dated but quality pieces of furniture, none of which had really shown the strength of the space. Now it was painted a light caramel shade, and although the sofa did not match the two fireside chairs, they seemed to complement each other. The huge fireplace was the most impressive feature. The wooden surround had been oiled a dark walnut shade, and at some point David had laid a new hearth of granite, picked from a catalogue of Andie's. The bureau's proportions meant that it remained in the large room, but it was covered in a new generation of photos. Stuart's eyes lingered there, and at that moment Hazel squeezed his hand and smiled a genuine smile of complete understanding. Maybe, someday soon, there may be an addition to those framed images. But the stillness was stretching, and David's knuckles were still being crunched. Hazel sat forward.

"Are you worried, Dad?"

"No," David replied, dropping his hands to his sides.

"You sure? Nervous, then. Just a bit scared?" she pressed.

He studied the seam of his jeans as he scratched it in silence and then, "I just want you to have this more than anything. And I want it to work, for everybody's sake."

Hazel grinned. "That makes four of us then! Come on," she stood and ushered David to his feet. "We're going to get dinner on the table. Yes, you're going to help. Are you up to the task?"

"Well, I'm not completely ignorant–"

"It's irrelevant whether you are or not. It's you and me tonight, father of mine."

When Kate and the dry-trousered Alasdair returned to the comfort of the sitting room, it was to find Stuart sitting forward on the sofa, studying the weather forecast on the TV screen. The boy immediately jumped onto the seat beside him and placed a small box in the man's hands. As Stuart began to look it over, Alasdair undid the latch and eased open the lid. Inside were keys of various sizes and degrees of rust. The biggest and rustiest was like a dumbbell in the boy's small fist, and he held it in front of Stuart's face, eyes wide. He seemed as impressed as his nephew by the collection, Alasdair eager to share the use and origin of all of them; and Stuart was happy to listen to the enthusiasm of someone whose imagination was capable of conjuring countless doors and padlocks. Kate left them to share their opinions and was in the process of heading through to the kitchen, when an unusually easy banter and laughter reached her ears. Hazel was teasing David, something about his hairstyle sparring with his age, and David was arguing his case without hesitation. There were no awkward pauses, and for a moment Kate hid in the relative darkness of the hallway, smiling to herself and enjoying the sound of a Scottish tongue on the air. From there, from the two rooms where she was not needed, Kate wandered back upstairs and into her son's bedroom.

The space was unrecognisable from the sparse, old-fashioned room Hazel and Kate had slept in on their first surreal visit to the house. But the double aspect remained, and she loved to stand by the front-facing window, watching the light and shadows from the sitting room beneath playing on the lawn. Many were the nights she had walked this floor with a colicky baby, pausing occasionally to try to catch the moon clawing its way from behind a cloud; and each time Alasdair had settled, she had stood perfectly still and let the shivers build, then roll away from her, enjoying the thought that in a mere minute she would be enveloped by a warm duvet and David's arms, where he did not even seem to mind her freezing feet. She laid her burning face against the glass, wondering if the flush was due to the wine or the medication she was currently taking. Her heart began to thud at the thought of the days to come, and for a brief moment her stomach clenched and she tasted acid in her mouth.

On paper it was easy. In two days' time Hazel, who herself had been receiving injections since her arrival two days into the new year, would be relieved of her "nicely pumped up" eggs, and Stuart would be asked to do his part. With luck, and help from people who knew the magnitude of their desires, an embryo might be produced. If Hazel's previous four pregnancies indicated anything, it was that Stuart and she were capable of creation; and if not for Hazel's pitifully incompetent cervix, they surely would have had a couple of toddlers creating havoc in their Camastianavaig cottage by now. So hopefully, that would be the easy bit. Those eager little sperm and an enthusiastic egg or two might forget the courting period and get straight down to business. Nothing complicated there, was there?

Kate took a breath in and let it out in one wobbly exhalation. After that, it would be down to her. On Friday, if all went well, Kate's uterus would be housing the newlywed couple. She had, after all, been artificially plumping and lining the space for the last month, and surely, surely Mr and Mrs Embryo would be pleased to settle there. She had prayed more than once in the last month that this should be the outcome. She had prayed more for this than she could ever remember praying for anything, even for David and her own relationship, for she had never doubted that; praying had seemed an unnecessary action in that instance, and she had felt in control.

This situation was different. This had to work. If it did not, she risked being sad for the rest of her life. She rolled her eyes at the dramatic content of this thought, until it struck her that it was honest and factual. If this failed, she would revisit the failure each time she cast her eyes on her own child. It was enough to make a person cry.

"Kate?" The voice on the landing was Stuart's.

"In here," she called, sniffing back the tears and wiping her face. She folded her arms quickly to seem less melancholy, and when his silhouette appeared in the doorway, she smiled.

"You can see the night sky better if you leave the light off."

"Right," agreed Stuart, hovering on the threshold. "Em, apparently, there's some problem with the gravy. I said I'd see if you were available."

"Oh? I didn't hear any carry on, must have been daydreaming," she replied, but in the next instant her eyes had grown wide. She moved towards him as she spoke. "Just tell me she didn't let David do it. Surely she knows better than that!"

As Kate made to hurry past him, with thoughts of a significantly less enjoyable roast without its thick sauce, Stuart shyly touched her arm.

"How are you feeling?" he asked.

She could have made a joke about David's lack of finesse in the kitchen, and he would have laughed and taken the hint. She had known Stuart since he was nineteen and he deserved more. She hesitated beside him in the doorway, then gave a nervous little snort and wiped her face properly.

"I'm scared that everything will work up until my part, and then I'll ruin it. I know they've said I'm ideal, and they've done so much to give me the best chance, but ... nine months is a long time for you to put your faith in me. God, I'm so scared, Stu."

"I did wonder. The pair of you finished that bottle in under half an hour. We were only sledging for about twenty minutes."

"Aye, well, it was stupid I guess. It was supposed to be just one little glass each, like to try and normalise the night. Bad news, though, now I've got a sore head, David has ruined the dinner and I'm still scared."

Stuart made an odd face. She watched as his nose wrinkled and then he ran his thumb over his right eyebrow and shrugged his shoulders.

"I really wish you wouldn't be so scared," the words did not sound as if they came from Stuart, so she listened intently. "We've been hopeful each and every time, Kate. This really isn't any different, except that we get to come here, and it's nice to be part of more than two for a while."

"Oh, Stu!" cried Kate, amazed. "Bloody hell, mate. You're a really lovely man, and I guess I always knew that, but wow. Thanks. Thanks for letting me try this. David wasn't sure I should."

"It didn't cause any problems, did it?"

"No," Kate suddenly blushed when she remembered how that particular argument had been resolved. "Absolutely not."

Stuart nodded, then grinned. "Look at us. Talking like grown-ups. When did that come about?"

"Don't know, but it's high time we put a stop to it! Come on, I fear carnage is being committed downstairs."

Later, when Alasdair finally admitted that he was tired and took himself upstairs, the four of them lounged in the sitting room, where the lamps and the fire were much more appealing than the brightly lit, dish-strewn kitchen. Hazel seemed on the point of dozing, her legs draped sideways over Stuart's knees as they occupied the sofa, and Kate sat opposite David, the pair of them flanking the fireplace. It was not an uncomfortable silence. However, after a minute or so, Kate rose and hunted through their collection for an appropriate CD. Hazel yawned audibly then forced herself to sit upright.

"So," she said. "Tuesday. Not long. I was just wondering. If it ... works, what are you going to say to wee Al?"

Kate looked across at David immediately, and if Hazel was aware of the question in his returned gaze, she did not let on. Perhaps it was the lack of his immediate reply which threatened a potentially dangerous topic, or perhaps it was the continued aftereffects of the wine; but before another second had passed, Kate had crossed over to David's seat and settled herself on his knee. For an instant, the room was totally still as if someone had taken a photograph, and then David wrapped his arms around her waist and she laid her head against his shoulder. Hazel's face was pink from surprise, but even she could recognise this as a regular occurrence, so comfortable were they both with the arrangement.

"We haven't quite worked that one out yet," said David gently. "It's not that we disagree, we're just not sure–"

"We don't want to risk it not working by talking about it," Kate interrupted, whispered what sounded like an apology in his ear for cutting off his words and then turned back to the others. "You can understand that, right?"

"Completely," said Stuart, determined that the silence emanating from Hazel should be covered up. "He's a good lad anyway. Right, Hazel?"

His wife nodded her head, before letting it fall back against the sofa. Still she did not speak, but watched instead through the eyes of someone on the outside as David and Kate sat completely motionless on the one seat, not in any way acknowledging her embarrassment.

Without speaking, Stuart took her hand and kissed it. Slowly, she relaxed and closed her eyes. "Well, no doubt you'll figure that out, and all the other things he needs to know. Just make sure he understands that this particular thing is a gift. What you're doing is amazing. Both of you."

"Okay," replied Kate, then, "but we're not talking about it, remember? We need to get through tonight and all day tomorrow, and I'd rather talk about anything else in the world. How about a game of Monopoly?"

Later still, whilst David loaded the dishwasher and switched off lights, Stuart counted his piles of coloured paper money and stashed them back in their box. Kate had settled the fire and was waiting for Hazel to hint that she was also turning in for the night, but her sister remained resolutely motionless; and when Kate frowned at her, her eyebrows creased in a definite question, Hazel folded her arms and rubbed Stuart's arm with her foot.

"Stuey, you go on up. I want another minute or two with my little sister."

"Sure," he replied, then, "but if you're going to keep drinking, try to keep the shrieking to a minimum for my ears' sake."

Kate held up her hands. "I'm completely done in that department. Pretty knackered, actually."

"Won't be long," Hazel assured him as he departed, but offered no such assurance to Kate, who was almost irritated by the assumption that she was willing to stay and take part in whatever was coming. She was tired, and even Stuart's childish enthusiasm for the board game had not completely masked how subdued Hazel had become. It did not bode well.

"Give me a minute, then," stated Kate firmly, and met David at the bottom of the stairs. "I'm just going to make us a hot chocolate, Dave. She's got something on her mind, and I'd rather get it over with tonight."

"Okay, sweetheart," he winked as he smiled and kissed her lightly. "I'll try to stay awake, but whisky on top of wine ..."

"You sleep, I'll be fine."

Before returning to the sitting room, Kate did indeed set a pan of milk on to boil in the kitchen. The room was cool in spite of the range's presence, but she refused to let herself shiver as she listened to the plumbing overhead. By the time the milk had produced tiny bubbles around the edge of the pan, Hazel had wandered through and sat at the table.

"God," she sighed, holding her head in her hands. "Have you got a paracetamol? S'been a long time since I had a hangover before I even got to bed."

As the soluble painkiller fizzed beside her sister's cradled head, Kate also placed a mug of pale brown sweetness within her reach. Sometimes, it was better to sit on functional wooden chairs at a solid table, thought Kate, especially if there were major issues to tackle. Yet Hazel was smiling as she sipped the hot drink, cursing only once as her tongue recoiled in pain. Kate sat opposite her, so she could assess her face properly.

"The fizzing has stopped," she pointed to the glass, "just get it over your neck in one go."

When Hazel finally stopped grimacing and shaking her head at the bitterness of the taste in her mouth, it was to find Kate watching her with a resigned look. Kate raised her eyebrows and spoke in a low voice.

"Is it something specific, or just everything?"

To Kate's surprise, Hazel's eyes were at once brimming with tears; and it was so unexpected, when she had imagined some sort of hard-edged confrontation, that Kate did not react immediately.

"Well now, I don't know," lamented Hazel. "I suppose it must be everything. And I know you don't want to talk about it, but I was watching Alasdair earlier and wondering, if it goes ahead, what he can possibly make of this unbelievably complicated mess? If not this minute, then a bit further down the line. Maybe ... maybe this extra thing will make things worse."

"Wait right there," Kate's tone was harsher than she had intended, but she did not alter it. "Alasdair's in no danger, and what 'mess' would you be talking about exactly?"

Hazel wrinkled her nose and looked straight at her sister. Kate smiled coldly.

"Wow," she said quietly, "it's been bloody ages since somebody called Dave and I a 'mess.' In fact, I'm not sure anybody has ever called us a mess except you. Well, it's nice that nothing has altered your opinion in all these years."

"I was thinking about your son."

"Jeez, Hazel, do you think we're not worried about him? We've been trying to figure how to explain everything to him since the day he was born. He's our only concern, so don't try and say we didn't think–"

"All right, keep your voice down!" hissed Hazel, immediately reverting to the Gaelic tongue. "Maybe you haven't noticed, but I never use the word 'dad' if Al is in the room. How d'you think that makes me feel, especially when I rarely see the man and I would quite like to spend some time with him?"

"So, who the hell has stopped you spending time with him? Not me and certainly not Alasdair! You've been here for three weeks, and you've hardly been apart."

"Aw shit. You know what I mean. Please, let's not nark at each other."

Kate sighed and was about to let it go when she caught sight of the clothes horse standing by the range. There were a few T-shirts of Alasdair's, a pair of David's work jeans and her favourite navy sweatshirt, all hanging together and contented to be sharing the same space, and she was immediately defensive again. This was their home. It was permanent and secure and where she wanted to be for as long as she could imagine. Hazel and Stuart had been invited into this home, yet still her sister treated them as if they were a joke or an ongoing experiment of some sort. Kate stood sedately, but then marched over to the noticeboard hanging by the back door. She removed the entire board and laid it on the table, edging Hazel's mug out of the way and causing a minor spill to dribble over her sister's fingers. Hazel grimaced and sat upright.

"This," said Kate, pointing to a scrap of paper, "is a note of Dave's appointment at the dentist. I made it for him. This is a photo of when the three of us went to a hockey game last year. Look, together. Here's the postcard you sent us, this is a note of parents' evenings coming up. My library card, Dave's ideas for the shed and the costs involved, Alasdair's first attempt at writing a Christmas list. Okay?"

"Okay what?"

"Okay, do you get it? This is the life we have. David, me, Alasdair. We're a family, like you and Stuart are. In fact, I happen to think that we're the best Scottish/Canadian combination since Bruce joined

Runrig, and you know how much I loved Donnie. We've built a life and it doesn't matter how much you doubt us, or worry about the damage it will do to our son, we're going to be together for as long as we have. What vexes me is that you would try to use the thing we're doing as a way of starting this particular conversation! Shit, this is for you, Haze. We decided, together, to do this for you."

Hazel, paler by a degree, sat completely still as Kate returned the noticeboard to its rightful place. Slowly, she massaged her lips together and stared at the mug before her. She could almost picture the skin from her face dripping like candle wax onto the table before her, so heavy and pliable did it feel to her. But the only marks on the table were two dark pennies where her tears had fallen, and she sensed that Kate had finally had enough of her. She had heard it in her voice and had seen it flashing in her eyes, and her sister was currently heading for the door and a better place than here.

"Don't hate me," she suddenly cried.

"Stop making me, then," replied Kate without hesitation, and left the room.

Very slowly, Hazel took her hands off the table and placed them on her empty belly. She looked down at the spread fingers and pressed them even harder against her. Why was she so intent on jeopardising the only chance she ever had of having a child, by falling out with her sister? Could she not, after eight years of watching two of her most beloved people make vows to each other, simply give them some credit for proving her wrong? Well, there was a reason she could not, a learned response which she could not leave behind. But Kate did not know this. She assumed Hazel was harbouring a grudge just for the sake of it, and she could not blame her for that. She could see for herself how much David loved Kate and his son, which should have made a difference to the way she felt. Maybe tonight it had. Maybe tonight she could have explained it once and for all, but she had driven Kate away, and with good cause.

"I'm sorry," she whispered to the void inside. "I'll try again. I'll make it right with her tomorrow."

When Hazel had switched off the remaining lights and trailed through to the hallway, she found Kate sitting on the fifth stair, her elbows resting on her knees and her glum face held in her hands. Hazel stood motionless, wondering if her sister had made it to the first floor and had then had a change of heart or whether the stairs themselves had proved too much of a burden on top of what she was already carrying.

Hazel crawled on her hands and knees up onto the same stair, nudging Kate slightly so that she gave up more space. Kate did so, but did not move her hands away from her face. The light above them caused their shadows to appear defined on the floor, and after a few moments of mutual sighing, Kate became aware that hers now sported a pair of bunny ears. Slowly she turned her head to Hazel, whose face was part apology, part hope, and without a word pulled her hard by the hair. The woman did not even cry out, but clasped her hands in her lap, accepting the penalty for being a horrible sister.

"I don't hate you, Haze, but I could kick your arse on many a day."

"I know," agreed Hazel. "Stuart says the same."

Absently, Kate rubbed her eyes, but she could not imagine how she was going to get from her present position to that of the edge of slumber, either mentally or physically, while there was still so much to address. She was trying to form sentences around her opinions, but even that was such hard work that she was grateful when Hazel leaned back on her elbows and stretched her feet out in front of her.

"You remember the Christmas game? You, me and Mum. That was magic, wasn't it?"

"The best fun," agreed Kate, recalling how, as children, the lead-up to Christmas had always included "rehearsals" for Christmas morning, involving dark rooms, candles and fairy lights. "I might start playing it with Al. He loves the tree in the house."

"I miss her."

"Yeah," agreed Kate, but her neck was beginning to prickle. "She was a fantastic mother. She just made a few mistakes with other folk, that's all."

Since this was a fact with which even Hazel could not argue, she slipped her arm through Kate's in acknowledgement of the truth. In response, her sister laid her head against her shoulder, an action which had been seriously neglected in the past few years, but was still completely natural, and allowed her eyes to begin their dance with sleep. But Hazel was not finished.

"Here's the thing," she said, softly. "I used to think about Dad far, far more than you ever did. And I know it's ridiculous, but in all of the pictures in my head, they were back together and smiling, like they were in their wedding photo. That's how I saw him. With Mum. That's why it's difficult for me. That's why I struggle with it."

Kate's eyes were wide, as if someone had snapped her back into consciousness, and she felt herself tighten the reins of control concerning her family once more. She was not stupid, what Hazel said was clear and perfectly understandable. But time had passed. Their mother was no longer part of their lives, and David was happy.

"I'm not daft, you know," Kate affirmed. "But, Haze, he and Mum were together for five years and then nothing, which was cruel. She took herself and both of us away from him, her choice. I've been married to him for eight years, living every minute with him in this house, planning and sharing, and, for me, nobody even comes close. Not you, not Neil, and not Mum, because if it wasn't for the way David loves me, I would have no life and no son. I'll say it. He's my whole world, and Al and I are his. It's up to you whether you can handle that or not, but it's never going to change."

CHAPTER 8

September 2003 • Vancouver Island

With Alasdair and Rose safely breakfasting on hospital fare, David guessed he had time to say what was on his mind, and better that he made it factual more than emotional, if this was at all possible.

"Kit," he began, "if I start to tell you something, can you listen to the whole thing without interrupting?"

He watched her wipe her face with her gown and could see that she viewed his words as improbable. But when she spoke, there was submission in her voice. "Well, I could give it a go. It's pretty much a day of firsts already."

David wandered to the window, which was disappointing, as Kate liked to take each and every opportunity to look into his eyes, and they were never more intoxicating than when he was using his serious voice. He cracked his knuckles.

"God," she said, trying to inject some levity into the stillness. "Is it that bad? Oh, sorry. That's me shut up."

Kate watched his face, at first with appreciation which evolved into curiosity, and then with the beginnings of a genuine fear. He was not talking, he was thinking, and eventually she placed her hand over her mouth simply to stop herself from asking yet another uninvited question. Even this did not encourage the words, and only when her brow creased into a desperate frown did David pull a chair up to her bedside. She reached for his hand at once, her other remaining clamped to her face below her wide eyes.

"Just give me a minute, honey," he frowned, his voice low.

When David finally began to talk, Kate felt herself sag into her pillows, her ravaged body relaxing inch by painfully breathless inch. No, she had not realised that he had been outside the delivery room when Hazel was born. It had never occurred to her to even think about that. Yes, she could understand that with both his daughter all those years ago and then with Alasdair, David had been handed a baby, clean and swaddled and perfect. To her mind this made him certainly in the minority, but where was this leading? She opened her mouth to ask if this was about the mess she had made on the sofa and the rug, but amazingly managed to keep the words inside. His face was earnest and surprisingly distressed, and he might take it as a joke, which in fact it was not. His hand tightened around her fingers.

"Look at you," he marvelled, "all strong and in control yet ... still hurting. How can twelve hours make so much difference? No, not yet. That was rhetorical. So. Kitty. My problem. I ... I don't want to see that again. I don't want to see you screaming in agony. I didn't know how to make it better, make you better, and you kept asking me to. I wasn't sure that everything was," David paused for a moment then forced out the rest, "I couldn't be sure you were okay or that it was going to work out."

He hung his head low, apparently seriously embarrassed, but Kate needed him to continue as soon as possible.

"I know this makes me sound pathetic and selfish," he mumbled. "I know I should get over it and accept that this happens a million times a day. I'm a grown man who knows a bit about life, but this one has me both beaten and ashamed."

Kate could feel her throat starting to ache with the effort of keeping the tears inside. She had put him in this position, for the best of reasons, but still she had done it. Here he was, leading her down a road she had no wish to travel. She shook his hand gently until he looked straight at her, and it was obvious that although he was putting his feelings before hers, he could not deal with them alone any longer.

"Since I've known you, everything that ever touched you or upset you, I was able to do something about," he explained, with the tone of someone resigned to completing this task. "I've never seen pain like that affect anybody. I thought I had killed you by agreeing to this, and I don't think ... I know I don't want to do it again."

Kate understood that David had not meant to cause her one ounce of anxiety, and that it had taken all of his strength to say the words in the first place, but the emptiness inside her at that moment made her nauseous. The hollowed out space where the tiny infant had been only twenty-four hours before had taken on a life of its own. It was an aching, mourning monster, black and solid, which she could not mould with her hands into something more hopeful. She had assumed that, with the fading of the physical pain, it would begin to whimper instead of wail and that eventually it would go back to sleep. Surely Hazel's delight and the fact that everyone was still alive and celebrating another life would soothe it back to its slumber. But since Alasdair had been born, this monster had been merely hibernating, and David was suggesting that they should perhaps make that sleeping state more official and permanent.

"It wasn't that bad," croaked Kate, trying desperately to forget that she herself had thought she was dying and that Al's expression had been that of pure fear.

David creased his eyes and stroked the inside of her palm. "I've been sick with this all night, but I couldn't think of a way of keeping it to myself. You see everything on my face, you always have, and you always make me share. So, even though what you've done is so incredible, I had to tell you today, because I couldn't have hidden it. I'm sorry, honey."

Kate, lying with her hand limp in his, tried to think of words which would make him feel better, but they failed her for what might have been the first time. Her mouth seemed to be filling with water, as it always did when she was losing control; but her throat would not let her swallow any of it, and slowly she took her hand from his and wrapped both of her arms around the slightly deflated bump in front of her.

"I'm sorry," David repeated.

"It's okay," Kate gulped at last and laughed lightly as she stared at the ceiling, her eyes not willing to connect with his for the moment. "Hey, I'm in no hurry to go through that again. Why the hell would I? I'm absolutely wiped out!"

There was a taste to the air which was almost metallic, as if Kate were running her tongue along a razor blade, but she was damned if she was going to discuss this when there was every chance that she would cry so hard that Alasdair would notice. She bit her lip for one second only and then turned to the man still sporting the desolate face.

84

"But she's worth it, right, Dave? The baby, she's perfect and she's worth it."

"She's precious," stated David.

"Okay then, I think maybe you should go and see what's happening. Make sure she's still doing fine. One of us needs to be watching her. She needs to know there's family in this place."

Thankfully, David did not prolong their awkwardness by asking her how she felt, because in truth she had no idea. She just wanted a little space, a small moment to soothe the monster and sort out the lines of thoughts in her head without his obvious worry tying them in knots. He stood and kissed her cheek, but she grabbed his chin firmly and pressed her lips against his, adamant that his words should not cause any more concern than was necessary. She felt him hesitate and then respond. His rough jaw was almost more than she could cope with. It had been ten months since they had done anything more than kiss and caress, a decision he had made as soon as the surrogacy plans had been agreed; and even now, with her body in shreds, she could remember it all and wanted it all. Slowly she pulled her mouth from his, and there was a tear on his face. David never cried.

"Oh, don't," she whimpered, using her thumb to dry the droplet, her fingers grazing his scar as she did so. "Don't do that, Davey, please."

"If I'd lost you, Kit, I wouldn't have survived. But you're disappointed."

"It doesn't matter!" Kate meant it at that moment. "We have Al, we've done this for Hazel and Stuart. That should be enough and I'll make it enough. But you can't be upset today, or I'm going to crawl under this bed and never come out. I'll stay there for good. I'll turn into some sort of inanimate hermit, surviving only on my own body fat, which will probably keep me going for a year and a bit, and it'll be all your fault. They'll have to shut this room off, probably the whole ward and—"

"Okay," he smiled at last and then took a deep breath. "Okay, I'll go and see the little one, see if Al would like to meet her. But we'll talk again. I love you."

"God," moaned Kate, rolling her eyes. "How long do we have to wait after this? Six weeks is it? Is that the law? Could we be arrested for doing it earlier than that? We've got ten months to make up for."

"Let's just see how it goes," David grinned, more than a little remorse in his eyes. "I won't be long."

When the room was still once more, Kate found herself detesting the whiteness of the walls and stared instead at the sky and concrete of the outside. But it looked equally monotone, and she wondered how green the bay was and whether her sister and husband had already popped a cork with which to wet their daughter's head. She frowned slightly, the notion that there was no actual baby within their physical grasp bringing another little tremor to her heart. She steadied it, clearing her face, but another revelation stepped up to the mark, and this one sparked a double beat.

If she was not very, very careful, she could ruin this entire situation. Had she gone to full term, Hazel would have been present at the birth, and surely her joy and relief would have eased the physical pain of the parting from the child Kate had nurtured. But now she was in grave danger of committing herself to her niece in their absence, and with David's feelings clear and defined with regard to no more "life-threatening" children, this was twice as dangerous and likely. Wrapping her arms around herself once more, Kate tried to recall how she had promised everybody that she could do this, but it brought her no comfort. Why did everybody sound so much more sensible than she did after the event, and why did they continue to believe her assurances?

When Rose entered the room a few seconds later, Kate sought her help immediately. It was anybody's guess how long they would be caring for the child before Hazel could get a flight, or indeed how long it would be before she took her home. Away from them. Rose was going to have to help her, elderly though she was, and Kate was going to have to accept that people would think her hard-faced. Well, there was no choice. She had brought them all to this place, and she had to ride out the consequences. It was exhausting her already, and after a few moments of discussion with Rose, Kate slid down the bed slightly and closed her eyes.

When she opened them again, the clock on the wall was reflecting the sun, and she had to move slightly to read the time. It was nearly midday and the room was empty, but there was an old combat jacket hung over one of the chairs, and Kate looked at it without recognition for a second. However, there was definitely a faint chemical smell on the air, and, true to form, Neil wandered in, careful not to spill the coffee he was carrying.

"She's awake," he grinned, setting down the foam cup. "How are you doing there?"

"I'm bushed," Kate smiled weakly. Never one to show affection outwardly, Neil stood with his arms folded across his chest, nodding as if he visited people in her circumstances every day in life.

It was not awkward; Kate did not expect him to enclose her in a hug. That action was rarely visited on anyone other than Andie and the girls, and she took no offence. He had made a significant journey two days in a row, which was enough to warm her inside, and she finally injected some feeling into her smile. He relaxed at once.

"What the hell happened?" he enquired. "This time yesterday ..."

"Think it was the shock. Who knows? The main thing is that she's okay."

"And you?"

"I'm fine."

With the pleasantries over, Neil sat on the chair by the window and sipped at his coffee. Outside, the sun had decided that it was more fun to play than to hide, and the room was even more dazzling to her than it had been. She shaded her eyes, looking at her father. What a puzzle of an individual he was. There he sat, a man who had learned that human contact could sometimes be deadlier than a nuclear bomb, but who had nevertheless decided to give himself over completely to raising two strangers. Who, in fact, had accepted her after an absence of eighteen years and who had no problem sitting with her today, not speaking, just being.

For the tiniest, briefest moment she felt total gratitude. She was thankful that she was his, because apart from Alasdair, this man had no connection with anyone else on earth. There was no genetic link with the previous generation, and his children were not of his making. But she had been made by him, she was his, and so his features and traits at least had a chance of continuing forward. Alasdair could never be mistaken for anyone's son but David's, but at least he had Neil's colouring. She was glad.

"Have you seen your grandson, Neil?"

"Rose took Sophie and him back to The Edge. His nose was streaming."

Kate's face fell. "Oh," she cried, "You brought Soph? Aw, I wish I'd seen her. She's so gorgeous, and she makes me laugh every time she opens her mouth."

"She's a spark," he agreed. "And ... I had to bring her. She nearly pitched a major one when she knew I was driving over again."

"It's no better then?"

"We'll get there, one day."

《•》《•》《•》

Sophie thought that Alasdair's bed was possibly the bounciest she had ever been allowed to jump on. It barely even squeaked as her activity gradually saw all of his stuffed dogs inch their way to the edge and then tumble to the floor. It had been thirty seconds at least, and still nobody had called a halt to her enjoyment. At home, Mom might have come marching in, hoisting her and twirling her until she screamed with laughter. Or Dad might have banged on the ceiling from his workshop below, shouting something which she could not hear.

Granma Rose had let them stay up here on their own, and they were making the most of the fact that Alasdair was feeling better and that her dad had brought her along. While Sophie bounced to her heart's content, Al was trying to find new batteries for his Battleship game. It had been ages since his mom had the desire to play it with him, and she nearly always lost interest halfway through. Today, he had the opportunity to teach someone who had no idea of strategy, so he was almost bound to win. If only he could find some batteries.

"Wasn't she tiny?" gasped Sophie, between bounces.

"And wrinkled," agreed Alasdair. "Why do people think babies are beautiful? Mom said I was gorgeous. Well, I must have been lucky, because that baby wasn't gorgeous."

"Aw, she was okay. Just small. Bet if we had been in the same room, she would have looked pretty."

"Okay. There are no bloody batteries anywhere!"

Sophie stopped bouncing immediately and sat down hard on the bed, eyes wide. Alasdair knew at once that he had impressed her and was equal parts embarrassed and proud. She was grinning at him, on the verge of laughter, waiting for him to say some more. Daring him to say more.

"Where the bloody hell are they?" he stood, opening his dresser drawer and starting to rummage, grinning to himself as Sophie shouted in glee behind him.

"You would be in big trouble if my mom heard you," she cried. But as he continued to pull open drawers and curse over and over, Sophie stopped laughing and began to think of the previous day. Her dad, hunting through drawers, had said something very strange indeed, and it had involved Al's mom. She was going to find out all about it when she was eight. That was a really long time to wait.

"I know!" Alasdair suddenly shouted. "Mom's sewing room has everything in the world in it. Bet she's got a ton of them in a box somewhere."

Before Sophie had time to ask anything, they were both running through to the back of the house, where Kate had created the workspace which had kept her busy for the last seven or eight years. The room had belonged to Neil as a boy, but the blue wallpaper was gone and had been replaced with a sunny yellow emulsion. This in turn had been covered in photos, fabrics, cuttings and an old OS map of Skye, so much so that very little of the colour was visible. David had built her a shelving unit of many individual compartments, which contained more books and magazines than anywhere else in the house, and a long wide table stood in the far corner. There sat her sewing machine, her most prized possession, which Alasdair knew better than to touch, since his distraction of her had once resulted in her piercing her fingernail. Man, she had jumped up that day, and he had fled as her chair had toppled. That machine was dangerous. Apart from that, he found the room quite uninteresting. Sophie had never been over the threshold and stood, open-mouthed at the colours on show.

"Smells like Mom's shop," she grinned. "But that's a lot tidier than this!"

Alasdair was too engrossed in his mission to comment, but he did not stop her as Sophie began to pick up scraps of material, something he had always been discouraged to do. He was almost positive that the girl would have clean hands, however, so there seemed no harm in it. Sophie's fingers were extraordinarily long and slender for a four-year-old, something which stood her in good stead as she let silk and cotton alike slip through them, back to their semi-folded state.

"Curses," muttered Alasdair, finally tired of actually cursing, "I'm going to ask Granma Rose if she knows where they could be. Do not touch that sewing machine."

But Sophie had already sunk onto the carpet and was staring at the reels of coloured cotton on the bottom shelf in front of her. They were pitifully out of order in terms of colour, and at once she began to rearrange them so that they sat upright and ran from white to black, like her box of crayons did at home. This completed, she hauled herself off her knees and began to look at the wall behind the door which had a giant pinboard covered in photographs, all unframed and all at random, jaunty angles. By dragging the wooden stool from the table, Sophie was able to stand at eye level with most of the images and study everything she saw there. It was better than a picture book.

There were more of Alasdair than anyone else, and Sophie stood entranced. He was her best friend, much better fun to spend time with than Abbie, who always wanted to play house by draping the tartan rug over the upturned clothes horse. It had been fun in the beginning, but Al was brilliant. He let her play in his tree house or organise his ceramic animals and had promised to teach her Battleship, if he ever found the batteries. And there he was, sometimes tiny with white-blonde hair, sometimes older with his head under a cap or sitting in the cab of a huge vehicle. There was even one of him in the bath, but Sophie was too embarrassed to linger on that one. The biggest, most central photo of them all was of Al and his dad. Their heads were together and they were so close to the camera that there was no background visible, but it must have been a sunny day, because both of them had their eyes screwed against the light and were wearing exactly the same grin. There was no colour in the photo, just shades of grey, and so their hair and eyes looked the same; but Sophie noticed everything, and she knew her Uncle David's eyes were green, where Al's were blue.

She liked this particular photo, because their heads were touching and they looked so alike. She also liked her Uncle David because he always spoke to her, asked her questions and smelled slightly differently than her dad. Dad smelled oily and dusty sometimes, Uncle David smelled of sap and sawdust. Back at home, Sophie had even more photos to look at than this. Their bedroom was full of them, some in frames, some stuck on the ceiling. There were the especially precious ones of them with their first mom and dad, but there were even more of their life now. All mixed up together, the way she wanted it. Abbie sometimes asked her about the early photos, but often the little girl was too busy building a house or trying to write her name, and in truth Sophie liked to keep some of her memories just for her.

At the bottom right-hand corner of the large black and white image, three or four coloured snaps of Al's mom holding a baby caught her eye. They looked like they had been taken on the front steps of this house, and the man standing next to Aunt Kate looked like her dad, except that he was really smart and had a tie on. Sophie was standing with her nose only an inch away from this photo when Alasdair came pounding upstairs, yelling that he found some batteries and to get her butt back to his room. When she had not appeared in the next full minute, he found her sitting on the floor of the sewing room, smiling at the small pile of photos in her lap. There was a tell-tale area of bright yellow wall shining into the room, and he stared at her apparent concentration, not understanding how a photo could be more interesting than learning how to play a new game.

"What are they?" he asked, edging closer.

"It could be you," she laughed, "it's got a blue hat on and it's your mom and maybe my dad. What do you think?"

Alasdair dropped onto his knees and took one of the images from her. "Yeah," he said knowingly. "That was my christening. There's another one downstairs on the dresser, except my dad's in that one."

"Look, my dad's holding you in this one. Hope he didn't drop you on your head!"

Alasdair was weary of this chatter. He had seen all of these photos too many times already. "Come on, or we won't have time to play before you go."

"Okay," grinned Sophie, standing and hastily pressing the photos back where she had found them.

In his bedroom, Alasdair's Battleship game was buzzing and flashing its lights, testament at last to the incredible power of batteries. Sophie was giggling as soon as she saw it.

"It looks a bit scary," she snorted. "Does it sting you when it buzzes?"

"No," scorned Alasdair. "But you can't sit beside me. You have to be over there."

Sophie finally settled herself and started to listen to what Alasdair thought she needed to know, but often he spoke very fast, and sometimes he sounded more like his mother than he did the rest of them. So she wrinkled her nose and thought instead of the carefully folded photograph which she was concealing up the sleeve of her jumper and what questions she was going to ask her mom when she got home. Just because her dad wasn't going to tell her anything didn't mean that her mom would not.

CHAPTER 9
Vancouver Island

David lay staring at his socks. They were made of Shetland wool, and Hazel had brought them over as part of his last Christmas present. Surprisingly, he had yet to put a toe through either one of them, and even more surprisingly, they did not itch. His Shetland jumper itched around his neck and he rarely wore it without the protection of a collared shirt beneath it, but these socks were a revelation. They were warm and comfortable, and he had been known to wear them two days in a row, if he thought he could get away with it. As his eyes stayed on them, propped against the foot of the wooden bed frame, he wiggled his toes and then tapped his feet together. He was still fully dressed, stretched out on top of the duvet, not acknowledging the passing of time but trying instead to enjoy as much warmth as he possibly could without moving from his position. It was after midnight, he had been awake now for over forty hours straight, and he guessed his socks were the only thing left to think about.

At one point, perhaps an hour previously, he had been almost in a dream state, although his eyes had never closed and the murmurings in his head had been recollection rather than fantasy. He had been thinking of their early days in this house, when it still bore the marks of a dated, lonely existence, and how Kate had flitted from room to room, making it come alive. From day one, she had called out to him whenever they had been separated by walls, an action which had invariably brought him from his own space to where she was. He had loved to watch her as she shouted out her opinions at an alarmingly Celtic pace, the words of which had occasionally required further explanation.

"Here, Dave, d'you remember that tree on Ben Tianavaig? You know, the bushy thing on the edge of the cliff? You'd better remember it. That was our tree in the bad days, and there's no reason why it shouldn't still belong to us, even if we only see it once every ten years. So, are you with me? You know the one I mean, right? David!"

"I'm in the room, Kit."

"Oh. Well, why didn't you answer?"

"I wanted to see how long you would actually talk. You've been known to go on for minutes, and sometimes I even get the gist of it."

"You can call it trealaich if you want to. I won't be offended and it is just pure and simple gibberish."

"Trealaich."

David smiled at this recollection, because Kate had laughed at his pronunciation and had asked him to repeat a further phrase in Gaelic, which he had refused without first hearing its translation.

Still she had teased. "I swear to you, if you say it, I'll tell you what it means. Please. It's Bidhidh a bhean agam a bruidheann torr trealich gun chiall ach tha mi cho mesail ora." With his Canadian intonation, it had sounded stilted and alien. Kate had guffawed at his many attempts before finally allowing him the satisfaction of knowing that he had declared "My wife talks complete and utter rubbish, but is still adorable." These moments had caused him nothing but joy. Joy that such a personality was in his house, in his life, and that he still seemed to make her happy just by walking through the door. There had also been, prior to that, the intensity of their wedding night, which teased his body whenever he revisited the memory.

The legal process of proving that there was no blood connection between him and Kate had taken all of his energy until the momentum of it had suddenly placed him on Skye, just days before the wedding. Kate's Aunt Beth, whilst taking a long walk around Camastianavaig Bay with him, had questioned the need for them to get married at all. He had been completely frank with the woman. He wanted Kate happy and he wanted Kate safe. He also wanted Kate but needed to make sure that people knew of his total commitment, even if down the road, Kate turned away from him. If it didn't work, he wanted her to know that he had taken her love seriously, however young she was. Beth had been surprised at his honesty, she had told him so there and then; but she had also accepted the situation, because it had been time for all of them to start their new lives.

And then there had been the day of the wedding. He had shaved without cutting himself, steadying his hand and heart by staring at his face in the mirror and telling himself that he could do this, she was worth it. After the ceremony itself, where her hand had been gripped in his the entire time, they had sat at a family table, trying their hardest to appear the one thing they were not: run-of-the-mill. What a pity that he had let her do that on the day where she should have shone brighter than any other being on the planet. He remembered that every time he had looked at her, he had said the word "wife" to himself, but even the recognition of this fact had not soothed his continued fear and amazement.

They had driven through falling snow to a hotel in the northeast of the island. It was the quietest she had ever been in his presence, but she had smiled the whole way, glancing out at the weather every few moments and offering to drive if he was nervous of the road. Oh, there had been nerves inside him all right, nerves which had nothing to do with the roads; but he had matched her smile for most of the journey and even handled the semi-concealed curiosity of the receptionist by standing as tall and as straight as possible. From that moment on, all of his half-formed plans had been shelved as a realisation had hit home; Kate was there in front of him, alone, in private, and he had no conception of how she would react to any of his words or actions. She occupied his every thought, had done for months, and had still managed to remain a divine mystery to him. For one ground-shaking moment, he had been truly scared of his ability to remain cool in her presence, not to mention the hideous doubts about the workings of his long-abandoned body.

But Kate had stood beside him, touching him as and when she had dared, her face so clearly showing her love before she had gone on to voice it, that he had merely replied in kind and it had felt easy. The air between them had been like crystal, and he remembered thinking that he had never been so aware of his environment, standing in the dim light watching Kate's face. She had asked him not to let her spoil the moment, he had asked her to trust him; and when at last her skin had lain against his, they had managed to hold each other in place as the world had gone spinning away from them. It had been their beginning, and it had been remarkable. Somehow, she had made him a player in his own life again, and in all the years since, she had continued to push him through risky doors, all the while following him with complete confidence in both of them. As a young man in his twenties, he had accepted happiness as his right. In spite of Kate, he would never do that again, and now, lying in their empty bedroom, he realised that he had taken his biggest risk to date. He had taken something from her at the hospital, purely to protect himself, and her disappointment had been dangerously apparent. It was little wonder that no rest was coming his way.

When David finally allowed his focus to reach beyond his feet, he saw the dull outline of a fleece hanging on the wardrobe door. If he stared at it long enough, he could almost see Kate standing there, hesitant, wondering if she was still welcome beside him after he had made his feelings known. He cursed out loud and shook the image away. He needed to sleep more than anything else, because the following day he had it all to face again: Charlotte's numb grief, Jay's injuries and Kate's thoughts, none of which were lying easily on his heart, or his stomach for that matter. There had been a substantial amount of grumbling and groaning coming from inside his body in the last hour, but even it had given up the fight at his stubborn lack of respect. However, if his brain truly had lost its ability to shut down, he figured he may as well go and find something to eat. Sighing, he put his feet over the edge of the bed and swung himself upright.

He allowed himself ten seconds or so for his brain to catch up, then stood and wandered over to the top of the stairs. Looking down onto the next landing was like staring into a dark well, but he took the stairway without the aid of the light, and his footing remained sure in spite of his fatigue. As his hand slid down the smooth wood of the banister, he could almost hear Kate giggle behind him.

"Not taking the stairs two at a time, Dave? What's wrong, you feeling your age?"

"I am tonight," he murmured and continued on his way.

In the kitchen, he turned the lights to dim and stood in the half comfort which they provided, his eyes still stinging inside his head. He wondered where to begin. Toast maybe. That would involve the least effort. Or there were those three dead sausages lying in state in the fridge– maybe they could be resurrected with microwaves and a bit of chili sauce. But the light from the fridge was dazzling to the point of hazardous, and so he quickly took the plate to the table and ate all three corpses without the aid of sauce or seasoning. They were totally satisfying.

The next time David sensed anything was when the mobile phone in his shirt pocket buzzed against his chest, and he hauled his head from the table and wiped his mouth, trying all the while to clear the fuzz from his vision. He pressed the answer button without even looking at the clock.

"Hello?" he said, automatically.

"Did I wake you up?" Kate's voice was low, almost a whisper, but it was neither frantic nor urgent, which was a huge positive.

"You did, actually," he yawned. "But this is a good thing. I fell asleep at the kitchen table."

There was a pause and a tiny sigh at the other end of the phone, then, "Dave, man, you need to go to bed. And I need to come home. Nobody in this place listens to a word I say."

"What's happening?" he stood as he spoke and stretched his stiff spine as much as he was able.

"It's not important. They've obviously no idea who they've taken on, I'll be fine. But I really want to come home," she paused and then whispered, "and they don't like me using the cell phone."

As he let her tell him of how the staff were bullies, even the young ones, and that the bed was too hard, too small and too lonely, he made himself switch off lights and head for the stairs. Somehow her outrage helped him to scale both flights, and by the time she had asked him his opinion on all of it, he was finally unclothed and in bed. She had to repeat her final question.

"So can you get me out of here?"

"The baby really needs to stay for a–"

"But I don't," Kate countered and then simply stopped speaking.

David rubbed his eyes, no longer able to contemplate any of the issues involved. "Okay, I'll be over in the morning. I'll see what I can do."

"Thank you," replied Kate, and even in his semi-sleeping state, David was aware that a hard edge outlined the two words.

Barbara Morris

"Will you be okay tonight, sweetheart?"

"Yes," Kate stated. "I just ... I want to be with my family. I need to be with my baby. See you tomorrow."

The phone beeped dead before he had a chance to answer, but he was only able to frown at it for a second or two, before his hand slipped to his side and he was finally asleep.

Later, as the sun began to rise on the hospital car park, shortening the shadows of the few cars still in situ, Kate was up and hunting through her locker for something to pull over her nightdress. Her pitifully inadequate "birthing bag" must have been thrown together by David rather than Rose, as it seemed to contain only two fleeces and a pair of socks. There was no extra underwear and no pads, which meant she was at the mercy of the nurses and so was forced to keep in with them. Her animosity towards the staff was unfounded and had initially surprised her; they were incredible people who cleaned up and took care and mostly did it with a smile, but they wanted to do what "was best," and Kate had stood her ground against it, mostly with a frown. "I'm not breast-feeding her and that's that," she had affirmed, "and if you can't understand why, then it's high time you had yourself a baby that isn't yours. See what your heart says then."

She had spent the half hour following this pronouncement weeping at her own horrible nature and had then walked along to watch as a trainee nurse sat cradling her tiny niece in her arms, patiently coaxing the newborn into accepting the plastic teat into her mouth. There had been glass safely between them, and when eventually the infant was sucking sufficiently, she had watched the nurse raise her head and look straight at her. For a second Kate had smiled in defeat, shook her head slightly and then moved away, leaving a handprint on the previously spotless glass. So, the baby was feeding, and maybe the next time or the time following that, she would give it a go.

As the sun rose higher and the ward began to rustle and sigh, Kate needed to be out of her room and away from the cloying demands of the people around her. She took a paper towel from the dispenser and scribbled a few words of reassurance on its surface, laughing to herself at her optimism; did she really imagine she would be able to get farther than a few yards? But she had pulled on her socks and a fleece in the meantime and slowly peered through the open door. The immediate area was clear, but this would not be the case for long, so she focussed on the nearest darkened room and slid her way safely into it. It took less than twenty seconds before her body began to throb, resenting her assumption that it was ready to go anywhere at pace, and the end of the ward began to stretch away from her. She paused at the window of the peaceful nursery, still within the bounds of acting perfectly normally, before she took her final step to freedom and escaped the ward.

In spite of the hour, there was a tremendous bustle of activity as she took in the clean floors and sparse interior around her. She had no recollection of the previous journey through these halls, but it felt good to be part of a bigger picture at last, where no other human in her sight knew her circumstances or wished to express an opinion on them. A porter nodded at her as she managed a wide confident smile in his direction and managed to reduce her hobble to a sedate amble for his benefit. She stopped beside a row of four seats and wondered if other such seats could be found at strategic places along the corridor, specifically spread out to encourage escaping prisoners to make a break for the next one. Either way, Kate sat tenderly for a moment or two, resting her aches, and tried to remember the reason behind her journey. Amazingly, about fifty yards in front of her, lay the answer. This was proving far too easy. Really, an escape should not be as technically effortless as this, and yet there was a small seating area next to a booth selling sweets and hot drinks; her ultimate goal.

Kate stood slowly, gliding and shuffling her socks along the flooring until the array of goodies were in front of her and the simple choices once again made her feel in control.

"Can I have a cup of tea, please? Oh, and some chocolate fingers. They've been my favourite forever."

The young man behind the counter grinned as he reached for a tea bag.

"Which part are you from?" his accent was even broader than Kate's, and she squealed in reply.

"Oh, from Skye! What about you?"

"Lanark. Or as near as damnit. I'm Tom. Would you like milk in that?"

Kate nodded, still delighted beyond words that a Scot was serving her, and watched as he tried to remove the bag without scalding his fingers. He failed and ended up cursing under his breath, sucking his thumb before he fished it out with a plastic spoon. Kate helpfully took the chocolate fingers from the stand and laid them on the plate on the counter.

"Are you a native now?" Tom asked, ringing up the total on the till.

Kate laughed at the word, then shrugged, offering her hand. "Kate. And I've been here for nearly nine years, but I point-blank refuse to lose this accent. Nobody in Portree would be impressed if I went back there with a twang. Oh, curses! Oh no."

"What's up?"

Kate's face burned with embarrassment as she patted her fleece pocket and realised that she was carrying no currency whatsoever. More than that, she was standing in front of a young compatriot, highlighting to both of them that she was dressed only in a nightgown, inadequate fleece and socks. She held her head in her hand for a moment, while Tom could provide her with no crumb of comfort.

"Kate?"

At the sound of her name, Kate's head flicked up and there stood Charlotte Forsyth, her face drawn and confused beneath her grey fringe. Kate's initial relief at recognising the woman quickly collapsed into complete despair as she remembered the woman's own circumstances, and all she could do was reach out and touch her arm.

"Charlotte. Hello. How ... how is he doing?"

Charlotte looked down at Kate's hand on her arm and then back at her face. She pursed her lips against the pain of her words and croaked, "Same. What are you ...?"

Kate closed her eyes at the complete awfulness of the situation and said simply, "I wanted a drink and I don't have any money."

Without a word, Charlotte made her way past her and took a note from her purse. She laid it on the counter without looking at Tom, handed the cup straight to Kate and sat at the nearest table, her hands instantly folding in her lap. Kate, dry-mouthed and mortified, could do nothing but glance once at the man behind the counter, then sit opposite her friend; she had not even been able to buy her a drink. Hesitantly, Kate pushed the cup towards her.

"You have it, Charlotte. I really just wanted a change of scene." Again, if Kate could have cut out her own tongue she would have. But the words barely seemed to register, and Charlotte scratched at the back of her neck and shook her head. She took a breath in and then eased it out slowly through slightly parted lips. Her hands began to move, and as she silently twisted her wedding ring round and around, Kate desperately tried to think of words. Adult words of comfort for this woman's plight, which seemed way beyond her reach. Instead, she watched the surface of her tea tremble as a porter hurried by with a mop trolley, and tried to lubricate the inside of her mouth.

"So, you've had a little girl, then?" Charlotte's words were no stronger, but at least she had raised her head in Kate's direction.

"Yes," replied Kate. "A bit early, but they think she'll be fine. Oh, Charlotte, I'm so, so sorry."

"I don't want to go home. I need to. The kids ..."

When a second cup of tea appeared in front of Kate, she raised her bleak face and, thanking Tom with her eyes, pulled her fleece a little tighter around her. Again, she tried to find a word or a phrase which might show how stunned she still felt at Charlotte's loss; but she could only equate it with losing her mother, and that had been such a long, expected passing that it didn't qualify. She almost forced herself to imagine that David had been hurt, to try and find a way of empathising, but she was nowhere near brave enough to travel that path, even if just in her imagination. So, she found herself sipping her tea instead, shivering slightly in spite of the heated hallway.

"Is she in isolation?"

Kate, thinking only of Jay lying injured and alone, was confused momentarily by the question. In the silence, Charlotte looked closely at her face.

"She must be," Charlotte answered her own question, "or why would you be out here, wandering about? Sorry, that was thoughtless."

Kate swallowed, the first fingers of true shame encircling her heart. "She's not. She's doing really well. I just ... I mean," she began to struggle as her hormones grew in density and fell like rocks in her gut. She put her arms around her own waist and tried to ease the heaviness there. But she could not stop her eyes from filling and her throat from aching. "It's just, I can't get too close, Charlotte. I have to give her away and Dave says .... Well, I know it's going to hurt a lot."

For the first time since the beginning of their conversation, Charlotte looked as if she might be registering the situation, and in the next few moments, Kate saw her narrow her eyes and lick her upper lip. Kate held her breath, but there was no comfort heading her way just yet.

"Please tell me you understand," Kate almost whimpered.

Charlotte shrugged her weary shoulders and fixed her frown on Kate. "I can't do that," she said firmly. "Not on this day."

Kate supposed she deserved nothing more and did not push for it, but hung her head as Charlotte got to her feet.

"I would dearly love to see the little mite," said Charlotte as she put her hand on Kate's shoulder. All the younger woman could do was to follow her as she began her journey towards the maternity unit. By the time she had slid along behind the woman for the length of two corridors, Kate was beginning to feel slightly light-headed, her body protesting in the strongest terms yet to her treatment of it. She slowed to a halt on the threshold of the ward, and finally Charlotte glanced in her direction, frowning at once. Her eyes opened wider still as she saw the thin trail of bloody droplets, some smeared into tracks by Kate's own socks, which had accompanied them on their journey. "Kate, are you in pain?"

"No," croaked Kate, then "I've got a stitch and I could do to lie down but—"

"You're bleeding. Come on."

Kate allowed herself to be guided onto the ward, more mortified than scared; that floor had been a shining example of cleanliness before she had leaked spots and smears onto it, and she wanted nothing more than to be somewhere private where she could hide her face and sort herself out. They had almost made it to her room when they were met by one of the day nurses, clutching the paper towel, her face set for a fight. Kate chose her attitude wisely.

"I need a new pad. I've made a bit of a mess, sorry."

"I can see that," the nurse agreed, then made a point of crumpling Kate's note into a ball and binning it in front of her, before taking Kate's other arm and escorting her to the toilet.

"Please," cried Kate over her shoulder to Charlotte. "Stay for a bit?"

Kate took her admonishment with reasonably good grace, pointing out (only the once) that she was not haemorrhaging but simply needed a fresh pad and agreed that perhaps she did know less than all the professionals on the ward and that most patients probably were more amenable and grateful.

"Well, I can see why you'd think I was a gigantic pain," she sighed at last. "I'm not all googly-eyed about the baby, and I've been a bit snappy. But I'm trying to do this the best way I can."

"You can start by getting back into bed and actually resting. Your body took some knocks, you know."

Kate could feel the tears and wounds as she stood to hobble to the bed, but stifled the need to be flippant and instead waited until she was propped against her pillow.

"Please, the lady who came in with me. She's just lost her husband and her son is in a bad way. Could you let her see the baby?"

The nurse did not even hesitate. "No, I can't do that, but you can. I'll bring her along and she can see her in here."

Even if the woman had not walked out at this point, Kate was not sure she could have argued, for there was a razor-sharp panic cutting through her and her impulse was to contact David and scream for help. The child in her arms would prove too much, nothing was more certain. But the phone was in her hold-all, and the pillows beneath her head and back were working their magic on the rest of her aches, so she merely stared at the empty doorway until Charlotte appeared.

"You're very white," Charlotte commented.

"I'm scared."

"So, you've never been scared before, Kate? I can't believe that, and yet you're still here, still surviving."

The words, said in anything other than Charlotte's even tone, might have had Kate climbing back onto her soap box, but instead she burst into real tears. It was the sheer defeat which felled her; the realisation that she could be as bolshie and as confident as she liked, but when it came down to it, she was fighting against the needs of her own body as much as the opinions of everyone else. She wanted to hold the child, she wanted to have another baby of her own, and she wanted David there in the room. Nothing was right if he was not "with" her; and she had been her usual determined, demanding cow to him earlier, when all he had needed was some peace. They were all trying to cope with a situation which she had initiated, and she was still trying to run the show.

"I'm such a terrible person," she murmured, as her tears dripped onto the bedsheet, "you know it and I know it. I'm scared that maybe Dave knows it now, too."

Whether she agreed or not, Charlotte allowed Kate to feel as she did until the tiny infant was wheeled into the room between them. With no action other than to hand Kate a fresh tissue, the staff nurse retreated and left the two women alone. Kate blew her nose, but did not lift her head until she heard a tiny sniffle near her ear, and there was the most perfectly snubbed nose and softly closed eyelids in front of her. She had nowhere to run to, and automatically her arms accepted the bundle, tears still rolling as she gaped at Charlotte. Before she could say anything, the older woman had sat close to her and put her arm around her shoulder. The baby smelled sweet and new and beyond familiar, and Kate had no choice but to whisper into the rare and beautiful face.

"Hello, sweetheart. Hello there," she cooed for a couple of seconds, before looking up at Charlotte, "I'm sorry, I'm useless."

"Kate, you're sore, blue and worried. Give yourself a break."

For moments which may even have been minutes, Kate and Charlotte studied the youngest human being known to either and marvelled at the effect she had on them. She had been in the world less than forty-eight hours and somehow had still brought a little pocket of peace to two anxiety-ridden women. Kate, feeling the small bundle's heat against her, closed her mind off to how the warmth was once again filling the void inside and instead tried to imagine Hazel's basic, pure joy at finally having a child of her own. There, in front of her, was possibly Hazel's mouth and a hint of Stuart's dark hair. A wave of shame hit Kate as she realised she had not even established the colour of the sleeping infant's eyes.

"Oh," she simply murmured and leaned her head forward so that her lips grazed the fontanelle. "They are going to spoil you rotten."

"That's what it's all about," stated Charlotte. Very slowly she rose from her seat, running her finger delicately one last time along the baby's forearm and kissing Kate on top of the head. "I need to go. Let her make you happy, Kate. She's here for a good reason."

Happy, thought Kate, as she watched Charlotte disappear. Happy sounded quite pleasant. Happy sounded more relaxing, and really, why not let your heart warm up and soften? That was better than this strong, hard shell keeping everything at bay, right? She could kiss this child, knowing that she had carried it for Hazel; imagine if this began to redress the balance? Imagine if the years Hazel had spent fighting her demons, losing all sense of rationality where food was concerned, and viewing every eventuality in terms of her father's relationship, could be aided simply by placing the bundle into her arms. Imagine if that were the case.

"Imagine if any of your ridiculously simple solutions ever come to pass?" Kate said out loud, "That would be the real shock."

When David crossed the threshold of Kate's room an hour later, his face wary and drawn, he found his wife asleep with a tightly wrapped pink body tucked into the crook of her arm. The smile jumped onto his face from where it had been hidden for too long, and he sat quietly beside the immobile pair, trying to arrange his scrambled thoughts around the scene in front of him. His wife, his granddaughter, Hazel's delight, Stuart's pride, Ally's curiosity and his own relief. It was enough to bring him to the brink of tears, but in the next second there was an insistent squawk, and both Kate and the child were moving again. He watched her concern turn to pleasure on seeing him, and he leaned over to kiss her before his heart did indeed overflow.

"I love you," they said it simultaneously and then laughed.

"Davey," said Kate, as he extricated the newly screaming baby from her sanctuary, "She has brown eyes."

PART II

Christmas Eve 2003

CHAPTER 10

Vancouver Island

"No, no, no!" cried Kate, thumping the dashboard of the SUV with her fist. "You are the most annoying person I have ever had to listen to! Please, please stop."

When there was no reply, Kate turned her face to David to find his green eyes, barely visible beneath his woollen hat, staring right back at her.

"It's Christmas," he stated evenly, looking back at the road. "I thought I could inject a bit of–"

"I can't believe," protested Kate, "that you're using the 'most wonderful time of the year' as the excuse for your, I'll say it again, appalling lack of ability in this field."

"Only the first line was right," added Alasdair from his seat in the rear.

"Okay, but did you or did you not get the gist of it?"

The remainder of the driveway back to The Edge was covered by both Kate and Alasdair enquiring as to how repeating "You better watch out" four times could possibly tell anybody that Santa was on his way. He bore the criticism in his usual manner, grinning through his eyes and keeping his mouth firmly straight to maintain some sort of dignity.

"And I'm sorry, Dave, but how is it possible that you cannot hold a tune?"

"Don't even know what you mean by that."

The debate continued until the Christmas presents for the Port Alberni crew were safely stashed under the tree and Al had curled himself onto the sofa with his Game Boy Advance. The fire looked as if it could be revived with a bit of work on David's part. Kate declared that the topic should perhaps be dropped until the next time the man wished to assault his family in such a way. As she headed towards the kitchen, the phone rang out in the hall and she changed direction, still smiling at the sight of David's incredulous face and solely personal belief that he was musical.

It was Rose, as Kate imagined it would be. The woman had a telepathic mind when it came to her family returning to their home. Or maybe she simply sat by the window, waiting for the headlights to fracture through the trees in the dusk, which was as good as a trumpeter heralding their arrival.

"They were worse last week," Kate answered the woman's first question regarding the roads, "I think there might even be a thaw in the air."

"Well, I was wondering what time you were thinking of collecting her. Tonight or first thing in the morning?"

"Oh, not sure. I did think about it, but I never got a chance to ask the boss. I'll ring you back after we've eaten– unless you are completely sick of her right now?"

Rose's voice sounded anything but fed up. "No, no, that's fine. We'll sit and watch the stars for a bit longer. Speak to you shortly."

When David wandered through to the kitchen, his pink cheeks showing that he had indeed managed to get the flames to roar once more in the fireplace, Kate pulled the hat from his head and laughed at his hair.

"That was Rose," she grinned. "She wonders if we want to collect the pup tonight or in the morning. What do you think?"

With the kitchen door safely closed between them and their son, David rubbed his hair back to normality and twisted his face in indecision. Unbelievably, neither Kate nor he had ever owned a dog of their own, and yet they had produced a child who was obsessed with all things canine and who probably knew more about how to look after a pet than either of them. David reckoned Neil was to blame for this state of play, allowing Al to commandeer his dogs on each and every visit. Then, after the wrench of handing over Hazel's baby had left even Alasdair a little subdued, Neil had hinted that a puppy would be a really great Christmas present. There was no arguing with the thought, although in his private heart David was a bit annoyed that it had not been his idea. So, here they were. Christmas Eve was upon them, the dog gear was safely hidden under the spare bed, and the only question to answer was when to bring the tiny spaniel bitch into the house. Neither was entirely sure how to handle the situation.

"Well, does it make a fuss?" David asked. "Is it likely to wake him up?"

Kate shrugged. "Haven't a clue and it's a she. I think we should just risk it. It'll be less hassle than in the morning."

"Okay," he agreed, then began to smile as he took off his inner coat, "God, can you imagine his face? Hope this pup is as patient with him as Neil's two are. He'll pet it to death."

Kate had turned to retrieve the previous day's meatloaf from the fridge, but while she was scanning the shelves for the foil-wrapped slab, she felt David's chin on her head and his arms around her middle.

"What you got me for Christmas, Kit?"

Kate laughed out loud, but held his arms in place. "You think I'm actually going to tell you, matey? It's less than a day to go, and I told you not to get too excited. You're worrying me."

"Don't worry on my account," he whispered into her hair, as the kitchen door opened. Only one thing could drag Alasdair away from his game, and, true to form, his little body joined them at the open fridge door.

"Are there any pickles?"

"Bottom shelf," replied Kate, finally pulling David's arms from her but turning to kiss him before moving away. The stubble on his face was still warm from the fire, and he winked at her as she messed up his hair one last time, purely to annoy him.

"Do you two want chips or baked spuds?"

As the preparation gradually evolved into a sit-down meal, Alasdair became increasingly agitated and loud. Kate gave him as much rope as possible, hoping that by running himself into the ground, he was more likely to sleep through the moving in of the pup. David also tried really hard for about an hour to accommodate the skipping and the shouting, even the dancing on the chair, until Kate had sent him into the sitting room for his first whisky of the day. By 8:00 p.m., when her son's enthusiasm had finally waned for a full thirty seconds, Kate took her opportunity and hauled him upstairs. His protests rang out until she turned into her sewing room instead of his bedroom and seated him on her sewing table.

"Right, Al. Time is marching on, and the fact is Dad needs to relax a bit before everybody descends on us tomorrow. So, grab that tape and we'll wrap this last present. After that, you go and say goodnight to him. Time you were in bed."

"But it's still early," moaned Alasdair.

"Fine, but here's the deal. The later you stay up tonight, the later you stay in bed tomorrow. Up to you."

Al reckoned that he loved his mom. She was pretty, and she liked to watch films with him on a Monday night when his Dad was at the Rotary. She regularly made biscuits, and when she was busy in her sewing room, he was still allowed to ask her questions and wander in and out as he pleased. But sometimes she was really annoying. Like tonight, when the tone of her words and the look in her eye meant there was absolutely no point in arguing with her. He frowned instead, picking up the clear tape and hunting in vain for the end of it, then watched as his mother retrieved a package from behind her bookcase and began to rip the brown paper from it.

"It's already wrapped," he pushed one last time and then rolled his eyes as the gift was revealed. More photos in a frame. He could have guessed as much.

Kate traced her hand over the professionally framed images, her grin finally intriguing the boy enough for him to slide off the table and join her. This frame was different from the clip frames she had all over the house; the photos were separated by a creamy-coloured card. However, the faces were ever-familiar and Neil would love it.

"Why do you like photos so much?" enquired Alasdair. "You can't do anything with them once you've seen them."

"I know. But look. Uncle Neil's going to love these. Sophie and Abbie and you."

Alasdair had already lost interest and handed over the tape. "I'll go say goodnight."

"Remember your stocking!" his mother shouted as he sloped off, "I'll be down in a minute."

When Kate joined her two men a mere five minutes later, David was trying to find the least inflammatory position on the mantelpiece from which to hang a fabric stocking. Although Alasdair was offering his opinion regarding the best place, he was also running out of steam at last, and a yawn obliterated his words. For the first time in almost a year, he lifted his arms up to Kate and she grinned broadly as she lugged him onto her hip; he was too tired even to object to her delighted surprise. By the time she had rolled the duvet up over his chest, his eyes were already drooping, and he kissed the side of her face in total submission. "Night, Mom. Will you come and find me in the morning?"

"You bet, Al," Kate smiled, recognising his father's tired expression. "It'll be just you and me, like always."

With maybe a totally unexpected addition, thought Kate as she turned off the overhead light. The last thing she noted as she closed the door was the silent flickering of snow through the gap in his bedroom curtains. Before returning to the sitting room, she shrugged herself back into her coat and hat and picked up her boots. She fully expected David to be dosing on the chair, his glass dangerously suspended above the ground, but he was hovering instead by Al's stocking. He seemed to be studying it, trailing his fingers over the snow-white fluff and red felt, and she slowed at the sight of him. What was he thinking? What thoughts had prevented him from sitting in his favourite chair and sipping at his favourite malt?

"You okay, Dave?"

"Never better," he assured, turning to her with a grin which did not quite light up his eyes. Kate raised her own eyebrows in response.

"Have it your way," she replied softly, then, "I'm going to take myself over there, unless you desperately want to go?"

David was quite happy to act as childminder but insisted on tying her scarf firmly in place before allowing her to disappear. When it was established that she would walk over, he wondered if they could risk leaving Al in the house by himself; for a man who knew the dangers of snow, he was surprisingly fond of walking in it. But another minute down the line and Kate was wandering alone down the driveway, her mitt wrapped around the big torch, trusting that David's quiet mood was due to tiredness alone. The snow was falling down in feathers around her, and the silence was divine. Peace. Snow always brought her peace, and she lifted her face to the sky and sighed. There would be precious little peace in the days to come, best to make the very most of this night.

And there was Rose's porch light, detracting slightly from the Christmas bulbs strung around the doorway. She saw a silhouette wave from the sitting room, and she waved her torch back in its direction.

"It's freezing again," Kate stomped into the kitchen. "So much for the thaw. Oh, baby dog!"

The pup came tripping through in Rose's wake, her whole rear end wagging from side to side, and Kate was down on her knees in a second. At ten weeks old, her brown and white face, head and ears were smooth and warm, and Kate could not stop kissing her. In response, the pup's excitement and delight caused her to freshly water Rose's pine floorboards, an action complemented by high-pitched yelping. Kate was in love, and she scooped up the struggling, squirming body into her arms and allowed the pup to wash her face with its tongue. Rose smiled and reached for the kettle.

"Well, there's no way you can hide her when she's this excited, so how about a coffee?"

Half an hour later, the pup was fast asleep on Kate's knee, and the heat from the wood-burner was threatening to lull Rose and her daughter-in-law into a similar state. It was just too comfortable. Rose's house may be full of the dated furniture which had once graced The Edge, but the fire was lighting up the seasoned pine walls, and every object on view had become just as familiar to Kate as it was to David and Rose. The coffee mug on the table next to her had been replaced with a small glass of sherry, and Kate was wondering how she would ever gather enough energy to pull her boots on and trek back through the woods.

"I can't wait to see Neil with those girls," murmured Rose, downing half of her sherry and licking her lips. "Have you noticed how he watches them when he's not preoccupied?"

Kate nodded and smiled, recognising the truth of the matter. But incredibly, she also felt a little arrow of envy enter her. It was possibly the first time that she had acknowledged this feeling, and it seemed a little ridiculous to be jealous of two individuals who had lost so much. She had never been jealous of Andie, so why did the two blonde sisters, or rather, Neil's devotion to them, make her feel a bit hard done by? She shifted in her seat, slightly ashamed and reminded herself that if she had known him as a child, she would be in a very different position. She had spent her childhood without a father, her mother had made such a figure seem superfluous, anyway; but she was lucky enough to know the man, know how things had been, and he was a decent person. Rose and Pete must have been really together as parents, moulding David and Neil as they had done.

"I wish I had known Pete," Kate stated, forgetting as ever that her companion had been ignorant of her thoughts up till that moment. Rose froze in her seat for a microsecond, her eyes wide, and then grinned.

"How on earth did you know I was thinking of Pete?" she asked.

"I didn't," laughed Kate. "I was thinking you must have been real partners, to bring Dave and Neil up the way you did. They're both strong men."

Rose settled herself back against the easy chair and allowed herself a small sigh of satisfaction.

"Well, I wish you'd known Pete, too. He was the person who propped me up. Some days it felt like my soul was thinner than paper, and he was always there."

Kate hesitated for only a second. "Did Pete know about Neil and Mum? Was he in on it?"

"He knew. I never told him at first, but I suppose somewhere along the line, he questioned Neil's reaction, where David was too lost to do so, and I couldn't lie to him. He never went near either of them with it, though. We couldn't allow it to be discussed in the house."

Of all the facts which Kate had gleaned during the years of coming to terms with her family's lives, the most difficult to accept was that David had spent many, many months isolated in his mind. At twenty-eight, his life had been changed beyond recognition with no justifiable reason, and he had been forced to get up each morning and ask his brain to think of a way of surviving the hours until he could sleep once more. How much time had he wasted, when his body and mind should have been at their peak, on the past and those unanswerable questions? It hooked and pulled Kate's stomach to the base of her spine when she considered this, which is why she rarely did so. She might go insane trying to picture David's confusion on his lean face. It was much easier to overexpose that image, letting it dissolve into white light, and see instead his positive eyes and mouth; the face that she knew now. She was lucky.

"I'm so lucky," Kate's voice was weary, but assured. "I get to see Dave at his best. Thanks for looking after him."

When Rose failed to reply, Kate stroked the head of the snoring puppy and added softly, "And thanks for letting me love him. I owe you for making it easy."

Rose shook her head gently then raised her glass. "Here's to you all. All of my oddly complex but treasured family."

They toasted her words.

"I should definitely think about moving," Kate murmured, not moving an inch. "It'll be Christmas Day in the good old UK already. Wonder how they're faring. Bet that 'leanabh beag priseil' has more presents than all the rest of them put together."

Rose knew exactly who Kate was referring to, and wondered if the girl continued to miss watching the progress of her niece. It had been eight weeks since she had been put on a plane with her natural mother and waved off into the dark blue sky. Since then, Kate had put her mind to getting rid of the "aftereffects of carrying another human" and had given a pretty plausible impression of someone who had accomplished something and was happy with the outcome. Only once had Rose seen her hug herself around the waist, bent double as she screwed up her eyes, but it had lasted three seconds at the most and had not been spoken of by either of them. It was anybody's guess how many other times her loss had affected her that way, but tonight she was dozing by the fire, a contented curiosity highlighting her face; and for the first time ever Rose caught sight of another young woman in her calm expression. It was extraordinary, and she could do nothing but hold her breath as Kate's inanimate eyes stared off into middle distance. It was not Fiona whom Rose recognised; Kate had so much more of Neil in her features, and tonight, when she seemed a mixture of intrigue and gratitude, there was another individual there altogether.

"Gracious," Rose breathed.

"What?" Kate's face was once more her own.

Rose sat forward, trying to calm the fluttering of her heart and remaining speechless whilst also trying to choose a path to follow. Kate herself sat up at the woman's hesitation and flushing cheeks. When she was still inanimate a few seconds later, Kate stood, the puppy sliding to the floor and only waking as the world fell away from under her. She hauled herself onto her four paws, shook herself better and wandered nearer to the wood-burner before flopping onto the much safer rug.

"Rose? What's up?" Kate was kneeling by her chair when finally Rose took a breath in and let it out in a shudder of sound. She let her eyes study her daughter-in-law once more, and it was all she could do to cup Kate's mystified face in one hand.

"I'm fine, my lovely Kate," Rose pushed herself forward to the edge of her seat and put her arms around her daughter-in-law. "But you should get yourself away through the woods before Davey sends out a search party."

Kate allowed herself to be held in a hug for just one more second before sitting back on her heels. "But you look shocked. A bit ill, if you want the truth."

Rose used her hand to suggest that Kate was talking nonsense, but did not follow it up with words. And although her original colour was back, she waggled her fingers in the air as she stood and wandered over to the fire. Kate watched her move; the woman in front of her was eighty-three years of age, suffering at the beginning of an arthritic journey, and yet she was pacing around the room, trying to look as if she was doing a normal sweep and tidy of her most comfortable space. Kate was not fooled, but held her tongue.

"My, honey, it really is getting late," Rose spoke evenly. "I'm fine. I just saw something that I haven't seen in years, and it was unexpected. But not unpleasant. Goodness, it's not even that mysterious. Go on, off you go. Otherwise I won't be up soon enough to share the excitement in the morning."

"It's only ten past ten. I know you're a night owl, but if you really don't want to tell me ..."

Rose remained undecided as she straightened photographs on top of her bureau and shook out the velvet curtains until they hung perfectly straight and free of stray folds. She almost laughed to herself; when had the curtains ever been so important? And still Kate had not moved from her kneeling position. As the seconds stretched, she could almost feel the girl begin to steel herself against whatever was coming, and, actually, she should be feeling apprehensive. As Rose moved to put another log on the wood-burner, Kate gave in to her curiosity and stood.

Instead of reaching for her scarf, however, she lifted the crystal glasses and filled both with twice as much sherry as previously.

"You'd better put more than one log on there, Rose, because I'm not leaving until you tell me what's going on. When I go back home, I want to be cuddling up to my husband, not sitting worrying about you. That's me being honest."

"You're never anything else," replied Rose, but she took the glass and gratefully seated herself once more.

The truth was, Rose had information that, since the passing of her husband, no other member of her family was party to. The knowledge had been neither a hindrance nor a blessing, it had simply been there for her to use or ignore. She had always ignored it, but lately, it had begun to creep into her thoughts. This might have been due to her recognition of her body's decline. Equally it might have been that she had never felt more secure or in love with her whole family. Tonight, it had been an expression on a dear face and that expression had not caused fear, but rather total wonder. Maybe it was time to share, to let someone else enjoy the knowledge; perhaps even make use of it.

"Okay," assured Rose, "I won't keep you, but I just had the strangest experience, and I can't think of one reason why it should happen tonight. So, I'll view it as a green light to go ahead and tell you. What you want to do with it after this is up to you."

Kate was listening closely, Rose could tell, but it was obvious that she was completely baffled by the words and more than a little bit anxious. There was a tiny lip of pink irritation appearing on her neck beneath her jumper and her spine was tense and rod straight. This reminded Rose that Neil's spine had a kink in it and that seemed as good a place to start as any.

"You know, Neil was in second grade before we knew about his scoliosis. It was very mild and it didn't seem to hold him back, but I was still mortified that I hadn't noticed it. A mother should know these things."

Kate shrugged as she paused, but relaxed slightly and eased herself to the back of the seat.

"I remember David being quite interested," Rose continued, "and it was the one time he acknowledged that Neil was born of someone else. Do you know what he said?"

Kate shook her head.

"He said, 'I wonder if his mom or dad had the same thing.'"

"But, it's not necessarily hereditary," Kate whispered, thinking of how mercifully straight and perfect Alasdair's miniature spine appeared to one and all. "I read all about it when I was pregnant. Also, Neil's spine is barely noticeable."

Rose smiled. "You're absolutely right, but here's the point. When David said that, I remember telling him that we'd never know and that we should concentrate instead on helping him deal with it."

Kate waited for her to continue, still mildly disconcerted that they should be holding such an odd conversation, when she had not one clue what had caused it or where it was likely to end up. "Okay," was all she could add.

Rose took another sip of the sweet liquid and savoured the taste as much as she savoured the silence of the moment.

"Do you feel safe, Kate?"

Kate levered herself out of the chair. "Look, you're really starting to worry me. What d'you mean by safe? Is Neil okay?"

Rose also stood and joined Kate by the stove. "I want to tell you something, only I seem to be making a bit of a meal of it. Of course you feel safe. David would kill for you and Al." She paused for one more second but could feel Kate begin to tense beside her and decided to go for it. "The truth is, I know for a fact that Neil did not inherit his condition from either of his parents. I knew them both, his mother very well."

Kate's eyes and mouth opened simultaneously. "Oh!" she cried. "I just assumed that it was all anonymous."

"Well, no, it wasn't, and tonight I saw an expression on your face that I've seen before on another girl. Neil doesn't know who she is. I don't know if he's waiting for ..." Rose paused to smile and then added, pointedly, "a more appropriate time, but he only once mentioned looking for his mother, and that was during the black days. Since then, he hasn't shown any interest whatsoever, and that's fine at the moment, but I just wondered if you had ever been curious."

Kate gave it a little thought. "Not really," she said eventually. "Maybe if Al ever– Oh God, Rose why are things so complicated? Sometimes when I think about all of us, it feels like there are all these long branches which started off straight enough and then got tangled up with each other, and I can't quite get through them. Going further back just seems like it would make it even harder."

"Fair enough, Kate," Rose patted her shoulder and moved away. "If you're happy with that, then I'm perfectly happy with that."

It felt like the biggest anti-climax of Kate's life, and she mentally kicked herself for causing the conversation to end as abruptly as it had begun. When Rose returned from the kitchen with Kate's coat and boots, she sighed and took them from her. Her hands were shaking slightly, and as she zipped the lethargic puppy into her coat, she knew that wandering back through the woods and then expecting to fall into a peaceful sleep were beyond her capability. Both women were silent as Rose opened the front door and allowed the chill of the night to cloak the pair of them. It seemed to freeze them for another shocked second, before the puppy yawned loudly and sniffed at the air, squirming already, and Kate knew that she had to leave. Rose kissed her cheek and then the nose of her charge.

"See you bright and early, the pair of you," she smiled, and began to retreat back to the heat. At the door, she was aware of Kate's eyes still peering at her from between the rims of her scarf and hat, and she could not close the door on the concern she found in them. "What is it?"

Kate bit her lip, and then, "I don't mind if you want to tell me. Some night soon, maybe?"

CHAPTER 11

Vancouver Island

David met Kate in the kitchen. "It's nearly eleven, Kit."

Kate rolled her eyes, unzipped her coat and gladly unburdened herself of the "monster." "We were almost on our way when she got her second wind, or fifth wind actually, so I wandered about outside for a while until she tired herself out. Sorry, that's our Christmas Eve buggered."

David was unable to reply, as the pup recognised fresh meat and began to lick his face. She stopped almost at once, however, when she realised that a hairy face was not quite as irresistible as a smooth one. "It's fine. Hell, if this is her tired ..."

In the sitting room, Kate noted that the fire was still comfortably alight and David had already filled Al's stocking, but she was shattered, and so fell onto the sofa, stretching out fully and throwing her arms over her face. David closed the door behind them and finally released the dog onto the floor. He watched in wonder as the tiny body covered the entire room in less than a minute, sniffing and nudging, skittering and halting only at the sight of the huge Christmas tree. She immediately looked it over and then retreated a couple of feet, before sitting and staring once more. David was so entranced that he did not notice Kate's attitude until he sat down.

"What's up?"

"Shattered," she mumbled into her arms.

From his seat by the fire, where he had waited patiently for most of the evening for her to return, David looked at her defeated frame and frowned. This was totally unlike her. Usually this near to midnight on Christmas Eve she would have taken over from their son in the excited stakes and would be flitting from room to room, ensuring that everything that could be organised was ticked off her list, before sitting on his knee until they could toast each other as the clock struck twelve. They were only a matter of thirty minutes away from that time, but it looked like she might just drop off to sleep, and he rubbed his face, surprised at how disappointing he found this. It was certainly not a night to share what was on his own mind.

"Is there anything you need me to do for tomorrow?" he offered.

"I'll be getting up early anyway," she replied. "It'll be fine."

As David scratched his knee, wondering which different tack to take, the pup made a valiant attempt to jump from the floor onto Kate's shins, but misjudged the height and bumped her face off the sofa's wooden frame. Only when she yelped in shock and retreated behind David's chair did Kate roll herself up into a sitting position and try to focus her eyes. David screwed up his own, still baffled by her deflated manner. A few hours ago she had practically skipped her way out of the door, as pretty in her winter gear as he had ever seen her. Now she was positively white.

"Jeez, Kit," he pushed himself to the edge of his seat. "It's your favourite night of the year, what the hell happened over there?"

The hesitation was miniscule and could almost have been missed as Kate forced out a grin in his direction and shrugged, but this man knew every tick, every expression, and he recognised evasion when he saw it. He also knew that his wife only kept things to herself when she was playing for time; and if he pushed at this point she would panic, analyse everything beyond the point of reason and finish the discussion by berating herself for being "a ridiculous person." Consequently, he let her be and spoke to the puppy instead, who instantly danced all over his socks.

"Watch!" warned Kate. "She pees!"

"Well, she's a baby. Of course she pees."

As the dog rolled onto her back and allowed David to scratch at her soft belly, Kate knelt beside them and, smiling, sat quietly for a few more moments. Twice, the pup stretched her head and licked at Kate's hand, but other than that the only movement was David's long fingers tickling and stroking the animal into submission. When she glanced up at him, he seemed equally entranced, and in the next second she realised that, on this particular night, she would very much like some of his attention. But he spoke first.

"Why don't you go to bed, honey, and I'll get her cage set up. One of us might as well get some sleep."

He had broken a spell he had not even known he had cast, but maybe it was for the best. Kate needed time in her own head, and it was even possible he knew as much. So, with no argument and with no advice as to where she thought the dog's cage should go or how he should go about abandoning the animal with the least fuss, Kate levered herself off the floor by leaning on his knee and wrapped his head in her arms. She loved the feeling of his hair in her fingers and his jaw in her palms.

"Think I'll just take a quick bath," she spoke languidly, "soak some of this tiredness away." If David noticed the invitation in her tone, he did not acknowledge it.

Later, as Kate played hide and seek with her toes in the soapy water, she alternated between listening for tell-tale signs of chaos downstairs and drifting back into her recently expanded mind. She was not so much exhausted, as astounded into immobility and was at a loss as to what to do or what Rose's motives had been on this particular night. There was a familiar feeling in her heart, one which she never did seek but which had a habit of visiting her every few years, usually when she was at her most secure and comfortable. And here it was again, that combination of disbelief and excitement which had the potential to alter ways of life if acted upon, but could never guarantee the desired outcome. There was always just enough risk involved to make you wonder, then doubt and worry.

"Why?" Kate murmured. Why did the world imagine she could deal with it? Her mother's mistake had needed to be recognised and sorted, and yes, she was the one for the job, because it was her story exclusively. But when Neil and Andie were in the depths of despair ten years previously, she had tried to shoulder the burden of their plans and it had almost crushed her. From nowhere, she had the most unexpected knowledge and had no idea where to go with it. Neil would be in this house the following day, and she seriously doubted that she could look him in the eye without him seeing some odd expression. Yet it was Christmas Day and not conducive to revelations of this kind. That was for some private moment down the line, when Neil and she were alone and in no hurry, which rarely happened if David had his way. Kate breathed out another huge sigh. David.

Well, she had to tell him. Keeping this from him was way beyond dangerous and a sure guarantee that he would see it as collusion. He already knew she was hiding something. However, just as awkward would be Neil arriving to find the pair of them subdued, maybe even jittery, and Rose worrying that she had done the wrong thing. Add this to the company of Andie, her reticent mother Iris, three excited youngsters, two old dogs and a new pup and the day was fairly singing to be born. Kate did what she usually did in this particular mood and these particular surroundings; she slid down the bath until her head was safely underneath the bubbles and the world was an unnaturally muffled place to inhabit. She dared herself to open her eyes, wondering how bubbles would look from beneath the surface, but knew that it would sting a bit; so she gave herself a break and lay motionless until her breath ran out. When she sloshed back up into the air, David was standing by the closed door. She smoothed her hair back and wiped her eyes.

"How's it going?" she whispered hopefully.

David gave her the thumbs up but apparently dared not jeopardise the situation by speaking. Instead, he leaned back against the door and folded his arms.

"She's asleep?" Kate asked.

David grinned and spoke quietly. "I wrapped your old hot water bottle in her blanket and she just drifted off on top of it."

"How clever are you?"

"I do my best," he replied.

In the moments that followed, Kate tried to rearrange the bubbles around her. Three months had passed since her body had gone from walrus to seal, but it was more the streamlined otter look she craved, and there were still too many areas of "extra padding" for her liking. The water was on the point of turning from acceptable to tepid, but her dressing gown was out of reach; and even after all this time together, she was aware of the disparity between the body she had at this moment and the one she liked to flaunt in front of this man. Rather than comment on her obvious attempt to conceal herself, David began to pick up Alasdair's jettisoned clothes, while Kate rolled the bar of soap up her forearms, rinsed them off and finally hauled herself out of the water. Her teeth began to chatter immediately, but David handed her the heated robe without looking at her, and she was soon wrapped tightly in it. In gratitude, she leaned against his back and folded her arms around him. She could feel the warmth of his skin beneath his jumper and suddenly the distance between bathroom and bedroom seemed more than she could endure.

"Is it Christmas Day yet?" she mumbled against him.

He did not answer but turned so that she was clamped to his chest. Kate's eyes were hooded as he looked down at her, but those grey irises were unexpectedly sparky. In fact, she was a bundle of mixed messages and attitudes. He was growing weary of it.

"What's going on?"

Kate did not even hesitate. "Rose told me something. Something that I want to tell you. But please, please can we go to bed before I do?"

Without a word, David took her hand and led the way. As she trailed behind him, Kate's heart sank slightly. If she handled this badly, she could ruin the holiday and that would be unforgivable. She had planned and baked and even tidied, which usually proved the biggest waste of time, and they all deserved to enjoy the fruits of these activities. So, she had to arrange her words carefully; she must not sensationalise this seed of information which could sprout with very little watering, but who was her main priority? Neil was her father, and he knew less about his ancestry than she did. That wasn't entirely fair. But David was her mate in every aspect– soul mate, bedmate, playmate– and he needed to know what she knew. Besides, all of this hiding and whispering and choosing whether or not to divulge was supposed to have ended years ago. She was tired of these burdens. She was tired, and the duvet was soft and cool against her face as she crawled on top of it. Her eyes stayed achingly open, however, as she watched David unbutton his shirt and ease it from his shoulders. She rubbed her toes together anxiously.

"So, here we are," David's voice was businesslike as he manoeuvred her around the bed until she was finally on the reasonable side of the quilt, and flopped in beside her. "Tell me."

For three seconds, Kate rubbed her cheek against the skin of his forearm then she sat up and brought the duvet up around their chins.

"We were talking about Neil's spine. Well, actually we weren't …
Rose had this funny look on her face, went a bit red, and then started
talking about Neil and his condition. It wasn't making any sense, and
then she just said it. Straight out. She knew he hadn't inherited the
scoliosis from his parents, because she knew who both his parents
were. She knows all about them."

At last, Kate dared to look at him, and she found his expression was
more of intrigue than anything else. She watched as his eyes widened
slightly, and then he shook his head doubtfully. She was about to add
to this statement when the howling began.

"You're kidding!" Kate cried, dismayed by the pup's timing, but
unable to stop herself from throwing back the duvet. By the time she
had reached the top of the stairs, the volume and pitch had increased,
and Kate nearly tripped over the belt of her robe in her anxiety to save
the situation. It was not until she was halfway down the second flight
that she realised she was alone in her mission.

In the kitchen, the pup ceased its protests as soon as the light was
switched on, and immediately started to jump in the air, creating just as
much noise albeit in ecstasy rather than agony. Kate knelt beside the
dog cage and shushed and soothed, but even as she slid back the
catch, she could hear quick, light footsteps on the stair. Oh well, what
was an hour or two in the grand scheme of things? As Alasdair came
skidding to a halt in front of her, she had managed to cradle the pup and
took in her son's face.

"Santa's been!" she beamed and felt her nose prickling instantly.

"Mo-om! Really? He brought me a puppy?"

"Well, I don't remember it being on my list. Here. It's a girl."

Alasdair sat full on the kitchen floor immediately, allowing the dog
to jump all over him. Kate watched the animal enjoying the treat of a
new chum, complete with fresh skin to lick, before her face fell and she
ran into the hallway.

"Dave!" she called, "You need to see what the man with the white
beard has left! Al is being eaten alive."

"Mom!"

"Davey!"

Kate moved back into the kitchen only when she heard the familiar
creak of her bedroom floor, and by then, Alasdair was on his knees. He

and the dog seemed to have merged into a blurry, fluid whirlwind, neither of them static for a second; and Kate, tying her robe properly around her once more, took a seat by the range to watch the show. The commotion was incredible.

Until that moment, Alasdair Neil Wilder could barely have been described as loud. He was prone to outbursts of energy, wild and frenetic, but usually only in the company of schoolmates, during the sledging season or if the Canucks were on particularly stunning form. Normally, he moved at one easy pace and his face was verging on the solemn, which had nevertheless enchanted Kate; he was a miniature David with lighter hair and she was in love. But tonight, his grin would not leave his face, and he was on his feet, bouncing and whooping, unworried by the little accidents which were occurring on the floor around him.

"What's her name?" Alasdair cried above the ruckus.

"You get to choose," laughed Kate. "Not my dog, Al."

As David appeared in the doorway, the pup bounded over to him, hightailed it back to the boy and then did a frantic tour of the room before tearing into the hallway. Alasdair practically bowled David over as he took off after her, and the pup's claws scrabbling on the polished boards of the hall added to the sounds of chaos. Standing beside David, Kate nudged her way under his arm, but did not try to catch his eye. The delight they were witnessing was still too intense to be interrupted, especially when they had anticipated it for days. The pup tried to negotiate the stairs, but kept bumping her nose, and Alasdair, like a professional handler, scooped her up and carried her back to where they stood. His eyes were huge.

"Dad!" he almost squealed. "Look at her. She's so brilliant!"

David knelt to give the newest addition the consideration she demanded, and the pup's whole head fitted into his palm.

"She's certainly a character," he agreed, then, "What are you going to call her?"

"Bertuzzi," he said, without hesitation,

"What?" cried Kate as David patted his son's shoulder, impressed. "But she's female!"

Alasdair's face fell momentarily. "But ... that's what I always wanted to call my dog. He's my favourite player."

When Kate looked up to David for assistance, he shrugged. "Well, he's married. Mrs Bertuzzi?"

"But without the 'Mrs' part," nodded Alasdair.

"Fair enough," said Kate, "if it gets to be too much of a mouthful, you can shorten it." Tootsie was an acceptably girlish name.

"Okay," agreed Alasdair, "Bert would do."

Kate could feel David silently shaking against her, determined not to laugh out loud at their son's thoughts which were still tinged with glee. It was comforting to her; it meant that her news had not affected his overall mood, and that possibility shed a more positive light on the coming day. At that very moment, a yawn took over her whole body and she sagged slightly against David's chest. Before another second had passed, her teeth had begun to chatter, and she knew she needed to sleep more than anything.

"What do you reckon?" she asked David.

"I reckon that Al should show Bertuzzi his bedroom. I'll bring up her bed. Okay, Al? It's still too early to be up."

"So, she's going to be sleeping in my room? For real?"

"Sure, why not," David replied, and Kate was too tired to even think of the future consequences.

Ten minutes later, Kate was into her tartan pyjama bottoms and vest, listening to David's low voice on the floor below issuing instructions and advice as if he knew all about dogs. She smirked, picturing Alasdair's patient face; he could run rings around all of them, but was still young enough to be kind about it. She pushed herself farther down the bed and let her arms fall loosely above her head. The dog had been a success, there was more hope of everybody sleeping if she was snuggled on top of Al's bed, and David was heading back upstairs at a buoyant pace. Her smile increased.

"They'll calm down eventually," he assured, then added, "probably around breakfast time."

David settled himself beside her and she wrapped one of her legs over his calves, willing his skin to match hers in temperature sooner rather than later. It was after twelve-thirty, and Kate thought of all that had taken place since she had dragged herself to the shower over seventeen hours previously. She had witnessed Jay Forsyth take his first few crutch-aided steps in his own home, his mother and sister breaking their usual melancholy to cheer and applaud. She had bought and collected the remainder of the Christmas presents in Duncan, wrapping and labelling them in one frantic half hour. She had listened in amazement to Rose's words and had just sprung the biggest surprise on her delighted son. Now, when she should have been weary to the bone, she needed to hear David's reaction to the news before she could happily put her body and mind to sleep.

"What are you thinking?" Kate asked softly.

David raised his chin and scratched at his throat. She had asked a question and the polite thing to do would be to answer her. He did not want to ignore the conversation, nor did he want to worry her by not replying, but he wasn't sure what to say. He was being encouraged to look at his brother from yet another angle, and like Kate, he wondered if there would ever be a day when they did not have to consider past mysteries and potential threats.

"Dave?"

Finally, he reached for her hand under the covers and held it close to his heart. He decided to play it safe.

"Nobody ever mentioned that they were local."

"I know. Well, I mean, I never assumed that they were. Suppose I thought he came from an ... orphanage or something. Man, do orphanages still exist ..."

David let Kate ramble on for a few moments, expressing opinions which were not radically different to his own in terms of disbelief and discomfort. It seemed that she was saying all that he needed to say, although he doubted if she would let him away with silence for much longer.

" ... known I would tell you. What do we do?"

"Do we have to do something?"

Kate sat up further in bed, ready to point out many things to the man; the enormity of their new knowledge, the gifts they could bestow on others, the potential extension of their family. Her mind had done its usual trawl of the facts as she had watched the pup sniff a trail through the woods, and she had some ideas. Since childhood, Kate had been the problem-solver in the family, and the only way she could deal with issues was to concentrate on nothing else, usually to the detriment of life going on around her. David had tried to dilute this self-imposed role by sharing responsibility, but had only partially succeeded because she could not fight the instinct to control and solve. Her success rate was mixed to say the least, and in spite of her own self-doubts at the start of every predicament, she could not ignore her urges to take on the task and make things better as time went on. So, in the space of an hour, she had made her way through the heavy despondency of the "I'm not cut out for this, stop giving me difficult jobs to do" to the relative optimism of another challenge, which might even have a truly positive outcome for people for those she loved the most and for others who still lived in hope.

"I'm not entirely sure," she said, "but should we not tell him?"

"Tell him what? What do we really know?"

Kate felt her shoulders nip with irritation. "Well, we know more than he does, and that's not fair. Would you like it, if he knew something about your life that you didn't?"

As she looked at David's face and heard again in her head the words she had spoken, Kate swallowed back her instant, completely heartfelt mortification, and cringed against him.

"Ah, shit," she whispered her despair into the skin of his arm, waiting for him to move or speak, and when he did, she remembered why she loved him.

"Maybe we should wait. Timing can make all the difference sometimes."

Kate remained silent, trying to encourage her flushed cheeks to cool down in spite of David's deliberate ignoring of her faux pas. She wanted the moment to pass quickly, for her incredibly insensitive phrasing to stop resonating in her ears and for it to be four hours earlier, when they had been hooting at David's singing. She wanted to take his fingers and entwine them in her own, for them to caress her as she had watched him do to the puppy. She wanted his attention. She wanted far more than she deserved.

"Tomorrow isn't the time for any of this," David's voice was low as he removed his forearm from her face and put it along her shoulders. He pulled her in close, and as she began to relax, she thought that he was probably right. They were heading into a day of celebration, a day which may hold unrealistic expectations for some and where the children may be overexcited and demanding. The adults might relax with the aid of food and alcohol, or they might realise that even a place the size of The Edge was not big enough to house all of their individual emotions. Equally, it may be the best and easiest day any of them had ever experienced as a group; there was always that hope. Whatever happened, there was no earthly reason to apply any more pressure. "So let it be," he continued, "just for a little while."

When David switched off the light, the blackness was like a comforter tucking them in for the night, and Kate suddenly realised the extent of her fatigue. David and his hands would have to wait, perhaps even until Boxing Day, but somehow she found the energy to find his lips with hers and laid her arm across his chest.

CHAPTER 12

Vancouver Island

"Well, she can have my old slippers now that I have these sheepskin babies."

Kate pointed her toe into the air, showing off the cream and grey-coloured bootees, twisting her ankle to emphasise their sheer beauty. David was nothing if not dutiful in responding to her "hints" for Christmas presents, but even she was surprised that he had managed to come up with such genuinely awesome specimens. She thought of the matching scarf and hat she had tried to knit for him in a traditional Cowichan pattern, and how perhaps the flaw would not be noticed if he wore the hat in a certain way. At least the scarf had been without error, although by the time he had worn it around his neck for the duration of the present opening, he had been scratching at his throat like a man possessed. She had smiled as she had unwrapped his irritated skin and thanked him with her eyes for not complaining about it.

As Bertuzzi was handed her ancient slippers to worry and tear apart as she thought fit, Kate eased back further onto the sofa and looked around at the members of the family in her presence. Rose and Abbie were curled into the corner of one of the two fireside chairs, their heads touching, as the toddler learned about how a girl called Katie-Morag practically ruled an entire island. The girl's eyes were locked onto the picture book, her right hand resting over her own head and entwined in Rose's fine hair; and for all her concentration, Kate could sense her complete contentment. Sophie appeared to have run out of steam at last and was occupying the opposite end of the sofa, her knees tucked under her chin and wrapped in her arms as she watched the only moving beings in the room: Alasdair and his pup. Even they had reduced their pace by a degree and were merely rolling together on the hearth rug, while David slept the sleep of the righteous in his chair.

Kate envied his ability to sleep upright in this way. It never seemed to matter how much background noise there was, or how dangerously hot his feet became as they rested beside the flames of the fire, he could be sound asleep within a minute of sitting down and remain as such for up to an hour. Even with his neck at a painful angle, one knee bent and locked, the other stretched and vulnerable to attack from animals and children, he was somehow able to relax completely. The same could not be said for Neil, at least not when he was in this house. The day had been the most successful Christmas to date, but the man was still unable to sit still in a room filled with these particular people, unless they were taking part in a physical activity, such as eating or unwrapping gifts. Today, they had done both and it had not been awkward, but just "being" was still not an option for him, and so after lunch, Andie, Iris and he had taken the Labs for a run in the woods.

"I wonder why Granma Iris doesn't read us stories?" Sophie's voice was more curious than offended. "She likes us coming to stay, because she always shouts 'come in, come in my lovely ladies,' but she doesn't read to us. Or play with us. Is she too old, d'you think?"

Kate looked over at Rose, who continued to give her full attention to Abbie, and so was no help at all. "I haven't a clue, Soph," she said, thinking how much younger Iris was than Rose and so discounting that theory immediately. "But I'll bet she would read to you if you asked her. Have you ever asked her?"

Sophie hesitated, then crawled across the fabric space between them. She glanced at both Rose and David as she did so, and Kate leaned in to listen, remembering how much Sophie liked to conspire. "Well, I was going to, once," the girl whispered behind her hand, "but she wasn't very smiley that day. Sometimes she's smiley and sometimes she isn't."

Kate nodded and put her arm around Sophie to show her total understanding. She had often considered Iris, had marvelled that a person could cope with losing a husband to a degenerative illness, and how that same person could then aid her son to end his own life, rather than follow the same route as his father. She had once or twice, usually when felled by the flu or a migraine, sweated through the scenario of losing David and Al in such a way, and could not believe that anyone had the strength to survive such an experience. The wonder was that the woman ever smiled at all. But she did. Iris was reserved with all of them, had none of Andie's hope or thrill at being alive, but she rarely declined invitations to join them, and was never impolite. The truth was simple enough: She found her joy in Andie alone, and she accepted the rest of them because she had to.

"Hey, I could tell you a story, if you want," Kate announced, "I've got loads of them up my sleeve. You in the mood for a story, right this minute?"

Where Kate expected to see excitement and delight in Sophie's eyes, she found doubt instead and it scythed her confidence in half.

"You make up stories?" asked Sophie, frowning.

"Indeed I do, missy," Kate assured, sitting up straighter. "Well, sometimes. Sometimes I make them up, but most of them are things that actually happened, and they're even stranger than the made up ones. Interested?"

When, an hour later, the three absentee adults walked back into the sitting room at The Edge, the fire was very low, grey ash and orange-pink embers lying undisturbed in the hearth. Neil halted just inside the doorway, his bootless feet making no noise, shushing the two women as they joined him. David, Rose and Abbie were asleep on chairs, Alasdair lay curled on the hearth rug, his head almost buried by Bertuzzi's straying ears as she matched his soft snores, and Sophie had her legs hooked over Kate's knees, her arms folded and her mouth open as she dozed. Irrespective of the sleeping bodies, Kate continued to talk in a low voice which had obviously soothed the majority into their present states, and acknowledged the recent arrivals with one small wave of her hand.

"... when we had finished, it looked like somebody had dropped a water bomb filled with yellow paint on it from a great height. Tiles, walls, curtains, towels, they were all sunshiny and bright. My mum loved it. We thought it might damage our eyes in time. In fact, Hazel used to leave a pair of sunglasses hanging on the door handle with a sign for visitors. It said something like, "To avoid retinal meltdown, feel free to use." Still, it meant the room always felt warm, even on wintry days," she paused as Neil and Andie crept further in, and then, "I think I've bored them all into submission. They'll be full of beans for the journey home. Ooops, never thought."

At the additional movement in the room, David slowly opened his eyes and stretched his entire body, still within the confines of his chair. The look on his face told a story of muscles which had contracted for too long and possibly even an overload of wine with dinner, but he managed to stop himself from actually groaning out loud. In the next instant, everyone was shaken from their slumber as Bertuzzi jumped to her feet and stood on Alasdair's, who in turn sat up and, before he had a chance to think it childish, crawled over to Kate and laid his head on her knee. The movement disturbed Sophie, who coughed as she rubbed her eyes open, and immediately, Abbie was awake and running off in the direction of the toilet. Rose, sedately, took a heavy sigh in and pushed herself up into a more comfortable position. Iris finally entered the room and seated herself beside Sophie.

"Goodness," she smiled, "what happened to the excited bunch of people we left behind? Did you all eat too much pie?"

Kate was heartened to see that this remained one of Iris' smiley days, and so she rose happily to put the kettle on for one more drink before their departure. Alasdair woke up properly as soon as Bertuzzi began to lick his face, but Kate reckoned that, in spite of the reanimation of the group, coffee was still required to get them all talking again. As she filled the kettle, she watched the dusk touch the top of the conifers outside, and as it rolled down the branches, it seemed to turn the bright snow into a deep turquoise. The kitchen was a disaster area, plates piled high and leftovers in dishes dumped unceremoniously near the sink from the dining room, but she stood motionless, ignoring everything around her in favour of watching the twilight work its magic. There had been no more snow, but the crystals had frozen where they had fallen the previous evening, and she could almost taste the cold freshness on her tongue as she watched them start to twinkle of their own accord. She was still holding the filled percolator in one hand, her other resting against the sink, when David wandered up to her.

"Look at that," she breathed, nodding towards the window, "what is making it sparkle? The sun's not touching it, but the snow's twinkling at us. How?"

David took the percolator from her and plugged it in, before leaning his hand on her shoulder and concentrating on looking at the trees rather than their own reflection. "Want to go out and solve the mystery?"

But Kate's eyes had already committed the entrancing scene to the background and was grinning at David in the glass. He had a very prominent blemish on his cheek where his hand had rested against it during his recent nap, and she reached up and tried fit her own palm into the shape. It was pitifully too small, so she cupped both cheeks in her hands and kissed him.

"Maybe we can take a walk later, when the moon has taken over?" she suggested. "I'd love that."

"Sounds like a plan," he murmured, hugging her to him before she could move away. "Today was really good fun and you made it all happen, so thanks, honey."

"You know I enjoy it all. Christmas is never a chore. This kitchen, on the other hand. Hmm. You know, if you really loved me ..."

"Well, I think I could manage to fill the dishwasher, if you need proof," David frowned/grinned. It was a combination which sometimes made Kate draw in breath at the depth of her attraction. He was fifty-five years old, but that was merely a figure, a way of quantifying years; and all Kate ever saw when she looked at him was the tall man whose eyes and hands could command her whole soul. She had no conception what others saw when they looked at him, she had only ever seen him through her eyes, and her perception was ruled by her heart. Eternally, she thanked God that he had trusted her enough to agree to be a couple. What if he had dismissed her? It hurt too much to think of that consequence, when she could stand there in front of him and simply enjoy his face. "Oh," she said, sliding her hands around the man's waist. "What on earth made you think that's what I meant? Sometimes you're too practical for your own good."

Before David had a chance to question her criticism, Kate had pulled his forehead against hers and locked her grey eyes onto his green. She watched them widen slightly as she dropped her hands once more and pulled his body against hers. In spite of her qualms at her current figure, Kate loved when she could fit her body against his, making sure that he understood one thing above all else: When it was just the two of them, when no others were demanding of their attention, she was his completely. He never had to ask, he never had to doubt, and he knew this. But sometimes, it was even more exciting to steal a "private moment" when it was least appropriate, and with the entire Wilder clan in the next room, this would surely qualify as one of those moments.

"What are you up to?" his question was innocuous enough, except when used in that particular tone. Her intentions were perfectly clear to both, and there was no need for her to answer, because his words had been followed by his lips on her scalp, where they moved slowly over her dark hair and onto her left temple. Kate was shivering already, never assuming that he would take part to this extent, and found herself on the point of total surrender, inappropriate or not. She steadied herself by hooking her thumbs into the belt-loop of his trousers, and leaning her face against his shirtfront. Today he wore white cotton instead of checked flannel, and her toes began to curl inside her new slippers as she felt his heat touch her cheeks. He had played her game and totally blindsided her. He was far cleverer than she ever gave him credit for. Even with the dishes and overhead light and the sound of laughter from the sitting room, Kate felt that they were already joined together, alone and on the cusp of their favourite trance. He raised her face with his hand and kissed her mouth, until she had to place both hands on the unit behind her just to stay on her feet.

"Pay no attention to them," Alasdair's voice meant that Kate's eyes flew open, but David made no such harsh movement, and took his time moving away from her. There was Sophie standing shyly in the doorway, sucking the end of her plait and staring at the two adults, while Kate could do nothing but draw in a breath and try to stand straighter. Her son fished a carton of milk from the fridge. "They're always kissing, you just have to let them."

Giggling, Sophie followed Al back into the hall, and David started to spoon coffee into the ancient percolator. When he turned his face in Kate's direction, she saw he was grinning, and still she found it difficult to gather her thoughts properly. Finally she sank into the chair by the range and watched as her legs trembled inside her linen trousers. Oh, the man still had moves, and suddenly her heart was soaring. Her mother had told her and Hazel as children that the key to happiness was having something to look forward to, no matter how trivial or seemingly insignificant that thing might be, and on this Christmas night, she began to grin as widely as she had done all day. Her son was totally bowled over by the addition to the family, Rose had enjoyed an easy reunion of her most beloved people, Hope had been the star of the show over in Scotland, and her father was about to take his own family back to the place he was at his most comfortable. They were all content and that was amazing. But the very best thing, her own nugget of joy and anticipation, was that later, when the house was finally devoid of visitors, she would remind David of their unfinished business. Life could be really quite grand, on occasion.

"I wonder if anybody wants Christmas cake," Kate tried to sound as if she was totally unaffected, but guessed that she failed miserably, and instead hunted through the wreckage of crockery for the cake slice. David made no comment, but reached into the wall unit for mugs. Their deliberate attempt to keep their distance made it all even more delicious.

"Mom! You're missing the story. Come on!"

Kate looked at David to see if Al had made any more sense to him, but he shrugged. "You take the cake, I'll bring the coffee."

"Okay," she agreed, but hesitated at the door. As she turned to look at him for one last time, he spoke for her.

"It's a date."

Alasdair and Bertuzzi met her at the door of the sitting room, her son's face a mixture of impatience and vexation that she was not already seated and enthralled like the rest of them. Once more, it was Rose who was speaking from her throne by the fireside, and Kate allowed Alasdair to guide her to the only remaining seat in the place apart from David's. It was a relief to sit slightly back from the others, where the window panes cooled her body a little and she could watch the proceedings without being studied herself. Al and Bert sat on the floor, their backs to the sofa, and she watched as Neil placed his hand on the dog's head once, patted it and then did exactly the same to his grandson. It seemed both natural and extraordinary, and Kate enjoyed the feeling.

"... when I appeared on the scene, they had managed between them to get his arm wrapped in a towel. To this day, I think they were more scared of my reaction than the blood on the floor."

"Did you throw a hissy fit?" asked Sophie, her eyes shining at the thought of Rose being the boss of her dad and big Uncle David.

"You bet your life she did, sweetheart," Neil shook his head at the memory.

"Well, I don't remember quite what I said, but I can picture your dad crying his heart out and David insisting that all it needed was a Band-Aid."

"Can you still see the scar?" Alasdair was once again on his feet, in search of his father's elbow to check where the bread knife had pierced his skin during a play-fight.

"Another one, Granma Rose," urged Abbie, delighting at the atmosphere in the room. "Tell us more about Daddy."

During the activity that followed, Kate did not move from her seat on the periphery of the room. She had been on her feet all day, and it was just too easy to sit and watch Andie act as hostess when David placed the mugs on the coffee table. She smiled as she saw him roll up his left sleeve, showing his son and the two other childish faces crowded near him the tiniest line just below his elbow joint. They were suitably unimpressed; it was a ridiculously mediocre example of an injury, and so David had to kneel beside them and offer his much better facial scar for their inspection. As they pointed and gingerly touched it, Rose began to speak again.

"I remember another day, even clearer than that one, Sophie. I remember the day I brought your daddy home to stay. He was only two weeks old, can you imagine him as a baby? He was only about this long." She spread her hands.

Kate almost felt sorry for David, as the thought of Neil as an infant made his blemish suddenly irrelevant to the girls, and only Al remained filled with pride at the sight. Abbie jumped back onto Rose's knee, where her form fitted straight back into the mould it had recently vacated, but Sophie hovered by Neil's side, waiting for him to acknowledge her. After a moment, he looked straight at her, and just as Andie was about to step in and offer her own lap as a seat, the man hauled her into the crook of his arm. Kate wasn't sure who was the most delighted by the move, Sophie or Andie, but it was nice to see.

"Now then, girlies," began Rose, in a voice which betrayed her own excitement at the telling, "This is one of those stories which is both true and special. Get yourselves settled in, because it's a good one, and you girls should know all about it."

When Rose and Pete Wilder were delivered of their first child in the summer of 1948, they had assumed it signalled the beginning of the gradual and joyful expansion of their family. David had lain awkwardly inside Rose, had been a longer than average baby and had to be taken from his mother by surgery. But he had been their joy, and as Rose had entered her thirties, she had not once shied away from trying to conceive again. This she had been able to do on two more occasions, both of which had proved so heart-breakingly unsuccessful that after the second bloody failure had been cleared away and mourned, Pete had withdrawn from his wife completely for a number of months. He had remained strong and protective but distant, and Rose had found herself aching to be more to Pete than a cook and housekeeper. It had taken almost a year for her to accept that a fine, strong son could be enough, and gradually, she had begun the re-courtship of her husband. She had not done this with skimpy dresses, she was not a skimpy dresses kind of lady; but she had begun to arrange date nights where they would talk and eat together in a crowded restaurant, which ultimately had proved more intimate than their cavernous, quiet kitchen. She had made him take them on picnics and began to grow her hair onto her shoulders and down her back, because in their early days he had loved to run his hands over and through her thick locks. Winter nights at The Edge could be long and cold enough, and people in love needed comfort and connection.

If David had noticed anything around this time, it was that his babysitter seemed to be there every week instead of every fortnight, and he had commented happily to this effect. The girl had been quite a good playmate, for a female teenager. Even more impressive to David was that she had sung in a band. Every Friday and Saturday she and her best friend had accompanied the lead singer in a dance band, and every Thursday, she had shared it all with David. He would laugh at her descriptions of the oldies dancing, and she would teach him her new songs. Apparently, he had an "interesting" singing voice for a child, and she had advised that he learn the drums to help him with his rhythm. Her dad had worked with Pete at the timber yard, and in the winter, her mom had driven her to The Edge rather than let her cycle over in the dark. They had all been the best of friends, until the teenager had become too busy at home with her own little brothers to help out with another.

In the summer of 1956, Rose and Pete had taken David camping up north and had spent more time with him than ever before. It had been great fun, Rose smiling each and every day and Pete showing him how to build fires and cook over them. And when they had returned home, suntanned and exhausted, Rose and Pete had delivered their news to him. He was due to get a baby brother, and David had been asked to help choose his name.

The infant had been two weeks old exactly when he had been introduced to David, and in the first few moments of laying eyes on the bundle, the lad had merely hoped he would grow some hair soon or people would make fun of him. According to Rose, all three of them had been lucky, because this baby's mother had known how much David had wanted a brother and had asked them to take care of him from that moment on. At eight, David had not realised that he had wanted a brother quite that much. However after a day or so, he had been able to consider the addition as a bonus of sorts; it made up for the absence of his babysitter, his mom had been at the singing, happy stage, and his dad had his "cutting crew sorted." But this had brought on its own worry.

"What if his mom wants him back some day?" David had asked.

"I'm his mom now. She wanted us to have him."

"But she could change her mind. I do all the time."

"I don't think she will. She's moved quite far away. Don't worry about it too much."

And that had been that. Pete had expressed relief that David finally had a playmate because siblings were important, not just in childhood but throughout life. Rose had been beyond contented because she had so much love to shower, and all three men in her life were standing underneath it; and David had been happy because everything seemed to be okay in the house again, even if eight years difference meant that his brother had perpetually followed his lead and had wanted things way before he was old enough for them. The Edge had been noisier and more settled than it had been for a long time, and Rose concluded by saying that fate had a way of bringing good times out of bad.

Throughout the tale, Abbie had alternated between playing with the beads around Rose's neck and watching her sister snuggle against Neil. She sat up slightly.

"Did baby Neil's mom die, like First Mom did?"

Kate could feel the heat rush to her face, and it took all of her effort not to stand and start singing "Feed the World" at the top of her voice. She sought David's eyes, desperate for him to recognise her anxiety, but he seemed as relaxed as the rest of the room until the very moment her expression registered with him. He sat up, frowning, but had no time to speak.

"No, no," explained Rose, "your daddy's 'first mom' couldn't look after him, so we asked her nicely if we could maybe give it a go. She thought, hoped, we might be good enough, and so that's how your daddy became my son; and now, you pair are my grandkids. I am so glad, what would I do without my little baby girls? Freddie did us a big favour."

"I'm glad, too," said Sophie and kissed the side of Neil's face. "I like this family."

Iris seemed to have sensed Kate's apprehension but had no idea of its cause and so did not acknowledge it. Andie, on the other hand, looked at the flushed face occupying the window seat and leaned forward. Before she could ask after her, however, Kate made an attempt at a wide-eyed "this-is-dangerous-let's-change-the-subject" form of telepathy, but Andie was neither David nor Hazel, and she failed to connect.

"What?" she asked outright, "What's up?"

As all heads turned in her direction, Kate immediately softened her features and laughed, "I forgot the liqueurs and I've been saving them for weeks. Just as well I'm on this diet, or they would have disappeared at least three days ago. Oh, curses, can you remember where I hid them, Dave?"

Kate reached the doorway just as her words petered out, but there was no actual escape on this occasion. Just as she looked over her shoulder, hoping against all hope that David was following her, Abbie yawned and said, "Who's Freddie?"

Rose did not even hesitate, and Kate, when revisiting the whole scene later, suspected that the woman had spent time setting this up, choosing a moment when the little people would ask the questions the adults felt too awkward or afraid to ask. It was unlike her to be quite so manipulative, but it did not stop her from wading in and answering Abbie's question.

"Freddie was Neil's First Mom."

Kate held her breath, her eyes flitting from Neil's still expression to Rose's lively one. The silence was broken by Sophie suddenly guffawing, an action which startled her sister into copying her, right down to the tone and volume of the laughter.

"How can a lady be called Freddie? That's ... ridiculous!"

"And that's a great big word for such a wee scrap of a caileag like you," cried Kate, which only sent both girls off into more screeching giggles. Nobody else said a word.

Alasdair slumped against the sofa, unimpressed by all of the carry on and could not even be bothered to wonder why Neil's left foot was tapping so fast. In his opinion, dogs were much better fun and much less noise than girls, and maybe it was time that all the guests went home. The thought of curling up on his bed with Bertuzzi would not leave his mind, and he wished for it sooner rather than later. As he rubbed at one of his pup's long ears, Alasdair let his eyes wander from the fireplace to where his dad was sitting motionless. He frowned. The man was not laughing. In fact, his face looked like it sometimes did when he watched the news: thoughtful, bordering on the seriously worried. The boy took a breath in and looked up at his mother.

"Can I go upstairs and play?" his voice was weary.

"I think it's time we all made a move," said Neil, manoeuvring both he and Sophie to their feet. "This place is just too comfy, and we need to get those dogs back and settled."

The most surprising thing of all was that there was no opposition to this announcement, not even from the girls; maybe each and every one of them had given the day their best shot and were happy to escape while they were all still smiling. Kate still hovered by the door, watching, incredulous that Neil was walking away from an apparently unrecognised opportunity, and that Rose was allowing it to happen. Then everyone was talking and acting at once, gathering bags of gifts, helping Rose to her feet, trying not to trip over each other, and the only soul aware of her agitation was David. He stood with his back to the fire, hands in his pockets, warning her with his eyes to keep her cool and let it be. She bit her lip and said nothing.

A mere five minutes later and the folks from Port Alberni were packed and strapped into the SUV, dogs in their cage, some leftovers wrapped and stashed, the girls yet again displaying fatigue in their eyes. Kate had hugged them all, including Iris, but hung on to Neil for just a shadow longer than anyone else. He seemed perfectly in control, there was no tremor in his body, and he rubbed her upper arm as he moved away.

"You put together a good day, Kate," he half-shouted over his shoulder. "Thanks."

As the others made similar noises, Kate acknowledging them all, she watched Alasdair retreat gratefully into the house with his near-constant companion at his heels, and she moved to where Rose stood huddled in her huge winter coat. They waved the vehicle away, listening to the snow crunching and groaning under its considerable weight, and David put his arm around his wife's shoulder. She shivered against him.

"Okay," announced Rose, pulling on her gloves. "That was a wonderful day, but I am beat. Totally, utterly. So I'm just going to wander back home. Kate, thank you for everything, and my cardigan is lovely. It's doing its job already."

"You're welcome," even to Kate, her voice sounded surprised, but David stepped forward immediately.

"I'll walk you home."

As he turned to retrieve his own jacket, Rose held up her hand.

"No, son, I'm fine. I'd like to go at my own pace. Get yourselves inside, relax and don't argue with me. I'll speak to you in the morning."

David appeared stalled in the open doorway, and Kate, after the roller-coaster of the last half hour or so, realised that there was about to be yet another indeterminate period of debate and wonder. It made her want to stamp her feet, to scream at the woman to just tell them everything, but before she could even throw her hands up in despair, David spoke into the icy air.

"Freddie Hunter? Honestly, Rose?"

CHAPTER 13
Vancouver Island

Only Freddie Hunter had come out of the situation with nothing to show for it; nothing to show, but plenty to feel in the late summer of 1956. Red raw panic had been the first emotion. It had slammed mercilessly into her chest as the first few days of nausea had confirmed her worst fears. How could something so spontaneous and reasonably unremarkable have caused such a mountainous disaster? It was bound to affect every single person she loved and admired, and their expressions would always be darker and less trusting from the moment the news broke. Next had come shame and the unbearable burden of someone else's disappointment. Only after all of these had almost broken her back did the pure fear come. She had been fifteen years and five months old when the shaking had taken over from the nausea and she had been forced to confide in her mother.

On the day of her confession, she had walked into the kitchen and stared at her younger brother as he had tried to attach a net to an old fishing pole. The boy was innocent, happy and would be an uncle before he was ten. She had vomited onto the floor at the thought, and her mother had been all concern and sympathy until the moment she had told the woman her news. The next image was carved into her brain; her mother on her knees, cloth and bucket beside her, her head twisted up, eyes wide and incredulous. It was her stillness which had been the most terrifying, and the following few days had brought them all to a similarly immobile state. Her father had taken himself off on a hunting trip. Freddie had never witnessed shock of that magnitude before, the kind of shock that took the life from eyes and the colour from cheeks. She had cried until her whole swollen body had ached and convulsed.

The fear had shifted perspective when the child inside had begun to move and she had considered the physical journey ahead. Her friend Trudy had tried to visit, but had been turned away with tales of an unknown malady, so she had seen nobody but her parents, and she had no intention of asking them anything about childbirth. She had awoken each morning to the realisation that one day she would be in pain beyond her current knowledge and that when the pain was over, there would only be days of responsibility and worry ahead. All of this, because she had no way of preventing it, either physically or emotionally. What a thoughtless, unparalleled mistake, yet it showed she was just as susceptible as every other girl in search of recognition.

As the time drew nearer, her brothers had learned more than any eight- or six-year-old should have to know, but her nearest sibling James had started to bring her cups of tea whenever she sat on the porch. She had never forgotten his kindness. It was then that talk began of moving back to Scotland, the country of her mother's birth and her own.

Fred and Martha-Jean Hunter had taken full responsibility for the catastrophe. They should have acknowledged her youth, they should not have allowed their pride in her singing voice to dictate her social life, they should have known better. Ultimately, they had an obligation to put this right. They had to give her a better future and they had to work together to sort it out, whatever the cost. So, on a late spring morning in 1956, Fred asked his daughter if she would like to go for a walk in the woods with him. Her face burning at the relief of being spoken to in such a soft voice, Freddie had followed him in a second.

When the house had finally allowed the trees to conceal it from view, Fred had begun to clear his throat and slow his steps. His boots had seemed to hold his interest for a long time and Freddie had begun to look around her, taking in the way the sun shone around them, splintered by the trees; whatever was coming, the sun would be there again the next day, warming the needles beneath their feet and letting the aroma rise around them. Nevertheless, Freddie wondered if she would still find comfort in this place after he had said what he needed to say.

"We've made a decision, Freddie." The man had not used his daughter's name in months, and she had found herself praying that this signalled a change for the better. "In the fall, we're moving back to Scotland. All of us. Your mom, brothers, you and I."

Freddie had not been able to speak, because she had been fighting to control the curiosity inside her. What were his motives in this? Was it a permanent move? Her face had gone on to betray the biggest question of them all. When he spoke again, her father's tone had hardened slightly.

"If you won't tell us, then there can be no wedding. No wedding, no baby. We'll sort it for you, and then we'll get you away from here. Nobody across there will ever know, and things will be better that way."

However she might feel in the days to come, at that particular moment Freddie Hunter had experienced nothing but intense relief and overwhelming gratitude. Her father had promised to take care of things and make it all bearable again. She had been so surprised, that she had not even asked him how. Perhaps she could return to thinking of new songs and hair-bands instead of how her life had ended with another's conception.

"Will it really be okay?" she had almost whispered. "Will, I mean ..."

"The job is set up already. We're going back to your mom's hometown, and the rest is ... being discussed."

"Can't you tell me?" Freddie had shivered even as a shaft of sunlight had tried its best to warm her bones.

"You'll know when it's sorted."

By the time the middle of August had dropped its sweltering blanket around the house, Freddie had been assured that things would be well, without having been given any actual details on the subject. Rose Wilder had begun to call round, and even though she had been a dear family friend, Freddie had been surprised that even one visitor had been encouraged into the vault that was their home. By her third visit, the plans had finally been laid out on the table: Rose would take the baby. As simple as that. It would be legal and final. Freddie had sat staring at the entwined fingers resting on her tight belly and had remained silent throughout the speeches and the preparations. Their tones had all been positive, especially that of Rose, but the girl had not been able to take part, as her mouth had been bone dry. She had loved Rose, thought she was a great mother and knew that she had suffered during pregnancies; but the fact remained that this woman was actually waiting with delighted anticipation for her to hand over her prize, the only precious item involved in the whole sorry state of affairs.

Nothing about the situation was fair; her parents had been broken-hearted, she had gone through more distress than she could ever have imagined, and the child inside her had gone from being a problem to a commodity. Freddie had pressed her palms against her tummy, trying to work out the position of the baby, and had begun to weep for it. Yes, it would be safe with Rose and Pete; but the fact remained that it had been viewed as an inconvenience for its entire existence so far, and at some point down the line, it might figure this out. Poor, confused baby. She had loved its dependence on her, she had been the only person on earth who had been able to nurture it, but this had been about to end, and that was worth shedding a tear over.

She had shed many more tears a week later when the pains had started. She had been hanging out washing, and had ended up tearing the line from the wooden posts as she had used it to try and stay upright. Her mother had found her on the ground, surrounded by white linen, moaning and curled into a ball. She had seemed so tiny, far too petite to be capable of creating life; yet a mere three hours later, there had been a bundle of wrinkled, pink skin which was as beautiful a thing as any of the Hunters had ever seen. Freddie had become instantly mute and would not let another soul touch him for three days. Her mother, perhaps recognising the magnitude of her daughter's anxiety, had taken her side against her husband and had allowed her to dictate this much at least. Rose had visited every day, but only to look and console. Then on day fourteen, she had let Rose take the infant from the house, and Freddie had begun the interminably long journey back to insignificance. Her bedroom under the eaves of the house had felt like a cave for two or three weeks, stifling and shadowy, full of prolonged silences and dust which would not settle. But eventually she had headed out into the sunlight, and had found her parents waiting for her with softer features and hope in their eyes.

Moving back to the estate in the Scottish Borders, where Martha-Jean had promised to spend time helping her daughter to get over the whole business, had sounded easy. It had appeared rounded and resolved, but Rose Wilder, who knew about loss of this kind, had made a point of meeting up with Freddie a week before they flew across the sea. The girl had appeared hard and determined, and their meeting was so short that a cup of tea had not even been poured. She had stood by the café table, looking down at Rose with a set jaw.

"Don't tell me anything about him," she had pleaded, "I don't want to know his name. I don't want photographs or letters through the mail, and I don't need to know that he's clever or handsome. I know he'll be all right with you and that ... Davey will look out for him." The mention of David's name had caused her the only tear. "Just promise that you'll tell me if you move somewhere else. Or if he doesn't make it."

Rose had tried to get her to relax for a moment, but she had merely grabbed the table to steady herself and carried on.

"I'll let you have my address," her voice had wavered. "Wherever I am, I'll let you have it so that later, if he wants to ... It's for him. I'm not going to bother you and I'm begging you, do not tell me anything about him. He'll have a great life with you. I'll be okay this way. I'll make do."

If you looked at the situation from a problem-solving perspective, then the vast majority of people had benefitted. But Rose had never forgotten the way Freddie had retreated from that table where the tea remained in the pot, her head down, her hands touching every chair to guide her safely to the door; and she knew that, one day, she would share it all with Neil.

Chapter 14

Vancouver Island

David's green eyes were dazed in wonder, and Kate, perhaps for the first time in their life together, did not try to prompt him into speaking. She had absolutely no idea what was going on, but felt that any perspective she might have would sound too trivial, so she settled on the sofa, crossed her legs underneath her and waited, chin in her hands. At least Alasdair had succumbed to his heavy day of excitement, and in her gratitude, she had left Bertuzzi lying on the foot of his bed before making her way back to this man. David must indeed be perplexed, as there was no nightcap cradled against him. Still she waited, watching the newly stoked fire lick at the wood and crackle. Thank God for David and his complicated system of drying out logs which had–

"Freddie Hunter. Hell, I haven't thought about her in years." The confusion was evident in his words as well as his expression. "Her mom was Scottish, I remember. She promised to teach me the drums. She was my babysitter."

"Ah," even to Kate the response sounded non-committal and she added quickly, "No wonder you're quiet."

If he were to speak the truth, Kate would learn that he had been trying to recall Freddie Hunter's face. It was a formation in his head; an unclear image, more of a feeling than a picture, but one which he regarded as familiar. He had worshipped that girl, had looked forward to her attention and had never understood why she had simply stopped coming over. There had been suggestions that Pete and Rose were saving up for a big camping holiday and so had decided to go out less, but that had not stopped him sulking for days at the way things had turned out. At the time, he had wondered what trip could possibly be worth cancelling his time with Freddie. She had indeed promised to teach him the drums. It had never happened. But he had a sense of her features and suddenly marvelled at the thought that Kate's familiar face may not solely be due to Fiona. Did his wife want to hear that?

"So, do you remember much about her?" Kate asked at last.

"I was under ten."

"That's not an answer."

David let his eyes close for a moment. "I may have wanted to marry her when I was seven," he paused and then, "My God. She wasn't that much older than me. How young must she have been?"

As he let his mind play with these thoughts, David realised that the information was connecting two people in his life who had never even been considered in the same breath before. It was bizarre. Freddie had filled the space of his missing siblings, at least for one night a week, and he had run the length of the driveway back to the house whenever she was due. She was always singing, had told him that you had to practise if you wanted to get anywhere at all, and that one day she would mention him on the sleeve of her records, "just for being my audience." Suddenly, her face was as clear as day in front of him. She had brown curls which she had hated and her eyes were grey. But Neil had come along later, and although he had filled the void created by Freddie's sudden disappearance, there had never been the slightest connection. The only thing they had in common was that they had each made his life less isolated. Yet it had never occurred to David to think of that until now.

"You okay?" Kate was watching him with an intensity he usually adored, but this shock was changing his reaction to it.

"Kitty," he sighed. "That girl brought Neil into this world. I'm finding that almost incredible. Yet he barely reacted."

Kate, who had been in such a fearful state at the time, tried to see Neil again, sitting in this very position, but could only recall his passive expression and active foot. Perhaps he had viewed the conversation as his girls had done: the telling of a tale from the past which had shown the youngsters that even the families created out of sadness could turn into happy families. Rose, although she had skillfully introduced the topic out of nowhere, had been content to allow everybody to take away the revelation and come back to her if they wanted to. Kate was astounded at this level of patience and almost resented the woman's ability. As she scratched her ear, she could only guess at the discussion Neil and Andie would be having later that evening. If any at all.

"Maybe he really isn't interested. Rose hinted as much. She thought I might be, though."

"And are you?"

Kate shrugged. "I don't need any more drama, if that's what you're thinking."

They fell into silence for another few minutes, during which the sound of the fire seemed to crescendo. Kate found herself pouring the last of the open bottle of red wine into their glasses to prevent her yawn from being noticed. So much for their date.

"Hey, Dave," Kate continued, having warmed the wine in her mouth before swallowing it, "do you ever wonder what it must be like to be a member of a completely conventional family? You know, the kind where the family tree is only made up of straight lines and individual names. No brackets or asterisks or long explanatory notes at the bottom? Ours is practically a cryptic crossword."

David finally smiled, but she pointed her glass at him immediately, anxious that he not think the initial question rhetorical.

"No, I mean it. Sometimes I lie awake at night and try to work out what our common thread is. How did all of us end up tied together? We're all flawed, I know that, but I'm sure most of us weren't before we bumped into each other. And you can't even say it's indigenous, because it involved folk from two different countries. Blimey," Kate paused, as another thought struck her. "Freddie's mum was Scottish? So actually, if I think about it percentage wise, I'm actually more Scottish than Hazel is. Oh, she'll love that!"

David leaned back in his chair and allowed her to blether. She recognised the action as one of compliance and immediately began to list the numerous associations and her thoughts on each one. Rose and Pete came out as possibly the most ordinary of partnerships, and Kate felt the need to commend them for finding passion and friendship amongst their own generation, and sealing the deal without the need for anxiety or vexation. Hazel and Stuart came a close second, having courted for over seven years and then throwing a big wedding in direct contrast to Kate and David's pitifully plain and private affair. But even they had not been immune, and only intervention had allowed Hope to enter their otherwise by-the-book lives. It seemed to Kate that every relationship she knew of had either attracted unwanted attention or caused some sort of carnage for its participants.

"And tell me how Andie and Neil found each other? Out of all of those students, this man with a damaged soul meets this girl with an indefinite future and they bond within weeks. Does it make you feel stronger, attaching yourself to somebody who might be more wounded than you are? Like, Andie looks at Neil and says, I can make a difference, and Neil looks at Andie and says, let me help you along the way. And on top of all the despair and the regret, they start to build something. Well, good for them, they're set in stone now, but what happened to just 'fancy this dance, gorgeous?' I don't know."

Kate set her wine glass on the floor and lay full length on the sofa, ignoring the abandoned toys cluttering the entire room and staring instead at the coloured globes adorning the Christmas tree. Many years previously, Kate had read a very personal account of how David and her mother Fiona had met, written in her mother's hand, and at the time had thought Hazel's unplanned arrival the only remarkable thing about it. That particular relationship had begun during this festive time and had floundered more or less exactly five years later. Five years. Enough time for David to enjoy the thrill of providing for a wife and daughter. Enough time for him to trust it to last forever and plenty of time after that for him to reflect on who and what had caused his particular devastation. Kate guessed that Christmas decorations did not fill him with as much pleasure as they did her and Alasdair, and yet he never complained about them. She closed her eyes and thought about nothing but flickering candles and how pretty the snow had looked, winking at her through the kitchen window.

When she opened her eyes later, the fire was still sparking, but the original logs had been replaced with a fresh set and David's seat was vacant. Kate shivered as she sat up, reacting to being left alone rather than to any fall in temperature. Her head felt a little thick, which could be attributed to either the alcohol in her system or the complexity of her dreams, and she did not move immediately. From her tentative seat, she noticed that the toys had been piled up and were back under the tree, her wine glass was gone and the two lamps were no longer lit. It was her ultimate Christmas backdrop, coloured bulbs and firelight, but the room had never felt quite so wrong. Where was he?

Kate wandered through to the kitchen and found the place tidy and clutter free. While she had visited her ancestors from her position on the sofa, he had tackled every obvious chore, and she had not heard a sound. Whilst she had sat amongst Mackinnon kin, dressed in both plaid and distress as they were shipped to a more bountiful land, wailing at their departing Scotia, David had loaded the dishwasher. As family members had wept at the rocking of the vessel and then screamed in Gaelic at the foundering of it on Canadian rocks, her husband had shelved leftovers and banked down the range for the night. And as a teenage girl in bobby socks and hair-band had stood on the shore, waving with all her might as a young boy jumped clear of the sinking boat, her husband had done all of these things silently, so as not to disturb her rest. Kate was suddenly more emotional than she had been all day, guilty that she was only awake because that young boy's ankle had snapped as it had made contact with the slimy stones of the New Scotland. The boy had looked like Alasdair, but with dark hair.

"David!"

When her cry did not immediately result in the puppy howling in alarm, Kate glanced at the coat rack. Both the brand-new leash and David's jacket were missing, and she wasted no time in lacing up her boots. Too late she remembered that her winter coat had been left on the stairs, and so, cursing under her breath, she grabbed only a scarf and hat.

Outside, the moon had created a world of deepest blue, punctuated only by the black of the trees and shrubs. It was beautiful, but not illuminating; and Kate, who had been positive she would find David stamping his feet, urging the latest member of the family to "get on and get it done," was struck by the stillness of the immediate area. He was nowhere in sight and she took off at a pace, to keep her temperature up as much as anything. Almost immediately, she regretted her haste, as the ground was harder and much less forgiving than it had been under the sun's influence. As she slid and grappled, the significance of the winking trees hit home, and in the next second she was on her back, cursing like a navvy. She stood with some difficulty and stared wildly around. David was not at the front of the house, and she could see no tall figure near the perimeter of the trees. Perhaps the little dog had slipped the leash and, at this very moment, was sniffing and bounding through the middle of the woods. She had no torch to accompany her, no coat, and her throat was aching with the icy air travelling down it.

"Dave! Where are you pair hiding?"

The only light visible in front of her was due to the houses in the distant Peter's Lane, and although that appeared a reasonable place for the man to find answers to his questions, it seemed unlikely that he would make the trip without telling her. Now, her rear end felt tender and her linen trousers were allowing moisture to seep through to her bare skin. Her misery conceived during her ridiculous dream threatened to bring the day to an unexpected and lonely end. Kate stopped walking. She could imagine her breath crystallising in the blue dark and stood completely still. There was zero movement on the air and no sound whatsoever apart from her breathing. What was she doing here? The thought caught the breath in her throat and she widened her eyes. There were stars in the sky above her, but they were not the stars Beth or Hazel would see. She stared at them, as her fingers began to freeze and her heart began to flutter. The longer she gazed, the more detached she became, and she simply stood there and let it happen.

The house behind her had been her home for the last ten years, and tonight it was a curiously alien place, hidden away in a strange country. Slowly, she turned full circle, searching for the familiar to bring her back from this weird realisation, but finding nothing but frozen, blackened shapes. The silence was unnerving; how was it possible that no vehicles were travelling the highway? On this particular night, at this particular moment, where were the people? Where were those who gathered together to sing their ancient ballads, in the only language that made sense of the melodies? They were certainly not in the middle of this clearing, thousands of miles from home and growing colder and more solitary by the second. Kate stood motionless again. A few minutes more and even the concept of moving became too big a challenge. She no longer acknowledged that her mind was misbehaving, and she remained inanimate as the night began to settle itself around her. Her eyes had fixed themselves upon the single bulb of light from Peter's Lane, yet in that very instant, it was extinguished. She accepted this, with no reaction at all.

When the temperature had begun to drop at an alarming rate, David had scooped the pup up into his coat, and it was this which had slowed down his return journey. As he emerged from the woods near the back door, he noticed that it was ajar and cursed; the house would be losing heat faster than the range could produce it. He had made it as far as the steps, however, before the stationary figure in the front driveway caught his eye. A nervous man might have jumped in fright, but David was merely surprised and curious. He had left Kate asleep by the fire. What was she doing?

"Kit?" the word produced no movement from her whatsoever. David more or less launched Bertuzzi through the door and closed it quickly. "Kitty!"

When she still did not react, David felt his stomach constrict slightly. She was standing straight, head upright, but looked so tiny and abandoned. Maybe she was sleepwalking, he thought. Every sleepwalker had a first time. He approached her slowly enough, but remained confused. Did sleepwalkers don and lace boots and wrap a scarf tightly around their neck?

"Hey, Kit?" He touched her cheek as he spoke and was instantly swearing wildly, forcing her stiff body into his arms. He didn't know or care what you should do with a semi-conscious person, he only knew that nobody's skin should feel as lifeless as his wife's had just done, and he half marched, half dragged her back towards the back door. "What the hell?" he spat into the air, trying to give her his heat as they walked. By the time he had negotiated the pair of them awkwardly over the threshold and into the comfort of the warmth and light, Kate's teeth had begun to chatter, yet she watched him with perfectly focussed eyes.

"Hi, Davey," her jaw seemed to have seized, preventing any major conversation. "Where were you?"

"Kate," he held her hands against his face, "You're way, way too cold. Here, come through to the fire."

She pulled back. "Chilblains," she frowned.

David rolled his eyes in the hope that it would annoy her enough to break this spell. "For God's sake, you need to warm up a bit. Listen to what I'm saying, even if it's the only time in your life that you do!"

Kate let herself be guided into the sitting room and placed on the sofa, away from the direct heat for the time being. David knelt in front of her, trying to put a name to her present state, but could not do so by the light of the fire alone. When he switched on the powerful central light, Kate immediately frowned and shaded her eyes.

"Why?" she mumbled, "You know how much I hate that light."

"Because I need to see your face when you tell me what the hell is going on."

Kate moved her eyes from his face to the fire to the floor. She was not aware of her body touching any surface, only of a tingling in her nose and fingers, and this proved a very odd sensation indeed. Even odder still was that David was standing in the sitting room, fully clothed in outdoor gear, including boots. Her own feet were similarly clad.

"Here," she murmured. "No boots in the sitting room."

She was about to attempt to loosen her laces when her husband knelt in front of her again. She touched his face because she loved it, and even though he flinched from her icy fingers, he did not move them away.

"You're frozen. How long were you out there?"

Kate shrugged, unperturbed by the question until she actually thought about it. David watched a frown form on her forehead, and she shook her head.

"Well, that's weird. I remember waking up on the sofa and figuring out that you were outside, then not much else. What time is it?"

"Does it matter? You scared me to death."

"Well, it wasn't my intention," she tutted and pulled his hat from his head. As always, his hair objected to such harsh treatment and remained angrily upright until she patted it down. "Think it's time for a haircut, matey."

He took her hands and rubbed them in his. They seemed smaller than ever.

"I think you will actually be the death of me, Kitty. One of these days, when I'm even older and greyer, you'll do something even more ridiculous and I will keel over. Here's an idea: Don't do it."

He stood, almost expiring from the fire at his back, unwrapped his scarf and threw his coat onto his chair. He flopped beside her on the sofa, where he looked completely out of place and put his arm around her. The chill coming from her was a complete contrast to the heat emanating from him, and gradually, their respective temperatures evened out. David stared at the fire, still shaking his head slightly, but unwilling to ask her yet again what she had been up to. Kate, not understanding very much about the situation at all, merely fitted under his arm and murmured, "I meant it about your hair. You won't suit it any scruffier. You're not Neil."

At that moment, they heard the sound of paws on wood, and into the room padded Bertuzzi, licking her mouth free of any residue of food and wagging her entire backside with glee. She whined slightly, used her tongue to wet David's offered hand and then put her paws up on Kate's knee.

"No, you don't," David said as sternly as the doe eyes allowed him to. "She's mine, Bert. All mine."

The dog cocked her head at the words, looked as if she would jump up anyway, and then took off out of the door. A few seconds later and she was manoeuvring herself rhythmically up the stairs, one at a time. Apparently, she already knew who appreciated her the most, and she wished to be back at his feet as soon as possible.

"What a very strange day," Kate commented, relaxing by the second but determined to keep her eyes open. Since just after six that morning, she had been in the company of others. She had enjoyed it all: the excitement, the chatter, the laughter and even the incredible storytelling which had seen her sweat with anxiety until the moment had seemed to pass with little damage done. The arrival of Bertuzzi had changed the usual order of her Christmas mornings, where she would normally wake Alasdair and watch him assess the gifts that were his, but there would be many more of those to come. Until he got older, of course, and refused to get up until noon. David's face was within kissing distance, and Kate felt she should take up the opportunity and remind him of their date, but was no longer sure she was capable of taking part. This was the most bizarre occurrence of the day, and she sat up, alarmed.

"Come back," David's voice was low. "I want to talk to you."

As she relaxed back against him, her blood swished in her ears.

"I've been trying to talk to you since last night, but first you were late back from Rose's, and then the dog and everything. Freddie Hunter has still completely thrown me, but it makes me acknowledge one thing. I'm really, really lucky."

Kate made use of the pause in his words to try and figure how he thought himself lucky. He had a wife who continually demanded his attention and made him raise his eyebrows on a daily basis, a son only a few years older than his granddaughter, a daughter who had lived out of his reach for most of her life, a brother who could not seem to ditch his past because of a mother who had suddenly felt it was "time to share." Kate widened her eyes, thinking that if it wasn't for his job, which he had always viewed as a vocation of sorts, he would most likely be insane by now. She was about to voice this when he kissed her hand and she held her tongue instead.

"Conventional, eh?" his voice was warm, matching the comfort of the room. "If you'd stayed in Scotland, what conventional life would you be living?"

The motive for his words could not be even guessed at, not when Kate had only really begun to think straight in the last few moments, and so instead of trying to work out what he wanted to hear, she merely answered.

"Depends. If you mean if Mum hadn't died, then I'd probably be teaching somewhere, maybe in a city, maybe in charge of a wee primary," Kate grinned at the assumption of her capability. "But if you mean what would I be doing if you hadn't seen sense and had insisted I was too big a risk, then that's easy."

Kate watched as finally the heat from the fire made it as far as the damp linen of her trousers and made them steam. She picked at her knee, trying to release the hold the material had on her skin.

"Feel like sharing?"

"Okay," sighed Kate, taking the hand that had held hers to kiss, and weaving their fingers together, which always seemed to work in spite of the size disparity. "But your lack of knowledge in this department leads me to suspect that perhaps you've not been listening every other time I've told you. You could argue that you've never asked me directly and I'd have to relent–"

"How about you just tell me, before Christmas Day becomes New Year's Day?"

Kate stretched her legs far out in front of her, watching a tiny sliver of ice drop and form a small puddle on the polished wood. She grinned, simply acknowledging that no matter what she said in the next few moments, she was in fact sitting next to David, his thigh resting amiably against hers, and so she had already won the battle.

"Well, I'd have made my bedroom into a fortress for a start, shutting everybody out of my life except your ghost. I suppose I'd be saving hard, probably still holding down three jobs and avoiding socialising at all costs, even though Hazel would be trying to fix me up with anybody under thirty who was on the market. Basically, I'd be getting more and more pissed off with people and killing myself inside at the thought of you meeting somebody else, somebody lovely, who would love you more than anything else."

The last sentiment had David doing his usual disbelieving "hmph," followed by Kate's habitual dismissal of it. But she had not yet finished.

"I'd be ill, because I'd know you deserved to be happy with that person, but I'd still wish that that person didn't exist. And I'd want it all to go wrong, so that you'd come back and look for me instead. God, what an admission. I think we should stop this before you realise what a truly selfish person I am."

David reached forward, but as he dropped her hand and began to unlace his boots, he turned back to look at her vexed face. "I wondered if you might have seen yourself in the arms of some fit graduate, a rugby player maybe, someone who shared your views on the use of advertising hoardings at Internationals." He moved his hands over to Kate's boots and began tugging at the wet laces. "Somebody who would buy you shoes once in a while instead of boots. You know, you'd be part of a 'conventional' young family, awaiting the birth of your third child, say."

He found Kate staring, her face flushing in front of him. "My, that was worryingly specific."

David hauled her feet out of her boots and onto his lap. Her socks were cold but not damp, and he peeled them off as she settled against the cushions in the corner. There were two areas on her body where Kate was ticklish. One was her right collar bone, the other was her feet, and David knew better than to caress them, so he simply held one ankle in each hand; cradled them, wanting her to feel valued as he spoke.

"You're not the only one who has been known to lie awake and wonder," David said, tracing his fingers over Kate's ankle bones, an action which had more power than he would ever realise. "You're smart, Kitty. You could have been out there, touching countless more lives than you do here, hidden away in this house. But every day when I wake up, you're with me. Sometimes curled into a ball, sometimes taking up more of the bed than a person your size has any right to, but you're warm and beautiful, and you smile as you open your eyes. So I relax and remember how lucky I am for another day."

Kate had kept her eyes open until that moment, because watching David move his mouth around his words, especially words which concerned his feelings for her, had always been a favourite pastime. He had been on the point of shaving that morning, as an extra Christmas present to Rose, but Kate had pouted and promised all sorts of rewards if he refrained; and in the past few moments of easy privacy, she had studied his green eyes and his salt and peppered jaw with her usual gratification. When his hands began massaging her ankles and lower calves, she had to close her eyes or risk not hearing his words at all; her senses could only cope with so much simultaneous stimulation.

"Lucky," she murmured. "I'm ... lucky one."

"In that case, I think we can afford to be 'conventional' as well. Here, this is for you."

Kate eased open her eyes but in the blur before her, could only see him holding a small black object. She sat up, genuinely curious, as David had long since given up on trying to surprise her– "I see all, I know all, so there's no point–" to find that the object was a tiny velvet bag with a drawstring. He dropped it into her palm and kissed her.

"You really thought slippers were your gift?"

"And why not? They're cool," she nodded, and then, "Oh, Dave, my fingers can't undo it. Please?"

When he held the ring up to the light, Kate's heart did an odd leap of pure nostalgia. It was neither as large nor as square as the plastic ring she had owned as a child, but the band was gold and the stone was an emerald. A winking oval of green, held between David's thumb and index finger, which had her grinning and shaking her head in equal amounts. He took her hand, trying to assess if it would fit, and then slid it carefully across her knuckles until it rested by the ring already there.

"Just because we did things in a hurry, doesn't mean I should have left it this long. So this is the start. Your engagement ring, madam."

"Dave, you're mad. I didn't care. But wow, it's completely beautiful."

David accepted the grateful kisses all over his face, but held tightly onto her left hand throughout. When she finally stopped and looked at her gift more closely, he moved the hair away from her cheek and held her face in his free hand.

"I have no idea what people actually make of us, Kit, and it matters even less. But I like the thought of appearing ordinary, to those who might still wonder."

Kate was truly surprised, but as she watched the firelight through the emerald's facets, she managed to conceal this by not allowing the smile to fade from her eyes. Of course, their family was unique at this point in time, but there were immeasurable global stories, past and present, of lives complicated by love; and as a couple, she and David had physically harmed not one person. Their issues with Hazel were gradually growing out, becoming thinner and weaker as her life produced its own situations and delights, and Kate had no doubts that the people who mattered the most had long since accepted them. But she remembered the first few weeks as his wife, and the realisation that most of the surrounding population had known David's entire sorry history. She had introduced herself many times to many different individuals in that time, and had always returned their curiosity with questions of her own. If David was with her, they would always walk close together, dodging attention by talking non-stop to each other, an activity Kate found as easy as breathing. They held hands in private, they stood close beside each other in public, and she had only ever found it empowering. How had he felt?

"Love you," she ventured, hoping it would express some sort of understanding as well as gratitude. "But I never want us to be ordinary."

David laughed. "Kitty, we're way past ever being that. But maybe to others it looks like we're still taking things easy, 'giving it our best shot,' testing the water. You know, quiet wedding, one token child ..."

"Hang on, there's no way we're having one of those second, posher weddings, matey," Kate would have been out of her seat if he had allowed it. But he held her tight, laughing as she struggled to prove how serious she was.

"Oh, agreed," he replied, his arms encasing hers like a strait jacket. "I was thinking of another, less tacky way of showing everybody how normal we are. Let's have us another baby."

Kate, who had been gradually thawing on the outside, managing to smother her shivers as she filed away her odd episode outside, felt a spark inside. It was that initial, disbelieving spark of excitement which occurred rarely but seemed soaked in fuel from the outset. It sprawled quickly, the fire within her, burning through the skin and bones of the "beast" in her belly and reducing them to blessed ashes. Her own breath had stopped momentarily, and she saw a sudden doubt on David's face, wondering if he had somehow misread every sign regarding the subject. She loved that doubt as much as she hated to see it, because it proved the serious thought behind the suggestion. But before his green eyes took on a totally vexed look, she spoke.

"Really? That's what you've been wandering around with on your mind for the last day or two?"

"Well, I thought about the ring for your birthday, but didn't have time to buy it. Now, I really like the prospect of another mouth to feed. If I can do it at forty-nine, I can do it again at ... fifty-five plus."

Kate finally relaxed her whole body and lay, languishing in the knowledge that a barrier had come down. Whether they would be successful in their attempt remained to be seen, but an obstacle had been removed, and that was what brought her the most joy.

"What time is it, Dave?"

"Nearly 10.30."

"Good," murmured Kate, grinning like a madman as her jaw relaxed even more. "I thought we might have missed our date, and that would have been a crime. I love you. Merry Christmas."

Chapter 15
Isle of Skye

"Happy New Year!"

Beth, as she stepped through Hazel's front door, did not for one second consider volume control, and at once there was a tiny startled cry followed by sustained bawling. "Sorry," she whispered, to the empty hallway, "I'm an idiot."

Stuart MacIntyre came grinning out from the kitchen with his three-and-a-half-month-old daughter Hope fitted over his shoulder. The noise seemed to snuffle to a halt as the baby tried desperately to raise her head, and Beth cringed in apology. She hoped that the bottle of Talisker whisky she held in her right hand would ease the pain, as the lump of coal in her left would almost certainly do no such thing.

"No harm done," Stuart let her off. "Bit early for that coal, though."

"I know, but I wanted to be sure to be the first first-footer. Here, let me wash my hands and I'll nurse her for a while."

A few minutes later, Beth joined Hazel in front of their sitting room fire, Hope gurgling happily at the relative peace and quiet. Hazel was dressed in a long velvet skirt and floral shirt, and already had a glass of white wine in front of her on the coffee table. Around her lay a changing mat, a baby seat and some discarded felt toys, but she seemed in no hurry to tidy up. Instead she leaned forward in her chair and pointed at Beth's feet.

"Whoa! Where did you get those?"

At forty-four years of age, Beth Mackinnon should have known better, but even when her waist was beginning to thicken and she needed to wear her glasses on a daily basis, she had not been able to resist the black patent leather boots she now wore.

"They're great, aren't they? Kenny seems to be under the impression that they're for teenagers, but what does he know?"

"Och away, anybody can wear those. Maybe I could borrow them sometime?"

Kenny wandered in, and Beth immediately offloaded her charge into his nervous arms. Not for him the casual placing of the infant on his shoulder, he needed to know that there was no earthly chance of her being harmed in the time she was his responsibility. He stood, tense and still, awaiting his next set of instructions; but neither Beth nor Hazel made a move to put him out of his misery, and instead the former reached in her bag for her camera and the latter sank back into the sofa.

"Aw man, Beth," Kenny groaned, "you're enjoying this, aren't you?"

"If you mean, I'm enjoying the anticipation of taking a lovely photo of you with your great-niece so that I can frame it and put it on the wall for all to see, then yes, I am. Now sit down and make sure we can see her face."

Kenny followed the orders with continued anxiety, lowering himself carefully onto the fireside chair to avoid Hope's precious head making contact with household objects. His face was beginning to glow with the effort, diminishing even further the colour of his already fading red hair, but finally he sat still and let out a breath.

"A smile would make it even better," suggested Beth and held the camera still by her face until he was relaxed enough to let his mouth turn up at the edge. "Much better. Relax, Kenneth. She survived being born a month early and a journey across the Atlantic in a metal tube with wings. What makes you think you are dangerous in any way?"

"Okay, but when she wakes up ..."

Hope did not stir for another hour and twenty minutes, by which time Beth had refilled Kenny's glass and fed him a couple of sandwiches. Twice Hazel offered to remove the burden, but he had shaken his head gently and declared himself a perfectly capable host. Although there had been many discussions in that period of time, ranging from Beth's footwear, to the conviction of the Lockerbie bomber, to the great dummy versus thumb debate, nobody's eyes had strayed far from the swaddled, contented little person warming Kenny's upper body. Stuart, when he studied his daughter, saw Hazel's profile even with the snubbed nose and smiled each and every time. Kenny liked to momentarily pass his hands over her ultra-fine hair, letting it tickle his fingers. Beth had a habit of simply gazing and sighing, and Hazel watched all of these activities, teaching herself patience. She was not the only one who had longed for this child, but perhaps because she had not actually carried her, she could only go so long without stepping in and reminding them that she was Hope's mother. The palms of her hands actually itched after a certain time.

She need not have worried. As soon as the infant uncurled and tried to open her eyes, her bottom lip protruding and her back arching against Kenny's suddenly tense arms, the man's face took on the usual anxious look.

"Eh ... Haze?"

"I've got her. My God, Ken, you poor bugger. When did she fill her nappy?"

"I didn't want to spoil the atmosphere ..."

"Well, she's one step ahead of you there."

Hazel lifted the pouting and stretching infant from his arms, reached for the changing bag and mat in one single movement and took the child out of the room, to the relief of those left behind. As Kenny gingerly unlocked his frozen arms and was handed a second dram, there was a loud bang on the front door followed by a very masculine chorus of "A Guid New Year," which was subsequently shushed by a very feminine reminder that the bells had yet to chime. However, both Bruce MacIntyre and his wife Catriona were laughing from the general occasion, or possibly the three or four drinks already consumed. There was much cooing and fussing to be heard in the hallway, followed by a hiccup and an uncomfortable wail, before the two adults finally made an appearance in the sitting room. Catriona wore jeans and a hooded sweatshirt, while Bruce, three years older and two stones heavier than his brother Stuart, was dressed from head to toe in full Highland dress, including fly plaid. He walked awkwardly, with a pronounced limp.

"And here we all are, together!" he shouted, raising his six cans as they all stood to greet the remainder of the party. "First time in God knows how many years!"

"Why?" cried Beth, pointing to his attire. "Why would you choose to wear that when you weren't playing in the pipe band?"

"Because–" Bruce began.

"No, let me tell them," interrupted Catriona, laughing before clearing her throat. "This is what Bruce wears on Hogmanay. He has worn this since joining the band in 1981, and he is not about to let an Achilles operation stop him from 'donning the plaid.' I think they were his exact words."

Bruce nodded his agreement before shuffling over to one of the fireside chairs. "Absolutely. Well done for listening."

"Well, you won't last long in this heat," replied Beth, settling the logs in the fireplace. "Better get you a drink before you expire."

In the room at the end of the hallway, Hazel was enjoying the relative peace of Hope's musical mobile. It seemed the kindest thing to do, to let the infant delight in the tinkling chimes when the changing mat was potentially the most hazardous place to be in the whole house. In spite of the chore, Hazel liked the way her daughter never took her eyes from her own for the duration. Maybe it was the string of soft words in their melodic framework which enchanted the baby, or maybe it was that her mother's eyes shone in any light. Whatever it was, Hope would join in the communication by moving her smooth limbs continually, sometimes to the detriment of the task in hand, and making the odd gurgling sound. Sometimes she even grinned, which usually had Hazel squealing for all to come and see. Tonight was just for the two of them, and as she fastened a fresh vest in place and eased her into her Babygro, Hazel felt her heart expand all over again. As she hugged the wriggling bundle to her chest, she thought that maybe a few more minutes of private time was required, and she slipped the warmed bottle into Hope's eager mouth where she stood.

Stuart had promised Hazel a rocking chair, for the simple reason that he had glimpsed it on one of the many baby food adverts they had historically changed channels to avoid, but trying to source such a thing on the island was not easy. In the meantime, Hazel had taken to settling herself on the wide windowsill for moments like these. She liked the cool glass, but more than that, she loved to show Hope the night sky. She was no astrologer, but something about the blue-blackness peppered with glowing rocks made her glad to be part of this particular planet, and Hazel loved the moon most of all. It had often accompanied her walks across the moor between Stuart's family farm and Beth's cottage in their younger days and had been a constant on her visits to Canada. It had also caused her to run her little car off the frosty top road one night, due to its brilliance, but she was willing to forgive this one transgression. She knew its phases as a matter of course and was aware that, even if the cloud had cleared, that there would only be a sliver of a waxing crescent to see this night. Nevertheless, she switched off the main light, leaving only the spot over the changing mat, took the child and settled both of them behind the curtains.

"You warm enough, my baby?" Hazel had Hope snuggled into her, but still the tiny hands were exposed and Hazel wrapped her own around them. "This is the life, yes? Who in their right mind would want to live anywhere but here? Look, there's Beth's outdoor light. When you can walk, you'll get to know the path very well. I might even let you go over the moor on your own someday. But not until you're at least … oh, probably never."

Hope had been trying to find her thumb for days, but with the bottle drained, she found her third and fourth finger instead and began to suck on them. Hazel watched in awe; somehow, unbelievably, her baby was replicating her own childhood habit. Her thumb had never come close to being acceptable, and as a toddler, Hazel would simultaneously suck her two fingers whilst twirling her hair with her other hand. Hope was months away from this possibility, but Hazel was transfixed nevertheless. From the second Kate had handed her over, Hazel had been searching for signs: eye colour, the shape of her nose and chin, anything to confirm their connection. But this was the firmest to date, and almost unearthly. Realistically, it could only be coincidental, but it did not stop Hazel from almost choking on her elation.

"Oh, you little miracle," she whispered against Hope's soft cheek. "Thank you for that."

As Hazel relaxed against the recessed wall, looking out onto the amalgamation of black heather and water, trying to distinguish the even blacker outline of Raasay across the bay, she thought of Kate and tried to picture The Edge on the final noon of the year. Would she be getting ready to entertain the residents of Peter's Lane as she had done for the past three or four years, issuing orders to her son and fretting over her lack of cooking ability? Was it snowing, the flakes covering the front lawns with yet another layer of white? Maybe Alasdair was tearing through the woods with his new dog, the period of time spent with his newborn cousin a distant memory. Hazel had to hand it to her sister, Alasdair had indeed seemed to be her focus again after the last year, and Bertuzzi had been a success by all accounts. But to someone who had only ever been in contact with working farm dogs, it had seemed a big commitment.

"Will you be a kitten, puppy or a rabbit baby, Hope? Maybe a hamster. We had a hamster once. It didn't end well."

Over the top of Hope's head, Hazel saw a pair of headlights crawling up out of the village, someone on their way to the Hogmanay celebrations in Portree more likely than not, and she absently waved at the travellers. They were over a quarter of a mile away, but Hazel liked to acknowledge people all the same. She wondered if they had their children with them, where they were planning on bringing in the New Year, and thanked God for her own situation. She did not have to travel, she did not even have to make an effort socially because every person she needed to have a good time was already in the house; with maybe one or two exceptions.

There was a blare of laughter from the sitting room. Hope jumped slightly in Hazel's arms, but before she could tense and wail, Hazel was whispering in her ear, her lips murmuring against the sweet, silky skin. In the next second, she felt a slight pressure on her foot and looked down to see one of Stuart's sports socks playing with her bare feet. Smiling, she tried to grab the material between her toes and finally, after a tussle of a few seconds, Stuart poked his head through the curtains to find her grinning, Hope droopy-eyed and tranquil in her arms.

"Here are my favourite ladies," Stuart's face was shining. "Beth thought you might have decided to crawl into bed with her."

"We're just watching for the moon," replied Hazel, which needed no further explanation to her husband.

"So, is there room for another?" Stuart did not wait for an answer but eased himself into the tiny available space remaining and sat, his knees pressed against Hazel's. "If somebody else comes looking, mind, they'll think we've lost our minds."

"Nice, though, isn't it?"

"I've got the best view," and placed his hand gently on the back of his daughter's head.

As a teenager, Stuart had maintained a huge circle of friends. He was a reasonable football player, joining the local team whilst still at school, and this had boosted his natural confidence with girls. No real effort had ever been required in that department, and Hazel, unlike the majority, had watched him only from a safe distance, listening and absorbing. She had shushed Kate into conspiracy as soon as her interest had become known, however, being determined that he should notice her without her having to flaunt and simper, and had only struck up a conversation when she had begun to serve him cakes across the baker's counter. His lines had kept Kate and her amused for many a long evening. Even during their first months as an item, he had been known to use words and facial expressions to flatter, encourage and eventually get his own way; but by then Hazel had developed moves of her own.

Twelve years into their relationship, the man used far fewer flowery words and rarely gave her a card on Valentine's Day, but Hazel could not have cared less. He had not given up on her. He had listened to her tirade of dismay and fury regarding her sister, not walked out on any meltdown due to her continued grief for her mother, or her irrationality towards eating. He had held her hands at every doctor's appointment and held her face at every subsequent failure. Stuart was no longer a lad, he was a man who had taken on enough to prove his worth and was still sitting beside her, their knees touching. He smiled, and gently she passed the baby to his shoulder. He took her easily.

"What a picture," breathed Hazel and then, "Hey Stuey. What do you think the chances are that one day we'll get a phone call from Dad saying he's decided to retire and he's moving them back over here? There are loads of houses for sale just now … apparently."

"Not that you've been looking."

"Dreaming, maybe," admitted Hazel. "I miss her, them, and I know Kate misses Hope. Rose said as much the last time I spoke to her."

Stuart shrugged slightly, determined not to let her to settle into this particular frame of mind. "I don't doubt that, but I can't see them ever coming back, honey. You know it's unlikely, right?"

"I hate when folk take away my options, especially the preferred ones."

Stuart's eyes dulled slightly in the dim light. At thirty, Hazel had more or less accepted that life was an entity who allowed you some input, an even lesser degree of influence, but which ultimately strung you along until it grew weary of the journey and turned to punch you in the gut instead. This acknowledgement could not, however, stop the bouts of pure despair at her inability to alter circumstances which, in her mind, would have ensured her the next degree of safety in a scary world. The worry was that the responsibility for said security fell to him, and he was as helpless as the rest of them.

"So, what do you want to do, Haze?" Stuart's voice was directed at Hope's head, who had taken so much comfort from her little fingers that she was asleep against the man's chest.

"Nothing I can do," replied Hazel, staring past the glass into the winter beyond. After a moment of frozen silence, she suddenly smirked and leaned her forehead directly onto the pane. "You've got to see the irony though. Dad was supposed to make sure we stayed close, and he's keeping her all to himself."

Stuart stood fluidly and released himself from the cocoon of curtain material. "I'm pretty sure she isn't a prisoner."

Hazel was at his side in a second. "Hey, hey, I was only thinking–"

"Leave them alone, please, Hazel." Stuart placed Hope gingerly beneath the miniature quilt in her cot, covering her loosely and awaited his wife's reply. When it did not come, he took his chance. "I'm never going to win an argument with you, but let me say one thing, as it's the last night of the year."

Hazel's eyes were wide, but instead of speaking, she began to crack her knuckles. Stuart took her hands and pulled them apart.

"I don't understand how Kate works. I never will. Hell, I don't really need to, since she seems content, and honestly, I think they really need each other."

"She's not a saint, you know," she interrupted, her eyes brimming.

"That makes two of you, then," he smiled, folding his arms. "Just let them be, Haze. I know you were imagining family dinners, cousins playing together, the pair of you maybe even eventually running that B and B you want; but it wouldn't have worked, and I think you have to see that."

She wondered if Stuart had the nerve to explain the remark further, and in fact made a face to encourage this, but he did not take the bait and began to wind up the mobile instead. In the absence of his verbal opinion, she put it together in her head anyway. Kate may slot back into their lives, bringing her husband and her son with her, and everyone they knew would rejoice. Until the day that Hazel decided she should be more important to her Dad than Alasdair was, that he owed her years of time and that in the absence of her mother, he alone should be at the end of a phone, ready to drop everything for her. Then the bickering would follow, Kate's hurt expression turning to one of offense, then defence, finally resulting in full-blown resentment and division, from which there would be no boarding of a plane to escape. It was one way of looking at it, but recognising it was not the same as agreeing with it.

"What if I don't have to see that?" she asked.

"Makes no difference. David sees it and Kate sees it. No way are they going to risk what they have for you. Sorry, love. You coming through?"

"In a minute."

As Stuart left the room, Hazel leaned back against the wall next to the cot and let out her breath. Her husband did not always speak his mind, unless it was to shout at the shinty game on the radio, and even then it was rarely articulate. He made jokes and sometimes he teased her until she lost her temper just so that he could watch her eyes flash and her arms flail. He only really looked at her for a prolonged period of time when their bodies were locked together, ironically the only time when she felt free enough to let him do so; the rest of the time, her body was for her scrutiny alone. But when he laid facts out as barely as he had just done, she knew that he needed her to accept them much sooner rather than later.

Fighting back the tears, Hazel leaned in to watch her daughter's mouth still working on her fingers and held on to the sides of the cot. "Hope," she whispered, "listen to me. Very occasionally, your daddy can be wiser than your mummy. Sometimes I can be ridiculous, but I mean well. Yes, you heard, your mother can be ridiculous, and it might take a long time for her to recover from the affliction. Just warning you."

Beth stood as soon as Hazel entered the sitting room, and insisted she take her seat. She took it willingly, rubbing her arms as she did so, deliberately avoiding Stuart's face. It was easy enough, with Bruce's voice dominating the entire space and Kenny throwing in his views whenever he got the opportunity. Catriona sat forward laughing.

"Here, you'll never guess," she paused to haul her sweatshirt over her head and hook it on the back of the sofa, "Hugh the post got engaged last night. I mean, who gets engaged two days before New Year?"

"Never on this earth," exclaimed Beth, "he's only twelve."

"He's twenty-one in March, wants to get married on that very day, and the lass is from South Uist. Aw, you should have seen him. That gorgeous young face was shining like a beacon. Oh, and wait, the best bit. He shouts back from the gate 'and she's not even pregnant.' Hellfire, there are going to be some broken hearts on our island this night."

Hazel began to relax, and by the time Beth and Catriona had simultaneously celebrated with and mourned the loss of the young Hugh, she was ready for a drink. The clock read just after nine. No doubt Kate was trying to get Alasdair to eat something substantial whilst she concentrated on cooking for the supper party. As she allowed her face to react to the two different conversations within the room, without joining in either, Stuart slipped a glass of wine into her hand. He said nothing and she replied in kind, but he sat on the floor at her feet, and she settled her free hand in his hair.

An hour later, when empty bowls of curry covered the surface of the coffee table and Bruce had stripped to his shirt sleeves, the phone rang in the hallway. Hazel frowned. It was too early for the Canadian call, yet when she picked up the receiver, it was indeed Kate's voice she heard.

"Oh, thank God!"

"What's going on?" Hazel enquired, aghast at the anxiety in her sister's words. "What's happened?"

"I tried Beth's house first–"

"What the hell is it? Is it Rose? It's not Dad."

"Eh?"

"Why are you ringing this early?"

There was a pause and then, "Because I need to ask Beth about her cheesecake. I'm on my third attempt, and there are no more lemons in the house. Jeez, why are you shouting?"

Hazel shuddered. "Can you stop saying 'Jeez,' please? You sound like a Canadian."

"Is that better?" Kate replied in Gaelic. "Anyway, I'm assuming she's at yours? There's a bloody disaster taking place around me, and if you want a decent, sensible phone call at midnight, I need to speak to her now."

"Just a minute," Hazel rolled her eyes even though her sister was unable to appreciate the gesture and turned to find Stuart in the doorway, eyebrows raised. "Kate for Beth."

As her aunt took up the summons, Hazel pulled Stuart through the hallway into the kitchen and shut the door. He held on to her hand, grinning, ready to play out the final scene; the scene where Hazel apologised, not so much with words but with facial expressions and grateful embraces.

"Right," Hazel sounded excited rather than apologetic. "Here's the plan. I want Kate at the christening. Let's get her over, even if it's just her on her own."

Stuart sighed his confusion.

"I know, I know," continued Hazel, "Catriona and Bruce will still be the godparents, but we could have one more, surely, and I bet I can talk her around eventually."

Stuart looked at his wife in genuine disbelief, recalling a surprisingly recent discussion. He could picture the evening easily, as it had been Hope's first night in this house. Hazel had sat on the sofa, almost buried under baby paraphernalia, her eyes never leaving the tiny bundle held against her. She had been full to brimming: full of awe, full of an altered future, full of luck, full of love. There had been happy tears accompanying the tales from Canada and disappointment that Kate had declined the initial invitation to be Hope's godmother. She had wanted only to be an aunt to the baby she had fed, changed and comforted for the first three weeks of her life. Kate had been totally inflexible on the point, and Hazel had accepted it in spite of her lack of understanding. Her mind was made up, there was nothing clearer.

"Okay then, I just need her to be there," Hazel spread her hands wide. "Maybe you're right about my silly, rose-coloured version of what it could be like; but even if she's just here as her aunt, that would be great. Better. I'll pay for the ticket. She's paid for everything else, let's face it. What do you say?"

Stuart was not exactly sure what he wanted to say, apart from "I know what you're up to, but let's just live a simple life, for a little while at least," and so he remained silent until he saw Hazel's hope fade a little at his lack of response. He sighed. Was there really any harm in it?

"Well, "Stuart replied, "you can ask her. It'll be up to her, mind."

"I know," Hazel allowed, "but I'm going to try my bloody hardest."

CHAPTER 16
Vancouver Island

Alasdair Wilder opened his eyes to find only a tiny crack of light at one of his bedroom windows. But light it was and it made him sit up and listen. No radio sounded in the kitchen below him, no vacuum cleaner, no washing machine, no doors opening or closing anywhere in the house. Bertuzzi's yawn ended in a stretch, accompanied by the thumping of her tail on the base of her cage, but other than that Alasdair wondered if he had been abandoned. In the spirit of his environment, he rolled back his duvet and quietly tiptoed over to release his best friend from her prison. It was all a bit spine-tingly, a word he had picked up from the TV a couple of days earlier, and could not believe his luck in being able to apply it so soon.

Out on the landing, Bertuzzi clicked her way to the stairs and began her descent, never assuming for a moment that he would not follow and let her outside. But the boy stood motionless by his door, trying to detect other signs of human activity; and in the snow-white light of the new morning, thought he heard a sneeze above him. Alasdair smiled. It was his mom and she must still be in bed.

Three stairs from the top of the second flight, however, Alasdair also heard his dad's deep murmur, followed by reference to his own name. He halted and sat immediately, intrigued. Why was nobody up when it was full daylight, and why were they talking about him when he wasn't there to help them with their questions? Silently he remained just out of sight and tried to gather information from their hushed voices instead.

"He'll be in school then," his mom said softly, "much better if he stays here with you. You can have boys' nights, beers and hockey. You'll probably end up dreading the day I come back."

When his dad did not answer, Alasdair raised his head until his eyes were level with the top stair. The space before him was nowhere near as dark as his room, but at floor level he could not see his father's reaction. He saw instead the fringes of a blanket trailing from the bed, a pair of trainers and socks at the base of his mom's chair, and a magazine lost under the chest of drawers.

"It's a lot of time I can't afford," his dad's voice was so low it made Alasdair frown and stretch his neck. There was the man's head lying lazily against the headboard, staring straight in front of him; he was wearing his worried face. His mom's delicate hand appeared and touched his dad's chin.

"I'm quite capable of going alone."

Then his mom turned the face towards him, and Alasdair guessed that she was kissing him. It did not take as long as it sometimes did, and his dad looked no happier for it.

"Oh, Davey. This trip, the christening, is just the natural ending to the whole of last year. That's all it is."

There was a pause, then, "Well, that and the ... real possibility that she is there for the finding."

Alasdair shifted on his knees as his dad pushed himself into a sitting position.

"Kit, I wish you would, just for once, look at the negatives involved."

"Why is looking for the missing link negative?"

"The missing link? For God's sake."

Alasdair slumped back to his original position. Living in this house was okay. The woods were really cool, and his friends were jealous that he had his "huge" bedroom all to himself, with only Bertuzzi to bother him. But sometimes he wished for a brother or even a sister, someone to turn to and say "What d'you think is going on? Is this something to worry about?"

"Dave, we are sorted. We know all there is to know, every last detail of where we came from, but this isn't for us. If there's even a tiny chance that I can meet Freddie Hunter, see her face-to-face and hear her story, then we'll have something to give Neil. And Freddie."

"And what about Rose?"

Sometimes it was easier to leave his parents to it, especially when both of their voices started to get higher and louder, and Alasdair crept down to the landing. Bertuzzi met him at his bedroom door and waited with her usual impatience as he pulled on his clothes from the night before, adding a thick jumper because his good shirt was not enough for a walk in the snow. Unexpectedly, the kitchen was tidy, considering the amount of food it had produced for the previous day's celebrations, but Alasdair did not look in the fridge. His Granma Rose would feed him and talk to him, not about him.

"Hey, Al, you going somewhere?"

Alasdair was relieved to see that his mom did not seem to be weepy or mad, just curious.

"Why am I the only one dressed? It's late."

"Yep, well, you're allowed to get up late on the first day of a new year. In fact, it's the law."

Alasdair finished tying his boots and tried to unhook his coat without success. "I'm going to Granma Rose's for breakfast. Bert needs a pee and I'm starving."

His mom pulled his coat from the peg. "Well, I hope you were going to leave us a note, Mr Independent."

"I was," he replied, his face burning slightly at the fib, and allowed his mom to zip his coat and hug him as penance. "Come on, Bert!"

He was halfway across the front lawn when his mom called out one last instruction.

"Stay there until I pick you up, bud! I need to speak to Granma Rose about something."

PART III

March 2004

CHAPTER 17

Northumberland, England

The single-tracked road was tarmac with a layer of fine abandoned grit, the camber quite severe at the edges, but with relatively few potholes, and it wound its way out of the town at a formidable gradient. On either side, the farmland was edged with hedgerows bursting with buds and tiny flowers which would eventually produce berries to colour the scene. Kate pretended to herself that she had stopped by the five-barred gate to look at the patchwork of fields below her, but really it was nerves which had halted her. She was glad that she had taken the time; the country before her was a milder-looking landscape than Skye, with no serrated ridges. Neither was it enclosed in trees like The Edge, but the vegetation was fresh for early March, and the slopes rolled smoothly down towards the road. Kate appreciated the gentleness of it. She leaned first her elbows upon the rough wood of the top bar, and then her chin, letting the breeze fan her hair. How on earth was she going to approach this woman? Yes, Rose and Freddie had agreed that they would always know where each other was, but she had given this person no warning of her arrival. That wasn't fair. It was equally unfair that Neil knew nothing about this, but she was prepared to forgive herself in this instance, unless it went terribly wrong. She had travelled this distance; something was pushing her forward. Still her stomach rumbled on.

As Kate allowed the nearest group of sheep to disturb her with their calls for food, she also heard a set of defiantly healthy footsteps behind her, and on turning was surprised to find their owner was much older and definitely fitter than she was. Kate stood upright and rubbed her chin where she could still feel the imprint of the wooden bar, noting that the woman was tall and obviously used to climbing this hill on a regular basis, as her stride was long and unlaboured. She glanced in Kate's direction.

"Good afternoon," her pace never altered.

"Hi," replied Kate and then turned her burning face immediately back to the entirely safer view of sheep and grassland. There was nothing whatsoever to suggest that this woman was Freddie Hunter, except perhaps her age. Kate felt her heart begin to thud a little louder. By the time she had watched an old ewe nibble and tear at the head of a thistle, she had breathed herself steadier and thought that perhaps she should just wander back down to the town. If this was her reaction to meeting someone who may be completely inconsequential, then there was a chance that she would not hold it together should she ever meet her grandmother. Her watch told her it was heading for four o'clock, and indeed the sun was low, approaching the summit of the nearest hill; but what stayed her feet from heading back was the thought of sitting alone in another bed-and-breakfast establishment for the second night in a row. At that moment, she felt her mobile buzz against her hip. It was a text. From Neil.

"No way," stated Kate, as she pressed to open the message.

"Kate. How goes it in the land of kilts and weird pipes? We've got snow. Soph wondered if you had too. Said I would ask."

Kate grinned. One of these fine days, Neil might actually stop making excuses for contacting her and merely enquire if she was okay. But for today, it was a convenient little sign which had her heading off uphill instead of downhill as she tried to concentrate on the tasks of walking and texting. As quickly as she could, she constructed her reply.

"No but it's cold. Out for walk. Lots to see. Thinking about you sledging with S & A x."

As she watched the moving arrow which assured her that the message was flying across the ocean, The Edge's number appeared as an incoming call.

"Hello family, and who am I speaking to this morning?"

It was Alasdair, and Kate settled the rhythm of her walking so that she could hear his monotone without her shallow breathing drowning it out. He was bored. School was dull and Dad was hopeless with bacon. How was Hope? Rose had a cold and couldn't get out of bed. He needed some new trainers. When was she coming home? Kate tried her best to raise his level of enthusiasm before he left for school, and answered every question except his last one, before David's voice took over. His deeper tones had never been so welcome, and as she passed two low houses, she stopped so that she could give her full attention to the man.

"Al seems a bit fed up," she said, scratching her eyebrow.

"Yeah, well, he misses you. Makes two of us. And who knew that bacon could only be cooked one way?"

"Dave. Guess what. I might have just seen her. I think I should just do it. What do you think?"

There was a pause during which Alasdair's voice could be heard shouting about the imminent arrival of the school bus, before David replied, hurrying his words along slightly.

"Yeah, just do it, Kit. Al and I, we're missing our ordinary days, so find this lady, do what you have to and please hurry back to us."

Kate frowned slightly at the door of the nearest cottage, noting that there was a definite strain to his words which she had not heard since she had first thought of making the trip. Surely, after all this time, he had faith in her and her return.

"Okay, then, I will. But you need to grow a spine, David John. Can't believe somebody as tall and strong as you can't get by for a week or—"

"Got to go, or he'll miss the bus. Call me later?"

"Okay," Kate agreed, but watched the phone until the little green icon had gone and the connection was broken. She guessed that the man she loved did not have the luxury at that moment to think about their odd little communication, but it didn't stop her from doing so. Of course they were missing her. She was missing them. You didn't spend your lives cocooned in the woods with the same adored faces and bodies for there not to be an obvious wound at separation, but she had a persistent inkling that what David was actually missing was her attention. He always became slightly anxious whenever she switched her focus to Neil, and this trip was more for her father than for anybody else. Well, it made a sort of sense. David and Neil were fine together when in the same room and were mutually supportive in times of real crisis. But she still had some work to do before their family took on a totally normal coexistence. God, would she be forever manipulating others until they behaved themselves?

As she stuffed the phone into her back pocket, Kate glanced for one final time down the road towards the town, then turned and continued uphill. The sun was low in her eye-line, but it continued to heat her face as she climbed higher; and if her instructions from the post office staff were correct, then another few yards would show her the house she was looking for. So, to business. What should she use as an opening gambit to ensure that the woman did not faint dead away at her feet? She needed to ask her if she was Freddie Port, nee Hunter; that went without saying. Maybe she should ease into a dialogue by mentioning Rose's name and asking her if it meant anything to her? As the road passed under her feet and she realised that after another three tiled roofs she would arrive at the last house in the row, she tried to decide. What if she just whipped out a photo of Neil and said "Do you recognise anybody, lady?"

"God's sake," murmured Kate, keeping her eyes on the end house. As she watched, the front door opened and a figure deposited a black bag into the nearest plastic bin. Kate slowed her pace as she saw that the fit lady was indeed the inhabitant of the last house before the open hillside. Freddie Hunter, birth mother of Neil, her grandmother by blood. Kate's nose suddenly felt irritated and she knelt immediately, pretending to tie her bootlace, while she tried to swallow her fear and her wonder.

When, a few moments later she could stand once again, the woman had disappeared back inside; and Kate, suspecting that she might not move until dusk had settled around her, forced herself forward. Just a few more steps and it would be all over. Either she would welcome her or she would not, and it really was up to her. Rose had reckoned that she was a decent person, but had also not seen her in nearly five decades. There was no way of knowing how life had affected the woman, but if nothing else, both of them would know that the other existed, and knowledge of that kind usually proved quite positive.

"Oh, curse and swear," moaned Kate. This really was intolerable. She was standing on a country road, staring at the front door of a house which she had never once set foot inside. It looked like a reasonable enough front door, painted a high gloss black with a heavy brass knocker, the likes of which she had never seen since her Skye days. But why did it have to be so brutally black? Thank God for the rose trellis surrounding it and the stone cat curled on the side of the step. Kate moved slowly over to the gate which enclosed the garden, fiddled with the latch until it released, and stepped across the boundary. Okay, so she was completely invading this woman's territory, and it was in no way acceptable to take up space in her tidy garden without announcing her arrival. Watching her own fingers in amazement, Kate raised the knocker and dropped it twice, hitched her backpack until it lay straight on her shoulders and ran her fingers through her hair. She had time only to rub her hands together once before she heard an inner door being opened; and as she held her breath, the black door was pulled inwards, and there was only air between them.

Kate studied the woman's face for as long as was politely appropriate, but it was enough time for her to note the colour and shape of her eyes. It was disconcerting to her that this lady, in spite of the soft, pale skin surrounding them, could pin her to the spot, and she knew exactly why: Because the eyebrows lay in a straight line, the eyes below them triangular in shape, and she saw this combination every time Neil turned his face towards her. The irises, however, were a slate grey, and this made Kate smile. She blinked automatically, willing the woman to see what she saw.

"Hello? Are you lost?" The intonation was strange, slightly melodic with a definite burr, but not Celtic.

Kate cringed slightly and wrinkled her nose. "No. I think I might have the right house. Am I speaking to Mrs Port?"

Winnie moved forward across the threshold and stepped out from under the rose trellis. She glanced at Kate's hands, took in her small backpack and frowned slightly. The girl could have been a walker without a map, but no walker worth their salt wore jeans in the hills. She was slightly built, innocuous enough looking and apparently was happy to wait for some sort of response.

"I'm Mrs Port," Winnie volunteered at last.

Kate's smile grew wider, but she had to clear her throat before speaking. "Well, that's the first hurdle over then. I mean, I was pretty sure my directions meant this house, and then I actually did have the nerve to knock on the door, which is ... a bit impressive. I'm not usually that forward."

"You were looking for me?"

Kate nodded, but offered nothing else. Instead, she clenched her fists once and then shoved her hands into her fleece pockets. Winnie's eyebrows shaded her irises further before she took a deep breath in.

"You're Scottish?"

"Yes."

Winnie looked intently at Kate's face, moving studiously over every inch of her features before finally relaxing and letting her expression soften. She shook her head gently. "Sorry," she sighed. "I wasn't expecting anyone, and then, I wondered ... So, how can I help?"

Kate was suddenly intrigued to see a tiny pink area of irritation on the lady's neck, and she self-consciously touched her own throat where the skin had been tingling for the last ten minutes or more. She stared at the mark until Winnie herself lifted her hand to acknowledge it. There was another moment of complete stillness before each of them was startled by the appearance of a tiny border terrier at their feet. In the next second, a Lycra-clad runner pounded past, greeting the pair of them and shouting for the dog to heel in the same jagged breath. The dog sniffed once more at Kate's boots, then took off at speed. Winnie followed the dog's journey for a second and then stared more assertively at the girl before her. Kate finally outstretched her hand.

"I wonder if you would be willing to talk to me, Freddie. My name's Kate Wilder."

It was the most fluid movement Kate had ever witnessed, and she thought she would probably remember it for the rest of her life. Winnie's eyes gradually widened, synchronised completely with the slow journey her fingertips made to her lips, where they stayed until a clear pool of liquid finally spilled over onto her cheek. Kate's face fell immediately and she dropped her hand.

"Oh no!" she cried. "It's nothing sad. I hope. I didn't mean—" Kate stopped talking as soon as Winnie grabbed her wrist to steady herself, and when Kate cupped the woman's elbow in her hand, it felt almost as if they were holding each other upright. "Hello," she whispered into Winnie's bowed head of greying hair.

"But," Winnie's voice betrayed a tremor, "you're Scottish."

186

At last, the thoughts behind the statement penetrated Kate's comprehension, and she squeezed Winnie's hand. "I am, but only half. I grew up on Skye, but my dad is Canadian," she hesitated, then, "from just outside Duncan. BC."

"You know Rose and Pete?" Winnie's voice croaked with emotion, but in the next instant she had lifted her head and cleared her throat. "What do you know?"

Kate slid her hands into the woman's warm palms. "I know that Neil Wilder is the most amazing person, and if you want me to, I can tell you all about him."

《•》《•》《•》

Winnie scrutinized the young woman in front of her through the steam from the newly made cup of tea. She watched as Kate cradled the mug in her palms, marvelling that she sat there in her kitchen, transforming it within half an hour from something ordinary and unremarkable. Now, it was filled with a source of energy which was making Winnie's heart jump every three minutes or so, and she knew she was staring at the girl: her face, her hands, her short, dark hair. And yet the subject did not seem to mind this level of attention. Instead, she was looking around her, maybe even committing it to memory, and Winnie suddenly wished that she was a better housekeeper and that she had managed to emulsion the walls the previous month like she had intended to. As she continued to put away her groceries, Winnie was aware that the evening had the potential to change all that she regarded as private and cherished and that this seemingly calm individual was not nearly as nervous as she was.

Kate was indeed happy, delighted by her surroundings and unable to prevent her eyes from wandering across every surface and decoration. There was one long shallow window situated at her back, which allowed the dying sun to illuminate the room with moving golden fingers; indeed the addition of an electric light might prove too much for either of them at this time. But it did not conceal any of the room's delights. There was a deep red cooking range (which Kate had fallen in love with on sight and which reeked heat) slotted into a tiled alcove. The pale green tiles surrounding it carried on as splash backs, and it reminded Kate a little of a stick of rhubarb-flavoured rock she had enjoyed as a child. It made her smile to think that this woman also liked the combination of colours.

They sat at a tiny pine table on chairs that perhaps had seen better days, but it was a comfortable room. Kate imagined it buzzing with family and friends, wine mulling and snow falling outside. The wall opposite seemed to play host to a variety of terra-cotta birds arranged randomly, and by the back door was a low boot rack overflowing with walking boots, trainers and one pair of wellies. Kate's eyes widened. It really was high time she took her own fitness more seriously.

"Is your tea to your liking?" Winnie asked, breaking into Kate's musings and cutting the atmosphere with her low but determined voice.

"Och yes, it's fine," replied Kate and sipped once more as if to prove her words. "It's the best cup I've had in two days, if you want to know. Had a bit of a convoluted journey."

Kate stopped speaking as her mobile phone made a buzz in her pocket and she cringed, embarrassed.

"Please," stated Winnie, "feel free."

Kate fished the phone from her back pocket, blushing as if the thing had gone off in a packed cinema. It was a text from David and it simply read, "With you all the way xxxx." Kate visibly relaxed at its content.

"Looks like you appreciated that," observed Winnie.

Kate grinned then shrugged, as though they might already be at the point of intimacy, and laid her phone on the table.

"It was my husband. He was wishing me luck with ... well, with this conversation, actually."

Winnie sat forward, intrigued. "You're married?"

Kate grinned a second time but before speaking, she laid her mug on the table and tucked her bottom lip between her teeth. "Listen, there's so much I would willingly tell you, because you seem very nice, and I'm sure you would be a kind audience. But that wouldn't be fair, unless I knew you wanted to hear it. If you'd rather we just let it be, I could walk away from here knowing that at least my gran seemed a person worth meeting."

Winnie felt her throat tighten and realised with amazement that the tears caused by real emotion were quite merciless, and would not be stopped by sheer will alone. As she reached into her cardigan pocket for a hankie, she stood and switched on the lights surrounding the range in the hope that the five tiny bulbs would take Kate's attention away from her face. She wiped her nose and hovered by the window.

"Sorry," Kate's voice was almost ashamed as she turned to speak. "I have a not altogether acceptable habit of saying exactly what I feel. I forget sometimes that it can alarm folk."

"I'm not alarmed."

"Well, that's good, because I've known people who have wasted time instead of enjoying it, just because they were too scared to open their mouths."

Winnie looked down at the face before her, surprised that this scrutiny did not make the young woman look away, and there were her own grey eyes staring back at her as the light faded behind her. The girl did not have a mass of brown curls, but there were curves and shapes in her face that were familiar, and it was surprisingly comforting to look at them.

"Honestly," continued Kate, "I'm not here to hurt a soul and I can leave now, if you want things to stay the same for you. I mean, you have a beautiful home and maybe family that you want to keep safe."

"So," Winnie tried to keep her voice from rising with the scepticism she felt, "you would really travel from Skye to here and still leave if I asked you to?"

Kate's eyes flickered but she answered almost immediately. "Yes I would, although if we're going to be honest with each other, I actually travelled from Canada. I live there now."

Perhaps it was the second mention by name of the country Winnie had missed for all those years, or perhaps it was the fact that this girl lived amongst those dear people, enjoyed a culture she might have been part of had life been less harsh, that made up her mind. But truly, had there ever been a choice? She knew there was no way she could turn down this opportunity. If she did, that date in late August would mock her from here on. Without another thought, she stepped away from the sink and smiled.

"Let's go through to the sitting room. I think that we should both be as comfy as possible if you're going to tell me this story."

Kate was on her feet in a second. "I would love that. Just bear in mind that although it's a bit unconventional, we are honestly quite a normal set of folk."

"That's fine," replied Winnie. "Oh, and people know me as Winnie."

Kate's face betrayed her lack of understanding.

"I was christened Winifred Alice Hunter, and I haven't been Freddie in nearly fifty years. Freddie Hunter is now Winnie Port."

"Okay then," smiled Kate, "well, I was lucky. When I got married, I got to keep the name I've always had."

CHAPTER 18

Northumberland, England

Kate lay perfectly still, breathing rapidly and marvelling at the fact that you could be brought out of sleep in an instant even without the classic movie action of sitting upright and sweating. It was just as scary to be heart-thuddingly awake by merely opening your eyes and staring straight ahead than it was to dramatically scream and wake the household. She swallowed back the totally unexpected fear and eased herself slightly up onto the pillows beneath her. She was in a pitch-black room, which in a way might have doubled for her bedroom back at The Edge but for two major differences: David was not by her side, and there were far too many pillows. As the crick in her neck began to fade, she remembered what had fired her along the tunnel from slumber to awareness, and she reached blindly for the lamp switch. But when her eyes grew accustomed to the light, the unfamiliar objects and alien decoration made her feel even more displaced, and she closed her eyes once more, revisiting her recent dream.

A black panther, all green eyes and white fangs, had been hiding in a bush near to Beth's cottage. It had been dark, but the moon had allowed her to distinguish shapes and movements as Kate had hurried along the foot of Ben Tianavaig, a path she knew better than any other walkway. The drops and boulders had not fazed her, but near the gate at the bottom, the panther had attacked at her thigh, sending her sprawling. She recalled the smell of the grass, but had no time to appreciate its cool freshness before the monster had sprung and sunk its teeth into her throat. Before the fright had a chance to turn to pain, Kate had opened her eyes and was breathing in shallow pockets of air to aid her recovery. She shook her head against the recollection, mystified. Animals had never frightened her, but this one had been vicious, and it must mean something. Her throat was dry, and she tried to recall if she had been particularly worried as sleep had approached. Nothing came to mind.

Winnie had been a receptive if hushed audience to all things "Neil" and an exceptionally hospitable woman. She had insisted, before Kate had been in the house more than an hour, that she must collect all her belongings from the bed-and-breakfast in town and move them into her spare room. That way they could talk until the sun came up if necessary. At first, Winnie had listened more than she had enquired, allowing Kate to run along strings of details, stopping and changing direction when she had a mind to. Winnie had insisted to Kate that she wanted to hear it all, that nothing was irrelevant, because each word Kate had used, whether descriptive or opinionated, was in some way answering unspoken, unasked questions: Years and years of wondering and guessing, hoping and willing, and here was this blood relative of her own sharing this knowledge. Once or twice it had looked as if the woman was on the verge of tears, but the grey eyes never did spill any liquid, and Kate wondered if she had inherited some of her steeliness. Maybe what Kate occasionally viewed as stubbornness in her own character was more strength. That and her grey eyes were two things she had been happy to share.

But, at just after four in the morning, all of her strength seemed to have evaporated on account of a ridiculous dream, and she would have to trawl back through all of her previous words and ideas to recognise its source. It may take the rest of the night.

Along the corridor, the lamp had been burning since just after midnight. Winnie had found Kate chatty and amusing until that moment, sharing a bottle of wine as the evening had progressed. But at the turn of the day, the girl's eyes had begun to lose their sparkle, and she had almost dropped off in front of the fire. When Kate had retired to the spare room, both of them grinning at this totally surreal moment in their lives, Winnie had settled herself in her own sanctuary of a bedroom and had merely sat on her bed for an unknown number of minutes. She had let her eyes roam over her entire room, every familiar object still sporting the same colours and shapes, but looking so entirely different that she had then wandered from surface to surface, picking up trinkets and turning them in her hands. That morning, she had wondered if she was fit enough to take on Cheviot this year in the annual summer challenge and whether or not she should even attempt such a test in her sixties. Now, she had met her granddaughter, and amazingly, she felt half her age. How was that possible?

Sleep had deserted her, but she was quite happy at the prospect of merely resting in the peace and silence which accompanied the night, after the extraordinary evening they had put in. Kate appeared to be quite an undemanding companion, and remarkably Winnie continued to feel no awkwardness at having a stranger in the house. But the story the girl had managed to relate in her still-broad Scots accent had been full of as many surprises as anecdotes. She was married to Davey Wilder, her playful little companion of another time, who had apparently "brought her through the worst moments of her life." Kate had admitted that theirs was an unusual alliance, and yet she had spoken about the man in no extraordinary manner. She loved him and she harboured no doubts about him. For her own pleasure, Winnie had been replaying Kate's words all night, trying to picture her in the arms of a man who must continually be shielding himself from the next bombshell. Yet, ten hours later, she found her heart still fluttering in her chest and her hands refusing to lie quiet. She thought back to the truly scariest moment of the entire period.

"I have photos," Kate had said softly. "I had to bring them, but it's up to you ..."

In the few moments it had taken for Kate to run along to the spare room, Winnie had stood in front of the fireplace, her hands clasped tightly behind her back for fear that she might snatch the precious items from Kate on her return. To her credit, Kate had been speedy and had looked fit to burst as she had jogged back to her seat. Winnie had done nothing but stand motionless, and eventually Kate had caught her apprehension in the air and pursed her lips, willing herself to stop smiling quite so much. She had stood again immediately and began to open a small folder.

"A word of warning," the girl had begun to babble, "Neil doesn't ever shave, just sort of trims his face occasionally. Well, he once shaved for my benefit, but it was a disaster. Dave's not much better. It's just not part of his daily routine. Point is, they might appear a bit scruffy, but they're not really. Oh, let's just have a look."

Kate had handed over a photo of David and her on the front steps of The Edge. The image had shown Kate standing two steps up from him so that their heads were at the same height. She was behind him, her arms around his neck and her face touching his. David had wrapped his hands around her wrists and they were both grinning. He was lean and tall, traits she could have guessed at knowing the family, and yes, she had still seen the boy in the man. She had studied their attitudes for a moment or two, finding their expressions a mixture of pride and contentment and marvelling in it, before asking, "Does he ever sing?"

"He is totally without talent. It's actually painful to listen to."

"I didn't like to tell him. I suggested the drums as an alternative, but I don't know if it ever happened."

Winnie had held onto that particular scene tightly because it was safe and not intimidating. Kate had handed over a school photo next, showing Alasdair half-smiling, and she had not been able to stop herself exclaiming. Alasdair was the David she remembered, but with blonde hair. She had laughed out loud. Kate grinned with her and then made a point of catching her eye.

"Okay?" and then handed the rest of the bundle to her in one go.

The first photograph of Neil had shown the man standing by a trailer full of felled branches, and Winnie's lips had parted involuntarily as she had looked on his face. His mid-blonde fringe had tried and failed to conceal the blue eyes, their shape uncannily like her own, and she had felt a tug inside which threatened to fold her to her knees. Instead, she had locked them tightly and gripped the image to steady her hands. His face had indeed been lightly covered in a scrub of hair, which had made his age even more obscure. The man's arms had been folded against his chest, his sleeves rolled up to the elbow, and she had marvelled at the strength in those manual arms; in her mind's eye, she still saw the silky, pink limbs of a fretting infant. Kate had appeared slightly bunched against the man, her face serious, but he had leaned his head down towards her, possibly to reduce their height difference. He had also obviously known the photographer very well, as his eyes and mouth smiled together, and Winnie had been speechless, staring until Kate had spoken for her.

"That was about ten years ago, when I was eighteen. He was really good to me, to Dave and me, that holiday."

"He looks as if ..." Winnie's throat had closed almost immediately, but she had somehow continued, "... he looks like he cares. Oh God, he's so handsome."

"He is, isn't he?" Kate had laughed. "If you keep looking, you'll see him with Andie. She is gorgeous."

The photos had caused an odd reaction. Inside there was a core of pure elation– elation that her completely defenceless baby had made it through the minefield of childhood diseases, had survived learning to drive and the daily danger of using a chainsaw, and had found someone to share his life with. He had made a family, unintentionally on both counts, but was currently thriving because of his relationship with all three of his daughters. But that core, shining and diamond-tough, faded outwards to a frailer pewter grey as she recognised the dreaded regret. She had missed so much. She had missed it all. The face she had seen, rough yet striking, could have been grinning at her in all those years, showing her his feelings, but he had graced another with that gift. Sitting in her flannelette pyjamas on an easy chair, the photos still lying in her lap, she caught her breath. The man was not only alive as she had always hoped, but he was suddenly available to her. She repeated this notion again and again, because it brought her great joy. A Red Letter Day, indeed.

Her throat dry, Winnie padded past the door of her spare bedroom and into the kitchen. As she switched on the alcove lights, her eyes fell on the two wine glasses by the sink. It was testament that she had a visitor other than Charlie, who was a vodka man, and she felt that rush of wonder all over again. A girl had dropped into her life with no warning. She was in the house this very minute. She would be chatting, smiling and eating breakfast with her in a matter of hours. Did she have enough variety of food in her house for a visitor's breakfast? Winnie pulled open the fridge, enjoying the extra illumination the action offered, and relaxed. There were at least a dozen eggs, and they surely afforded enough choice. Only one carton of fresh orange remained, however, so she placed the kettle on the hob instead. Tea was always the best thirst quencher, anyway. In the silence, Winnie raked out the AGA and re-stoked it, aware of how the sound amplified as soon as you were trying to be quiet. As the kettle began to hiss gently, Kate appeared at the door. Her arms were folded across her body.

"I couldn't get back to sleep," her voice was an apology.

"Quite a night for the both of us," Winnie replied and reached for a second mug. "I was making some tea. Would you like some?"

Kate nodded, not sure if they were still at the level of intimacy they had reached the night before. The woman remained a stranger, and Kate was cold and tired, missing David more than the eleven days away from him truly warranted. Maybe now that the nerves and the anticipation of the meeting were behind them, there would be a painfully self-conscious period before she retreated to the ease and comfort of Skye. And there were still hours of this period in front of them. She glanced at the huge kitchen clock and thought of Alasdair preparing to retire to his room with Bertuzzi. It seemed a beautifully simple life he led, and she longed to be in that very place, shooing the dog from under her feet and imploring her son to put away at least some of his Legos.

"Take a seat, Kate," Winnie smiled, aware of the awkwardness the girl had brought along the corridor with her. "I was a teacher, you know, English and History. When we came back from Canada I read and read and read. Books, magazines, newspapers. I wanted to read about other lives, so I wouldn't have to think about mine, and it stood me in good stead. Teacher training college was a piece of cake."

Kate began to relax as their voices filled the void. "I wanted to be a teacher. I fancied going to Edinburgh, but when Mum got sick, everyday things seemed pointless. People at school seemed ridiculous to me, and I couldn't imagine being a student in a big city without her back at home waiting for me. Then I met David, and I didn't have to worry anymore."

When Winnie did nothing but smile warmly at this declaration, Kate sat forward slightly.

"I'm so used to people's jaws trying not to unhinge when I explain our relationship or when they see us together for the first time. You don't seem bothered at all, which is lovely. Actually, I don't even know why I said that, it makes me look like an attention-seeker."

As Winnie joined her at the table, the two steaming mugs bringing much-needed warmth to the pair of them, she seemed to be organising her thoughts before replying.

"Well, it's clear from what you've told me already that you've never been worried by it. But if you don't mind me saying, he must have been a very brave man when you started out."

Kate felt her back straighten slightly, ready to defend herself and her man, but Winnie was not finished.

"I mean," she continued, "you say he runs the family business, so he must have had quite a few friends and colleagues. That's a lot of shock and criticism to invite."

"Oh," Kate said quietly, feeling genuinely surprised that Winnie had been so bold. The woman knew nothing about how it had been, and yet she was offering views. "Well, people had their own ideas. We never really put ourselves on show, but we didn't try to hide, either."

Winnie shook her head as she swallowed her tea. "Hey, who am I to comment on anything? I'm only thinking of how some people react in situations like this. Vulnerable woman, older man. The public will always need something to talk about. Take it from me, they love to assume and they love to label."

Throughout this speech, Winnie had been concentrating on scraping a piece of wax from the underside of the candle holder on the table, but when she paused and looked up, she found Kate's eyes wide and fiery.

"Is that how you see this? Is that what you think about us?" There was a tremor to Kate's voice, a vibrato which signalled either fury or distress, and which became quite obvious in the next second. The girl pushed her tea away from her and stood. Winnie was instantly repentant.

"No, absolutely–"

"I liked the fact that you didn't seem to have an opinion on this, and then you come out with things like that. Was it your first thought when I told you? My God."

"Kate, stay a minute."

But Kate had walked away, down the corridor and straight to her bedside cabinet. Inside, her fatigue was creating pressure and utter despondency at her inability to escape it. When Winnie, mortified, made a similar journey, she found the girl seated on the unmade bed, frantically punching the keys on her mobile phone.

"Please," Winnie remained by the doorway, in her own home, feeling like the worst kind of elderly idiot. "That wasn't what I meant, not at all. I was trying to explain why I thought he was brave."

"Brave to be seen with me? Brave to be labelled as God knows what? Cursing hell, why do you think he married me? He wanted everybody to take us as seriously as we took each other! And that's another thing: Remember that out of most of my immediate family, yourself included, I was the only one a virgin on her wedding night! God's sake."

Kate stopped speaking and texting simultaneously and laid her phone beside her thigh. Her words still ringing in the air between them, she could not raise her head and stared instead at her bare feet staining the floorboards with condensation prints. She was exhausted. Not for the first time, her mouth had run away with her, but she doubted if she had ever said anything quite so personal to someone she had only just met. Whilst sitting in her home. When the woman had invited her in and fed her. Kate took a couple of deep breaths and bit her lip until the threatened tears were decidedly shoved back from where they had come. The muscles between her shoulders ached with heat, and she found herself caught between dire embarrassment and sheer sorrow that David was so very far from her. How the hell was she going to rescue this, using her arguments alone? She had never felt more like curling up and rolling away.

"Well, you have a point there," Winnie remained by the door. "Although, I'm pretty sure Rose wore white authentically."

There was the tiniest invitation in Winnie's tone, an invitation to lighten the mood; and Kate thought that, with no choice at her disposal whatsoever, she really should make an effort to cooperate.

"Maybe, who knows?" she raised her head once and then dropped it again, still uncomfortable. "But I still think I deserve the biggest accolade. I mean, David is gorgeous and he made me hold out for it. That's how much he wanted to do this properly."

Finally, Winnie walked farther into the room and hovered by Kate's knees. "Shall I bring your tea in here?"

Kate shook her head, pushed herself onto her feet, scooping up her mobile as she did. "No, I'd like to go back through. I'm feeling a bit ridiculous. I'd rather not feel like this again in the morning. I'm sorry."

Winnie stood back so that Kate could go ahead of her, but before they had reached the warmth of the kitchen, Kate's phone was ringing in her palm. She glanced back at Winnie, her face vexed at the timing.

"It'll be Dave," she explained, frowning. "I asked him to ring me."

"Sit down, I'll leave you to it."

Back in her bedroom, Winnie mentally kicked herself for not listening to her own words in her head before uttering them. She was used to Charlie, his take on things and his reactions. She was used to the fact that his age and life experiences meant that he was more or less of the same mind-set. She was not used to debating with a girl in her late twenties, who had probably built up a convincing defence of her life over the last decade. Nor was she used to that defence being constructed into three or four cutting, yet accurate, sentences. This truly was the most surreal night/early morning she had put in over many a long year, and it had woken her up from the inside out. She wondered if a small brandy might steady her stomach, but the sitting room seemed miles too far away. Winnie looked out of her window. The stars were invisible, but the moon had decided to hang out by itself anyway in the heavy sky. Weird, weird, weird, thought Winnie and let the curtain fall back across the glass.

She tried to recall her initial feelings when Kate had tentatively told her who her husband was, how they had come together and that they had a six-year-old son. What had she actually thought at the revelation, and had those thoughts unintentionally produced criticism? She remembered trying to imagine how the girl at eighteen, bereft of her mother and thrown into the middle of an identity crisis, had possibly had the confidence to set her sights on such an unlikely figure. Perhaps from there she had tried to picture David and Kate's own wonder at it all, and had attempted to attach others' reactions to this. Whatever had occurred in those first few minutes of knowledge had somehow made it out of her mouth in a mistakenly unfortunate way, and she really should try to explain herself better.

But instead of forming arguments, Winnie allowed a grin to return to her face. Her baby had been named Neil Peter. He was tall and good-looking with strong arms and a worker's body. Imagine that. She had been speaking to a girl who was part of him, had spent time in his company and had shared some of his life. The girl, tied to her by blood, would share more with her if she allowed her to. She thought she would maybe allow her to, if she had not already cut that tie in two. As Winnie was hunting in her drawers for a sweater, Kate appeared in the doorway.

"Erm," she began, rubbing her eyebrow, "Dave would like to speak to you, if you want?"

Winnie stared at the girl. Her face must have betrayed all of her uncertainty, because Kate quickly covered the phone with her other hand and moved towards her.

"I didn't say anything about our … discussion. I said we'd been up all night blethering and that I was missing him." Suddenly Kate grinned. "He asked to speak to you. He sounded quite hopeful that you might want to."

Winnie watched her hand reach for the phone, simply because it was an action which was the least awkward in this ridiculous situation. Why were they both not tucked up in bed, sound asleep?

"Hello?"

The voice at the other end did not even hesitate.

"Is that Freddie Hunter? You owe me about twenty-five thousand drum lessons by my reckoning. I could have been a rock star."

Winnie's hand flew to her cheek. "Oh my God. Davey Wilder, listen to you. Your voice has broken."

Kate laughed in unison with her husband, and settled herself against Winnie's chest of drawers.

"And yours is as strange a trans-Atlantic mix as I've ever heard." There was a little pause and then, "How unbelievable is this?"

Winnie sank onto her bed, wishing he would say more. She had not heard a deep Canadian accent in so many years, and the idea that this voice belonged to a boy who had sat by the window, watching for her arrival, filled her to capacity.

"Actually," she breathed, "it's quite wonderful. And insanely out of this world. I'm not sure if I've ever understood the word speechless until this second. I find words are useless. They can't say what I feel."

As Kate listened to Winnie trying to express herself and the murmur of David's replies, she saw the woman's face gradually open up like the petals of a watered rose. She was smiling as she talked of the absurdity, the insecurity and the sometime harshness of the world, making it appear as if they were positive things. But who was to say they were wholly negative? Kate, who hated clichés with a passion, could not get the phrase "things happen for a reason" out of her head, which was a sure sign that she was on the verge of exhaustion. She slid down the front of the chest of drawers, pulling her knees to her chest as soon as she was seated on the floor.

"So, Freddie Hunter," David's voice took on a new tone. "You should know, Neil was a pure gift. He followed me everywhere, tried to outsmart me at every turn, and in a way, filled the gap that you left."

"Oh," Winnie could hide the emotion in her voice no longer, "I couldn't keep him, Davey. They wouldn't let me and that was the way it was. But I knew he would be okay with you. Thank you for being his brother."

Kate could be described as many things: determined, outspoken, devoted, eccentric to a point, stubborn, and a risk-taker, but never as particularly soft-hearted. Rarely did anyone but David see the tears which sometimes claimed her in the name of love, passion or regret. However, listening to the first signs of heartache coming from the woman in the room had brought silent, steady drops falling onto her pyjamas, and she had hidden her face in her knees. Winnie was telling David what she had already told Kate, but it was less factual and more personal, as if to a confidante; and Kate was happy to simply sit immobile and let it take place around her. From behind her closed eyes, she saw Alasdair perched on David's shoulders, hands in the air and giggling. She felt herself beginning to fall into the accompanying darkness and was not bothered by the realisation.

"Well," David said at last, "I'm sure you pair must be nearly asleep on your feet. We can talk at a more sociable hour anytime, you know."

"I know," Winnie reached for the hankie up her sleeve and wiped her nose dry. "I think Kate might have dropped off already , I should let you speak to her again."

"Before you do," he spoke quickly, "I'll say this tonight, because it will probably never feel right at any other time. Kate's mother might have broken my heart, but Neil and she gave me Kate, and that's all the that matters. He and I are close enough again, I have a wife and son who give me more than I ever had before, and I know how lucky we are as a family. If you want to share it, you're welcome to. But it's your call."

CHAPTER 19

Vancouver Island

As Sophie swung herself easily in the hammock, an old hat of Neil's shading her eyes against the late morning sun, she wondered if her mom could make her a huge long cushion which might stop the rope from digging into her. It was the only thing spoiling her day. The snowdrops were bunching in the paddock, her birthday was only "just over the next hill," and Abbie had finally given up on her habit of following her to the toilet. Even better, Ally and his dad were coming over for the day, and they would be able to play outside for hours and hours without any parents watching. Al had an idea to build some sort of a den in the woods; and although Abbie would almost definitely insist on joining in, she could be useful in gathering bits and pieces, and Sophie could be her boss, just as Ally was hers.

Christmas had been great, much better than last year when they had missed First Mom and Dad so badly and had spent most of the day sandwiched between Now Mom and Dad, watching the cartoon channel and eating chocolate. When Abbie had been sick around tea-time, nobody had seemed too worried. But this last Christmas had been the best fun ever. Granma Rose had told some great stories, and Auntie Kate had been on a diet, passing every extra cake or treat her way, making sure that nobody else knew. She was pretty sure Al would have been jealous, which might have been a good reason for her to spill the beans; but the woman had made such a fuss of making sure it was their secret that she had joyously gone along with it. Dad had made her a rocking chair with her name carved on the back, and Abbie had been given a slide which fixed onto her bed. Abbie loved slides and swings, and now she had one of each. Dad was a clever man, which is why it was highly unlikely that she would ever be able to trick him into telling her more about Auntie Kate. It was only her fifth birthday next, how could she wait until her eighth?

Sighing at her failure in this mission, Sophie poured herself out of the hammock, allowing only a moment for her legs to come back to life before shouting for Cuban to follow her indoors. The golden Lab, who had been snoozing in the shade of the hammock and its occupant, looked pained as she followed the youngster up the wooden steps; and Neil, watching the journey from his workshop door, felt his heart dip slightly.

The dog was showing her age, just as her brother was, and Neil feared that when their time was up, it would prove harder to face than ever. He remembered the hole left when Dougal, their Bernese Mountain Dog, had succumbed to one of the many conditions which seemed to plague the breed; how he, Andie and the two Labs had moped for days at the enforced absence. But this would be fully worse. Sophie and Abbie were generally a happy pair, settling at last into a pattern where life was fairly even, where the physical act of travelling was more commonplace and acceptable and where rainstorms failed to find them sitting wide-eyed in the same bottom bunk. But death, with its unbearably inflexible consequences, was such a potential hazard, that all he could hope for was as much time as possible. Time for those girls to fully trust them as parents and to see that although there might always be sadness and loss, there might also always be a way through it.

Neil closed his eyes momentarily. How was it possible that he, whose experience of dealing with life-altering events was to retreat completely from the world, was being entrusted with the job of guiding two children to adulthood? If Andie, herself a soul broken by a cruel world, had not appeared early in his student days and forced him to allow her inside his hand-crafted igloo, he doubted if he would have reached the age of thirty. But here he was, nearer fifty than forty, and his task was to instil optimism as much as it was to nurture the sisters. Optimism, he thought, it was laughable. And yet, the world itself should be optimistic, simply because Sophie and Abbie were in it. They were both such characters, so nippy and smart, and the world should be pulling itself together and arranging great moments for them to enjoy.

If the world could not be bothered, then it was up to him to do just that. It was not impossible. He could do it.

"Hey, Dad!" The voice came from out of his sight above him, but he moved round to the foot of the stairs without hesitation, twisting the chisel he was holding between his palms. Sophie was perched on the top landing, the soles of her blue trainers caked in spring mud, Cuban lying beside her. "How long before they get here?"

"Could be in the next minute, could be nearer lunch, Soph. If I was you, I would aim more for lunchtime."

Sophie made a huge deal of sighing and shaking her head, before jumping to her feet.

"Oh, and buddy? If you want to stay in Mom's good books, you'll take those trainers off at the door."

"But they're double-knotted."

"Your choice!" Neil cried as he ducked back into his workshop and tried to remember the last thing he had done before his daughter's movement had distracted him. It was the type of distraction he did not mind, especially on a day when the sun was shining and Andie was on-site. He liked those days as much as Sophie did. He loved the feeling that every face he ever wanted to see or every voice he longed to hear was within ten seconds of where he stood, and even if he never made use of it, it did not alter the fact. The one person he was missing was Kate, and only because she had gone across the ocean, back to her previous life. Today, when her son and man were about to arrive, she seemed very far away indeed. He paused by the workbench, which was badly in need of re-oiling, and wondered what she and her other family were doing on Skye, where the dusk would be rolling in from the sea. Were they talking about the old days? Almost surely they would be reminiscing about Fiona. Or maybe they were simply enjoying the new addition, cooing over little Hope as if no other child had ever meant so much. Well, they may be right, but in his heart he thought that Kate herself had probably claimed that prize, at least where he was concerned.

"What d'you think Auntie Kate's up to?"

He managed not to show how startled he was at Sophie's sudden reappearance, her question bringing him instantly back into the room. She was standing in the doorway, watching him closely as she was prone to do, her laces a mess of tangles, and he almost blanched at the thought of her teetering on the unforgiving wooden stairway as she descended. He inhaled quickly and bent to try and aid her failed attempt to release her feet. But the knots might as well have been set with superglue, and after a moment or two, he hauled the shoes off her feet as they were. She grimaced slightly, then put her arms around Neil's neck as he hoisted her onto his back. "You said that was the lazy way out," she murmured past his hair into his ear.

"And it is," he agreed, as her sock-clad feet tucked themselves into the side pockets of his padded shirt. "But sometimes you just feel like doing the lazy thing."

"Your rules are funny," she sighed, and then as Neil made for the stairs once more, he felt her straighten against him. "Dad, why did Auntie Kate go away without Al? Bet he's thinking she's never coming back. Bet Uncle David doesn't even play with him."

Neil hesitated, hitching her farther up, and then turned to look down the driveway. No sign of them yet. "I don't think she could take him out of school. That's what vacations are for."

There was more than a grain of truth in this, and certainly it was what Kate herself had explained to Alasdair over a series of fraught days, during which time he had felt left out, then annoyed and then upset enough for Kate to doubt the wisdom of the whole affair. But Hazel had wanted her at Hope's christening, and Alasdair would get over it. She had offered slightly more information to Neil the last time he had seen her.

"I don't care if it is only for a week or two," she had confided, as they had cleared the table after one of Rose's once-a-month Sunday gatherings, "I'm not taking Ally away from David. I promised him I would never do that, and I know it makes me sound dramatic and over-sensitive; but I can't settle over there for one minute if I think he's waking up to an empty house, wondering if this is the one time I don't come back."

"You're kidding," Neil had offered.

"No, I'm not. It's taken every minute of our ten-plus years together for him to realise that I'm not going to go looking for a better life elsewhere. Why in God's name would I? He's more or less on that track at last, but he knows that Skye is special. So, if he can't get away, then at least he'll have Al at home, making his days as normal as possible. I'll take Al one day, when we can all go together."

So Neil had accepted the explanation, just as David had agreed that it would be less "disruptive" if she travelled alone. But it had left Neil feeling slightly differently about the man he had considered his indestructible role model for his entire life. He remembered a day around the time of Kate's eighteenth birthday, when David had arrived unannounced at this very house and Kate had stood motionless, watching him climb out of his vehicle. There had been a period of utter stillness between the pair, until David had taken the first step towards her, and she had covered the distance between them with a look on her face he could only describe as bliss. From then on, every time he had been in their company, he had witnessed what they could not hide, something which caused reactions wherever they went, shocking the majority and delighting the minority. He had never doubted their connection, even when Andie had queried its viability and mere acquaintances had talked behind cupped hands, because he had seen a steel strand in Kate and he knew what it meant. It meant that wherever life took them, Kate would rather die than betray David, as her mother and father had done.

Yet Kate had suggested that the man was still vulnerable, still unsure of his long-term future; and it had caused a quiver in Neil, the kind that had the power to send Neil somersaulting into the pit– the guilt pit, which had practically been abandoned in recent years, but would almost certainly be twice as rancid and stagnant if he revisited it again. He had caught that quiver and squeezed it in his fists until he had assured himself that he had not brought David to that place by his never-forgotten past mistakes, and that time would cure him of every doubt. As the truck announcing Neil and Ally's arrival pulled onto the driveway and Sophie struggled from her position on his back, he told himself to concentrate. He must not think of David as a nervous, self-doubting individual, but as a man lucky in love, who was the reason Kate smiled as much as she did.

As Sophie finally managed to slide to the ground, Andie appeared on the landing, so she, too, witnessed the excited child run five or six strides in her socks until one of them was sucked off her foot by a softer than average mud mound. Only then did Sophie halt and look down at her feet in dismay. Tucking her lip under, she stared back at Neil, who held up her trainers.

"I forgot," she smiled, hoping that the action would ensure his forgiveness. Dad never really got mad, unless it was at himself, but maybe running through mud without shoes was a crime. As the truck drew closer, however, Neil simply brushed the hair out of his eyes and retrieved her one pink sock from the earth.

"Must have had something else on your mind," he replied mildly, and this time lifted her onto his hip. "I do the same sometimes."

"I'm just like you," Sophie grinned and brushed the hair out of her own eyes to prove the point. When he smiled straight back at her, she kissed his chin and wrapped her arms around his neck. Neil glanced up at Andie, hoping that she was sharing the moment. She gave him a thumbs-up, and he sighed contentedly. Hugging people was becoming less dangerous by the year.

Sophie could see Alasdair moving about in the rear of the truck, apparently already out of his car seat; and as Neil deposited her on the mud-free stairs, she began to hop from one foot to another. Abbie immediately began to do the same on the level above them, and by the time David had set his son free, the stairway was practically bouncing. On seeing the excitement of the girls, Alasdair immediately cooled his own enthusiasm and wandered over to them with the air of the far more mature and superior. Sophie didn't care. Now the fun could begin. Or it could as soon as her trainers were back on her feet.

In less than five minutes, Sophie was wearing clean socks and wellies, Abbie had been fitted into a fleecy waistcoat, and Alasdair was leading them as sedately as possible towards the woods, removing his rucksack as he did so and assuring them that plans had already been drawn up for their den. David watched them for a moment, his mouth turned up at the easy friendship, then took the external staircase two at a time.

"Man," he remarked on entering the open space, "what is that amazing smell?"

The interior of Neil and Andie's home was to all intents and purposes open-plan, the kitchen incorporated at the far end of the room, with only the two bedrooms and bathroom separated by walls. The aroma from the eating area filled the whole room, and David smiled widely; today he and Al would feast on more than scrambled eggs and fried potatoes. Andie beckoned him nearer and held out a wooden spoon for him to taste. When the meat touched his tongue, he pulled back slightly at the temperature and then accepted the whole spoonful. He opened his eyes wide as the texture and taste registered and the juices filled his mouth.

"Moose?" he enquired.

Andie grinned in response. "It is! We haven't had it in long enough, and then I remembered there was some at the bottom of the freezer. Thought you might like to share it with us. Can't have you fading away on us, Dave."

David acknowledged the truth of her observation as she gave him a very pointed look, but any words he might have had on the subject of missing Kate in every capacity were stored away when Neil came through from the bathroom, drying his hands on his shirtfront. Instead, he swallowed the rest of the stew and placed a wicker basket on the table.

"Rose sent a pie."

"I really hoped that she would," replied Andie, "but didn't like to ask for one. Great! It's still a bit too cold for ice cream, and that's all we have."

Neil reached past Andie to move the coffee pot onto the range, before turning and leaning against the sink. He, too, ran his eyes over David's frame but merely rubbed his thumb under his chin as he always did in every conceivable situation, then leaned over and took a long look at the pie which had successfully survived the journey from The Edge.

"I'm surprised she didn't want to come," Neil said, his mouth already watering at the sight of the crisp, egg-washed pastry.

David frowned and wandered to the window, just in time to see Alasdair and Sophie haul the smallest of the three youngsters over the fence and disappear into the wood. "She's not very well, actually. Jessie Morgan is going to pop in mid-afternoon to check on her."

"That cold still hanging on?" Andie settled the stew in the pan and began to fill the mugs with the strong black liquid. "Is she still in bed?"

"She's up, but not really moving very fast. I think I'll ask her up to the house until Kate comes back. See if Al can perk her up a bit."

"We should try to get over more," Andie said regretfully, simultaneously trying to conceive of how their present lifestyle could possibly accommodate this. It was nigh on impossible with Sophie committed to pre-school, and with Neil, Iris and herself juggling Abbie and work. They tended to use the weekends to catch up with each other, ensure that the girls were getting enough fresh air and company; and travelling the miles between Port Alberni and The Edge would cut into those precious hours. Immediately, Andie felt her face fall. That was no excuse. Rose was eighty-four years old, had been fit and strong her whole life, and now that she was suddenly reliant on her family, they could not seem to "fit her in?" "Oh, Neil, babe. We should make more of an effort. What were we thinking?"

Neil, who had been stirring the logs at the bottom of the burner, suddenly stood tall and turned to them. The movement caught David's attention.

"It's just a cold, right? She gets a cold every time the spring comes."

David shrugged, slightly surprised that Neil spoke with quite so much unease. "She's fine, just been a bit flat since Kate went."

Neil lifted his head in acknowledgement, happy to accept this as the reason. Anything rather than imagine Rose as anything less than immortal. She may be shrinking by the year, her hair more of a snow-white skullcap than a sandy bob; but she had always had the strength to pull Neil out of various dark holes, and her health had never been an issue in all those years. David sipped at his coffee, watching his brother pat Crisis, the chocolate Labrador, until his concerns had abated sufficiently. Should he share with them his real worries? Should he tell them both how Rose no longer marched but shuffled, how her eyes seemed watery and pale, and that she shivered even when the wood-burner threatened to set the flue alight? Perhaps this little family really should try to visit more often; perhaps Rose needed to look forward to more than she had at present. Those two little girls would make her day and maybe even spark the light in her eyes once more.

Three hundred yards from the house was a clearing in the wood where Neil had been retrieving firewood for years. The grass was long and unruly, there were stumps and scrub dotted and strewn seemingly at random, but it was ideal for a play area in terms of light. The sun meant there were only dark, scary areas near the perimeter, and that left plenty of open space for them to start planning the foundations of a den. Alasdair had brought a sketch pad of Kate's, which he was almost sure she had finished with, and a couple of pencils. All they really needed to agree upon was the material and the size. Their imagination would create the rest as soon as they were inside the structure.

Abbie was out of sorts. She would become four years old a month after Sophie turned five, and yet whenever Ally was on the scene, she was treated as a baby and a "pain in the royal behind," a term she wasn't quite sure she understood but guessed it did not mean a helpful and fun person. Was it her fault that the fence was just a bit wobbly for her to manage? Ally had been laughing at her attempts to climb it, but her sister had just kept calling her silly names and looking to the sky for some reason. Now the pair of them had a pencil each, and while Al used the pad to support his paper, Sophie used Al's back as an easel. They were both scribbling and laughing, and there was absolutely nothing for her to do. Looking around, she thought it might be a good idea to start gathering some lighter pieces of branch and twig, like birds did when they were building a nest. Maybe then the other two might see her worth.

"Dad says you need a flat piece of ground or else the whole thing will tip over, and it can happen to the best builder," said Alasdair, confident in his statement.

"My dad says you can build anything with wood, you just have to know how," Sophie's tone matched his, then, "He's the best builder I know."

"Yeah," ventured Alasdair, "but he's not your real dad, is he?"

"Well, he is now. He must be, because my name's Sophie Anne Jones Alexander-Wilder, and it used to be Sophie Anne Jones."

"You're called what?" Alasdair lowered his pencil and turned his face around to hers, the first genuine expression of awe on his face he had ever allowed her to witness.

Sophie repeated the name, adding that Abbie had a similar title and that both Andie's and Neil's names were there, which proved that they were their mom and dad, and it was an eagle.

"What does that mean?" asked the boy, still reasonably impressed that they had five names to his three.

"Don't know," admitted Sophie, physically turning his head back to its original position so that she could continue her sketch. "Dad said it was eagle and we could call them Dad and Mom if we wanted to. I like them, so I wanted to."

"Fair enough," allowed Alasdair, using one of his Kate's stock phrases. "Cousins should have the same name, or nearly the same name. Even new cousins."

Sophie laughed. "We're all Wilders!" she cried, as if this made their relationship even more firm and secure. She liked to feel secure. After a moment, Alasdair put his sketch pad down and turned his whole body to face her. He was frowning, his lips twisted to one side in confusion.

"Why Alexander? That's a boy's name."

Sophie dropped her own piece of paper and sat immediately, crossing her wellied legs and clearing her throat. She had the answer and she could explain it.

"Mom's name is Andie Alexander. Dad's name is Neil Wilder. Abbs and me are both– Alexander and Wilder– so that one of them doesn't feel left out. She told me all about it."

"Okay," Alasdair nodded, "but why's her name not Andie Wilder?"

"Because, silly, Dad never asked her to marry him," Sophie spread her hands and laughed. She just managed to stop herself from saying "easy peasy," because that would have been rude, but it felt lovely for a moment to know more than her older, wiser cousin. She watched him digest this information, frown until his face turned slightly pink just above his cheek bones and finally shrug.

"That's why they didn't have kids of their own," he stated and jumped to his feet, tired of the domestic chat and eager to start on their project before somebody came along and called them in for lunch. He picked up Sophie's scribbles and held the paper next to his own heavy-handed design to see if they could be merged together. Her drawing was tiny, tucked away in the bottom corner of the page, but he liked the triangular shape which was mirrored in his own sketch. He sighed.

"Which one?" asked Sophie, brightly.

Alasdair's instinct was to choose his own. He had, after all, spent the whole morning on the idea and had altered it several times. But he could be generous when the sun was shining, and they had already spent too much time on the preparation. Better just to agree to use both plans and to start collecting materials right away. As he instructed Sophie to this effect, he himself began to drag bunches of thin twigs away from the flattest area of grass on show. She, in turn, placed both of her hands under a limb she thought might come in useful later, and began trying to urge it into the circle of their activity. It was harder work than she had bargained for, and in her desperation, she shouted for Abbie to come and help. When there was no answer, she stood up frustrated and turned to where her sister had been. She was nowhere in the immediate area, and Sophie shaded her eyes to see farther afield. The shadows near the trees yielded nothing, fading from dark green to black with no sign of the purple waistcoat; and when Sophie did a full inspection of the clearing, there was only her and an unaware Alasdair nearby. Why was Abbie never here when she was wanted?

"Abbie!" shouted Sophie, "We need you!"

Alasdair glanced up momentarily before trying to stack the brush into a manageable pile, but when she called again, the pitch louder and higher, he stopped and passed his eyes over the area.

"Maybe she's gone back," he cried.

Sophie wandered nearer to the wood. It was very still near the trees, no breeze tilting the long grass and certainly no signs of life anywhere nearby. As she picked her way over the stumps, Sophie's irritation was giving way to something even less positive. It was an odd feeling, this anxiety sitting on top of loss, and it was the last thing she had expected for this particular afternoon. Alasdair wandered to the other side of the clearing, looking carefully ahead into the gloom for any signal that Abbie had walked that way. But when he heard the rhythmic rustling of feet through the grass to his right, it was David's boots who were walking in their direction. His dad was smiling as he raised his hand in a wave.

"Lunch, kids," he said, then, "Where's Abbie?"

Chapter 20

Northumberland/Isle of Skye

The train station at Berwick-Upon-Tweed was no warmer than Waverley Station had been three days before, but on this occasion, Kate could not stand still, and so her continual movement was keeping her cosy. It was hardly conceivable that she was on the move again so soon, but Beth had to be appeased, and if she was ever to get a good night's sleep again, she needed to be back on Skye. She needed the familiar and the easy to balance out the mind-boggling and the complex, but she also needed to see the jagged skyline and smell the sea. She wanted to climb the Ben in the silvery blue light of dawn and sit by the tree she had claimed as her own; a little tranquillity was all that was required, to ponder everything she had heard and all that she had felt in the past two days. It needed to be contemplated upon, sorted, filed and shared, and the anticipation was once again snapping at her heels. Winnie wandered towards her with a cardboard cup and a bar of chocolate.

Kate thanked her and they stood in silence once more as the grass across the rails tried valiantly to stand tall against the breeze from the archway. They had said so much in the last night and day that both were content simply to stand and smile at life and its peculiarities. Winnie had offered to drive her to Edinburgh and treat her to a night in a hotel rather than an anonymous Travel Inn, but Kate had always preferred to do her travelling alone; and since she planned to collapse into a coma as soon as she got there, the expense of a hotel seemed ridiculous. Winnie had accepted the argument, recognising that she herself probably required solitude and peace so that she could begin to consider the offer both David and Kate had made to her, separately. They had left their door open to her, but in spite of this generosity, she could not walk through it without the permission of her son. Only he could invite her over the threshold, and why on earth should he, when the woman who had raised him was more than enough and deserved nothing less than his total commitment? There was a lot of serious thinking to be done, but still it made her grin. There was an option there, which had not been there for the last forty-odd years, and it pleased her heart.

When the train at last appeared and eased to a halt at the platform's edge, the pair of them froze. Around them, travellers gathered and hauled and stood poised. Who knew why they were travelling or how far? Perhaps each and every one of them was embarking on an adventure which would change their lives. Every human on earth was taking part in some story or another. Still, it seemed that only Winnie and Kate were totally in awe of what their farewell signified. Kate lowered her rucksack from her shoulders and opened her palms to her newest friend. Winnie, laughing out loud, held her granddaughter tight and felt the arms around her back begin to rub and caress her. If she had learned anything from the girl, it was that she was a compact little fighter; but with many more facets to discover, and she wanted to be a part of her extraordinary life more than anything else. She was a great-grandmother, for a start. It was something she imagined her own daughter would find quite amusing, if she ever dared to steer her through the rest of the mines hanging in her particular ocean.

They promised each other contact and time. Kate said she would email, Winnie said she did not own a computer; they agreed that pens and paper were a fine way to communicate. Then Kate was seated on the other side of glass, her eyes wide but full of life, the same grey as her own. She pressed her fingers against the pane for a second and then curled them and turned the gesture into a gentle wave. Winnie did the same from her position four feet away. Ordinary seconds stretched for the two of them, bringing every thought and word back to them as they held each other's gaze. Finally, as the train jolted and then settled into its smooth glide, Winnie reached into her handbag and brought out the photo of Neil and Kate by the trailer of wood. She held it to her face, grinning and Kate laughed to herself. As she waved one last time, she thought that all three faces looked quite good together.

As a youngster, Kate had imagined her life as an Edinburgh student, and perhaps, if her mother had lived, she would have spent many a chilly hour waiting for the transport system to kick into gear and deliver her from the sandstone buildings back to the mountains. In truth, she had been in her country's capital only three times, and what she had once thought would become familiarly ordinary in time, still had the ability to make her open her eyes and take note: the spring sunshine hitting the Castle's rock, the jagged silhouette of the Scott monument, made even blacker by the sun behind it, and the sheer volume of pedestrians on the wide pavements. All of these had tended to make her walk a degree slower, drawing her eyes up from her feet and into the clear air, where the history of the place was obvious in the pillars and arches and courtyards. It was all beautiful, but it was not where she wished to rest her head at that moment in time.

Kate blew on her hands as she headed for her Travel Inn destination, secure in the knowledge that every mile covered had been worth it; but the cold was forcing her skin to creep away from her clothes, and she felt as if she was disappearing from view. She closed her eyes momentarily as a further draught cooled the right side of her face, and she could hear Beth's voice immediately, not quite reproachful but definitely bordering on the offended.

"Four days away. Really? That's getting on for half of your time over here."

"Yes, well, it's not a straightforward journey, and when I get there, it might take a bit of time. On the other hand, I could be back in a day if I chicken out; but I really hope you're not wishing that'll be the case."

"No, course I'm not, but folk here want to see you. It's been ages since you were here last, they want to hear all about Ally ..."

So it had been agreed. Kate would travel down to Northumberland by bus and train on the Wednesday after the christening and spend Thursday to Saturday in the company of a stranger. If all went well. Should it fall apart at the initial meeting, or if Kate suddenly felt it was a bad idea, she would be back on Skye by late Friday. Beth had baulked a little at the unnecessary cost, until her niece reminded her that she rarely bought posh clothes, never went on fancy holidays or burned cash in the form of cigarettes, and that this particular adventure would be her own money well spent. Kate guessed that Beth would think the costs of the current situation to be less financial and more mental: a cancelled journey due to flooding, an unexpected night in Glasgow and an attempt to catch up on a day's delay by catching the earliest train possible the following day, only to miss the connection in Edinburgh. But she had survived the whole thing and allowed herself a small commendation. She had a final night before catching the bus back to Skye, and then, late on Monday afternoon, she would be back in the air, Canada bound. She laughed slightly to herself; she was heading *home* one day and then heading *home* again the next. Some people were homeless, yet she had two. Kate tried to see this as lucky and not greedy as she bent her head against the wind.

CHAPTER 21

Vancouver Island

David glanced at his watch. They had been looking for Abbie for less than five minutes and had covered very little of the area beyond the clearing, so there should not have been any real cause for worry. But he had also been calling for her, throwing his voice in every possible direction in as calm a manner as he could, and the lack of response was beginning to make him feel queasy. In spite of his understated calls, Ally had left his rucksack and plans fluttering in the breeze and had wandered over to David, concern troubling his face. Sophie was crying.

"Hey, Soph, come here, sweetheart."

The girl stumbled over a stump in her effort to reach David's outstretched hand, which did nothing to stem the tears; but when he lifted her into his arms, instead of laying her head on his shoulder and allowing herself to be comforted, her lip trembled even more.

"She was just there," she explained. "She was moving branches."

"And we'll find her," he assured. "Al, do me a favour and run to the house. Think we need an extra body on this."

Alasdair took off at speed, glad to be able to think about how he was helping rather than how he had forgotten about Abbie altogether and let her sneak off. David kissed Sophie's wet cheek and lowered her to the ground, taking her hand in his.

"Let's go this way. I'm pretty sure she wouldn't head towards the road."

Sophie jogged beside her Uncle David, grateful that his hand was warm and that he seemed to be far less worried than she was. They skirted the perimeter of the clearing. Every few steps or so he would stop, and when she looked up at him, he would be scanning the scrub.

The wood beyond them was dim then dark, but suddenly Uncle David was pointing to a nearby spot.

"I reckon she's gone in here. Look, it's flattened down a bit," he looked down at her for agreement and instead found her streaked face showing signs of uncertainty. As he watched, she gazed farther into the darkness and took a slight step backwards. "Do you want to stay here, Soph? I don't mind going in on my own, but you would have to promise me not to move from this spot."

The option to stay out in the sunny daylight was very tempting. Sophie loved to go for a walk in the woods at The Edge, but it was full of interconnecting pathways which had been formed by years of family outings, and the trees were much more spaced out. This was a plantation, tightly packed with commercial timber, and the forest floor was uneven and tangled with growth. Worst of all was the darkness and the smell of sun-starved vegetation. It was not an area they had ever used for playing; if their dad allowed them over the fence with him, it was usually to play jump the stumps while he spent ages just surveying the area and rubbing his chin in thought. Cuban and Crisis would sometimes accompany them, alternating between playing along with their game and sniffing out new and exciting objects from the unruly grass. The clearing was a much nicer place than the woods. But Uncle David's hand was keeping her from crying, and she owed it to her little sister to take part in this. At least it wasn't raining.

"I want to help find her," she uttered at last. David squeezed her hand and led the way.

At the sound of Ally's rapid breathing and boots clattering on the stairway, Andie smiled to herself. Every time he visited, he found an excuse to race the girls. His long legs and slight age advantage meant that he always won, but it never stopped the little ones taking part. On seeing his face, however, she frowned in surprise.

"Hey, Al, you look—"

"We can't find Abbie! She wandered off somewhere and Dad needs somebody."

Andie did not run. She simply walked quickly past the boy and headed out into the air.

"Neil!" she called through the open treads to the workshop. "You there?"

When there was no response, she realised that the lathe was in full flow, and so she ran up to the doorway, her hair bobbing in its braids, and waved frantically at the man. Neil killed the motor at once.

"Abbie's wandered into the plantation. Not sure how far, but Ally seems scared."

Alasdair did not even argue but watched Neil lay aside his tools and begin the hike down the driveway. Both adults walked smartly, but only when David's voice could be heard calling for the girl did both of them break into a run.

Back in the wood, Sophie had stopped crying and was echoing each of David's calls. She found that the interior was not quite as dark as she had imagined, more a dark brown than black, but their voices sounded dead, as if the trees would not let them travel very far. David stopped for a moment and listened carefully.

"Abbie, honey. Lunch is ready."

"Abbie! Mom needs to eat on time, remember!"

David looked down at Sophie, impressed by her argument. She misunderstood his expression.

"It's true. She gets wobbly if she doesn't eat on time."

After another moment, they moved forward again, and this time David injected a little sternness into his voice.

"Abbie! Answer me, please."

At the alteration of his tone, Sophie did not repeat the words but instead began to sniffle once more. She held her breath as the sound of approaching feet hit them from behind, but on seeing both Neil and Andie's worried faces, immediately began to wail. She dropped David's hand in an instant and ran straight towards her parents. She could not look Neil in the eye, however, and ducked under his arm, losing herself in Andie's hug instead.

"She was– there, then she wasn't," Sophie's level of anxiety was heart-breaking to listen to, and Andie cuddled her close.

"Sshh, Soph, it's okay."

Neil had stopped in his tracks, vexed that his daughter had somehow feared his anger or disappointment, and moved to David's side.

"Could she have gotten this far?" Neil asked.

"Well, she has to be somewhere."

Neil held his brow, trying to sort his thoughts. She had wandered, she had been bored and had sought an adventure, she had run for the road; the heavy Saturday afternoon traffic filtered through to his brain. His head flew up. Andie, Sophie and Alasdair were walking back to the safety of the brighter clearing, his partner's voice soothing the children and telling them that there was no need to panic. At her choice of words, his hand slipped over the gathering sweat and his heartbeat wavered.

"Not now," he groaned, through gritted teeth, his eyes screwed as tightly shut as they had ever been. "No, no, no ..."

David watched as his brother grabbed his left wrist in his right hand, unable to hold his head upright any longer. The alarm David felt was joined by regret; it had been so long since he had witnessed anything like this, but there was no time to give it the attention it deserved. Andie was out of sight, Rose was miles away, and each second was becoming precious. He had no choice.

David took one step forward as his brother began to shake and put his arms around the younger man's shoulders, pulling him forward into a tight grip. He felt the resistance immediately, but Neil was trapped. David tightened his grip. He could hear Neil muttering profanities into their combined shirtfronts, but the more he cursed, the less he struggled; and finally David felt him take a broken but deep breath into his lungs. As he exhaled, David released him, before the need to acknowledge the episode proved necessary. Stepping back, Neil wiped his face and eventually opened his eyes. His brother was already on the move.

"What was she wearing?" David called over his shoulder.

"Purple fleece," replied Neil and stumbled after him.

In terms of acreage, the plantation was not huge, and that was the scariest fact of all: There was no conceivable way that Abbie was out of earshot, so either she had to be hurt, or she was long gone. Neil felt a fresh film of sweat coat his neck and back. True fear, with its ability to scald and to cut, was making his skin slick and his eyes sting; perhaps he was even bleeding, he could not tell.

"Abbie! It's Dad."

There was not even a hint of movement; the air seemed thick and deadly in its silence, but Neil pushed through it.

"Hey! Lunch is on the table, and you need to get your skinny little butt out here right now!"

To their left, there was a faint rustle and an even more welcome giggle, which was instantly stifled. David raised his eyebrows, grinning at Neil, who held up his hand to make sure he did not move.

"Well, Dave," Neil's voice had a tremor which he forced himself to control, "it looks like that little punk baby has done it again. I swear, there is nobody like Abbie at hiding. Only wish we were as good at seeking, because I hate the fact that she's going to miss out on Granma Rose's pie. Come on, let's go."

"Dad! You found me!" the purple fleece with Abbie inside it suddenly jumped into view. "Punk baby!" she cried loudly and then started giggling harder than ever.

The two men looked at each other for one last moment, before David patted Neil's shoulder and walked away. Neil made himself cover the distance between him and Abbie at a normal pace and found her still laughing, her face painted with delight and pride. But when he hauled her off her feet, he held her against his chest and showed his relieved expression to the inanimate trees only. Abbie enjoyed the contact for about five seconds before she was squirming. She leaned back, pulled at the strands of his beard and laughed one last time, "You said butt. I won't tell."

When they reached the clearing, David was helping Alasdair to gather his belongings into his rucksack and Andie was lugging Sophie on her hip, already more than halfway back to the house. It seemed that nobody wanted to talk about the little misadventure at that point, at least not all together, at the same time. Abbie was still bouncing in Neil's arms, her glee at having fooled everyone and having been christened punk baby making her oblivious to the subdued mood of the rest of them. Ally did not even look at her as he followed his dad over the fence, but that was normal. It was a little odd that Dad was shaking so much, but at least she hadn't missed lunch. And she had won the game of hide and seek without any real effort.

Neil placed Abbie on the house side of the fence, her feet flattening the spongy grass, and she waited while he vaulted it effortlessly. But rather than following the other two couples immediately, Neil knelt beside her and held both of her hands in his. She grinned in response.

"Hey Abs," he began, "I need you to do me a favour."

Abbie's face did not even falter, although she wasn't sure what his sentence meant or why his eyes were not as happy as they usually were when he spoke to her.

"I need you to promise me something. D'you know what a promise is?"

Abbie shrugged. "What people say?"

Neil sighed. With Sophie, who had been able to hold an argument with any member of her family for as long as she had been with them, he felt sure he could have done this. But Abbie was three and still let her sister decide which type of milkshake she wanted. He decided not to sugarcoat it or dress it up with analogies.

"If you say something and promise it, then you have to mean it and do it. So listen up. You can only play hide and seek if we all know about it. We thought you were lost and hurt, and we were all really, really worried. Sophie was crying."

"She was crying?" Abbie's eyes were suddenly wide, blue pools. "Why?"

"Because Uncle David couldn't get you to answer him."

"I was hiding. You keep quiet."

Neil slowly straightened his legs and eased his back into alignment. He leaned against the fence and rubbed his thumb under his chin. Abbie tilted her head to one side.

"If you speak, they find you," she explained, although she was beginning to feel a chill inside. She took his free hand and looked up at him, hopefully.

"Okay," he replied, "but listen carefully, because this is important. You– and Sophie– can only hide from us if we are all playing the game. And if Mom or I or any other grown-up asks you to stop hiding and to answer them, you have to do it. Those are the rules, from now on. You have to tell me you'll do this, and you have to mean it."

Abbie thought about what he was saying. She supposed that it had been a pretty boring time, sitting on the floor of the forest, waiting for somebody to come, and that if they had all been playing, it would have gotten to the exciting bit sooner. She remained impressed that Uncle David had not been able to find her, and he was the oldest person here today; but Sophie had been crying, and that wasn't so good. On top of all that, Dad was looking at her with his serious face, and she much preferred it when he was laughing with her. So, she nodded.

"Okay."

"Okay what?"

"I'll jump out and shout 'helloooooo.'"

Finally, Neil rewarded her with a grin and she clapped her hands at the sight.

"Shoulders, Dad?"

As Neil lifted her body above his head and settled her in place, she waved her arms in the air, loving her ability to balance and appreciating the fact that her Dad seemed to have stopped shaking at last. She might have fallen all the way to the ground if he had not, and that was a really long way to fall. What a day it had been so far. She had won at hide and seek, she had made a promise to her dad and he had called her a silly name, but a name that she loved to bits. By the time they reached the stairway, Abbie grabbed handfuls of Neil's hair she was laughing so much. When he pulled her to the ground and brushed the last of the wood's debris from her fleece and jeans, she ran ahead of him up the stairs. At the top she turned and threw her arms wide.

"Punk baby," she cried and ran inside.

Later, when Abbie had fallen asleep on top of Cuban, and Ally and Sophie had retired to the girls' room to build a scaled-down, indoor version of the den, Neil lowered himself sedately onto the sofa beside the sleeping couple and stretched his legs out in front of him. As he stared at the flames behind the stove's glass, his hand reached out and absently stroked Abbie's hair. She slept the sleep of the triumphant, and Cuban's smooth, warm flank ensured that his fingers did not disturb her. David was drying the dishes across the room, when Andie quietly took the towel from him and nodded in Neil's direction. When he failed to catch her drift, she shooed him away from her. He took one of the fireside chairs and waited until Neil moved his eyes in his direction.

"Man," was all Neil could muster. "Man."

David nodded. Fear like that took it out of you, no matter how short its duration, and even the strongest, most stable individual could be unsettled by it. In Neil's case, more than one terror had touched him that day, and David guessed that his reaction was playing with his mind as much as losing Abbie was. There were no chips or medals available to mark the years of panic-free survival; only the sufferer and their nearest were even aware of it. Neil gave David a wry smile, guessing his thoughts.

"It's been awhile. Disappointing."

David wanted to reassure him that it had been an exceptional circumstance, but stopped himself. Where youngsters were concerned, each day had the potential to be exceptional, and there was really no comfort to be had in those words.

"I've seen it a whole lot worse," offered David.

Neil's fingers continued to entangle themselves in the fine silk strands belonging to Abbie, and as he did so, his mouth twitched to the side as if his nose was bothering him. His eyes looked more desolate than disappointed.

"When Jayney and Don asked us to be guardians, we were flattered. You know, it was a gesture of friendship and the girls knew us, but nobody ever really thinks it further than that, do they?"

David shook his head. "Hell, no. No parent wants to visit that place."

Neil seemed willing to accept this assurance and hitched himself onto the sofa, leaning forward on his knees. He needed to share; David recognised the signs.

"They're so amazing. They just ... join in as if it was the most natural thing. And I'd forgotten. I had forgotten how funny little kids can be. And generous!" Neil wiped at his chin. "Our life is great, Dave. But ..." he paused for a second time, "but we're all they have, and one of us is me."

"Kids play hide and seek, brother."

"I'm talking about my reactions. Look at me, I'm middle-aged and I can still sweat and shake like an adolescent on a first date. What use is that to them?"

"Tell him, David," soothed Andie, sitting on the arm of the chair. "Tell him how lucky those girls are to have him."

Before he could say anything else, the phone in David's shirt pocket began to play a very definite Scottish melody on the air, and he rolled his eyes in apology.

"Kate?" asked Neil and David nodded, rising and moving towards the door.

"Sorry, it's late over there, I'd better–"

Neil waved him on with a weak smile and leaned back against the sofa, not particularly comforted by Andie's words, for as adamant as she was, he had heard them so many times before. As he closed his eyes against all of his headache-inducing frustrations, Andie slid from the arm to the seat and settled herself opposite her man's face. She watched him. He was an adult, it was true; a man who had enjoyed a free and happy childhood and in the last ten years had allowed others to forgive him before forgiving himself. The years in between had left scars, but who did not carry ridges and fissures on their soul? She reached out and poked his foot with her toe.

"You're wrong, you know."

"They're children," Neil frowned. "If I let you down, I'm an idiot. If I neglect the dogs, they bug me until I behave myself. But these two have already been injured in the worst possible way. That's something I think about all the time, and today I sent those kids out without really–"

"We," Andie emphasised. "We sent them out. And yes, we were a bit thoughtless because they were really excited. But we did it, not you. And we learned from it, right? End of story."

Neil still could not raise his eyes to hers. Somebody had to take responsibility for Sophie's terror-stricken eyes and Ally's peaky face, yet they were all insisting that all was well and that everyone was safe in the place they should be. These were indeed the facts, but what had they learned? To think twice? To pay more attention? All Neil had learned was that in any true crisis, and there were bound to be many more of them, he had the potential to seize up like an oil-free engine on a three-lane highway, and this was a dire situation. The word liability would not leave him be.

"God in heaven," his breath was hot with that same frustration, and he hammered his knees with his own fists. In the next second, Abbie had raised her sleepy head and was rubbing her eyes.

"Hey, Daddy," she croaked, delighted that he was sitting beside her in the middle of an ordinary day, and climbed over the unperturbed Cuban into his lap. Neil's face remained annoyed for as long as she was preoccupied, but when Abbie pulled her fringe away from her eyes and smiled up at him, he matched her expression. "Where's Sophie and Al?"

"They're building a den. The kind you can make in your bedroom."

She watched him for a moment or two more, until she was completely satisfied that he still loved her, then she rolled onto the floor and jogged away from them. Andie raised her eyebrows in a very how-long-are-you-going-to-sit-there-and-self-flagellate manner, and he may have even thought about answering the query, if David had not come nodding back into the room, spouting assurances down the phone as he did so. In the next second, he had handed the phone to Neil.

"Neil!" cried Kate, her voice surprisingly chirpy for someone still up at midnight. "Heard you had a bit of a drama. What a carry on!"

Neil stood as he spoke, rolling his eyes. "Yeah, well, it was good of Dave to share that one with you."

Lying in her Travel Inn three-quarter bed, where the sheets were so tight around her she felt mummified, Kate began to speak. The recollections took about ten minutes, and it was anybody's guess what the figure on the phone bill would be at the end of the month, but Kate did not omit one detail. Neil wandered around the open-plan living area, his head sometimes raised, his arms sometimes emphasising his counter-arguments; most of the time he just listened. Listened to how Kate had once fallen out of a tree and bit her tongue almost in two, how her appendix had been on the point of bursting and flooding her body with toxins just as they had removed it. He learned of Hazel's temporary "disappearance" at a Highland dancing competition, when she ended up taking part in the sword dance wearing a tutu, and her appalling record behind the wheel of the car which had meant many a sleepless night for their mother. More recently, Ally's unhealthy interest in the site of Dave's accident was discussed and her growing terror that "in a decade or so he'll be dating!"

"The point is," Kate yawned, needing to sum up her argument before lack of sleep slurred her words any further, "my mum was on her own with her fears, and she survived all of them. Well, all but the worst one. But I'm luckier, I've got Dave. When I'm shivering with the night terrors, he puts his arms around me. You've got Andie. So stop being a bloody martyr, father of mine. Having those pair is still better than not having them, isn't it?"

Neil wasn't entirely sure how he felt at that moment, apart from peeved and robbed of his usual defences. Oh, David was smart, there was no doubt, using Kate to tell him how they all felt. Before he answered her, he glanced around the room and saw the air clear a little in front of him. Andie was still seated by the fire, her legs draped over the arm of the chair, but her eyes were locked on his movements. David had moved Cuban from the sofa and was also watching, his face blank and very obviously, purposely so. He was twisted in his seat. They were watching and waiting. They cared. He turned away from them and wandered through to the girls' bedroom.

"You still there?" the voice on the end of the phone at least had the decency to sound slightly less confident.

"I'm here," he replied, his eyes taking in the destroyed bedroom. Blankets, duvets, boxes and pillows had all been made use of, and all he could hear were muffled discussions coming from deep within the confines of the construction. Abbie seemed to be singing a non-rhyming song, the other two were arguing over who should be the one to have the beanbag. Their voices were light, and in spite of their dispute, there was no malice in their words.

"Well, I'll just say this then," Kate continued. "I've been talking to folk about you. Telling them all about my dad and how he is such a special person. I'll keep on telling them just that, until they're lucky enough to meet you in person. Now, can I speak to my son?"

As the phone was passed over for the last time, Neil listened to Alasdair's initial monosyllabic answers change to a free-flowing speech. How did mothers know just which questions to ask? Sophie blinked both her eyes on emerging from the dim den, and waved at the man. She was unharmed by the events of the day, and when he finally left the three youngsters to it, his heart felt light enough to let him hold up his hands and admit defeat. Maybe his mind was not disabled, maybe it was just a little under the weather.

"Do you lot never get tired of joining forces against me? It's a bona fide conspiracy."

David answered from his seat. "Someday you'll accept that resistance is pointless. God, I hope it's soon. I'm not getting any younger."

As if to add weight to that argument, David glanced at his watch and frowned. The comfort of the sofa and the crackle of the flames in the burner were far more enticing an environment than the interior of the SUV and the Kate-free Edge that awaited Al and him on their return. He sighed and closed his eyes for one more moment. It was a sunny Saturday in spring, and he tried to hold onto the promise that came along with this. Kate would be home at the beginning of the following week, Ally would be instantly more settled and chatty, and surely Rose would be cheered by the latest developments across the pond. She had, after all, set this up, and there was every hope that things would turn out reasonably okay. But, more importantly, Kate would be back in his sight, and he would once again feel normal. When he finally encouraged his eyes to open, both Neil and Andie had disappeared. David levered himself onto his feet and stretched his arms high in the air. At that moment, Alasdair came whooping into the room.

"Let's go, Dad!" he shouted. "Where are the coats?"

David looked baffled. "You're set to go?"

"Yes, but come on," the boy urged. "If we go now, we can get Bertuzzi back from Granma before they get there."

Alasdair was into his jacket and struggling back into his boots as Abbie could be heard howling in the background. David was lost, confused by the reactions taking place around him, and then Andie appeared beneath a pile of coats and other clothes, Sophie bouncing at her side. David held open his hands as a question.

"Neil's taking them to see Rose. I would come, but you know Sundays belong to my mom."

It made sense, apart from the gradually subsiding wail, and he looked past her for an answer.

"Neil caught her hair in her coat zipper," she explained, then grinned slyly. "He seemed to deal quite well with the disaster."

"They can camp in my room," shouted Alasdair from the stairway. "Dad, we need to go!"

David genuinely grinned. They would have company after all in the big old house, and Rose would be pleased beyond belief when they all piled into her little kitchen. Best of all, they had already eaten a decent meal, so with any luck he would get away with adding a tin of sauce to some rice or pasta. As Neil wandered through with Abbie, her hair safely braided down her back, David hugged Andie.

"Thanks for that amazing lunch. Oh, and give my regards to Iris. See you soon?"

"You can count on it," Andie replied. "I want to hear all about Kate's visit from the horse's mouth."

"Okay," David turned to Neil. "See you back at The Edge. This is going to make Rose's day."

Neil smiled wryly as he stuffed the clothes into a duffle bag. "Hey, it's all for my benefit, brother. My ma is the only one who ever gives me any sympathy. She's one of a kind."

CHAPTER 22
Isle of Skye

The light finally began to fade in earnest as the bus climbed up and over the bridge linking Skye to the mainland. Kate felt her stomach somersault at the descent, but that was possibly due to the inadequate provisions she had bought at the station. Equally it could have been due to the crop of Sunday drivers who were holding up the coach and turning the journey into one of those dreams where obstacles and uncooperative limbs hindered your every step. However, she had enjoyed the entire experience. Fort William may have been a little grey, but prior to that Rannoch Moor had been washed in sunshine, making the reeds and mosses fresh and spongy to the eye, and Glenshiel had been startling in colour. Kate had never seen so many shades of green this early in the year, or such clearly defined contours. She had pressed her face against the glass and tried to commit it all to memory. As the countryside changed again, edging through translucent blues and glowing pinks, she began to relax. Half an hour farther up the road and home would be on the horizon.

Kate smiled, not-so-patiently awaiting the spot just south of Sconser, from where she could glimpse Ben Tianavaig. As a child, travelling back from singing lessons in Broadford, she had thought the Ben had resembled a sleeping dragon, its jagged spine curved as it rested. The ridge always looked fearsome from this angle, and yet the physical climbing of it proved a joyously simple ascent, which was worth every breath. Kate loved that hill beyond reason, she knew that. But then, it had been her friend for all the days she had lived. Her mother had trailed her up there in the sunny days of her Skye childhood; it had spelled just as much adventure as the Storr or Quiraing had done. But she had also run the length of the ridge, shrieking and bawling at the injustices of terminal illness; and then, in the hours when she had felt at her most isolated, with no David beside her and a hundred reasons not to go home, it had been a place where they could sit together, thousands of miles between them. The rabbit trails, heathery patches and rock-faces were all used as markers and sanctuaries for her, and, years ago, David had asked her if she was sure she could bear to be parted from it. He had known her spirit even then, and that was only one of the reasons she had been able to reassure him. Even so, nowhere on earth felt as good to her as the surface of that Ben, and she followed its outline for as long as the surroundings permitted.

When it had disappeared into the gloaming, Kate settled back to the thoughts she had been playing with since she had left Edinburgh that morning, and nursed the ever-present fluttering inside her. What an uncommon person Winnie had turned out to be, in spite of her years and apparently steady life. She had trained as a nurse, married a colleague, moved to England and retrained as a teacher. She had a daughter, Emma, who was thirty-three and who had not one clue about Neil or his child, but this had not even shaken her. She had not been scared by Kate's appearance, neither had she been meek or even overly emotional until David had spoken to her. Maybe she had to build a wall, just as Kate had been forced to do in the past.

When Winnie had spoken of her life since Neil, it had sounded a contented enough existence. If she had suffered, she wasn't about to share it; and Kate had found herself looking at her over her coffee mug, acknowledging the differences in her ancestors. She had lived in the same house as Mary Mackinnon, her maternal grandmother, until her death in 1986, and her overwhelming memory was of organisation and routine: baking days, washing days, the Memory Game, and tea in china cups on a Sunday night. Kate had no idea if the woman had ever even set foot on the mainland, and until she passed away, the house had been run as it had since Fiona and Beth had been children. They had been two different but strong and determined women, her grandmothers, and Kate wondered if such strength and wisdom came only with age, as it was certainly not hereditary.

Kate pulled her mobile phone from her pocket and pressed the rubberised buttons with both hands:

JUST PAST SLIG. SHOULD I GET OFF AT ROAD END OR PORTREE?

She watched as the phone struggled to send the information with its intermittent signal, and when it had failed after two attempts, she laid it aside. Another half a mile and the lights of Portree were glinting in the distance, allowing Kate to grin at the promise of the minty air which would accompany her departure from the bus. In the next second, she had hauled her one rucksack to the front of the vehicle and had persuaded the driver to leave her at the road end, whether a car was awaiting her or not.

As she held her breath until the fumes of the disappearing bus had cleared, Kate felt a familiar elation: the kind that always grew inside her at times like these, when the sky remained the palest yellow where it met the land and no clouds smudged the breathless indigo above it. Where, even at this distance, she could see the lights of the town reflected in the bay and nobody was talking, interrupting or damaging her appreciation of it. There was no vibration on the road as Kate crossed over and began the hike down the narrower route to Camastianavaig. It seemed likely, with every step, that her text message had not yet reached its destination. Either that or the reply had decided to take a tour of the island before parachuting back into her waiting phone. Kate wondered how that was possible. She thought she probably understood how telephones worked, although emails were beyond her; but where on earth did text messages go between being sent and being received? Did the information hover like a swarm of bees, until they got the go-ahead to connect with the appropriate recipient? And when a signal did not allow this to happen immediately, where the hell did the words go? The answers would forever allude her.

At the dip in the road, Kate stopped to peer over the bridge at the black water. She could see nothing, but the sound and smell of the river allowed her to picture it anyway. The first time she had made this journey alone in the dark, the bushes near the bridge had proved the only scary thing about it. They had rustled at the very moment she had passed, and she had sweated her way up the brae, grinding her teeth and reciting as much of Poe's "The Raven" as she could remember. Kate grinned to herself, trying to imagine a more ridiculous choice in poetry when waving bushes were making a person nervous; but then everything her English teacher Mr Ellis had liked, she had liked in those days. She thanked God that somehow she had learned to develop opinions of her own since, but she could still recite most of the first half of the epic without hesitation.

By the time she had reached the turnoff for Penifiler, Kate had moved on from gothic literature to thoughts of Beth's gingerbread and then to the journey back across the ocean the following day. Where had the two weeks gone? The first few days had been spent in a whirl of smiling reunions, waving and crying out to friends across the Portree streets, dropping in on all of her ex-employers and proving to them that she had not turned into a lumberjack.

Beth had taken the week off work, and the pair of them had spent a lot of time at Hazel's cottage, wandering through rooms, lounging on the sofa, taking their tea wherever the action was, even if the action sometimes was as basic as a nappy change. Hazel had been attentive to her sister, to the point where Kate had been forced to take Beth aside and enquire after the woman's mental health.

"She think she owes you."

"Well, that's beyond ridiculous!" Kate had hissed.

"Tell her that then. You're the only one who can."

Hazel, when tackled about her overbearing and frankly creepy politeness, had pretended to misunderstand for as long as it took for Kate's eyes to force her to come clean, which was all of eleven seconds. There had followed a very odd afternoon, where Hazel had as good as thrown herself at Kate's feet and washed them with her hair. Kate had gaped at her sister's words, listening to how she had changed their lives, given them so much and made them into a real family.

It was not the sentiments themselves, but rather the courteous manner and phrases she had used, which had Kate pulling her up short and asking her outright who in God's name she thought she was talking to. Yes, it had been years since they had shared a bedroom, but that did not alter the fact that Hazel was still the one person who knew her inside out, and there was no need to be so civil or obliging. Kate remembered mentioning the occupation of her mother's womb at one point, as if to emphasise her argument; and it was soon after that Hazel had dropped all attempts to ease her sister into her way of thinking, and just told her straight. She loved her, she missed her and could think of nothing better than watching their children grow up on the same side of the Atlantic.

Kate had been touched by the idea, delighted in fact that Hazel had wished to visit the pre-disease, pre-David, pre-division days of their youth but, of course, had committed herself to nothing. The idea that they should live happily within reach of each other in the place of their simpler lives appeared to consume her sister entirely; and as Kate hit the even narrower road, still well over a mile from Beth's cottage, she had to wonder at her own lack of response. Skye was in her soul, sometimes her blood sang with how much she longed for the wind at the top of Ben Tianavaig to blow her off her feet into a giggling, rolling heap. The place was so highly coloured at times, at others it was like a black and white image of itself as sea blended with sky and mist. It was then that she had to remind herself what she had willed David to believe the day after they were married: that it was only grass and rock and water if she was there without him. So yes, she was attached by her heartstrings to the island and would never try to alter this. But she needed David and Alasdair to be hers alone, selfish though that may be, and she needed to be part of the life that they alone had created. In a way, it had been a relief to escape south of the border for a few days, just to avoid Hazel's pre-occupation with the plan.

Kate stepped off the road onto the wet verge to let a set of rumbling headlights pass unhindered, and as they illuminated the road in front of her for the briefest of times, the sound of her phone rang out to cheer her. It was Canada, and Kate grinned once more into the gloom.

"And who am I speaking to on this fine, clear, yet black-as-ink night?"

"This is David Wilder, may I speak with my wife please?" David's reply had not even missed a beat.

"Davey! Your voice is like a fine malt. Gets better with age. Man, I miss you!"

"Snap. You back on the island yet?"

Kate's steps quickened as she swapped the treacherous grass for the safer tarmac, and David's voice made her long for the physical miles between them to explode into dust and for him to be standing at the brow of the next hill. But their reunion was still far too many hours away, so instead she took the time to ask him specific questions just to hear his voice on ordinary, basic family life. No need for analysis or debate, or worrying if words would kill conversations or break already tenuous connections, just the joy of hearing the man laugh while talking to her alone.

It would now be late morning at The Edge on a sedate Sunday, and so there was no need to hurry the words between them. It was what Kate had missed in the last frenetic fortnight, talking to only David in a safe, familiar room. That and his arm along her shoulder, his hands on her face.

"So," said Kate, as the road temporarily widened into a passing place, "are you going over to Rose's for lunch, or are you and Neil aiming to create a masterpiece between you? Oh, I can't believe I'm going to miss that."

"Ah, well," David sounded sheepish enough to make Kate snigger, "bit of both. We've got Rose installed here to cheer her up, and Andie sent leftovers, so it's just a matter of bulking it up with veg and bread."

Kate shivered as the road altered course and a breeze met her face-to-face on the hillside. "It's time I was back," she sighed, "and I will be tomorrow. Dave, I've got so many stories to tell her, she'll be back on her feet in no time. She needs a project to occupy her. Here! I'll help her. It'll be a joint– dare I say it– Master Plan."

David's reply was lost as the horn of a Defender started to sound in staccato bursts behind her. Thankfully, Kate's alarmed reaction also went unheard. The man behind the wheel could be an idiot at times, but he was also the one who had just been to Portree to pick her up, so she waved gently as he pulled up onto the verge.

"Listen, Dave," Kate raised her voice above the rumbling of the engine, "I'm going to ring you from the house. I'll speak to Al then, but Kenny is here and he's polluting the entire countryside as we speak. Give me ten minutes. Love you."

To his credit, Kenny had cleared the tools and clutter from the passenger footwell in her honour; and in spite of his unnecessary six-mile round trip, his face was lit up as she shoved her rucksack onto the middle seat and climbed aboard.

"Sorry, sorry, sorry," apologised Kate, "my fault. I should have just sat tight for the whole journey."

"Needed fuel anyway. You all right?"

Kate nodded, then laughed out loud. "I am, officially, dead beat. Weary to the bone. I may never travel again. Alternatively, I might decide to get up at six o'clock tomorrow morning and fly back across the sea."

Kenny slowed the vehicle to negotiate the hairpin down towards the village. "But it went okay? 'Yes' would be the best answer here, because only total success on this will convince Beth it was worth it."

"It was worth it," confirmed Kate, giving up on ever locating the seatbelt. "Tiring but worth it."

"Thank God for that."

Kate's watch read just after 7.30 p.m. when Beth met the pair at the cottage door, and there followed the few mandatory moments of explanations and excuses regarding text messages and the immense kindness of one Kenneth Elliot. As if to add weight to this, he insisted on bringing her baggage inside, not even allowing her to carry her coat. In the sitting room, it felt like her entire kin had gathered, and for one second, Kate wondered if Hazel had been recruiting for the Keep Kate on Skye Party. However, everyone seemed tension-free; and when Kate was settled near the fire, a mug of tea placed in her hands, the questions were all about the woman she had just met. Consequently, it was a good half hour before Kate returned David's phone call and managed to speak to Alasdair. As his answers to her questions became shorter and distinctly less interested, Kate asked to speak to Rose.

What struck Kate the most was the thinness of her mother-in-law's voice. She seemed excited and anxious to know Kate's perception of the situation, but she sounded like an old woman, and Kate could barely picture her as such.

"I took photos," Kate told her. "Loads of them and I was thinking, if you're up to it, we could maybe take it to the next step. But only if you still want that."

As Rose declared it a great idea and even began to ask her what she had in mind, Kate felt Hazel at her elbow. Another few moments, and she had passed the phone to her sister, finding herself grateful to do so. It had been a long day, with the prospect of an even longer journey to follow in a matter of hours, and bizarrely, Kate's knees were aching with fatigue. She thought of the duvet in the guest bedroom and wondered if she could just grab ten minutes of peace before the compulsory winding up and analysis of the past two weeks took place. There would be wine and no doubt the odd tear, but it was an exercise steeped in love and affirmation. Life was good, life was worthwhile, life carried on whether it was or not, and there was satisfaction in speaking to the people who mattered the most in it all.

Kate had thrown herself onto the bed in a style reminiscent of her teenage years, and was gazing dubiously at the remainder of the belongings still needing packed, when Beth appeared in the doorway. "Hazel's wondering if you need to speak to David again."

Kate, behind drooping eyelids, waved her hand. "Tell him I'll phone him when I'm back on his side of the water."

As she was once again left alone, Kate rolled away from the door and tucked her knees under her chin. "Life carried on," she thought as her eyes closed of their own accord.

When Kate next opened her eyes, she found the pink of the faux patchwork duvet cover the most welcome sight before her. Then there was the dresser with photos of her mother and the blessed anaglypta wallpaper which Beth had announced would hold up the walls until the end of time. She could hear the murmurs from the sitting room. She was safe on Skye and had obviously been missing for the shortest time permissible by her family. A shadow crossed her vision and Hazel leaned on the door jamb, as she had done years before. She looked equally as awkward today.

"Hey, besom," she smirked. "You grabbing yourself a wee forty winks?"

"I'm bloody knackered," Kate admitted. "Man, what I wouldn't give to be able to teleport."

Hazel finally wandered over the threshold. "Yeah, that would make it easier all round."

Kate stretched her hands in the air as she stood up, and then started to hunt for any stray clothes which might have decided that Skye was a better prospect than Canada. "How did you think Rose sounded?"

"Bit breathy, maybe. Dad sounded great, though."

Kate for once did not mentally edit her feelings before speaking. "God, I've missed him. You know, the last time I slept in this room was for your wedding. Al was in that ancient cot, and Dave's feet stuck out the bottom of the bed. Being here on my own, in this room, reminds me of the bad old days."

"Aye, well," Hazel allowed, "the bad old days are nearly ten years back. It's better now, right?"

Kate, trying to match up socks from her clean laundry pile, let her mind wander to the time when she had occupied her late mother's room for more than a year, trying to pacify family and thinking of David's face as she closed her eyes on yet another frustrating day. Then those same four walls had suddenly sheltered her and her husband for a week after their own wedding; and the previous wallpaper, as floral as Fiona had been able to endure, had become one of her favourite designs. She piled the underwear into her second, larger rucksack.

"Yes, it is. But don't start on again about what you owe me. Hope is a little cherub and I was happy to do it. With any luck, she'll have another Canadian cousin one day soon."

It was a bit of a cheeky move on her part, as Kate knew that her sister could still be silenced by some aspects of that particular relationship. Yet even she was surprised by the length of the pause. She grinned over at Hazel, to assure her that David was aware of the plan and that this was a joint and pondered decision.

"Really?" Hazel said at last. "You're still ... you're actually trying?"

Kate grinned even wider and put her hands on her hips. "At every opportunity. Och, Haze, come on!" Kate could not prevent her laughter as her sister walked from the room, and shouted after her, "You asked for that, you know."

"Shut up and come get some wine!"

When Kate eventually re-joined the company, the banter was as she had suspected, but with the added logistical debate regarding her forthcoming journey to Glasgow airport. Beth was to drive her, Hazel could tag along if she wished it, but it would be a long day for Hope. Hazel piped up that she didn't need to do any such thing, since her sister was a painful specimen of a human being and deserved none of her precious time. Kate raised her wine glass in response. By 8:30 p.m. Kate had yawned herself silent, and Beth finally sighed her acceptance that their time together was coming to an end, before suggesting that the woman turned in.

"I'll see you all in the morning, though," Kate groaned as she stood and moved into the corridor, "I won't go without wasting at least two more minutes of your precious time."

Her goal was in sight. She had cleaned her teeth and ran water over her face. She had also packed everything except her pyjamas and her travelling clothes and had set the alarm on her phone. The bed would hold her between sheet and duvet, and she could, perhaps for the last time in her life, lie alone in this double bed and try to picture Dave's face. As she laid her watch on the bedside cabinet, there was a very distinct knock on the back door of the cottage.

"No," whimpered Kate, and as if her movements would make the unwanted visitor go away, she dived into bed and switched off the light, shouting "Unless that's David Wilder I am well and truly asleep!" Whoever had come to wish her a safe journey would have to come back early the following day. This was her time, and even the opportunity to tease Hazel further was less essential than letting sleep work its magic on her. Yet it was less than a minute before Beth came bustling into the room, her very silhouette giving off rays of concern as Kate raised her head.

"You need to get up, Kate," Beth whispered, uncovering her niece as she did so. "I mean it."

Kate could hear that the woman spoke the truth even through her fatigue and, unusually, did not argue. What she did think, as she followed Beth through to the sitting room and saw the identity of the visitor, was that shock had the incredible ability to shake every ounce of weariness from a person in a split second.

"Hello again, Kate," Winnie stood as she spoke, "I was wondering how it would be if I came back to Canada with you?"

CHAPTER 23
Vancouver Island

David sat at his desk in the timber yard office, surrounded by unopened mail and dirty coffee mugs. In the years since this cabin had passed from the care of his father to him, it had not changed in size or even orientation– the location of the stove had put paid to that– but he could not remember it ever being quite so disorganised. After Pete's death, he had split his admin time between the office at the top of The Edge and this place, and the system had worked well enough. Then Kate had landed on him from a great height, and before the first bruises from this contact had a chance to fade, she had assuredly and mercilessly bated his heart until he had submitted. As a consequence, he had gradually moved the majority of the work back to the timber yard's office, simply because he now had two distinct aspects to this life where there had only been one long, undefined existence before. There was work and there was home, and the exhilaration he had experienced at this developing situation had somehow allowed both to prosper. Currently, he was sitting very much alone within the most familiar of wooden walls, feeling ridiculously abandoned.

He sighed and looked at his hands. They were not remarkable in any way other than his nails were bitten below the fingertips; he cracked his knuckles when agitated and chewed his nails when deep in thought. So, ordinary hands, but hands which Kate loved. She loved them entwined in her own, she loved them as they caressed her face. She loved them on her waist and in her hair. He stood up before he could travel that particularly dangerous road further. He was here to work, to sort out the mess accumulated over a fortnight of spending spare time with Alasdair, and not to picture Kate and himself together, not when he was another four tedious days away from her touch. The stove was cold and grey, but since it suited his mood, he ignored it and instead filled the sink with a kettle's worth of boiling water, soaped it up using the cold tap and added every dish/mug he could find to the mix. As the crockery steeped, David turned up the radio to a volume he could only just bear and forced himself to keep going.

Papers were filed, invoices put in order, cupboards cleared of out-of-date material and surfaces wiped. By the time he had finished, the room was starkly tidy, and he had suffered only two paper cuts and a coughing fit from inhaling the disturbed dust. But he had made progress. It was 11:15 a.m. on the second Monday in March, the day on which Kate should have been returning. His entire being had been geared to her return on this day, and it was reacting badly to the delay being forced upon it. He wanted to curse out loud and throw a well-aimed punch at any surface that would not hurt him; but instead he refilled the kettle and finally raked out the stove, Kate's conversation of early that morning threatening more than ever to break through the wall he had built to contain it. He could not afford to replay their words yet, because he would end up an even bigger mess of doubts and fears; it was safer to fill the hours with mundane tasks. As if to aid his distraction, the phone suddenly tried to compete with Outkast's "Hey Ya," and he was glad to exchange the annoyingly cheery singing for a live, interactive conversation. His relief was suspended when Rose's voice reached him, however. Her diction was low and her breathing surprisingly shallow, but the worst thing were her attempts to hide both by asking questions specifically designed to make him smile.

"So, today's the day," she murmured. "What time are you setting off?"

"Ah, Rose," he scowled into the room, annoyed at himself for not having yet passed on his news. "Change of plan. I spoke to Kate earlier and she's not travelling until Thursday now."

There was a very prominent pause, the kind filled with confusion, disappointment and worry. He knew this, because it was how he had felt on speaking to Kate five hours previously. Yes, he had very much minded that she was staying in Skye for another three days, and no, he had not really understood her reasons, even though she had been sure that he would. True, it was a chance to spend some time with someone newly discovered, and the rest of the family were grateful for the extra hours available to them; but their son needed her back here, and Rose was not well. Of course, little of his sentiments had been passed to his wife; she had already urged him to "grow a spine," and he had not wanted to risk hearing that again. So he had uttered his "understanding" and had "seen her point" before trying to express his regret like an ordinary lover. He was not sure yet that she had fallen for it.

"Oh, that's ... a shame," Rose indeed sounded a bit unnerved. "Is it the weather?"

It was a reasonable assumption, when the northern hemisphere was only just emerging from winter. The roads in Skye could be hazardous, and David considered using this excuse momentarily before lifting the tone of his voice.

"No, no," he offered. "She ... I think she's feeling guilty about the little time she gives them. She says Hope is gorgeous and just wants a few more days. It's understandable."

This time Rose did not even hesitate. "I want her home. I can't settle until she's here."

David felt himself sit. "Rose? What's up?"

"Nothing. Oh, there's Jessie with my mail. I'll speak to you later."

He was not sure what shocked him more, the emotional kinks in her words or the fact that she put the phone down on his concern. He marvelled for a second or two, more and more convinced that he should have ignored Kate's plea to keep Rose in the dark about Winnie for the moment. But the yard, which had been so still since the men had departed, was suddenly filled with the dust of an approaching vehicle, and there was Rob rolling out of his truck, looking uncharacteristically upbeat. David met him at the door, suddenly glad of company.

"Cleared it!" Rob shouted, wiping his pink face. "Brush, limbs, the lot, and still half a day to spare. Not every crisis has to be a disaster. You can thank me by getting me a long, cold glass of beer. Failing that, some tepid water."

As David took one of the sparking mugs, proudly showing Rob the stain-free interior as he did so, the man took off his jacket and folded it before laying it over the back of a chair. David could sense his confusion from over two metres away.

"It was long overdue," David said, without clarification. "Invoices are in the invoice file, ashes are ready for spreading, and the mud your feet left under the desk has been scraped off and removed."

Rob looked momentarily at the current state of his boots, then tucked his feet out of sight as he sat. He swithered whether or not to point out the stray cobweb moving gently on the stovepipe, then switched his negative to positive and admired the mug he was handed. On good days, when spring sunshine and a successfully cleared woodland track allowed thoughts of Mike and Jay to stay on the perimeter, they could afford to take pleasure in ordinary domestic matters.

"Is your house looking as good as this?" grinned Rob, gulping down his water. "Nearly three weeks without her. I can guarantee mine would be like a war zone."

"Hmm. It's not so bad," David pondered the question as he sat. "We've been pretty much based in the kitchen, so you know, it's not that … shit, it's not great, either. Neil's lot didn't improve it much. Still," he sighed, "I guess I have a few more days to sort it now."

Rob shrugged his response, then chuckled, "Neil with two kiddies. How is he doing?"

As the conversation trailed over old rocks, involving comparisons of times and reasons for optimism, David felt no obligation to mention the minor attack his brother had experienced two days previously; far better to concentrate on the panic-free months prior to that. They had all but decided that Neil should qualify for Father of the Year for the foreseeable future, when the office phone began to ring. There was the tiniest pause as both men looked at each other.

"Technically," Rob groaned as he eased himself out of his chair, "I'm not even here."

The sun was warm on Rob's face as he emerged from the office, inhaling deeply and hitching his trousers up as far as his stomach would allow. Spring. Timber, needles, dust, all bathed in thin, young light. Nothing smelled or looked better in his opinion, and as he had cleared the road ahead of schedule, it was a day for whistling, he reckoned. As he bent to tie his bootlace, David appeared at the office door.

"So, what were your plans?" David asked, his frown back already.

"As a matter of fact, I was going to bag up some sawdust for … nothing that can't wait, Dave. Something wrong?"

"Can you give me a couple of hours? Rose isn't well, I should get her checked out. Way beyond time I did."

"Go, go," Rob gestured to similar effect. "The phone is mine for the day. Might even take the opportunity to mess up the office while you're gone."

But David did not smile, and all Rob could do was step back and watch him jog over to the truck. Rob, never having risen above a brisk walk in twenty-odd years, guessed that if he had a wife under thirty and son who never sat still, then he too would probably move at pace and be leaner and fitter, if not taller. Kate was a firecracker, and little Al seemed to spend most of his free time at David's elbow, from what he could see, so the man had to remain on his toes. However, David also had a mother who was failing in front of them, slowing down by the day, and occasionally Rob saw more than pride on David's face; sometimes, there was resignation in his green eyes, even settled in the creases around them.

《•》《•》《•》

If someone had told Rose, eleven years previously, that her new neighbour Jessie Morgan would one day have to carry her through The Edge's hallway, one steady step at a time, both of them trying to catch their breath, she would have severed their relationship there and then. Rose had made a career out of loving her family, she had no problem whatsoever in showering them with her attention and care, but friends were allowed only to step so far into that arena. She had opened her doors at Christmas, held barbecues in her backyard throughout the summer and had looked after a range of Peter's Lane's children over the years. But cup-of-tea chats had never delved into the truly intimate, and Rose had honed her skills at steering conversations away from any such dangerous ground, skills which had been born way back when David's world had first disintegrated. Friends were not family to Rose, they were friends, and it vexed her greatly that this particular friend had to see her so very debilitated.

But the news of Kate's continuing absence had made the pressure inside her almost unbearable, and Jessie found her seated at the kitchen table, the heel of her hand pressed into her chest, crying as she cringed in pain. Her nausea and embarrassment had not allowed Rose to answer any of Jessie's frantic enquiries; and, eventually, when she could no longer sit or stand in comfort, Jessie had picked her up and carried her through into the sitting room. Neither of them had spoken until Rose was laid flat out on the sofa, where she had finally found a position which allowed her to take in an effective breath. From there, all she had said was that it was time to get David, and Jessie had acted at once, the older woman's tone cutting out the need for further questions.

Lying in the less-than-pristine sitting room, Rose tried to control her breathing by inhaling through her nose and counting slowly to five on exhalation. Her eyes remained shut, and, although Jessie hovered, she had the sense not to bother her with questions. Instead, she babbled on about her own experiences of chest infections, lured Bertuzzi back into the kitchen with a handful of treats, and eventually just sat at the woman's shoulder in silence, watching each laboured breath. She only moved when David's truck could be heard crunching to a halt outside.

Rose listened to the woman's retreating footsteps, not yet ready to open her eyes or sit up, and in the temporary silence, chased a small dot of light around her mind instead. It was so quiet, so completely soundless in the room, that Rose stilled her own breath and felt herself begin to float. What if, against all odds, she could make the last part of this journey of hers in relative comfort? What if it could be a peaceful road, a series of small, hourly steps when pain simply walked beside her and did not crawl all over her back, weighing her down so heavily that her knees gave way and her rib cage burned? She wondered if God would give her that much, or whether he was just teasing her with the concept of it.

"Rose?" sometimes David's voice was so like Pete's her heart jumped inside her. "Ma?"

It took a couple of seconds for Rose to focus on the face in the room, the image of her husband melting away instantly as she did so. Yet she loved the figure she saw in his place, had laid her eyes on those features nearly every day of the man's life and only frowned now because of the worry she saw in his expression.

"Oh, Davey-boy," Rose did not sit up, but her voice was strong and clear. "I'm glad you're here."

Sighing, David hunkered down until his face was level with his mother's. He took her hand and shook his head slightly. "Will you please just tell me what is going on?"

"Yes, I'll tell you," replied Rose, "but don't ask me to sit up, not just yet. I'm quite the most comfortable I've been for some time. Jessie?"

Jessie, who had been planted on the hallway side of the door since David's arrival, scuttled forward.

"Jessie, thank you for getting me this far and for bringing the mail across. I would have been in a bad way without you today."

If Jessie was waiting for a "but" and further explanation, she was left disappointed; and once David had echoed his mother's words, there seemed no reason to stay. The man made a grateful face in her direction to emphasise his thanks and saw her to the door, reassuring her that he would keep her informed as soon as he found out what the hell was happening. On his return to the sitting room, David shivered and figured like most people in his position would do: light the fire and make the room comfortable and warm. Rose spotted his intention immediately and held out her hand to him.

"Come here a minute, son."

To David, his mother looked too tiny to be the woman he knew her to be. He gazed in dismay at the outstretched arm, the skin devoid of muscle merely hanging from her bones; and when he took her hand in his, it felt unreasonably light, as if a puppeteer were holding it aloft on her behalf. It caused him to bite his lip, suddenly aware that what Rose was about to say was factual and irreversible, and he did not want to hear the words. If he heard them at this quiet moment, while she lay incapacitated, there would be no room for misunderstanding, and more than anything else he wished to misunderstand her. He wanted his fears and assumptions to be wrong, and he wanted his mother's words to be ambiguous.

"Aw Dave," Rose patted the floor beside her until he sat like a teenager, his back against the sofa and knees pulled into his chest. Releasing her hand from his, she laid it gently on his head, which he accepted without comment; some moments needed no clarification, and in the silence, David finally let his shoulders relax.

"I don't want you to be angry or sad, Davey Wilder, because both of those faces make me twice as maternal and remind me that it's my job to protect you." Rose felt so full at that moment, so totally in control, that all she could do was to keep speaking. "Then I remember how strong you are, and I sit back and wonder instead how I can say the words without making them into a drama. This is not a drama, it's just the way my life has turned out, and I'm grateful for every bit of it."

David leaned his head back against Rose's arm, staring at the ceiling as he took in a strong, uninhibited breath.

"You didn't think I could help you?"

Rose let her hand slip down to his shoulder. "Shall I tell you what I thought? I thought some of us had been there before, and some of us shouldn't ever have to go there again. And I didn't want Alasdair thinking I was some invalid. I wanted him running and jumping at me like he always did, or life really wouldn't be worth … this."

David silently wiped his face, and Rose, too, felt herself falter slightly. She would have loved to have seen Alasdair as an adult, just so that once again she could marvel at how time and care could allow precious infants to grow into treasured men. She guessed he would stir hearts, as his father, grandfather and great-grandfather had all done. She smiled at last.

"I'm looking forward to being with Pete. I think I deserve his company again."

At last, David turned his face towards her. The green eyes were curious.

"You don't really believe in that, Rose?"

It was a fair enough question. Sundays at The Edge had taken the form of picnics out at the lake or treks up into the mountains, yet here was Rose ready to be reunited with her love in some other ethereal dimension.

"I get to choose what I believe in. It's the one perk of all of this, so let's not talk about it."

David slowly stretched his legs out in front of him, his boots almost shouting out their presence to the one woman who could not bear them in this place. Even on this day, when he had no conception of how the last five minutes had emerged from a relatively ordinary day, he leaned forward and began to unlace them, because it seemed the most normal of actions to take.

"Maybe you should leave them on, Dave. You'll find a number on the phone pad. I think I may need to go see somebody, for the pain."

Rose knew at once that she should not have used that particular word, for it rid her son of all further hope and doubt. He made a point of holding her gaze until she punched him gently on the arm. She shrugged her shoulders.

"You know how many Pete smoked in a day; you know what took his life. For whatever reason, I don't really care why, it's in my lungs and I can't do anything about it. I'm not saying the word, and you don't ever have to acknowledge it to Kate or Hazel. I'm old. My body has run out of steam, that's all they need to know."

David tried to swallow the information, but his mouth was too dry. His hands looked old and useless, lying against his thighs, and far too still to be helpful. But what was the next step?

"How much does Neil know?" he asked, without raising his head.

"Nothing. Dr. Hendrie, some lab technicians somewhere, and I are the only ones. Why would I tell Neil and not you?"

"Why wouldn't you tell either of us?" David threw back at her, still not looking at the woman.

"Because there was no point, when no amount of treatment would make a difference and when everyone would want to talk about it all the time. No thank you. I am not going to be cosseted or canonised, so get used to it."

David finally looked at the woman, whose adamant words did not quite tally with the frailty of the body who spoke them. She was right about one thing. It was all very familiar, this reaction to news that could not be altered. He had heard it in his first wife's telephone voice and seen it in his present wife's younger face. What he had considered nobility in both of them, now struck him as just plain desperation. David saw the thin, white hair covering his mother's skull and knew that within its walls was a brain that was nowhere ready to stop dreaming and enjoying. She may indeed be old and tired, but she was also still inspired by her family, had countless ideas for their future, and was still trying to hold it all together in the midst of it falling apart. Something suddenly fused in David's mind. He heard the connection and the fusion and wondered if age was slowing him down. How had this bypassed him?

"So this thing with Neil's … mother. It's because of this?"

Rose finally rolled herself up into a seated position, her face immobile as she concentrated on maintaining a neutral expression for David's sake. His stomach turned in response, and he jumped to his feet simply to stop the wail of despair coming out of his mouth. But Rose was not ready to stand yet, and all David could do was to prop as many cushions as he could lay his hands on behind her thin shoulders. It took her a moment or two to gather sufficient breath to speak, by which time David was already suggesting that nothing mattered enough to risk her discomfort. She looked up at him.

"You know," she said quietly "you probably think I'm doing it for Neil, or maybe even Kate who seems to like adventures, but I'm doing it for me. I want a little adventure of my own."

David shook his head, failing to see how she regarded it as an adventure.

"I always meant to meet her again. I needed to tell her how she helped complete my family, and I wanted her to know everything about him, because …" Rose swallowed as best she could, "I remember her face the last time I saw her. She was so deep in shock, and scared witless. I swore I would see her again and make her feel better."

"God in heaven," said David, suddenly, and moved over towards the fireplace. Through his thin, spring jacket, Rose watched his shoulder blades separate and his hands reach to the mantelpiece to steady himself. He hung his head. She had seen this stance before, where he looked as if he were strung up between two flogging posts, but only on two occasions. Once, when he had felt his entire family was keeping him in the dark regarding Kate, and once when Fiona had told him that she could not stay with him, that she had betrayed him in the worst possible way and that she was not capable of dealing with it. Both of these times had been critical and painful, and it surprised Rose that he was viewing this situation in the same way.

"David," she began, "I'm seeing Kate finding the woman as a really positive–"

"No!" David almost shouted, "No, it is not. What the hell is wrong with this family? Why in God's name does every piece of devastating news have to be viewed as a way of … of reuniting or compensating for something that can never be compensated for! Jesus, some things just need to be screamed at!"

And he was clearly not finished. In all the years since David had been able to string words together into sentences, Rose had never heard language like it come from his mouth. It was not all profane, although it was punctuated by some choice adjectives, but it was all bitter, thankfully directed at the world rather than at Rose. As she listened to the words being spat into the cold grate, Rose could not even argue with them. Indeed, if she had the strength she would have jumped up and matched him, expletive for expletive, throwing her arms in the air and screeching out the fear and frustration. But that had been beyond her even in the beginning, so instead she watched her son's face grow red and damp, and waited until the one sentence he had been struggling with was out in the open. In the following silence, David's breath was as shallow as her own, but for sadly different reasons; and Rose sat like a statue, seconds stretching in the room, until gradually they were both aware of the clock ticking in the hallway. Rose finally spoke, just to cover up the very obvious draining away of time.

"My, my. That little speech didn't just occur to you in the last ten minutes."

"Well, I guess you're right," David replied eventually, his voice calmer but not in any way apologetic, "but there's a chance I picked a bad moment to offload. And maybe I didn't have to … maybe I could have chosen my words better."

Rose allowed her tentative smile to develop into a chuckle. "Dave, I've never heard anything so honest in a long time. If you need to vent like that again, don't hold back– oh! Oh son."

David was kneeling beside her in a second, but even his hands taking hers and his eyes pleading close to her face could not stop the racking, burning pain in her chest. She heard him asking questions, she felt him disengage from her and heard him running through to the telephone. But it took all of her presence of mind to speak when he at last came back into the room.

"I wanted Kate home today," gasped Rose. "I wanted to hear everything she had to say, right here in this house. But I don't think I can stay here any longer."

David wiped the excess moisture from his mouth. "I called the number. I can take you right this minute, if you think the SUV is comfortable enough."

As Rose edged herself forward, her loose dress bunching up underneath her, she concentrated all of her efforts on looking at David's face and pursing her lips to keep her face frown-free. By looking at her son, she was able to ignore the room she was leaving. She managed to keep her eyes on her feet as he shuffled her away from the furniture and the photos and the hallmarks of their lives. But she was not so lucky in the wide hallway. David and Kate had redecorated the house throughout since their wedding, but they had not touched the staircase. The seasoned oak was too beautiful to even strip back, and Kate liked the way the sheen complemented the grandeur of the space. Pete had treated and cared for that wood on an annual basis, and Rose had chosen the design of the spindles. It was their staircase, and she was unable to divert her eyes and keep her composure. By the time David had helped her over the threshold into the redesigned, overly modern kitchen, Rose was weeping from her very heart.

"Do you have any pills here?" David croaked, holding her to his side as if she were a taller than average ragdoll.

"In my purse," she whispered. "But I'm not ..."

In a way it was the kindest thing, oblivion taking over. In one fading moment, the physical pain of her diseased lungs and the emotional grief of bidding farewell to her home let her feel nothing but David's arm around her waist. When she awoke again, her environment was white and sterile and mercifully devoid of memories.

CHAPTER 24

Vancouver Island

Vancouver International Airport was bright and airy, and Kate felt her face burn with anticipation. Winnie, hovering at her elbow, also seemed alert to the point of agitation, and Kate grinned her easiest grin at the woman, before turning it towards the whole of the crowded terminal. She had such a soft spot for this particular place, where the sunlight through the glass walls threatened to blind the unwary, but also had the power to warm many a weary, travel-sick heart. Many years previously, David had held her tightly against him and instilled in her a hope that she had never lost: the hope that she would always belong to him. The sights and sounds still had the power to make her insides quiver, and, apparently, her face flush with pleasure.

Yet Kate had imposed the delay on their reunion herself, by agreeing to wait until she and Winnie could travel together. The older woman had insisted on paying for the new seats, citing that she had been saving all her life for this particular journey and that if Kate argued, she would risk disrupting the way she viewed the trip. Kate had no argument, especially since Beth and Hazel were delighted by her extended stay and at the opportunity of hearing Winnie's story. Kate, in turn, had spent most of the time furnishing the woman with details, some intricate and personal, some merely factual and informative. To her credit, Winnie had wanted to hear everything, or at least Kate's take on it, and not simply the aspects which touched on Neil. But it had to be acknowledged that her features only became truly alive when the younger woman talked about her father.

"Andie's really smart," Kate had informed, as the aeroplane seats had tried their best to allow them to relax. "I do a bit of sewing for her, and she's so different at work compared to home. At work, she's completely independent and really in control. Finds clients, sells herself, speaks on the phone while wandering about, being ... organised. Then she comes home and lets those babies crawl all over her, lets them help with the cooking and stuff and uses a totally different voice. Neil has followed her lead and ... he touches people now."

Winnie had wiped her mouth and asked to look once again at the photos of Neil's lover. She continued to wear her black hair long, but it did not obscure her features, and Winnie thought her babies would have been angelic, as her two inherited daughters appeared to be. Kate caught her studying the family of four.

"Jayney worked for Andie in her shop. Sophie has her looks without a doubt." Kate had heaved a sigh into the cabin and lowered her head slightly. "Some things are just woefully unfair."

Winnie had not been able to argue with that particular statement and had been about to add weight to it, when Kate had turned her whole body towards her with a more positive expression.

"But Neil adores them and I think it's mutual. Tell you what, Winnie. The Wilder men are nothing if not resilient. Both of them ending up with young families later than was really necessary, and yet they seem to be enjoying it all. How are you feeling about meeting him?"

Kate's sudden change of tack had stalled Winnie for merely a second. "As soon as he's given his permission, I'll tell you exactly how I feel. But I don't want anybody putting pressure on him, so in the meantime, I'll keep that to myself."

Kate had eventually stopped trying to think of ways of getting the far more astute woman to admit to her feelings and turned the conversation to her recollections of her own mother. It had been an odd journey of thoughts. Whilst she was alive, Kate had completely defended every one of Fiona's actions; but this had not merely shifted as the truth had come to light, but had blurred as Kate's understanding of love had developed. Mistakes were made by many people in many different ways, and all a person could really do was to try to reconcile all those concerned with their individual reactions. She had passed through a period of disbelieving despair at the woman, unable to forgive what she had done, until she had accepted that she had been younger and much weaker willed back then. Yet how that creature had managed to break two good men and destroy an entire generation was still beyond her understanding. She had toyed with the idea of telling this to Winnie, but as the woman had said herself, perhaps it was better to keep things close for the moment. After all, Fiona had given Kate everything, including her desire to make things better for everyone.

As both women awaited the arrival of their baggage, Kate dialled David's mobile number, and as soon as it was ringing, put her arm through Winnie's and did a little dance on the balls of her feet.

"Oh, man," Kate giggled. "I'm not sure what I'm more excited about. Seeing Dave again or seeing if he recognises– David! I'm back. I'll be out as soon as this bloody conveyor belt thing coughs up my rucksack!"

Winnie could not help but grin as Kate's voice was the loudest in the vicinity, then grinned ever wider as her ears became aware of more and more Canadian accents on the air. So many years had passed, with only the soft tones of her father to remind her of this country; and even when it would have been quite safe, when she could have visited the eastern arm of her family and seen sights which were not familiar, she had not allowed herself to return. But she had made the journey, and in the days before her, she would lay eyes on the trees, the river, the lakes and the mountains of her childhood. She was still grinning as Kate removed her arm from hers and moved away from her. The girl was most definitely smiling no longer.

"But, you said she was comfortable," Kate wandered to the moving belt and hooked the strap of her rucksack onto her arm. When she turned to alert Winnie to the arrival of the bags, her eyes were black and her forehead creased. Winnie retrieved her suitcase and busied herself with trying to release the pulling handle; Kate was clearly not happy and she felt her euphoria dip slightly. Her suitcase sorted, she had no choice but to look up and found Kate's whole face was distressed.

"Oh, okay, well, that's that then. I should have come back on Monday, I'm sorry. So, what about a ... what?" Kate dropped her arm and the rucksack, so tightly packed that every seam was straining, rolled away from her slightly. Kate covered her free ear with her palm and very obviously turned away from the older woman. "What did you say?"

Winnie glanced at her watch. Perhaps this was an opportune moment to call her daughter, before the meeting with David took over the rest of their day. She had begun to fish in her hold-all for the knitted phone case when she saw Kate throw her free hand in the air, then pull her rucksack a few feet across the tiles. Winnie no longer pretended to ignore the scene and followed the retreating figure. Before she had reached her side, however, Kate had slowed to a halt, and Winnie had to side-step so as not to fall over baggage. The girl looked positively white, with only the tips of her cheekbones flushed red. This motley appearance did not look good on her youthful face; but before Winnie could enquire, Kate desperately shook her head in her direction, her eyes filling with panic-laden tears. Winnie stood back, but did not move her eyes away. Once, Kate felt her brow and then closed her eyes. In the next moment, she cleared her throat and swallowed.

"You're right," she nodded slowly. "You're completely right and I've arsed it up again. It just seemed better to travel together, so that Rose would be surprised, and I didn't think she would still be in hospital! But I can handle it, I'll do it. It'll be fine. See you later."

Winnie watched Kate kill the phone call and then take a moment to switch the phone off completely. One tear fell onto the plastic cover before she swiped it away and lifted her face. Was that guilt, fear or embarrassment written on her face? Her voice suggested all three.

"I really need a cup of coffee," she began. "Shall we get these bags through and try to find a seat?"

Ten minutes later, Winnie watched as Kate failed to relax in her chair. The girl stirred the mug of cappuccino until all the froth dissipated, and still no explanation was forthcoming. As Winnie opened her mouth, however, Kate's voice broke the silence.

"David can't collect us. Rose is still in hospital and he can't leave her."

"Oh," Winnie frowned. "So, is Rose very poorly?"

Kate shrugged her shoulders. "She's had this chesty thing since Christmas. I suppose she wasn't brilliant before I left, but she was desperate for me to find you, and I had to go to the christening. I had to leave her. Ah, shit."

"So, she's in the best place?" It was the first time Kate had heard the Canadian inflection in Winnie's words, and she almost smiled at how little time it had taken for the woman to make use of it. But it was not the moment to smile.

"Yes, she is, and I'm glad she is. But it makes the rest of it kind of awkward. Well, not kind of, bloody awkward, and I'm really, really sorry."

"Hey," soothed Winnie, not quite finding the courage to squeeze Kate's hand. "I'm sure we can find somewhere to stay the night. Or we could look at public transport. We might get halfway today."

Kate looked at her watch and groaned, pushing her coffee away untouched and laying her head on her folded arms. Winnie, not recognising this as a typical move on Kate's part, sat dumbfounded. She sipped at her tea, wondering if she was expected to take charge of this, whatever this was. Around her, the world continued at pace, family meeting family and embracing, suited gents running for the best taxi cab and others simply standing watching, searching, waiting. There was a sniff from beneath the folded arms and then Kate was hunting for a tissue and biting her lip.

"Oh, God above," she sighed. "Dave was right. In fact, he's right more times than I am, and I think I'm always right. But this time, there's no argument. It's worrying, this habit of mine."

"Habit?" Winnie enquired.

"Habit of landing myself– and sometimes others– in situations that are not always ... helpful or even endurable. Oh, Winnie, don't get mad. Neil is coming to pick us up. He offered and David accepted the offer."

Winnie felt both of her legs immediately start to tingle, and the shock must have registered on her face because Kate immediately screwed her eyes shut and began to babble.

"I know, it's a bloody cosmic joke. I'd like to know why I was allowed to get so far with this and then have it end in tears. I mean, I found you straight away, we got on with each other pretty much immediately, and then we managed to get this flight. Now, it's all going to crap and we've got, I reckon, about half an hour to get used to this. I'm so, so sorry. Is there anything– ?"

"I'll book into a hotel," Winnie's voice was low and assured. "In fact, I'll go immediately. The sooner the better."

Kate watched her stand, about to abandon her, and did not like the darkness of her features. She had truly messed up this time. Winnie had pulled her arms into her coat and zipped up her handbag before Kate had even joined her on her feet, her control slipping further from her by the second. What should she do here? How was it going to be from this moment on?

"Oh, don't!" cried Kate. "Please, just sit for a minute. I'm sure this will be fine."

"I won't just sit here, Kate. It's not fair on him," Winnie was adamant. "I can guarantee that you will not come out of this unscathed if it goes badly, so for your sake, I'm–"

"Kate Wilder! Is that what you call a Scottish tan, or have you just not washed in three weeks?"

Winnie sat immediately, staring at the table in front of her, her face the colour of faded brick; and Kate for the first time in her entire life felt her heart sink at that particular, jovial voice reaching her ears across the refreshment tables. Neil was early.

"Ah, curses, no," groaned Kate, but to ignore the man was more than she could do. He had, yet again, come to her rescue. Yet how would he ever be prepared for what was about to happen? Kate turned her head, saw the man's grin making its way towards her at no great speed, and in panic she crossed the ground to meet him. She tried to smile, but even an upturned mouth could not compensate for the lack of colour on her face. He grimaced as he punched her arm in greeting.

"You okay, there?" he tipped his head low, trying to read her face. "Are you sick?"

It was true, Kate had only felt nausea on this scale whilst pregnant, but the lurching of her insides was nothing compared to the thought of making this particular man uncomfortable or upset. She felt her nostrils flaring as the tears came and could hardly stand the compassion which crossed his face at their appearance. But she had to rescue this, and quickly.

"I'm fine," she sniffed and put one arm around the man's neck in as much of a hug as she thought he might like. The only thing to be happy about at that moment in time was that he did not flinch in the slightest. He was wiry, like David, but smelled only of staining oil and just for a second, for one tiny period in time, God sent too much Kate's way. She was going to cause this man distress, just as she was causing his mother distress, and David was not there to stand beside her. Kate could feel Neil's hand on her head and then his old flannel jacket was damp with her tears, and embarrassment was added to the mix.

"God, Kate," Neil's voice remained cheery, "is it jet lag? What the hell?"

Kate stood back and wiped her face with her sleeve, but could not look anywhere but at her feet. "Sorry," she sighed. "I thought Dave and Ally would be here, and I really, really wanted to see them. Then I get his phone call about Rose and ... and–"

"And you ended up with me instead," she could hear the grin in his voice. "Well, I guess I'd be pretty gutted, too."

When Kate looked up, intent on making sure he was not offended, she found that his eyes were focussed beyond the immediate area.

"You fancy another coffee? I need a break."

Before Kate could speak, Neil had moved towards the table which boasted only two half-empty cups and her propped up rucksack. She looked around her. There was a hankie next to one of the cups, but not one sign of Winnie. Kate barely managed to stop herself from gaping at the woman's absence and in the next moment was taking her seat once more. It was still warm, but if Neil noticed anything similar about his, he did not say anything.

"But hey, I mean it," he stated. "You look a bit peaky. Have you eaten?"

Kate could not remember the last time she had opened her mouth and spouted such inane rubbish whilst trying to figure out what the hell she should be doing. Less than an hour previously, Winnie and she had been anticipating David's grin and more, and her charge had now disappeared. Her heart was fluttering, her eyes flitting back and forth across the café tables and chairs, and all she could do was gibber on about aeroplane food and the songs she had listened to mid-Atlantic.

"They were on a loop, and not all of them were in English. French some of them, and honestly I don't care if I never hear even one of them again. But yes, if you want to eat, I could happily eat a small pachyderm. I don't mind sitting for a while. What do you fancy?"

《•》《•》《•》

From her seat, Winnie recognised that the cramp threatening her right calf was probably stress induced, and so she forced herself to calm her nerves and massaged it the best she could through her trousers; the last thing she needed was for the present company to watch her hop about in agony, clutching tables and scaring the rest of the clientele. She forced herself to look around her, hoping that the blandness of her fellow travellers' less significant days would rub off on her. It was only partially successful.

She assumed the couple opposite her were on their outward journey. They were dressed smartly in outdoor gear, exhibiting none of the crumpled edges or saggy features of the newly arrived. A toddler strapped into a high chair at the next table had fallen asleep upright, as her parents held hands and used the few moments of peace to catch up on their lives. Winnie had an idea that the man in the superfluous sunglasses and baseball cap may be a celebrity, as his face was familiar. Either that or he was nursing a hangover. In her eyes, however, they all seemed strangely beige. There was only one person in the entire area who shone brightly, in spite of the dark green checked shirt and navy jeans he wore.

Kate was unaware that she was still in the vicinity, and Winnie tried to use the time wisely, making herself take hold of her anxiety and shake it until it dissolved into wonder. This adult male, engaging in conversation with his daughter, was mesmerising. She had known he was tall, but had failed to appreciate anything much more than that. Yet here it was, all of it in front of her eyes: fair hair, blue eyes, his father's grin, hands which moved restlessly over his lean face and through his hair at regular intervals. He was still muscular, very probably fit, but best of all, he clearly cared for the girl who sat across the table from him. Winnie could see from her arm movements that Kate was talking at speed as she cleared her plate of all food, yet she could do nothing but study her son. At that particular moment, Kate's chatter was irrelevant. Once, Neil caught her eye, but thankfully he continued to chew and his gaze moved on just as quickly, allowing her to recover in peace.

Winnie thought of Emma, trying to find the odd facial similarity in Neil, but she recognised nothing at this distance. As her daughter's name and face entered her mind, however, she suddenly felt a little desolate and lonely. Somehow, probably due to the gap between pregnancies, Winnie had dealt admirably with the emotions involved in giving birth to Emma. And after the initial surprise at surviving it, she had thrown off the career cloak for a decade and taken everything that the child had to offer her. In Emma's case, she had deserved to be happy, had been entitled to take pleasure in her life, and she had done so with gusto.

But the fact remained that the girl who had partially glued her maternal soul back together knew nothing about her half-brother. She had assumed herself unique in the eyes of her mother, and yet she was not the only one who had tugged at her heart; she had not even been the first to do so. It pained Winnie that the joy she felt at seeing and acknowledging this man might hurt her relationship with Em. The truth remained, however. The first being to open her soul was sitting within shouting distance of her at that very moment, and the attachment was still there. Why had she not just explained it all already and invited Emma along? She, too, could be watching the man in wonder. Instead, the girl was wondering why on earth her mother had chosen this particular moment to make a journey home.

Neil leaned forward in his chair, the lines at his eyes folding into creases as he spoke.

"Hey, don't react, but that lady you were talking to earlier? She keeps looking over here. Were you in the middle of a conversation or something?"

Neil watched Kate flick her head in the direction he was looking, in spite of his request to do no such thing, and he saw the connection in their eyes before the woman once more dropped her head and touched her lower leg. Kate did not turn back to him for at least another three seconds, by which time a certain desperate look was erasing itself from her face. This was becoming wearisome, and Neil raised his eyebrows to signify this situation. Kate spoke immediately.

"Oh, I wondered where she'd gone. It's actually quite funny," Kate's neck was a livid red, yet she did not even pause to wonder at how easily the lies were flowing from her mouth. "I met her at the carousel, her suitcase was hooked onto my rucksack strap."

Neil shrugged as she stopped to inhale, so she followed it up with what she prayed sounded like an authentic statement.

"Aye, she's visiting family in Duncan, who would have believed it, and I was going to ask David if she could have a lift; but I'm sure she'll be able to find her own way back. I don't think she's in any hurry."

Neil let his eyes land on the woman in question. She seemed enthralled by the contents of her shoulder bag, but suddenly Kate was blocking his view as she stood, deliberately engaging his vision.

"I'm just going to tell her that there's been a change of plan. It's fine. I'm pretty sure it'll be okay."

Neil sat back and stretched his right leg out to the side of the table. He guessed that his relationship with Kate would never be as close as if he had sung her lullabies or driven her to hockey practice, her teenage hair flying behind her as she slammed shut the door of his truck; but he liked to think that they were open with each other. Today, she was definitely on edge, and he was missing her usual effort to put him at ease. In the space of ten minutes, he had witnessed tears, agitation and a bizarre notion that she had an obligation to an acquaintance of mere minutes. He rubbed his thumb under his chin as he watched Kate pick her way through the tables, immobile until he was forced to move his leg out of the way of the young girl clearing away cups. Three weeks in the country of Kate's birth did not seem to have relaxed her in any way.

As he continued to caress the bristles under his chin, Neil was aware that his features had settled on a frown in spite of his reunion with Kate, and all this time he had been looking for her to lift his spirits. He had persuaded his brother that he should come, simply so that he could focus on something other than Rose's frail chest rising and falling; and David, having descended into a truly sinister level of calm, had taken him up on the offer without hesitation.

Now, after four hours behind a wheel trying to figure out how Rose had pulled the wool over their eyes for so long, of trying to imagine how her active mind was reacting to her failing body and with the prospect of Kate's return the only ray of light amidst it all, he was beginning to feel seriously tired. The open road had long since lost its appeal, and for the first time ever, he was experiencing the frustration of being pulled simultaneously by the generation above and beneath him. It was exhausting and induced nothing but guilt at all turns. There was his beloved mother struggling to fill her lungs, yet he had run to the aid of his adult daughter because the thought of her stranded made him uneasy. When she was clearly out of sorts and strangely nervy, he could think only of Rose and the tedious road he had to travel to see her again. Neil stood and made his way to Kate.

"Hi," he announced his arrival, "everything okay?"

"Absolutely," grinned Kate, her neck throbbing, "I was just saying to ... Mrs, em ..."

"Port," provided Winnie, suddenly standing and extending her hand.

Kate watched as the couple made contact and, unusually, could think of no way of salvaging normality, although only she seemed to be disturbed by this.

"Pleased to meet you," Neil's face was pleasantly neutral, before he looked back at Kate. "Look, if Mrs Port doesn't mind the odd stray shoe or dog hair, she's welcome to a ride back down the road. But if you're finished eating, Kate, we've got a long journey."

Kate looked from Neil to Winnie, allowing no thoughts to form. "Erm ..."

"That is very kind of you," Winnie's voice was clear, her mixture of accents intriguing. "But I wonder if you see it as an imposition. I'm perfectly capable of making my own way, if it's too much."

Neil studied the older woman for what Kate perceived as far too long a time, and she could only giggle with relief when he finally let his facial muscles relax.

"It's not a problem," Neil assured her, then "Is this your suitcase?" Without awaiting an answer, he picked up the suitcase and added, "Kate doesn't need a hand, she's like a little pack horse. I've seen her carry a fully grown Labrador on her back before."

At this, Kate, her face gradually ceasing to radiate heat, hauled her baggage into her arms and allowed herself a weak smile.

"This is my dad, by the way," she spoke quietly to Winnie, sharing the smallest of apologies at the conspiracy with her eyes. "As you can see, he's one of the good guys."

As all three moved away, Neil looking ridiculous carrying a beige suitcase as if it weighed no more than a paper bag and Winnie holding her head high in his wake, Kate finally took on board the magnitude of her misjudgment. Her plan had not been foolproof, too much had been left to chance, and yet she had blithely gone ahead with it anyway. And the reunion, for those who had been aware that it was such a thing, had been an awkward, potentially dangerous anti-climax. Due to the change of venue, Neil was being deceived, and she risked his absolute fury, or worse, devastation. Also, Winnie was almost certainly as disappointed and vexed as Rose herself would be. Rose. Kate once more felt sick to the stomach.

"So, Neil?" Kate raised the level of her voice, "How bad is she?"

The man barely turned his head. "She's not great," he replied, and quickened his pace.

CHAPTER 25

Vancouver Island

To the relief of all three generations, Winnie had insisted on sitting in the back of Neil's vehicle; and within thirty minutes of leaving the city's boundary, she had closed her eyes and feigned sleep, a state she remained in for the rest of the journey. It was the only way she had been able to disengage herself from the situation, even if mentally she had stayed on the verge of combustion. "Years," she had thought, "years of wondering and imagining." Yet in the space of less than two weeks, her solid existence had been cracked, then split open; and she was not even trying to gather the fragments together yet, because she remained intrigued by how its demise had come about.

The instigator of it all had sat directly in front of her for the last few hours, and in spite of their current little conspiracy, they remained on the outskirts of any real intimacy. The perfume which her granddaughter continually wore was becoming so familiar to her that it was almost lost on the air; but she was aware of it when Kate opened her window for a few seconds, and she had breathed it in while the girl and her father had talked, wondering how this journey was going to end.

"Dave was a bit short on the phone earlier," Kate had stated at one point, "How is he doing?"

At Neil's hesitation, Winnie had wondered if he had been assessing her conscious state before replying; some things were perhaps too personal to say in front of strangers. The truth was, she had no interest in the contents of his speech, she had simply liked to hear the sound of his voice. It had added a sole layer of pleasure to the little mound of worry and nerves which were growing with each mile covered, and, behind her closed eyelids, Winnie had let herself enjoy the soft vowels and deep tone. But the hum of the road disappearing beneath them had also signified the passing of time, and soon she would have to face the man and watch as his expression changed. Until that point, his expressions had been reasonably open, certainly only superficially interested in her as a human. However, there was a possibility that it might alter for the worse, that it might even take place that day, and Winnie had known that the only way to retrieve some kind of hope was for her to speak to Rose first. Alone.

Kate was floundering, losing grip on the situation, with only the ability to relate semi-amusing stories of her Scottish trip to maintain her dignity. If Neil could sense her reticence, he had either chosen to ignore it or had put it down to worry about Rose, David or her son. But in fact she was developing an ever-increasing nausea inside which always accompanied anxiety. It had proved a quicker trip than she had imagined, and Winnie sat upright in the back seat, making a show of stretching until Kate caught her eye.

"Heaven help me," apologised Winnie, "I'm so rude. Just please say that I didn't snore."

"You didn't snore," Kate assured, "and we're very nearly there. We're going straight to the hospital. I hope that's okay with you."

Winnie began to confirm that it was all perfectly fine, but her words were lost as Kate's phone rang out into the cab. Winnie's words trailed off, and she gathered her belongings instead.

"Hi, Dave," Kate said loudly. "Seriously, we're here. Neil has just pulled into the car park. Great, we'll meet you at the door."

With Neil trying to locate a space where the truck would fit, Kate snapped shut her mobile and turned back to Winnie.

"Well," Kate tried to look optimistic. "It's been a long road home."

"Yes," agreed Winnie, then to Neil, "and I appreciate you getting me this far, Mr Wilder. Thank you so much."

"I have to say," Neil replied, "I think you might be the quietest hitchhiker on the planet."

Neil pulled on the hand brake and turned to grin at the woman. It was only a grin, but it tightened the air in the cab, and Kate sat on the very edge of disintegration. Winnie, however, did not pause, hauling her coat onto her back and reaching for the door handle instead.

"I'll call my friend from here," she replied, but all hopes of a quick escape were thwarted by an unexpectedly locked door. Her face switched instantly to a truly horrified frown.

"Child lock, sorry," Neil groaned and jumped from the cab. There was the tiniest intake of breath from Winnie as he did so, and Kate leaned over the seat.

"It's fine," she urged, as the door finally opened.

"Here," said Neil in turn, offering his hand. "It's a bit of a step down."

Kate could take the heat under her skin no longer. Fresh air, that's what she needed, not to be cringing against the pressure and mortification of this self-initiated situation. Outside, the air sprayed her with a gust of light rain, and she unzipped her jacket, desperate to cool down. Her relief was short-lived, however, as she watched Neil point Winnie towards the main entrance of the hospital and began to accompany her along the way, suitcase in hand. Kate gaped at them through the rising wind and rain as they all picked up pace, and there stood David on the other side of the glass, illuminated for all to see. But, of course. Of course this was going to end in the worst, most awkward manner. How could it possibly go otherwise? Kate was suddenly furious, although unsure at whom, and she was damned if she was going to let the control slip away entirely. She had set them all up, she owed them her best time and effort; and if she had to face individual versions of disappointment and disbelief, then at least the shocking words would come from her own mouth. She lifted her feet and sprinted past them.

David hovered inside the foyer door. Whatever she had expected to see on her return, it was not the drawn face or dull eyes which remained even as she arrived at his side. All he did was open his arms and hold her against him. Her own arms had not made it around his neck, and as he was barely allowing her to breathe; she was forced to stand awkwardly, clamped to his waist instead.

"Where have you been?" he shuddered into her hair, his voice bringing one more thud of anxiety to her, but the smell of him neutralised it immediately.

"The whole thing just took off," Kate tried to explain. "I'm sorry. How is Rose?"

At last David released her, but when she looked up into his pale face, he was staring past her at the two people shaking rain from their clothes as they crossed the threshold. His expression had hardened.

Kate felt sick. "He doesn't know who she is," she whispered. "But I'll sort it. Let me sort it."

Looking back, all Kate could remember of that particular instant was Winnie's raised eyebrows as she locked onto David's gaze. It was fair enough. He was, after all, the only one amongst them who had known the younger version of the woman, and whilst the other two were connected by blood, he must have felt like the only true support to her right then. At least that is what Kate imagined as Winnie seated herself and took in her surroundings. What David saw was an added complication with a familiarly shaped face, and what dismayed him the most was Neil's ignorance of it. He stood away from Kate as his brother came towards him.

"So, what's the latest?" said the younger man.

David tried not to see the optimism in Neil's step, but it was definitely there, and somehow he had to dispel it quickly. He shook his head, opened his mouth to speak, then closed it again, lost for words. Only when Neil's eyes crinkled up tightly did they come out at last.

"You two should go up there. Andie needs a break."

"Andie's here too?" Kate asked, surprised.

"Yes. Go on. I need to call Jessie, see if the kids can stay the night with them. It won't be a problem."

Neil began to move away, but Kate grabbed his arm and halted him immediately. She stared at David's stony face and her eyes were suddenly full of water.

"You look awful, what's wrong?" Kate's voice was a tiny echo in the cavernous foyer. "We … can't be losing her. We're not, are we?"

David looked down at his wife, for the first time ever unwilling to wipe the fear from her face. She had been absent for three weeks, with no conception that the woman was dying. He almost envied her innocence. "She's not coming home, Kate. She's waiting for you two."

"She has a cold," Kate argued, feebly.

"She has lung cancer," David softened his voice as much as he was able, which was not much at all. "Just go. Hurry up."

As Kate stood immobile, her eyes morphing from disbelief to despair, Neil took a step forward and hissed at his brother. "Shit, Dave. We didn't know, how was Kate supposed to?"

Kate could not take her eyes off the grey face that belonged to her husband, the stubbly hair above his lip beaded in the stark lighting. He looked worn out, his clothes hanging on his frame rather than dressing it, and it seemed inconceivable that he was looking at her through cool, hard eyes. Her own limbs seem paralysed, and she had no idea what to do next. David finally looked at his brother.

"If she'd been here, she would have known," he said. Without clarifying this to either of them, he bit his lip and then spoke to Kate specifically. "This is happening. Nothing else matters right now."

Until that moment, Kate had never really understood what it felt like to be small, yet in the space of three seconds, she saw herself as the smallest speck of humanity, a liability, an irritant with the ability to hinder and annoy, and it caused her jaw to slacken. She felt tiny beside these two taller, older men, with not a scrap of argument to put forward in her defence or to raise her to their level. Her face was burning, the surface of the floor shining back at her as she fought for thoughts to put into words, but nothing could get past the aching golf ball in her throat. Not even an apology. In the next second, Neil had grabbed her hand and was hauling her away from David's steely presence. She looked back once as she tripped after Neil, and then they were both gone.

It was impossibly quiet in the foyer as David rubbed his forehead, trying to ease the pain inside his skull. Or perhaps the sounds and activities had been sucked from his mind alone, but he was too tired to open his eyes to investigate and only did so when he felt a hand on his elbow. Freddie Hunter had Kate's eyes, set in a far more mature and empathetic face, yet it still caused hopeless shame to creep over him. Kate had not deserved anything he had said to her, but he had not been able to stop the sentiments spilling out. Freddie moved next to him with not even a hint of reproach in those eyes, which made him think of Rose and her endless understanding. It was too much.

"Davey Wilder," Winnie barely spoke as David's eyes screwed tight shut. "Let's sit."

As David moved across to the nearest seat, and Neil pulled Kate through yet another sanitised corridor, Alasdair Wilder lay curled as comfortable as possible on a low Z-bed, wishing with all his might that Sophie would stop talking. Earlier, he had sat picking at the food on a very shiny plate. Beside him at the table had sat Sophie, although she had to be propped on two cushions to reach, and poor Abbie had looked ridiculous in a plastic high chair. But, as ever, his smallest cousin had not seemed to care about anything so embarrassing and had concentrated instead on picking out mushrooms from her sauce and eating them before moving on to the carrots. Sophie, on the other hand, had shovelled her food in like she hadn't tasted meat in a week, little trails of gravy all around her mouth as she had talked and talked and talked. The kitchen belonging to Jessie Morgan, long free of her own children, had a glass table, and rather than eating, Alasdair had spent most of his time gazing past his plate at his own two feet. His socks had been hand-knitted and dark blue, but not nearly as fancy as those Granma Rose had given him last Christmas. They had been Canucks socks, his pride and joy, and he had really wished that Bert had managed to merely nurse them instead of chewing them to death.

"Would you like some milk, Al?" Jessie had asked at one point, wiping Sophie's face.

Milk had seemed quite a nice idea. "Yes, please."

"Soooo," Jessie had drawled, for no apparent reason that Alasdair had been able to see, "I was thinking that you might all like to sleep in the same room, keep each other company while your moms and dads are at the hospital."

"My mom is flying home today," Alasdair had offered.

"She's already here, she's on her way to meet your daddy."

"Okay," he had replied, and for the first time in three days, Alasdair had felt his insides begin to ease off and relax. Mom was home, well nearly. Bert would be over the moon to see her, and would probably sprinkle the kitchen in her excitement, even though she had not done so for weeks. He had smiled. "Okay."

After dinner, the girls had been ushered into the bath while Alasdair had pulled on his boots and let Bertuzzi sniff around in the woods for as long as she had wanted. Leaning against Jessie's fence, he had looked over at his granma's house. It had been black and bulky, quite scary without a light on, and had seemed a bit like a straight-edged lump of coal to his eyes. He had wondered if Jessie would let him go and sleep there on his own instead of with the "Noisy Sisters," but then had remembered that the heating system made an odd roaring sound when it came on, and he would rather hear Sophie's chatter than a machine breathing in an empty house. He had liked the house, but not that much if Granma Rose wasn't there.

"Alasdair!" Jessie had called from the house, "Your turn!"

Mercifully, the woman had not waited for him to respond, nor had she seen his suddenly flushed face in the darkness. Surely Jessie had not meant that he, too, was to have a bath? In her house. When he had no idea where the towels were kept and when his pyjamas were still at home. For the first time since his mom had been gone, Alasdair had felt like seriously crying; but he had not possessed a tissue, and he could not have faced any concerned questions about his snotty nose. Sophie would pounce on him, probably laugh and then go all wide-eyed when he didn't join in. Instead, he had whistled for Bertuzzi and shuffled back inside.

After Jessie had quietly slipped his pyjamas through a crack in the bathroom door and he was at last tucked beneath a duvet on an ancient Z-bed, he felt warm and tired enough to fall off to sleep. But Sophie had other ideas. She seemed to have an entire toy box packed into her little pink rucksack, and one by one she was pulling out individual "activities," assessing what Alasdair felt would be the most fun, without him actually speaking. Abbie was lying in the other twin bed, trying to braid her own hair, and obviously not interested in anything but doing so; and Alasdair wondered if Abbie was in fact his favourite cousin. He flopped back against his pillow, tucked his chin under the duvet, and finally Sophie got the message.

"What's wrong?" Sophie asked, truly not understanding how the boy could be so dull when they were all together in a strange and exciting place.

"Don't want to play anything."

Sophie looked over at Abbie to see if this state of affairs made any more sense to her, but her sister's eyes were entirely shut, and, as if to draw all discussion to a permanent close, Alasdair turned away from Sophie and let out a long breath. Although stalled in her mission to make this bonus of a night special, she did not immediately try to argue the case. Ally was brilliant, but sometimes he just stopped being. Sophie wondered if other boys were like that, as Abbie certainly was not. Abbie could be persuaded to take part in everything, except when she was asleep, of course. But with their mom and dad still a car journey away, and both of her allies unwilling to keep her spirits up, Sophie surprised herself by letting it be. Instead, she eased back on the bed and curled herself onto her side. Some of the trinkets and puzzles she had unloaded rolled and thudded onto the carpet, but her rucksack remained firmly clutched in her folded arms.

The room had once belonged to Adam Morgan. It still had both his childhood and young adulthood stamped on it, in an interesting mix. There were some triangles painted on one wall in lots of different colours, framing a noticeboard overflowing with cuttings and photographs. The wall opposite Sophie's bed was completely cleared; Jessie had taken framed posters down and stacked them, subjects towards the wall, but not before Sophie had caught sight of the last one, which looked like a big insect with water dripping from it. The other wall just had a window and a TV on a corner shelf, and the wall behind her head was decorated with blue and white badges, which Al had said belonged to a soccer team who wore white hats. To Sophie, the room was as uninteresting as her present company, and after a moment or two, she unzipped the front pocket of her rucksack and pulled out her matching pink wallet. She switched one of the bedside lights back on, cringing against possible objections, but none came. From inside her wallet she pulled several photographs and lined them up in front of her. Mom and Dad would be back soon, and in the meantime, she would be reassured by their smiling faces.

The middle photo was creased down the centre, and as she tried to straighten it, Sophie saw that it was the photo of Alasdair's christening. She studied it even closer as she remembered the day she had tried to ask her mom about Kate. Just for a moment Sophie had thought she was getting somewhere. She had shown her the photo and told her that Kate had called her dad by the same name. She had then wondered what Mom thought that meant and had smiled at her so warmly that the woman had surely been bound to tell her. Mom had asked her what she had heard, giving every impression that there was indeed news to be had; but when Sophie told her the whole story, she had rubbed noses with her and said, "Last time I looked, you were five, not eight." It had been really disappointing.

"Why'd you put the light on again?" muttered Alasdair.

"I'm looking at my pictures. I love pictures."

"You can't draw," Alasdair observed, but not unkindly.

"Not those kinds of pictures. Photo pictures. Look, this is you."

Alasdair had seen the photo before, and since it really could have been any baby in the world, he remained annoyingly unimpressed. Sophie began to lose all hope.

"Your mom calls my dad 'Dad' sometimes," she stated quickly. "Maybe her dad looks just like him."

Alasdair barely lifted his head. "She doesn't have a dad."

Sophie could have cried. She had been saving this piece of information for months now, trusting that when she had a chance to use it, it would prove at least interesting enough to talk about. Maybe she hadn't made it clear enough. Abbie had snorted, sneezed and then settled on her side before Sophie spoke again.

"Well, she calls him dad. Just like I do. And he's going to tell me a story about it when I'm eight. Then I'll tell you."

"Okay," replied Alasdair and that was the end of that.

《•》《•》《•》

Kate knew that the head of white hair belonged to her mother-in-law, but the face of the woman had changed in the saddest of ways, and in less than three weeks. She had managed not to gasp out loud at the sight, but she had been unable to stop the shock crawling all over her face as she had stood, taking in the brightness, the tubes and the pastel shades. The atmosphere was overwhelming– warm air tainted with disinfectant and breathless decay, a combination she could barely stomach. But this was Rose, and she had neglected this woman for far too long. As Kate edged past the tubes and machinery which were keeping her mother-in-law from slipping away, Andie stood slowly, unfolding her stiff legs from under her chair, and touched Kate's shoulder as she retreated. As ever, she ended up sharing Neil's air and looked totally at home there, if not at ease.

"Rose?" Kate spoke softly, trying to find the woman's hand amongst the folds of her sheets. "It's Kate."

When there was no movement, Kate leaned over until her own overheated cheek touched Rose's soft, cool skin; and even in the present sterile environment, Rose smelled of sandalwood soap. Kate whispered directly into her ear.

"Rose, I'm sorry I wasn't here sooner. Please say hello."

There was not even a flicker of an eyelid, but Rose's hand moved within Kate's grasp and at last Kate let out her breath. She hooked one foot around the chair, pulled it underneath her and without embarrassment, held the woman's hand to her face.

"Little Kate," murmured Rose, "love that voice."

It should have been so easy to simply cradle Rose's hand and let her tears add moisture to it, but Kate was unable to let that happen. Her chest felt like stone, and she had felt this way since David had looked at her with cold, disappointed eyes. She had brought Winnie into the middle of the biggest crisis in eleven years, was risking cutting her ties with Neil and Andie, and was watching Rose losing her spark, right in front of her. So there were no tears, but a pain in her gut that she completely deserved, and an urgent realisation that there was so much to tell. So very much to tell with not nearly as much time as she had imagined.

"I should give you a real telling off, you know," Kate's voice was soothing, in contrast to her actual words. "But I've got some news for you, if you're not too tired."

Finally, Rose opened her eyes, and Kate was surprised at how focussed they were. The woman looked straight at Neil, who was equally as startled by her gaze and moved nearer to the bed immediately.

"Hey, Rose," he smiled, "How are things?"

When Rose did not answer immediately, Neil, having witnessed the calibre and standards of the nurses on duty, took his greatest risk of the day and sat on the end of the bed. The woman continued to study him, breathing as evenly as she could manage, as he moved closer to his daughter. Even now, when time was reduced to a series of conscious moments ruled equally by pain and medication, Rose found joy in looking at the two faces in front of her. How could she possibly find the words to say to either of them what she saw there, when the emotions were so overwhelming? Neil's expression was open and encouraging:

blue eyes beneath blonde eyebrows, a straight jaw hidden by a surprisingly trim beard, mouth closed in a slight smile. Then there was Kate, with her short, dark hair cut close to her face, grey eyes full of knowledge and her lips parted, anticipating the reaction to her news.

They had come a long way as a family, and Rose knew that throughout the difficult years, including the little crises of the last ten, she herself had been the glue for all of them. David and Neil's mutual respect for her had prevented them from destroying each other on more than one occasion, and somehow they had learned to live with their situation. They had little choice, when Kate herself had needed the love of them both, and Rose had dearly hoped that when she left them, Kate's presence would keep all of their relationships intact. However, Kate had information, gathered at Rose's own suggestion, and it was the type of information which might form more connections. Alternatively, it was the type of information which might cleave her family in two. But a promise made to a desperate girl more than forty-five years before was not something to be forgotten or laid aside lightly, even if it had only been made in Rose's grateful mind. Kate had taken herself off on a mission and had news for her. It was a pleasant sensation, anticipation, and Rose had feared that she would never experience it again. Time was short, however, and she wanted to hear the words spoken out loud.

"Was she pleased?" Each word was painful and nauseating, so Rose chose them efficiently.

Kate looked once at Neil's continually passive face and squeezed Rose's hand.

"She was delighted. Really excited. She even spoke to Dave," Kate sucked at her lip to stop it trembling. "Rose, I think she's been waiting for this. She has his birth date tattooed on her wrist. You've done a great thing."

In spite of all the aches, those in her head, in her chest, but mostly in her heart, Rose smiled and shifted her eyes from Kate to Neil. The man looked bewildered but not uncomfortable and smiled straight back at her. He was surprised as her nostrils flared and a tear found a channel to travel along, but he made no comment. There was too little time and too much about this woman that he would miss. Not just her physical presence, but what she stood for– love, support, forgiveness.

He felt his own throat constrict as he viewed her, but Kate was speaking again, and her words continued to make no sense to him.

"Rose, can you hear me? There's something else." Kate waited until Rose finally dragged her eyes from Neil's face. "I brought her back with me."

Rose sat forward, until the pain stopped her in one sledgehammer blow and she fell back, breathless. Both Neil and Kate were on their feet in a second, but in spite of her discomfort, Rose did not close her eyes or cry out. Kate touched the woman's shoulder.

"She said she would love to see you, maybe meet him, but only if he wanted to and … oh, curses! He doesn't know yet."

Rose's chest heaved involuntarily and, just for a second, Kate imagined that her mother-in-law could see the entire situation from her point of view. Rose was smart, the smartest woman that Kate had ever encountered, and surely she could recognise her discomfort and despair; the potential to make cherished people happy had been there, she had simply been unable to deal with the unexpected. Could Rose understand this? The woman finally took in oxygen and breathed, "Where?"

"She's here, downstairs, talking to Dave."

When Rose asked to see Winnie, Kate realised that the time had come: that she was going to have to turn around and look into the face of her father and tell him several things. She was going to have to tell him that he had just spent over four hours in the company of the woman who had given him life, that that same woman was sitting talking to David, a boy she had known years before, and that Kate herself had put them all in this position, without asking how they felt about it. She was truly scared. But time continued to rule them, and Rose deserved to be put first in this.

"Neil … Dad," Kate choked out the word, then stopped. Whatever happened next, she could not afford to let the man run away from her or try to deal with it on his own. She hated the ignorant Before, especially when the knowledgeable After was so risky and imminent. "Will you come with me? Please? I need to tell you something."

The pair were nineteen steps into their outward journey when Neil finally spoke.

"So? Are you going to open your mouth anytime soon?"

Kate slowed to a halt, her boots beginning to trail dangerously, but she was damned if she was going falter in front of him. She was damned if she was going to cry; David was the only man who had the right to see her so exposed. Instead she folded her arms as a barrier between them and steeled herself.

"The woman we gave a lift to. Winnie Port. She's been waiting to meet you since she gave you away to Rose, two weeks after you were born. Please, please don't hate me."

Chapter 26

Vancouver Island

Poor Andie, all day waiting here with me, trying not to look too upset. She's probably been counting the minutes until Neil's return, and she sees him for less than ten minutes before the other woman in his life lays claim and takes him away. Still no complaints. Bless her. Neil looked good, tired, but alive. Sophie will be relieved.

Ah, Andie. Divine little elf, not even showing a fraction of your age on your face or figure. Thank God for you, you'll always be there for him. And he for you. You've proved that already. You have to be together, so this is going to be fine. Fine. Lord above, this is really happening, right now. I'm going to see Freddie and she's going to see him. She's seen him already. I wonder what she sees. I see a face made up of every one of his experiences. She probably only sees bits of his father and herself, which is all she really has to go on. Whatever she looked for, she would see something to make her proud, for sure.

Look at my useless legs. Two thin strings under the sheets, but I bet I could run a mile if I could use this joy as fuel. Can still wiggle my toes, after all. Oh, but I can run through our woods, jumping and skipping over puddles or even splashing through them, if I want to. Thank God for dreams, the only place I can move around unhindered. Where I can even fly. Never expected this feeling so late in the day.

"Rose?"

I'm not asleep, Andie, I just wanted to fly for a moment. Got lots still to see before I sleep. Breathe slowly.

"Andie."

She takes my hand, which is exactly what I want her to do. How did she know? Her hand is warm. Pete used to hold my hand in the cinema, in the dark, where nobody would see him for the old romantic he was. Well, of course he was romantic. My Pete. Big strong man who held me up in my grief. Big strong man who laughed at Davey's attempt to outwit Neil with words alone. Big strong man who cried in my arms when he knew he was leaving us. You're happy about this, aren't you, my darling? I've done the right thing and I'll share it all with you when I see you. You're going to want to hear it all.

"Rose, are you … peaceful? Do you feel peace?"

Only Andie would ever ask anything so personal, and I know why. She knows death, has been able to slide herself into someone else's shoes for a few moments, in an attempt to share the burden. Is she trying to understand why I didn't fight this harder? She knows the choice was mine, just like it was Fiona's, just like it was Pete's. Just like it was the choice of Dale, her twin brother. What she doesn't know is that I've always had a feeling, a manageable fear that this would happen. You witness the stages of a disease, watch your life-mate deal with information and try to accept it, and you travel that road with them. You begin to accept the probability for yourself, even without the information. So every decade survived is a bonus, and I've never taken any of them for granted. Peace. Peace is too simple a term. Gratitude for my time, realisation that soon the heavy, disease-soaked pressure inside me will fade along with my senses, almost delight that I will take with me my memories and love and let the earth have the body I can't control. But peace will do, if that's what she wants to hear. I should nod my head.

"Dale said the best thing was the peace. It was like a physical pillow. That's what he called it."

Look at her beautiful face. The last face her brother saw.

"I said to him, surely you mean a mental pillow, one that you can imagine, but he said no, it was physical. He could feel it beneath his head, cushioning his face, making his life more comfortable. But I never felt that peace, even though I really wanted to."

She's stroking my hand, I suppose she did the same for him as he eased himself away from her and from his short, pre-determined life. She thinks I'm going, too. She's making it as pleasant as possible, putting herself back into the role of enabler, but I'm not ready yet.

"He's going to need you. So is Kate."

She probably thinks I mean because I won't be there anymore, but that's only part of it. I wish I had the stamina to tell her the story myself, I would enjoy that so much. God, my eyes are so heavy, but I hear voices. Lots of voices, distant, most of them familiar. Pull yourself together, Rose, this is it. Focus. These people are here for you. They're returning the favour.

Well, she's tall, maybe as tall as I used to be. The brown curls have disappeared, but I know that face, that look. Wanting to smile, fearing the worst. And my Davey, holding her arm and showing her the way. Pete, you made that boy into the man, not me, but only I saw him shine. So much to tell you about him. Oh, and finally Andie has her man in her arms. I don't mind if he doesn't look at me, he will before I go. Watch your breathing, don't scare them.

"Fred-die."

"Mrs W," Lord, she never could call me Rose, "This is completely beyond …"

I try to raise my hand so that she doesn't feel the need to fill our time with the unnecessary, and she catches it in hers. She is kneeling on the floor, her face next to mine, and nobody is pulling up a chair. Where are my boys' manners? But only David is here. There's Neil's shadow in the hallway, Andie's too. Where is Kate? Why is my heart sore?

"Thank you," my voice sounds like I'm under water. Maybe my hearing is going. It couldn't matter less. "Been a joy. Every minute."

Chair, David. Finally. You're a good man, son. When did I last tell you this? Freddie is talking, Red Letter Day, I really should pay attention.

"He's a remarkable man, from what I've seen. Which is pitifully too little, but I knew. I knew that he would be fine with you, and I know how lucky I was, just to have that knowledge. Thank you, thank you. My God, just to be able to say that. You have no idea."

It should be me telling her this. Her touch is so light. Still no sign of Neil, I want them in the same room. Is it too much, this that I'm asking? He's within shouting distance, but my shouting days are over. Is he mad at me, disappointed? What about Kate? Freddie. Time has been kind. And there's black ink on her wrist, I touch it and smile. She smiles back, God love her.

"My penance," she's still smiling, "except, not really. More of an indulgence. It was a connection, and it made me remember every little detail that I had. Now, you've given me so much more."

David knows what I want, knows why I look at the door. Surely I don't have to tell him? But he looks exhausted, maybe he needs me to be clearer.

"Neil?"

At last the man is here. Andie is shaken, keeps looking at Freddie. Well, I'm not surprised. It's a lot to take in. But what does Neil's face say? That's it, son, come closer.

"Ma," here come my tears. He chose that word. "You're the steady one. What's this for?"

Oh, son, it's for you, for me, for her, for all of us together. Freddie's fingers are tight around my fist. I raise our hands together. His face, blue eyes, lines creasing above them. See it for what it is, Neil.

"For thanks. She deserves it." That's all I can manage. Freddie squeezes my fingers, it hurts a bit. All these people, how long have I got? My sons are my life, never a burden. No time to tell them this, no wonder my body hurts. "Rest is … you."

《•》《•》《•》

The room's dimmer, thank God somebody turned off that big light. And emptier. Only David and Kate, sitting far too far apart. And very little pain. I can handle that. Here's Kate, I do love that face.

"Rose," but her skin is as white as the wall. "They're talking, and I'm pretty sure it's going okay. I thought you'd like to know."

Oh, my favourite couple, both faces in this little ring of light. My lips, too dry. Thanks Davey, that's better. I'll just watch for a while. My eyesight hasn't gone at least. And they can look at each other for years and years yet. So lucky. Too much to say. Kate? Please?

"She's a lovely woman. He'll like her, he's bound to. He's surprised, but I think he'll survive it. That's what you want to know, isn't it? You've made her happy, and he will be okay. So. You're debt-free."

"Kate," why is David's voice so thick? His eyes are angry, but she's not looking at him. "Don't!"

Strange, watery taste in my mouth when David doesn't smile. She speaks to me anyway.

"You can leave, if you really have to. We'll just stay behind here and keep going. Keep raising those babies and keep telling our stories. You'll be there in all of them."

Kate looking at David's face, she never backs down. "I'm going to go and get them, Rose, and we're going to stay the night with you, all of us."

Kate's smart. Smart cookie. Beautiful cookie. David's eyes are so black, the only face here now. They will be fine. Oh, son, she did it for me, don't look like that.

"Do you need anything?" always practical, man of the house. But not my man. My man never has to ask. My man makes me warm inside. Nothing I need, anyway.

"Be happy," that's all I really need. For all of them. They'll stumble, but they're capable. Oh God, be happy with each other. Don't waste time. Stop worrying.

Here they are, five faces. Come close. Five radiant faces. Connected in a line.

Love in a line. In a circle. So warm.

All capable. All in love.

Men. Women. Children.

Capable. Beautiful.

Radiant.

Family.

Chapter 27

Vancouver Island

The sky to the east looked like pink ribbons had floated down onto a pale blue lake, the clouds forming tiny islands amidst the still water, and Kate was glad she was driving so that she did not have the opportunity to appreciate the colours too much. Such a dawn was too inspiring, and she did not want the distraction, this early into their grief. David, unusually for him, was scrunched against the glass of the passenger door, completely unconscious, arms folded and head tucked into his shoulder. She viewed this, too, as a blessing. It was one thing to be in a silent vehicle when your companion was asleep, an entirely different experience when they were awake and choosing not to communicate. This felt as reasonable as she could hope for, the dawn breaking on a frost-free morning and the steering wheel helping her to stay upright in her seat. The trees seemed taller than she remembered, black and needle sharp as they lined the road, but they confirmed her route, which was nothing but helpful.

About fifty metres behind her, Kate was aware of Neil's truck, the lights appearing and disappearing as the bends in the road allowed. She wondered if Winnie was asleep, or whether all three of them were actually chatting. She sighed. Chatting was a stupidly informal word. It smacked of the breakfast table or the queue for the hockey game, and that was ridiculous. Nobody was "chatting," not on a day like this. They may be enquiring or sharing or even explaining, but there was no way they could be chatting. In the days ahead of them, Kate supposed there would be discussions, lots of them, but there would be no Rose to mediate. Maybe they would let her take on that role, allow her to feel good about some parts of the situation she had helped to create. Or maybe Neil would shut the door in her face, there was absolutely no way of telling.

Back at the hospital, when he had finally understood what she was telling him, his face had just stopped moving. Every muscle had stalled for about five seconds before his hand had rubbed them back to life. In all of their time together, whether as a guest at his house, or any of the sporadic, informal moments of "family time" since then, Neil had not looked her in the eye for longer than a second. She had never sought further attention, they had always treated each other as friends, which was ultimately the safer option; but when he had studied her at length earlier, breaking one of his own rules, she had appeared to be the only one disturbed by it. His eyes had been their usual blue, but she had not recognised any other part of them. No twinkle, no actual presence. He had said nothing in response to her revelation, and she knew her face had been scarlet during the interminable silence.

Even when he had moved downstairs to the foyer and stood in front of Winnie, she had no idea what he was feeling. David had stood, Winnie had stood, and Kate had hung back against the wall, sick with anxiety. It had been intolerable. No hugging or crying or expressions of surprise. Just Neil standing over the woman and David glancing in her direction. Thank God she had heard nothing of the exchange, and, within a few moments, they had each made their way past her inert figure, concentrating on getting back to Rose as quickly as possible. All this for Rose, she had reminded herself then as she did now. For Rose and for Winnie. Only, it was just Winnie today, and it had all fallen apart.

The end had come too fast for them. They had not been prepared for any part of it. The seams had not yet been sewn up properly; they had almost gotten there, they had almost been tacked together, but still they remained loosely unattached at a dangerous level. Kate let a shiver take her over and was glad to finally see the gateposts ahead. Whatever happened, she would be given the opportunity to take part again. David would surely speak to her if they had guests in their house. Neil would surely speak to her if Andie took the lead. As a group, they would all have to speak to the children, and she was absolutely convinced that where the youngsters were concerned, there would be a united front. Truly, the only thing she wanted was to feel the thin arms of her son around her neck and his legs around her waist. She wanted the soft of his pyjamas under her chin, his blonde hair tickling her cheek and his low giggle in her ear. However, that would be later, at a decent hour, when they had decided together where to go from here.

As The Edge began to emerge from the gloom of the wood, its white clapboard still a deep slumbering blue until the headlights startled it awake, David began to unfold his body, groaning as he did so. He did not open his eyes until Kate yanked on the hand brake, however, and as his face was unreadable in the lack of light, she did not wait around to be ignored any further. Her leg eased open the door as she pulled the keys from the ignition, wasting as little time as possible in escaping the cab and its occupant. But David was already at the front of the vehicle. Kate halted immediately, her boot inadvertently kicking some loose gravel straight at the man as she slid towards him. Four weeks previously, he would have caught her hands and chided her for ruining the look of the driveway. She stood motionless before him, the man she had sworn she was lifeless without, wondering at what point she had forced him to cut her loose. Whatever he was about to say, he had no more than twenty seconds at his disposal.

"She's gone," his voice was strained but not harsh.

"Yes," Kate agreed, staring at her feet. "I don't know what to say to you, except I'm sorry."

David remained motionless. The sound of Neil's truck was already in the air.

"I thought that losing my mum was as bad as it could ever get and that I would be okay afterwards, because it was behind me." Kate could not believe that they were still standing two feet apart, but it seemed to be a time for words only, and so she continued. "Well, I was wrong about that, too. This numb feeling is going to fade and everything is going to hurt. But you know that already."

As Neil's headlights swung across the front lawn, Kate finally made it past David's bowed head and stumbled up to the back door. The keys cooperated in the semi-light, and inside the kitchen was already heating up for a normal morning's requirements, on this anything-but-normal morning. Kate looked around her at every vestige of her comfortable family home and felt the first of the pain, far, far quicker than she had imagined she would. The table was clear of everything but a couple of mugs and the floor looked like it needed a brush, but there were no dishes piled or clothes strewn. It was tidy and bright and completely soulless. No Bertuzzi, wagging her tail until she dropped, exhausted, to the floor. No Al trailing through from the sitting room in search of pickles or company. No David, whistling as he sliced bread. No Rose, asking if she could do anything to help. Clean, modern lines, subtle lighting, shining surfaces, and not nearly enough people. Kate for once let herself consider the cramped little house at Camastianavaig, where there was more noise and caper than there was space, as the preferred option. This, more than anything else, had her hurrying from the room, needing at least two flights of stairs between her and everyone else.

In her bedroom, their bedroom, the duvet had been smoothed down, but the cushions were piled on the chair next to the bed. David remained on the fence when it came to cushions. He had said he liked the colours but thought the constant moving of them on and off the bed was painfully unnecessary. He was very much a man where cushions were concerned. To Kate, the pillow on her side looked soft and, therefore, far too comfortable; the thought of having to pull herself up from there after far too short a time was only just short of depressing. She threw the cushions onto the bed and climbed onto the chair instead. As the sun began to crawl down the walls, Kate pulled her knees up to her chin and listened to the silence of her life.

《•》《•》《•》

"Would you like a whisky?" Neil spoke directly to Winnie, who was perched on the edge of the sofa.

She had learned to speak without hesitating in the last three hours. "Oh, thank you, but I couldn't. Don't let me stop you, though."

Neil twisted his face slightly. "I couldn't either. I mean, I could, but I don't. I thought it might help you sleep."

Winnie had no idea where to go next with the conversation. It was almost 8:00 a.m., the sun was growing brighter, and the previous night, combined with travelling across the Atlantic, did indeed suggest that sleep should be on the agenda. But how could that happen? Everything she did from now on would have to be at the suggestion of someone else, and the only person she felt anywhere near comfortable with had not been seen since the five of them had arrived back here. She could no more make herself at home here than she could expect this man to welcome her with open arms. Yet nobody else was joining them.

"Well, it's certainly been …" Winnie could not continue, and began to play with the cuff of her blouse instead.

Neil wandered over to the radiator and checked its temperature. "This room, it never really gets hot without the fire. Ceilings are too high."

Winnie nodded, letting her eyes wander over every surface. Framed photographs on the bureau, the odd piece of shaped glass on the mantelpiece, a newly padded window seat and many landscapes on the wall. The only original feature was the fireplace, so the place was barely familiar, but it was comfortable nevertheless. She just wished it had more bodies in it at this particular moment in time.

"I could light the fire, if you want to sit in here," Neil said the words as if it was the most natural thing in the world, which left Winnie with only one option: to be completely honest with him.

"It's not my house. I don't know what I should be doing."

In response, Neil slowly sat on the edge of David's chair. He stared for a moment or two as his feet, clad only in his two-day socks, then let his expression soften at the sight of Winnie's own trainers. He pointed at them.

"Rose hated shoes in this house," he began, his even voice bringing a tiny bit more light into the room, "but this hasn't been her place for ten years, and I'm pretty sure Kate won't mind."

Winnie offered to remove them, but he waved her words away. Instead, he settled himself back in the chair and stretched his legs out in front of him. The house became absolutely silent, and Winnie began to feel smothered. The man was being perfectly civil, but distant. Well, what else? He had just lost his mother. She watched him close his eyes for the first time in God knew how long, but perhaps the silence was also seeping into his bones, because in the next second, he sat forward once more.

"You came a long way," Neil said, rubbing his thumb under his chin. "I'm sorry you didn't have longer with her. I reckon it would have been quite a lively reunion, once upon a time."

Winnie smiled. The sight of Rose had been shocking; however, it had been almost exhilarating to see her surrounded by her kin, and to be invited into the inner sanctum had been so very comforting. But Neil was right, what she and Kate had planned as a surprise visit had taken a sad, awkward turn, and it was this which made her nose prick dangerously. During the odd moment where Kate had slept on the plane, Winnie had kept herself warm by picturing Rose in her little chalet, presenting her with photos and anecdotes of the man as a boy. The woman had made her life easier, not by taking him away from her, but by being the person she had been, and had remained. In all of her darkest days, Winnie had known that Rose would be loving her beautiful baby, and how many people in her position had ever had that luxury? There was nobody to ask.

"Was it Kate's idea?" Neil's face remained passive.

Winnie relaxed slightly; questions were easy, compared with silence.

"No," she looked straight at Neil, determined that she should not be intimidated by someone who had once depended on her touch and care for two whole weeks. "Rose started the ball rolling– I suppose now we know why– and by all accounts, Kate took up the challenge readily enough. She's a determined individual, put me in my place a couple of times. It was her idea to surprise Rose."

At last Neil grinned without fear. "I think she'll always be a mystery to me, but her heart's in the right place. She brought Dave back to life, you have no idea. I mean, I guess you know the whole story ..."

Winnie looked closely at his face. She marvelled at how many expressions she had witnessed in their short acquaintance. Right at that moment, he looked suddenly younger and less confident.

"Yes, I spent a week with Kate. I know how her life began."

Neil shrugged his admission. "Nowadays, I don't see her as my mistake, not in any way. But then," he shook his head, "back then, it was a black time."

He looked as if he might slip into reflection, but suddenly he was animated again. "My God," he marvelled, "I had no idea what to do. I had done something so ... cruel. I couldn't stand looking at my brother, from the night it happened until Fiona left. He was so confused." Neil took in a breath and then looked straight at Winnie. "I wondered if I should leave. I wondered if I should look ... elsewhere for a family. But that was too dangerous, and Rose couldn't stand the thought of me leaving like that. So. You should know. I never really needed to look for you. I'm sorry."

Winnie was on the point of daring to add her views when there was the sound of footsteps on the stairs. They were moving at pace, and as the woman gazed in the direction of the open doorway, she sensed Neil do the same. Kate's face was strangely blotchy as it appeared in the sunlit room, the red agitation on her neck not halting until it reached her lower cheeks. She looked straight at Winnie, switched her gaze immediately to Neil, and at once her expression crumpled in despair. Winnie stood, feeling the girl's emotion hit her like a hot gust of wind.

"I was looking for David," Kate said, concentrating on the floor a couple of feet in front of her. "I need to speak to him. I really need to see him, right now."

By the end, the pitch of her voice had risen considerably and she scratched frantically at her wrists. Winnie was aghast, the girl had never looked so undone. At their first meeting, she had been confident and assured, and it had somehow made her seem tall and able. Here she was, hunched into her own shoulders, her lips clamped in a thin, tight line. Winnie had watched the air shift between Neil and Kate more than once in the short time she had seen them together. What had started off as easy-going banter in Vancouver, had become a divisive shaft of cold shock at the hospital and seemed to have settled on this new and silent impasse. Kate was very obviously dying a death at the situation, had seemed to have lost her nerve altogether in the present company, and, yet again, Winnie was unsure of how to help. Kate finally allowed her hands to drop to her side and her head to tip forward. For the first time in years she also let the sound of her own keening breath be heard.

"Hey, hey, hey," Neil stood quite calmly, stalling Winnie's own instinctive movement. There could have only been a few seconds of stillness, but it was bitterly uncomfortable for all involved. Then Neil was moving over to Kate's slowly folding body. He touched her arm first, as if unsure of how she would react to even that, then hugged her against him. It was awkward, Kate's arms were folded in front of her and her head pressed into her own chest, but at least she did not move away. "You're okay, Kate. You're okay. Come on, now. Ally will be here in a minute."

Kate huffed in a breath immediately and stepped back. "Dave's gone to get him?"

"He and Andie, they've gone to get all of them. And it's going to be tough enough, so wipe your face, maybe?"

Neil handed her the less crumpled of two hankies, and she sniffed and wiped self-consciously until the man smiled at her and nodded. At that moment, the back door banged open and a babble of noise filled the room along the corridor.

"Mom! Dad says none of us have to go to school today! Is that the honest truth?"

Even the sight of Neil and an elderly stranger did not alter his pace, and Kate squealed his name as he launched himself into her already outstretched arms. Bertuzzi jumped first at Kate, then when this was ignored, sniffed at Neil's feet, shoved her face into Winnie's open palm and then began to paw at Alasdair's dangling legs. The boy held onto his mother for one prolonged moment, then leaned back and looked at her.

"So, really? I don't have to go? What's wrong with your face?"

Kate frowned. "I haven't been able to wash it for a day and a bit, Al. I bet it needs a right good scrub. Come on, I want to hear your news while I clean up."

As Kate carried the boy out of the room, Bert following on behind, her tail connecting with furniture along the way, Alasdair raised his head slightly and looked over her shoulder.

"Hi, Uncle Neil," he waved.

"Hi, Al," the man replied, but he was already looking past the retreating figures, and in the next second, Sophie was crossing the threshold, her coat half off and trailing behind her. As she wandered up to Neil, it caught on the fireside chair and remained in a heap where it landed, a soft pile of coloured cotton on the plain oak flooring.

"Hey, Dad," Sophie's voice echoed the frown on her face. "Is this Friday? If it is, you have to take Crisis to the vet. You said that was a job for Friday."

Neil hoisted her up onto his back as Andie came into the room, a very sleepy Abbie cuddled into her shoulder. Winnie stood at their entrance, but was too intrigued to move. The blonde girls were enchanting, and she saw that both their parents were equally as taken with them. Sophie wrapped her arms around his neck and kissed the back of his head.

"How were the roads?" she asked, watching Winnie from her vantage position. If the older woman was surprised by the oddly mature question, she did not show it, but it obviously struck a chord with Neil.

"Dry and empty, the way we like them. Mrs Port?" he offered her a chance to take part, "this is Sophie, and this is Abbie. They're our girls, and I'd like you to meet them. Soph, can you shake Mrs Port's hand from up there?"

Sophie did so, her eyes clearly assessing the woman. Winnie had taught school for most of her adult life and was not fazed by youngsters in any way. It almost put her at her ease.

"It's a pleasure, Sophie," she smiled, and the girl returned the gesture. As Winnie turned to Abbie, the smallest of all of them, the youngster wrapped her arms even tighter around Andie's neck and hid her face. Winnie made no move towards her, and Andie smiled at her consideration. Sophie, as ever, felt the need to explain.

"She's just woken up. She doesn't like waking up."

With Sophie clinging to him like a limpet, Neil walked over to Andie and smoothed down the back of Abbie's hair. She did not flinch but neither did she look around, so Neil kissed her head gently then held onto Sophie's hands, which had been absently rubbing his own hair into peaky tufts. Winnie watched with interest, guessing that none of the movements were unusual or for show, but the ordinary touches and gestures were proof enough for her. The man had grown up good; and no matter how much she had missed, how many experiences she had been unable to share with him, or how many of her mistakes he had been unable to learn from, this man was someone worth knowing. Kate had told her as much, and she had been right. Where was Kate?

"I'm going to light the fire," Neil stated, letting Sophie slide down his back onto the rug. "See if we can't warm this room up. Maybe if she sees the fire, punk baby will wake up and speak to us. What d'you think, Soph?"

Sophie thought for a moment, pursing her lips, and then frowned. "And what about Crisis?"

"Crisis will still be an old dog in need of a check-up this time tomorrow, and Granma Iris is there with her. Don't you fret."

Neil glanced at Winnie, wondering what on earth the woman made of the odd words being used so easily between Sophie and him, and gave her the best smile he could muster. Instantly, however, his shoulders felt heavy, and he wanted Sophie's small body back in his arms, where heat and a beating heart would remind him that life was bearable. Life was uncontrollable but bearable, and could on occasion even be totally surprising. But the girl was already moving towards the doorway, muttering something about newspapers and Uncle David. Winnie sat once more, and finally let out the breath she had been nursing for long enough.

By the time Sophie had returned with the paper, Alasdair had been encouraged into helping and was lugging the cinder bucket behind his cousin. As Neil and the youngsters began the process of raking and sweeping and rearranging, Andie sat beside Winnie and gradually brought Abbie out of her present state. The girl's hair was tangled in the front button of her dressing gown, and, very slowly and carefully, Winnie took the strands and eased them away. When she had finished, Abbie's thumb was firmly in her mouth and her slippered feet were moving around in small circles, as if a tune were playing in her head. When Winnie switched her gaze from the child to Andie, she found her looking straight at her. Kate had scrutinised her in the same manner, way back in her own kitchen, and she reacted as she had done then, with a hopeful smile.

Andie shook her head in wonder. "I can see it," she whispered, so that only the woman could hear. "The shape of the eyes."

Winnie nodded her agreement, thinking of Emma's face. Emma had always been her father's double, same chin, same black hair, but her eyes had been pure Hunter: straight eyebrows which would hood dramatically when she frowned, and beneath them, grey pupils which matched Kate's exactly. Neil's eyes were blue, it was the only difference, and, at some point in the days to come, she might tell the man about his sister. Winnie wondered if he had room for yet another female in his already female-heavy existence.

In the kitchen, Kate and David stood on opposite sides of the table, trying to absorb some of the familiarity of the room so that they could carry on with this particular day and all the days in front of them. Kate's face was composed beneath her puffy eyes, and David's was placid, if not downright waxy. There were adult and childish murmurings from the sitting room, but the thought of joining them, all being in the room together, was even less appealing than their present isolation. Kate was leaning against the warm range, her arms folded, staring at the crumbs on the table. Sometimes, when she was watching TV, either lying flat out on the sofa or settled on David's lap, she would notice one of Bert's toys making the floor space less than perfect. She would spend far too much time thinking about how she should get up to move it instead of relaxing and ignoring it. She felt the same way about those crumbs. They were all she could think about.

"Al missed you," David stated. "He couldn't sit still when I left him yesterday. I … I don't know how to tell him."

"Does he have any idea?"

David allowed a shudder to claim him, but instantly thought it might look contrived and moved towards the sink to cover it up.

"He visited her in hospital a couple of days ago."

Kate sighed. "Maybe we should tell him without the others. Just you and me?"

"I've missed you."

Kate held her breath and at last met the man's eye. It would take less than five steps to be back in his arms, to say a thousand sorrys and to let him forgive her for every stupid, arrogant assumption she had made about her family and their wishes. But what if he did not? Every single argument of the last few months suddenly stood in front of her face, waving and demanding acknowledgement. She could hear all of her opinions, her optimistic views on how people would "feel," but some other entity had stepped in and proved that she was not nearly as clever as she had thought. She also heard David's voice, reasonable, scared, wary and weighted with terrors from his past. She always listened to him where the house was concerned, the maintenance of the vehicles was handed over to him immediately, and she very rarely approached Neil without his prior advice on how to handle the situation. So why did she think she knew better when it came to their loved ones and their needs? Kate's head began to ache as she entered a state of exhaustion and fear, one born of her own stubborn enthusiasm, and she was scared as much by her own doubts as she was by this new threat of rejection.

"I need you," David spoke again. This time his voice was adamant, as if he, too, had been testing the water, but needed someone to choose a road through this. Kate had not seen that particular expression in his eyes since her own mother's funeral: that agony of unfinished business and the knowledge that time had run out for them. It was painful to witness, that total despair when the rest of his face was so typically David, and Kate felt dizzy that he could possibly be viewing their current estrangement on the same level. If she had given him that impression, then she needed to sort it immediately. As she moved towards him, her face creasing as the tears came, Alasdair bounded into the kitchen with Sophie at his heels. Their little bodies hindered her journey as they halted between them and her son took her hand.

"Mom, I'm starving," he began, dragging her back towards the sitting room, "but Uncle Neil says he needs to tell us something when we're all together. So come on. Dad! You too."

As the kitchen emptied itself, David finally pried himself away from the sink, cursing under his breath. He had been so close, had almost felt Kate's arms around his neck, her perfumed jumper comforting him as he buried his face in her shoulder. But there was too much free air in the room and nobody to wrap his arms around. Situations had to be faced, words said into quiet rooms and reactions witnessed, all this before any of them could take one more step. The hours seemed to stretch in front of his eyes, and he longed for a time when this house had only Kate and him rattling around its rooms, rarely hurting each other and laughing at their efforts to appear sedate when their hands would not behave themselves. Even walking seemed too much of a trial, yet in the next moment he was moving through the door of the sitting room, and there were seven familiar faces glowing and fading as the flames in the fireplace dictated. Freddie Hunter looked the most uncomfortable of them all, even with Kate sitting close beside her, and Neil immediately stepped aside so that David could take his rightful seat. What a mad, ridiculous episode they were taking part in.

Neil sat opposite David and raised his eyebrows. When his brother did not react, Neil held his hands open in a definite question. But there remained little movement, and finally the younger man sat forward in his chair, his elbows resting on his knees. He took a breath in.

"So, guys. Something really sad has happened, and we need to tell you because you are the people who matter the most in this family." Neil swallowed, then, "We can't hide how sad we are, and we don't want you to worry because things are going to be okay. We'll make sure things are fine."

Sophie, who had been sitting by Alasdair as he rubbed Bertuzzi's belly, stood and pushed herself onto Neil's lap, her face serious but not shocked. She put her arm around his neck and her head against his, as if to show that she could take whatever was coming their way. Abbie and Alasdair were silently trying not to fret, having no idea how to handle such melancholy amongst the adults. Neil cleared his throat.

"Granma Rose was really sick, and when you're that sick and old, sometimes you just can't get better again." Neil's face was a grey version of itself, and he wiped the sweat gathering under his chin.

Kate, weeping silent tears, her hands loose in her lap, did not see what was happening, but now David was speaking, his tone low.

"She died last night. I know you all know what that means, which is actually kind of a sad thing, too. But," David looked down at Alasdair, who had yet to raise his head, "it's better for her, because yesterday she was hurting, and now she's not."

There was a small pop as Abbie pulled her thumb from her mouth. "What hurt?"

As Andie cuddled her closer, David cleared his throat. "Her chest hurt, Abbie. It hurt to … to breathe."

Abbie thought about it for a moment, and then, "That's not fair," before shoving her thumb back where it belonged. Kate could not have agreed more.

"You're right," replied David. "But at least it doesn't hurt now. That has to be a good thing."

As Kate wiped her face with her sleeve, Alasdair finally got to his feet. There were no tears, just a certain intrigued look in his eyes. Since Kate had not taken part in the conversation at all, he wandered up to David's chair.

"But I thought hospitals took you in and made you better. I thought that was their job," he did not sound angry, just a little put out.

David leaned forward slightly. "A lot of the time they do. Some of the time they can't."

Alasdair bit his lip once and then moved towards the door. "Come on, Bert. I'm starving."

When nobody moved, Sophie turned Neil's face towards hers. For those who were watching, it was clear which one of them was the calmest. The girl kissed his cheek and then settled herself back against him. "I loved Granma Rose's stories. She had hundreds and hundreds of them. It's lucky I can remember nearly all of them."

Winnie, who was wedged between Kate and Andie, would no more have spoken out loud at this private moment than she would have run around the house naked, but Sophie sat looking at her, smiling. As all other conversations seemed to have come to a halt, Sophie tried her luck with the stranger.

"Did you know Granma Rose?"

"I did, a long time ago."

"Oh good," Sophie relaxed, "her long time ago stories are the best. My favourite one is the one where Dad comes to live here."

Kate stood as easily as she could. "Excuse me," she said and left the room.

In the kitchen, Alasdair had managed not to spill milk over the rim of his cereal bowl, but he was still frowning as he sat by himself at the table. By the time Kate had filled a glass of water and begun to drink it, he had turned in his chair to look up at her.

"So I can't speak to her ever again?"

Kate shook her head in reply. He turned back, his chin in his hand, and Kate wanted to comfort him more than anything in the world, but she could feel herself slipping out of control, and her legs would not move. God had pushed her many times before, but this culmination of guilt and grief was the worst yet. It had made her mouth dry and her feet immobile and, unbelievably, it made her useless to everyone in this house.

"Are you okay, Al?" Still she did not move towards him.

"Yes."

"We'll all be fine, you know. But if you want to ask me anything, you can."

When Alasdair finally turned around, his face was more curious than morose. "Why do you call Uncle Neil 'Dad' sometimes?"

Chapter 28
Vancouver Island

In the sitting room, the conversation had gradually moved on from the awkward to the practical, and as Abbie sucked her thumb and Sophie dosed against Neil's neck, the adults had begun to discuss the next steps. By the time Alasdair wandered back through with his half-empty bowl, the fire was settling enough to produce heat, and David and Neil were talking about time-scales and arrangements, which were just words and meant nothing to the boy. His dad looked tired and sad, his Uncle Neil not much different, and they seemed to be agreeing with each other rather than arguing. He frowned slightly at his two cousins, who had apparently claimed Bertuzzi as their own and were competing to see who could get the most facial licks from the dog; but he was actually more interested in finding out how the old woman beside Andie might fit into this whole scene. He sat down on the edge of the sofa. Andie smiled at him.

"You okay, Al?"

He nodded, wondering if people were going to ask him the same question all day long. He piled the last of his cornflakes onto his spoon and shoved it in his mouth. Slowly he chewed and tried to decide what to do next. He needed to tell his dad about his mom, but the man seemed tied up in important stuff, so he chose his second option.

"Where do you come from?" Alasdair asked Winnie. "You don't speak like us, or Mom."

Winnie smiled. "Well, I was born in Scotland, like your mom, but I lived here, just down the road, until I was nearly sixteen. Then I moved back to Scotland and then I lived in England for ages. I suppose I must sound a bit strange, after all of that!"

Alasdair shrugged. "I can understand you. Mom can speak a whole different language, when she wants to. Can you?"

"No, sadly."

"She's teaching me bits," he informed. "I can say a whole sentence. 'S'docha gur e na Canucks an sgioba hocaidh as fhearr air an t-saoghal ach is a geam rugbaidh as fhearr,' but I'm not allowed to tell Dad what it means."

Sophie sat up. "Say it again."

Alasdair obliged, and in the next second both Sophie and Abbie were giggling. Alasdair did not think it was funny. The Canucks were the best hockey team, and although he wasn't sure he agreed with his mom that rugby was a better game, the girls didn't have to laugh. Before he had time to tell them what he thought of them, Andie had stood and stretched a hand out to each girl.

"Come on, you two. Clothes and food. No arguments."

The room was sparse, down to four people and a lazy dog, and the school-free day was proving to be less enjoyable than anticipated. The humans were spaced out into four corners of a square, and Alasdair remembered his other task.

"Dad, I think Mom is ill. She said she needed to get some air, and I should tell you, just in case you were looking for her later."

His dad looked at him and eventually winked. "Okay, Al, thanks. Listen, bud, how about we show this lot how to make pancakes, the kind that don't stick to the pan? You up for it?"

Alasdair reckoned to himself that pancakes were about the best thing to make on this odd day, because they were easy and he had a chance to impress, which his use of Gaelic had clearly failed to do.

"Okay."

As two more bodies left the room, Winnie could sit no longer and wandered over to the window to watch the dew dissipate above the lawn and to take a few deep breaths into her lungs. The garden was beautiful, and although the abandoned trucks made it real rather than mystical, there was joy in the colours and mystery in the shadows. Her limbs seemed to have been either tensed or folded in the past two days, and she longed for the opportunity to wander around the house, trying to catch a memory or spy a relic of a previous life. But to suggest such a thing would be monstrously rude; she had no right to wish for escape from the situation. Behind her, she could hear Neil raking and refuelling the fire and suddenly wondered if he might view her departure as more diplomatic than rude. How long should she maintain this silence? Perhaps she should just let him off the hook and suggest that he go about his business, which he surely wished to do. He had his family to console and his dogs to tend to. She should just tell him to leave her be and that there would be time later when–

"Mrs Port. At some point today I need to get back up home. Things to do before we have to start sorting everything. But," Neil was standing only two feet from her, "I'm not really great when it comes to dealing with surprises and even worse at handling the unknown. The thought of us circling each other in the days to come is going to make this all the more difficult, so, do you think we could go for a walk, if you're not too tired? I would like to talk about this."

"If that's what you really want," Winnie replied, daring not to show too much hope on her face, "then I would also like that very much."

"Then, let's go outside. This family has no conception of the word privacy."

《•》《•》《•》

"My father was born in St John's, Newfoundland, in 1917. He was the middle of five brothers– Johnny, Jim, my dad Fred, George and Tommy, and each and every one of them cut lumber. My grandfather was their teacher, as soon as they grew tall and strong enough to pick up tools, and I think it was a reasonable living, but I never actually met anyone from the east to confirm that. Dad was quite a shy man, although his singing voice was incredible, but all four of his brothers were married in their teens and they left him behind. He had never had a girlfriend. Well, that's according to my mother, of course! So, maybe he felt like he had nothing to lose, when the call came for men to go overseas and help the British.

"They asked for lumberjacks to go, offered them some money and provided a little for the families they left behind. It was called the Newfoundland Overseas Forestry Unit, and I think it was such a great idea. The British were desperate for cut wood, you see, lots of wood to use as pit props in the coal mines. Coal was needed for the munitions factories, and pit props were needed for the mines. The Canadians were quicker, more efficient cutters, and so they were essential, even if not everybody was aware they existed. My mother was more than a little aware of them!

"So, let's see, Dad arrived in the Borders in 1939. Twenty-two years old, living in a basic camp with the men he had met on the boat across. He said it was fine, and it probably was to someone of his age and disposition. I daresay there were a lot of men missing their wives and families, but my dad used to walk the countryside in his free time and loved it. That's what he told me, anyway. They were based north of Langholm, a little town lying in a bowl of hills, and those hills were his best friends. He told me once that he would pretend to be somebody else between the town and the camp, somebody confident and outgoing, and if he met anybody out walking, he would be friendly and chatty. He always found the Scots easy to talk to– Mum said the townsfolk found the men fascinating in return and would have talked a mute into communicating. To them these foreigners spoke like movie stars! Sometimes the men would come down to dances, and my dad, so quiet amongst the workers, would talk easily with those he had met on his travels. That's when everybody found out he could sing. But it still took him over a month to speak to my mother.

"She was Martha-Jean McVittie. Viewed as practically on the shelf at twenty-five, she "saw right through" Fred Hunter's loud laugh to the quieter dreamer beneath and stared down any would-be rivals who came near. They met in October 1939, were married on Christmas Eve, and I was screaming at them by October 1940, almost exactly a year to the day they met. I'd like to think that it was an uncommonly romantic union, but, to be truthful, I'm not sure it was so unusual. There were a few single cutters and lots of marriages born out of that time. They were just one of many. What I like about it was that this man, who had never made any sort of impression on the folks back home, had been a minor celebrity at concerts in a small Scottish town. Mum had spied him and bagged him, and they seemed to get along well enough.

"After the war, when people were beginning to look forward again, to make plans again, Dad seemed to feel that living with his in-laws was just stagnating. He was grateful to them for housing the three of us, but Mum said herself that she didn't feel like she had moved on at all. She wanted independence as much as he did, and even though it meant taking their grandchild away from them, Mum was ready to leave her parents and follow Fred back to Canada. She told me she wanted to be the different one, the odd one out. She wanted the attention that a different environment would bring her. She actually told me that! She wanted a bit of excitement, like Dad had done when pretending to be somebody else.

"But we didn't move back to the east. Dad had cousins in British Columbia, and there was plenty of work out there, so that's where we ended up. They had James and Ian, two years apart, and we lived near Victoria until I was ten, when we moved up near Duncan. Our house was in the middle of nowhere, about thirty minutes' walk from The Edge, and I'm not sure if my mother ever did get the attention she craved, but lots of people loved her accent. There were one or two Scots in the area, and I remember there used to be Burns' suppers. I cannot bear whisky. I don't understand why people like to burn their tongue with the flavour, and I'm half Scottish; but they were well attended, so I guess I'm in the minority. Dad worked for Pete's father– William Wilder– because that's who his cousin Ray worked for. And that's how we ended up breathing the same air as the Wilder family. My God, I haven't spoken that name in years, and still it just trips off the tongue.

"We were like a little group of pioneers back then, Dad, Mum and me, heading out to the unknown. To me at that age it meant little. I was with my parents, so it didn't really matter where we were going; but for my dad, still not thirty and basically a shy lad at heart, it must have been a challenge. My mum chivvied him on, I guess. He wasn't like dads these days, spending time with their kids, taking them places. He worked and Mum took care of me. When the boys came along and we needed a bigger place to stay, he managed to secure a job at Wilder's, and I think that was the first place I really considered home. It felt like we had put roots down at last, and I started to make proper friends. David fell between James and Ian in age, but didn't spend a great deal of time in their company. If I think about it, he didn't seem to be needed in their relationship. They were really close to each other, he had no siblings, and so he didn't quite get the dynamics. But when I started babysitting, he really came out of his shell. Mum had told me about Rose's lost babies, so I knew David was more or less used to entertaining himself; but he was a funny little guy, tall for his age. He liked to hear me sing but was as tone deaf a child as I had ever met. I couldn't tell him, of course, he had little enough self-confidence as it was, so I kept teaching him songs and he could remember the words but never 'sang' a song as long as I knew him! Talking to him as an adult is really weird.

"I want you to realise something. My childhood was no different to any of my friends. I was not unhappy or lonely or neglected. I helped my mother in the house, and I babysat for pocket money, but I did have one extra thing that I loved more than anything else. I sang in a dance band with a school friend, Trudy Frazer, and we had the best time ever.

"My dad had been persuaded to sing at some function, a wedding, I think, or a christening maybe, I'm not sure. I was there, dressed up, and he pulled me up onto the stage with him. We sang 'The Rose of Allandale' in two-part harmony, like we used to do at New Year, and people loved it. My dad smiled so much that night. We might have sung another couple of things together, but I was thirteen, I don't really recall much except my dad's smile. The band liked me, though. Sometime later Dad asked me if I knew of a friend who could sing. It seemed the band wanted background singers, but there was no way Fred Hunter was going to let his daughter be the only female in a lineup of four men. So they pestered him, and he pestered me, until I suggested Trudy. Mum couldn't see a problem. If I tell you the honest truth, she liked to sit in on the rehearsals, sometimes she would teach them Scots ballads, and she sometimes drove me to where we played. It was like a little extra in her life, too.

"Trudy was my pal and she was very keen, so we did it together. She was the real star, not because her singing was any better than mine, but because she knew how to style her hair to the best effect, and even at fourteen she was a stunner. She could speak to men of any age, something that scared me to death; but all I needed to do was stand in her shadow, and people would come up and speak to us both. So it was a good time. We had a fiddle player, Sam, then there was Paddy on the piano. They were brothers and could have been anywhere between twenty and thirty, I have no idea. Matty Wilson was older, lead singer and the founder, I think; a real character, with plenty of chat for the dancers between songs. He was the reason we got so many bookings, and although the original lineup had changed after the war, they were still in demand. And Ned on the drums. I did love it. The lads took great care of us; it was like having four big brothers, and, you know, people applauding you, dancing to music you are creating, it's quite addictive. It might have lasted well into adulthood, if things hadn't turned out the way they did. I suppose that's what you really want to hear about.

"You know, I wasn't a fool. Trudy and I knew bits and pieces about sex, we were always talking about boys and dresses and who was good-looking enough to consider a second glance, so I can't attach innocence to any of it. Once or twice the band had to steer would-be suitors away from us, as a night of music and alcohol made even quiet young men brave enough to take their chances. And even this was fine by me, because fantasy was much less scary than reality in that department. As it was, I had just seen the *Dam Busters* and was totally in love with Richard Todd, so life was mainly helping at home, singing to keep the boredom to an acceptable level and dreaming of a life as an airman's wife. I wasn't precocious and Trudy, although easy-going and quite flirty, was absolutely straight down the line. Nothing like that was happening until a ring was on her finger, and she made sure everyone knew it. Matty used to tease her about the string of hopeful hearts she was wearing around her neck in the place of pearls, but she never strayed.

"I'm trying to paint a picture here, but maybe I should just tell it as it was and then you can ask anything you want. Here it is.

"Matty Wilson loved an audience, and the feeling was mutual. Wherever we went, girls would hang back while we were packing up our stuff; and Trudy, at more than fifteen years his junior, felt it her duty to 'protect' him from any untoward attention, which he seemed to accept with a kind of pride. Paddy and Sam had steady girlfriends, sisters in fact, so they more or less huddled together at the end of a concert, staying just long enough so as not to be criticised for rushing away and shirking responsibilities. That left Ned and I. I remembered him from school, which must have made him around eighteen. Where I live now, folk would call Ned a canny lad. But they were all canny lads, otherwise I don't think we would have lasted as a band for so long. Nobody likes arrogance, even in entertainers, and I loved everyone in that band. I just happened to share more moments with Ned, that's all.

"His dad had a car, and if my mum was unavailable, he would drive Trudy and me home. Of course, this could only happen once Trudy had ensured that Matty's honour was safe, and so we always had a little catch-up time with each other, waiting for her. I was never afraid of Ned, never even suspected that he liked me that much, because the band was the band. We were a group who sung together, and that was it. Usually, we played north of here where Matty was well known, and so I would get dropped off before Trudy, who lived in Duncan. But on a couple of occasions we found ourselves enjoying a journey of just the two of us. Do you want me to say that I loved him? Well, I did love him in that initial 'what-do-you-think-of' way, the kind of love that develops because you realise you have the same opinions and both find that a marvellous thing; and although he looked nothing like Richard Todd, I would watch his mouth while he spoke and wondered what it would be like to kiss it.

"On our third 'solo' journey, I waited until he had stopped his car at a crossroads and just leaned over and kissed him. If I was worried that he would be shocked or offended, his face put me at ease at once. He grinned and grinned, even more so when I asked him to stop well before we reached my house. He was a good kisser. He said I was, too. So, in the next few weeks, I made sure we made eye contact whenever possible, even asked him if he would teach David the drums in the hope that I could see him more than twice a week. Our first time was about a month later, as we were heading into the fall. James was sick with the flu, Mum couldn't drive me to rehearsal, and I could not believe my luck. More than that, Trudy's uncle was visiting and she couldn't make it. If ever there was a time to recognise signs, that was it. I made up my mind. Ned didn't stand a chance.

"He was very anxious, totally unsure. Yes, he loved kissing me, and yes, he loved me as a friend, but he didn't think either of us were ready for anything like that. I've had a lifetime to analyse why I did what I did; and, I'll admit to you, all I could think about at the time was that I had been given an opportunity to feel special, more special than Trudy would let herself feel, and I wanted to be a step ahead of her for once. Ned was a young man, a man with just as many feelings as I had, and so we gave it our best shot. I loved him before that night and I loved him afterwards. But we had only one other night like that before I realised what was happening. And immediately I cut him dead. It was cruel and awful, but nowhere near as awful as it would have been if my dad had found out who was responsible. I had to make sure there was no connection to him, so I left the band because my mum 'needed me at home,' and nobody was allowed near the house.

"I'm not sure even now if Ned knew what had happened, because by the time I told my parents, I had even stopped babysitting, and not even Trudy visited. She tried a couple of times, but was turned away. It was so important to them that I should be protected from other's opinions, I realise that now; but all I thought at the time was that my world had ended, and I was being hidden away. That year, my life was only lived for you, growing you and trying to plan for the future, within the parameters allowed by my family. My dad was so angry that I wouldn't tell him anything, but since they didn't want everybody knowing, they didn't go asking around, either. All he did say was that no groom meant no wedding, and so no baby. But he would have hurt Ned, I know that, because I was too young. Far too young. Ned was a lovely man and people would have condemned him, not me, so I couldn't hurt him, nor could I let him be hurt.

"I suppose you're thinking that it was okay to hurt you instead. It wasn't like that at all. I had spent hours and hours of time willing things to work out, because I knew before you were born that it was going to change again. My dad had presented me with a chance to return to my original life, by taking the whole family back across the sea. That was a major undertaking for them, and I was just as guilty as I was grateful; but it felt like at least they still cared enough, and that became the most important thing to me: to know that I hadn't disappointed them too much. So really, we were making plans to move, and I will be honest, I was looking forward to going. The icing on the cake, if you can call it that, was that Rose wanted you so much, and I loved Rose. They were desperate for David to have a brother or sister, and I knew he would be the best big brother. So, it began to look like an easy solution.

"But then you were born, and the time I had with you was unfeasibly short. They gave me two full weeks. I couldn't believe what was going to happen. I mean, at one point even my father seemed to find you intriguing, and I had a tiny moment of hope that you could stay. But the 'escape route' remained non-negotiable and final. I was going to get on a plane and disappear, and I was going to have to leave your little body behind. You had barely had time to open your eyes, and I was going to have to let you go. I had even learned to put my small arms around your body, which wasn't as easy as you might think, because you had long legs which wouldn't stop moving. But Rose was so good to me. At first she would just watch us together, then I started to let her hold you, and then she simply took you away. You were a couple of miles down the road, in someone else's arms, and I couldn't do anything about it. A month later we were gone.

"I asked Rose not to keep in touch, because the thought of hearing what I was missing made me physically sick. But we had an agreement. We would always know where the other person was, just in case some day you wanted to find out more. The only thing that made sense out of all of it was that you would be with David. I don't think I even considered Ned in this, I had cut him out of it and only thought of him the once, when you were first born, because it really wasn't fair that he didn't know that he had such a perfect son. I have no idea what happened to him. I told nobody at all about him, yet Kate seemed to think Rose knew who he was. I suppose she must have spent the odd moment wondering whose son she was raising, but I never mentioned his name to anyone, before or after. Ned had to be safe and I had to be safe. I knew you would be safe, so life carried on."

《•》《•》《•》

Pausing by the gateposts which signalled the entrance to The Edge's estate, Neil ran his hand over the wood, then stooped to clear some of the weeds away from the base. The red wood stood brightly against the dark green of the forest, and Winnie stepped up to them, taking in all four of the sides and remarking on the craftsmanship. Neil screwed up his eyes.

"It took me a long time, you should have seen the first attempt. But I needed to concentrate completely on something during the worst couple of years. And I couldn't let myself forget what I'd done. Anyway, Kate loves them. David understands what they're all about, and yet he still lets them stand here."

Winnie let her eyes roam the area. The highway, although close, was mercifully free from traffic, and the trees themselves were upright and uncomplicated. No noise, no drama. It made a pleasant change, and she was not sure she wanted to pollute it with more explanations; but she was equally sure that she had not expressed nearly well enough the feelings which had accompanied her life without him. The pine scent in the air and the sun on her face made her want to throw her arms out to catch it all, but she risked appearing unhinged and so she inhaled deeply instead, hoping that the extra oxygen would allow the telling of her story to continue.

"I guess we've both learned lessons the hard way, but seeing you here, seeing Kate and the way you are with those little poppets, how could I possibly have any regrets? All I really wanted was to have this opportunity, some day. Not to walk back into your life, but to listen to Rose's experiences and let her tell me how wonderful a son you had been. Hopefully see your face as an adult. Now that she's gone, I see it all. It's not the same, but it will do, and it means everything."

Neil began to walk down the driveway. "Let's go back. It's quite a hike on foot."

Winnie followed him, matching his easy pace, remembering the kinks in the driveway which only allowed you to see so far. She wondered how her own childhood home had stood the test of time, and if someone had made it into a happy, family home in her absence.

"You married at some point," Neil stated, indicating her wedding ring.

"Yes, when I was twenty-five. Sandy Port. He passed away in his early fifties. Heart attack, no warning at all. We argued morning, noon and night, but I loved him to bits."

Neil kicked at a large piece of gravel, and they both watched it tumble and roll to a halt before she spoke again.

"I have a daughter. Emma. She's thirty-five."

Neil's feet did not stop but he turned his face towards the woman, then also turned his mouth into a smile. He raised his eyebrows slightly, then slipped his hands into his jeans pockets and shook his head, laughing.

"Man, you couldn't have given me another brother? Thank God for David and Ally. That's all I can say."

Chapter 29
Vancouver Island

In Rose's sitting room, Kate was lying on the sofa. The room was not cold, apparently nobody had thought to turn the heating from timed to off, but it was empty and it was quiet. It was the only place she could be, where she could think and where she could try to ride the waves of guilt as they came at her, one at a time. The ceiling was still a brilliant white, not sullied in any way by the smoke of the wood burner, so obviously Dave had fitted it efficiently enough. She thought she might like to look at that ceiling for the rest of the day at least. Her neck hurt slightly, probably from the plane and then the stress of the night, but what did it matter? It didn't matter if she contracted yellow fever, things could not be any worse than they were at this moment. Rose was gone from them. It was just wrong.

She removed the fleece throw from the back of the sofa and arranged it around her. The clock informed her that minutes were passing, but time had long since ceased to be any kind of ally. She had been without her husband or son for almost three weeks and had missed them on a daily basis. Within an hour of seeing them, she had felt lonelier than she had since the Bad Year, and so the hours could do their worst. She was useless, she served little purpose; and somehow, seconds or minutes or hours down the road, she was going to have to face her entire family with these facts, at least those who were left. She had abandoned Rose at the end of her life, and she was hiding from the woman's family. She had to start thinking straight.

Today, or maybe tomorrow if she was lucky enough to be left alone until then, she needed to have discussions with David on how to talk to Alasdair. They needed to be together. They needed to be sensitive.

They needed to say the words "Neil is not actually your uncle, he is your mom's dad. Oh, and while we're on the subject, your dad was once married to your mom's mom." If that did not send him into some sort of screaming fit, then he was a better man than all of them. She could not do it alone. She was a coward and could not even attempt the words if David was not on her side. David was not on her side, she was almost positive about this. David was at last realising that being married to an irresponsible, thoughtless, capable-of-seeing-only-one-perspective moron was less than acceptable. He was apparently sharing his life with a foolish person, who was constantly testing his patience and actually contributing very little to his life except company. She wondered at what point this had begun to dawn on him, but it was too confusing a thread to follow. Better just to stare at the ceiling and keep warm.

She was a terrible mother. Alasdair was no doubt fed and comfortable and would be talking to whoever occupied The Edge about some weird and wonderful subject. But he was also probably, hopefully, missing her and wondering where she was. She needed to open up her cosy cocoon and start the walk back through the woods. They had been spectacular this morning, the trees, and the needles under her feet. Her feet had ached in spite of the spongy moss. Everything had ached. Everything still ached, nothing made sense, and she was hiding from it all. Alasdair would be wondering where she was.

She liked the way the sun was hitting the circular cross sections of wood on the fireplace wall. Did they warm up when the fire was on? She had never investigated this, in all the evenings she had spent chewing the fat with Rose; and that was really upsetting, because Rose was now missing. She was permanently going to be missing, just like her mother had been, and Kate could hardly bear it. Rose had been such a good friend to her, loving her from the beginning in spite of her doubts. Ally would miss out on her face, her company and her memories, and Rose would not see him grow. She was indeed unexpectedly and abruptly gone.

The last time she had felt as grief-stricken as this, David had been her saviour. But he was now aware of how she worked, and maybe that knowledge was about to prove fatal. She loved him so much. Rose had loved him, too. His presence was everywhere in this room, from the photographs to the bookshelves to the perfectly fitted stovepipe. His mother had projected him and her entire unique family onto every surface and wall. The room, for all its relatively short life span, was crammed with mementos. Yet it was nothing but dead when there was nobody there to look on them fondly and smile. It was a dead space.

Kate let her mind slip away from the Wilder-soaked mausoleum around her, and as she closed her eyes, she tried to put Neil and Winnie in the same frame. Winnie seemed a reasonably sociable person, she had been able to talk to her stranger-cum-granddaughter well enough; so maybe if Neil let her stay in the same room as him, there might be the chance of a connection. He was certainly a different man these days. Different from the nervy/laid-back enigma of their early encounters, but did she really have a clue as to what he would make of this? And who had set it all up, who had taken one woman's idea, compiled it with another woman's desire and shoved it in the face of a man who had only just recently thought himself strong enough to meet life full on? She had. She had done it, in all her glory. Kate bit her lip. Lessons learned, that was a joke and a half.

She was self-centred. David had married a self-centred, egotistical tyrant who needed to constantly show people how amazing she was. Ironically, she was also someone who could not be bothered to get up and sort out the mess she had created. Yet why should she even be surprised that she had turned into this person? She was weak and childish. Kate put her head under the fleece where it was stuffy and dark. It reminded her of the travel rug her mum would drape over her whenever she was sick. Back then, it had muffled every annoying distracting sound, and she needed that now.

"Oh, for God's sake, Kate!" she screamed, throwing the fleece through the air and jumping to her feet. "I hate you so much sometimes!"

In her coat pocket, her mobile phone was switched to silent. There were three missed calls and a recorded message. The frustration she felt would not allow her to listen to a voice she could not reply to, but she gave herself permission to look at the time. She had left their house three hours previously, and either they had never considered that she would take refuge in this place, or they had decided that life was easier without her. Well, they were right. But the place was suffocating her. Kate pulled her coat on and let herself quietly out of the back door, just as she had let herself in, willing Jessie Morgan to be far from the place. The driveway was indeed deserted, and, gratefully, she jogged to the safety of the wood. Once amongst the trees, she could easily go off the path and wander through the brush. She only needed to find a quiet spot for two or three more minutes, before she found the appropriate face and words to take back with her to The Edge.

Before her, on the path, stood David. He was staring straight at her and she stopped immediately. How long had he been outside, had he been searching, had he been calling her name, was he even pleased to see her? She thought that he might have changed clothes since the last time she had spoken to him, but could not be positive about this. She wasn't sure of much that had happened since their return home, only that she had yet to touch him. But he was there, completely motionless, hands by his side, and she recognised the stance. It was one of uncertainty, because she was holding her body in the same way, not sure whether to run forward or slope back. His head was uncovered, he wore no coat, but his jeans were clean, and his Shetland jumper must surely be irritating his neck. His boots were not even laced. His face was more relieved than happy. When he spoke, only his mouth moved.

"Where were you?"

Kate swallowed. "I went to Rose's. I didn't mean … I just wanted to be somewhere else."

His feet still made no movement, but he began to slowly massage his right knuckles in his left hand. It was the most familiar action she had seen him take since her return, but it did not help her to break the silence. She had no idea what to say to him. If she was strong, it might make her appear cold. If she was weak, he might question their whole time together. As she looked over his hair, his eyes, his mouth, Kate suddenly had the clearest thought of the past month, and because it was so very crystal in appearance, she knew it could not be fought against. No more hiding, or trying to excuse or justify her actions. It was time. He deserved to know what was behind all of her good intentions, and he deserved to know now, before he silently condemned her on the evidence of the past week alone. She finally spoke when he was about to start massaging his other hand.

"David," Kate's voice sounded hollowed out. "I don't know how to do this. Not properly, anyway."

She watched his eyes take on their worried shape as he folded his arms. She could have cried at the softness of his voice.

"What don't you know, Kitty?"

Kate felt her insides begin to shudder– the oddest sensation which usually hit her when her emotions seemed unable to stay within their own confinements and insisted on jumping the fences and joining in one great universal game of tag. Her breath was coming out in shallower and shallower gasps as she tried to stop herself wailing. It was too soon to cry, she had not yet said her piece. But as she tried to tell him her problem, the tears did form a slow, silent accompaniment to her words.

"I don't know how to be this person anymore," she let her head fall slightly, no longer sure if she should even be looking at him. "I hoped I was a good mother, but I left my son today to cope with sadness. I thought I might be a good daughter-in-law, but I wasn't there for her. I tried to be a good friend to Neil, but I put him in a dangerous situation. All that is bad enough. But," Kate looked up, "I know I used to be a good wife, Dave. I used to be able to give you everything, yet I walked away from you at the worst time. It's pitiful."

Kate shrugged her own acceptance of the facts, and, very slowly, she turned away from him and rubbed her cheeks dry with the heels of her hands. Best just to walk back to Rose's house and try to choke down the pain in her throat. She took a step in that direction but found her vision blurring yet again. If she had any strength left in her body, she had to find it now. Perhaps if David watched her move sedately away instead of running for the hills, he might still respect some part of her. Her feelings had been the rawest, most honest she had shared with him. There had been no bold statement of intent, no assurances that life could not and never would be able to break her, and no promises of a better existence to come if he would only believe in her. Those words had belonged to the child of ten years ago, when she had permanently been ready for battle.

Today she knew better. She knew she was vulnerable and ridiculous, as indeed her whole family did. She also knew that she still sought a parent's wisdom and that nobody was there to deal it out, and she knew that she had yet to tell him her truth, but her courage was failing her as she ached. Finally she moved one foot in front of the other and could see the edge of the wood ahead of her. Her tiny goal was achievable. She felt David's hand take hers from her side.

"Come on," his voice was low, as he walked her back across the driveway to the house she had just abandoned.

The spare key she had used on Rose's back door had a tartan lanyard, and as the coloured silk hung down from the keyhole, Kate supposed that the next owner would probably untie it and throw it away. She must remove it long before that was allowed to happen, and keep it safe. In the kitchen, David looked around him and automatically felt the radiator. Kate imagined he, too, was thinking of the immediate practicalities; and as she watched him, he opened the wall cupboard and flicked off the heating. So as not to appear as dead as a standing stone, Kate removed her coat and hung it on the chair. With nothing further to do but wait for him to say what he thought, she sat down.

"You should know," he leaned both hands on the back of the chair opposite as he spoke, "Neil is fine. He seems non-plussed, but not angry or upset. They've gone home. They'll be back sometime over the weekend. You haven't hurt him."

"Where is Winnie ... em, Freddie?"

David's eyes glinted for just a second. "Al is showing her his keys. And his ceramic dogs. Bertuzzi is joining in."

Still Kate did not smile. "I thought it was going to be Rose and Winnie, blethering and laughing. That's how I saw it. Rose was going to explain it all to Neil and everyone ..." Kate sniffed loudly, shaking the tears away aggressively, "everyone was finally going to be happy and ... full."

As David watched, his wife clenched her right fist and pressed it firmly against her teeth. Her eyes were tightly shut, but before she could permanently mark her own skin, David pulled her hand away and held it. There was a pine table between them, but at least he was holding her hand.

"Kitty, I know you–"

"You don't know anything," Kate interrupted, standing, her hand detaching from his instantly. "That's how I saw that part of it. But that's not why I did it, and when I tell you, you're going to realise what a fraud I am, what a bloody child I am, Dave. But if I don't tell you, we're never going to be real ever again."

Kate retreated to the sitting room, leaving David suddenly wishing he had left the heating alone. There was a real chill spreading through his gut, and when he heard her thundering up the wooden stairs, boots and all, he had no option but to follow her. He found her in Rose's plant-dominated bathroom, trying to unpick the end of a new roll of toilet tissue. The plants sagged sadly, devoid of water if not light; and as Kate blew her nose and flushed the rubbish away, David stood right next to her. At last, Kate felt she was breathing the same air but could not risk contact before she had said what was on her mind. He tried to help her out.

"Tell me then. It's me, Kit."

Kate sat on the edge of the bath, amidst the drooping leaves of the neglected vegetation, and focussed on the man's hand. It hung by his side, at her eye level. It was his right hand, and there was a smudge of ink on his thumb. Well, she had to tell him, and when she had, she deserved whatever came next.

"I really couldn't believe it, you know," Kate's lip wobbled as she spoke, "when you turned up at Neil's all those years ago, looking for me, saying you wanted what I wanted. But I knew I could make it work, as long as I stayed strong and never stopped making an effort."

As Kate wiped her nose and tried to swallow the tremor in her voice, David knelt beside her, real anxiety clouding his face. "You've had to put effort into this?"

Kate grabbed his face in both hands. "No! No, of course not. No, you have to believe me that's not what I meant. Loving you is all I do, it's so easy and still so amazing to me."

"Then what?"

"When Al was born, everything I felt for you multiplied and multiplied. Like somebody had squared it then … whatever the little three is called, did that to it, too. I wanted that again."

David removed her hands from his face and held them tight. "And we can have as many babies as you want."

"It wasn't having a baby," Kate shook her head, loving his hands cradling hers. "It was making you proud of me. Don't hate me, just listen for a minute."

Instead of protesting her words, David remained mute.

"Working for Andie, I wanted to show you I could do that and be a wife and mother. I know, I'm pathetic. But there's worse. Honestly, Hope was just as much for my benefit as it was for Hazel and Stu. And Winnie was just as much for my benefit as it was for Rose or Neil. Because I wanted you to think I was an incredible person. I wanted to prove to you that I was ..." she hesitated, but had to finish, "that I could be just as special ... as she was."

David, frowning, massaged her fingers in his. Kate wasn't sure if he was astounded by her deception or by her honesty, but she was pretty sure he had yet to catch the meaning of her last sentence. Suddenly, simultaneously, David's fingers stopped moving and his eyes opened wide. He tilted his head slightly and finally said, "No."

Kate nodded.

"No, Kate, no," David was on his feet, holding his head against the realisation.

"I know. It's appalling. I am appalling."

David began to pace the tiny bathroom, brushing through the "rainforest" like Dr Livingstone himself. Kate could say more, but needed some guidance on his state of mind. Eventually, he looked down at her face.

"Tell me you just made that up, because you couldn't think of anything else to say."

Kate felt the hurt in her chest and could not keep it from spreading to her face. "I can't do that."

When David swore, he never did it without feeling, but Kate had no idea which feeling was behind his present mutterings. She just sat with her head down, her fingers curved around the edge of the bath until eventually he pushed aside some of the foliage and leaned against the wall. The very worst thing about loving someone this much was when you had to sit in the silence of a reaction. It made the air tingle and the heart thump.

When David spoke at last, his voice was dull. "Did you think I was going to make comparisons? Did you really think that?"

Kate looked up at him, trying to find him in his odd, alien expression. "Let's be honest. She was your wife, too. I know how you felt about each other. How could you not compare us?"

David's eyes turned black, and Kate braced herself. But he did not speak. He stared ahead of him, letting his gaze wander over the shelves and plants and settle on the windowsill. His face was set; she watched him swallow something, hoping it was anger rather than hurt– anger she could possibly dilute, if he ever spoke to her again. When he did not, Kate stood up and cleared her throat.

"On the night of our wedding, you said that I was unique and that you hadn't … been with anyone in a long time. Do you remember?"

When David still did not open his mouth, Kate tried again. "The 'unique' part made me feel exactly that. The rest of it made me think about Mum. But that wasn't even a problem. It's never been a problem. I never wanted to beat her in any stakes. I just wanted you to love me as much as you had her."

After a moment, during which David's face remained unfathomable to her, he moved away from the wall, walked slowly out of the bathroom and along the landing. His steps were steady, he trailed his hand along the dado rail as he walked, and then, just as slowly, he sat down on the top stair. Kate watched him sit, saw him rest his chin in his palm. Was he about to explode or was he about to cry? Never having witnessed this in any form before, Kate felt the safest action was to ensure she could see his face. She walked up to him and sat beside him. His chin remained cradled in his left hand, his eyes closed. Again, he swallowed.

When David opened his eyes, Kate's body was near enough to embrace. He did not touch her, but studied her instead. Her face must have formed that particular concerned expression many times in all of her twenty-seven years, yet he had only seen it as an adult. He continued to appraise her, the woman who had walked beside him for the best parts of his life, had tossed aside the constraints of normality and encouraged unexpected delights into his house. She had done it all with confidence and a beautiful smile. He had not seen that smile for going on a month. David moved his right hand to her bottom lip and rubbed it gently, trying to tease the edges up. She kissed his thumb and tasted ink.

"I never compared you. You were nothing alike," he whispered.

As Kate held his hand against her cheek, he knew she deserved a fuller explanation. But just for a moment all he wanted to do was to look at her. She was still wearing her travel clothes, looking rumpled and more than a little exhausted; but the sight of her face in his presence still had the ability to ease his aches, and he had many aches at this particular time. He should be acknowledging that they were sitting in his mother's house, a place she would never grace again, but instead he was just looking, just being grateful. Her cheek was cool beneath his palm, and her knee was grazing his thigh as they sat.

"Fiona depended on me for everything, she followed my lead and tried to fit herself into my life. I loved her and we were both naive enough to think that we could just walk towards the future. I don't understand yet why she didn't think like that on that particular night. She took my faith from me. She shut me down. That was my time with her. But you," he dropped his hand to his side, "you slapped me in the face from the second you looked at me. You stood there, testing me, telling me what you thought, and most of the time I was a nervous wreck."

Kate bit her lip, internally cursing her own ridiculous carry on at the beginning of their relationship.

"Then suddenly you were asking instead of telling, then eventually trusting. I thought we could be okay with each other, but I died when you left. With us, it was much, much worse, because I knew we both wanted to be together. She never had your courage. She never had your determination or generosity. She certainly never had the guts to do what you've done in the last ten years, whatever your motives. You didn't try to fit into my life, you took my life and turned it on its head."

Kate could feel the tears but shook them away. She touched his knee.

"I'm sorry I wasn't here for you in the last week," Kate murmured. "I wanted Rose to see her again, and I wanted Winnie to see him. But nobody thought about you in any of it, did they? Have I ignored you, Dave? I don't even know if I have, which is unforgivable."

At last David put his arm along her shoulder. She moaned in relief and pressed her face into his neck.

"Oh, God, Davey. Tell me I haven't spoiled us. Please just tell me that much."

David could feel the shivers start to build as her lips moved against his skin. The heat from her words as she spoke confirmed that three weeks apart had not only taught him patience, but had also reminded him of the power of longing. He wanted her cradled against him, tucked into his arms, back in the embrace only she could create. But it was a time for honest words, and before he did another thing, he needed to give her something back, something to make them equal again.

"You could never spoil us, not by being you. The second cancels out the first." He kissed her temple. "I'm just amazed I haven't ruined us yet. I have my faults, I just never wanted to point them out, in case by some miracle you had yet to see them."

Kate sat forward and looked him in the eye. He held her gaze without fear, and she wondered if it was too soon to try and lighten the mood. Well, it was a day of taking risks, what was one more? She touched his cheek.

"This scar isn't a fault. I love it."

He smiled, but had no intention of letting himself off the hook. "I want you all to myself. I've tried to curb it and Ally has helped, because I don't mind sharing you with him. But sometimes, it's still difficult to watch you with others. You enchant them and I worry."

Kate frowned, fondly touching the hair on his chin. There were only so many words she could use in this area, and she had used them so many times before. He guessed her thoughts and shrugged his apology.

"Let's try a deal, then," Kate lay back against his arm. "I will be with you, in love with you, for the rest of our lives; and in return, you will be proud and happy to be my husband. That way, I can calm right down and stop trying to run the world. I'll be happy just being us. See, that was easy. So, is it a deal?"

"I love you."

Kate let him run his hands over her hair and thought it the most relaxing sensation. It allowed a little optimism into a day which had not truly moved on from heartache. She let her eyes close and thought of his hands, with their abused knuckles and tell-tale ink spot.

"Davey," she murmured, "please, will you wash my hair for me?"

Rose's landing had never seemed so bright; the walls seemed to spark and hum as they returned to the "jungle." Once more Kate sat on the edge of the bath, her mind and heart a million miles away from the last time she was there, as David unlaced her boots and peeled off her socks. She leaned forward at one point, wanting to kiss him on the mouth, but he made her stand instead. The sound of the shower running, the steam insistent upon making his image less clear, did not affect her, because he was pulling her sweatshirt gently over her head and unbuttoning her shirt. Still his mouth was evading her, and she began to worry that she would die before he let her have what she needed. When there was nothing left to clothe her, David helped her over the lip of the bath and handed her the shampoo. Before she could protest, he had hauled the jumper and T-shirt from his body and pulled off his boots and socks. Somehow there was nothing to protest about when he was standing so close to her.

He took the bottle from her hand and turned her away from him. She shivered as the suds ran down her shoulders and back, the water working its magic on the fragrant liquid being massaged over her scalp. She felt her hands reach out to the wall in front of her for support, watched as the water flowed from her face to where their bare feet were almost touching and wondered at how black his jeans had turned with the spray. She felt his hands move to the base of her spine, and finally he eased her round to face him. Her face was wet, his dry, and at last he was kissing her. Usually, Kate would throw her arms around his neck, but she did not have the strength to even reach up. So she gripped his wrists as he held her face, determined not to halt what was happening. Their feet were entwined, their body heat combined with that of the shower was almost too much, and suddenly David's mouth had released hers and he had stepped back, blinking and throwing water from his hair with two wild shakes.

"Kitty," he laughed. "This might work in the movies, but if I'd wanted to do this in a rainforest, I'd have shipped you to Borneo."

Normality had taken a holiday. Wet footprints on an upstairs carpet were perfectly acceptable, as was the discarding of sodden jeans in a rarely used spare room. It was okay that daylight was highlighting every glint in their eyes, and that Kate's hair was monsoon wet on a sunny day. It was not even noted that the sheets were icy cold on their radiator bodies. Such detail was not relevant when David's hands were at last on his wife's body, his head next to hers as she insistently demanded more kisses. Three weeks without her. He was tempted to ask her for the third time where she had been, but he could not speak. It did not matter. She was here, he was inside her, she was reaching her hands into his hair and she was shouting his name. What else was there in this ridiculous, unpredictable, incredible life?

CHAPTER 30

Vancouver Island

On the Saturday before Winnie's departure, The Edge was a reasonably passive place. Kate had taken Alasdair and his cousins to the library in Duncan, and David had decided that it was time to rotate the woodpile. Although it was not an unusual activity for the spring, it was exactly the type of task he took on when in a reflective mood, and nobody argued or even looked surprised when he announced his intention. Neil had taken all three dogs for a wander in the woods on the family's arrival and remained somewhere on the estate as the rain fell, thin but steady. It was still just a little too cool to sit on the porch swing, and so Andie invited Winnie to accompany her to Rose's house.

The sorting of Rose's possessions had taken Kate the best part of a week, and, finally, it was up to Neil and his partner to decide what they wished to make their own. The woman's will, although renewed in the last six months, dealt only with the house and the shares in the business. She had wished her personal items to go to whoever wanted them, had even stated this in the document itself, and urged them to share them as they thought fit. So far there had been no arguments, because it didn't seem to matter where they were, as long as they were with family. Kate had put aside several books, a couple of paintings and Rose's engagement ring for Hazel. Nobody had seemed overly keen on the glass paperweights, although Kate had thought that one perfectly matched the colour of Winnie's range cooker, and so it was slipped into her hands, irrespective of her own taste. Some days had been quiet, some had been riotous. Winnie had spent her time divided between The Edge and Port Alberni, and if Kate were to be honest, the easiest days had been when she and David alone had tackled the job. It had not mattered if they had burst out laughing at some ridiculous item, or the story attached to it, but when others were present, it had felt inappropriate. Now it was Andie's turn to pack their allocations, and Winnie seemed delighted to be asked to help.

Andie had lit the fire on entering the silent archive of a house to make the task more pleasant, but Winnie was pleased just to be reviewing and revisiting little scraps of memories as she packed the items for keeping into movable, named boxes. Occasionally, the woman would share these with Andie, just because there was joy in sharing.

"What do you think of him, then?" Andie suddenly asked, as she taped bubble wrap around the final painting. Winnie looked up, wondering if the question was as basic as it sounded, or if Andie was asking from a deeper level. "I mean, is he what you'd hoped for?"

Winnie finished wrapping the small figurine she had admired as a teenager and laid it aside, rubbing her hands free of a piece of stray Sellotape. It was a reasonable question, and she supposed that if anyone should have views on displaced children, then it might indeed be Andie. But where did she start?

"Oh, my dear," said Winnie, leaning both hands on the bureau. "Will it sound really strange to say that I didn't take it that far? I handed him over, I gave him away; and all I really thought about in all these years was how soft his hair was and how his little fists would find his mouth when he needed feeding. I didn't hope for anything. I just wanted to hold him again."

"Oh," Andie seemed thrown a little. "Well, I guess I can see that. I've never really known a newborn, but I can see how you would get used to a little body and how it felt."

"When Kate showed me his photograph, I did allow myself to imagine him properly for the first time. But the plan was to reconnect with Rose and then ask him if he wanted to take it further. It had to be up to him. Didn't turn out like that, though. I'm sorry."

Before Andie could begin to protest the need for an apology, the back door opened, and Neil called out to whoever may be around. Andie, who had spent three or four days watching Winnie react to the man's voice, caught her eye and they smiled at each other. Winnie was the incomer, was here at the invitation of the Wilders, and was a woman who had lived a life full of as many dramas as the rest of them. Yet they had asked her very little about anything except those which involved Neil. She was more than one-dimensional. Perhaps it was time to ask her about the rest of her life, if they were ever going to keep this connection alive in the future. Andie put her hands on her hips and looked at Neil's figure in the doorway.

"Well, we're nearly done, of course, babe. How did you time it to perfection like that?"

Neil looked around at the sparse room, the boxes almost filled, the bubble wrap and newspaper and spread his hands.

"I have many such skills. Anyway, looks to me like there is plenty left to do."

Andie nodded at his point. "Well, you can start loading the truck, if it's stopped raining. Oh, and there are two boxes of photographs upstairs. Too heavy for us, babe."

Winnie watched him wander between the crates and up the stairs. She watched his hand on the banister, gripping and trailing, her eyes remaining on the stairway even when he was no longer visible. She felt no real need to move, enjoying instead the warm cushion of certainty within her heart; in another minute or two, her son was going to appear again, and she could watch him retrace his steps until he was once more in the same room. It was such a luxury, but one which she could afford on this, her last day.

"I'll tell you the truth, Andie," she smiled, still watching the stairs. "He's a gift. David called him that, and it's exactly what he is."

In Rose's bedroom, Neil did not allow himself to dwell on her absence. It was easy enough: He had never really pictured Rose in this house, anyway, and to his mind, her furniture still looked a little lost in the immaculately painted, beautifully basic room. There was nothing of her here, and so no need for him to prolong the job, trying to remember her face when he would pick her up and dance her around, just to bring her out of a blue mood. This day was for clearing the house and packing it away. There would be time to think of Rose when the woman downstairs had departed and when this house had been sold. Then he would allow himself time to grieve, to remember, maybe even reminisce with David. But not yet. Things were too new, and David needed to concentrate on Kate for a while. Instead, Neil picked up the nearest box and headed towards the door.

At the top of the stairs, Neil felt the base of the box start to give under the weight of the photo albums and frames, and he had to adjust his hands to keep it intact. Whoever had taped the bottom had seriously underestimated its strength and adhesive qualities, and by the time he had reached the foot of the stairs, his face was pink with effort. Just as he held the box in the direction of the bureau, its contents came clattering down onto the floor. Luckily for all concerned, Neil's curses were lost in the melee of noise, and in the next second, all three adults were kneeling on the floor, dusting off covers and checking that no glass was cracked or broken. Two of the frames had split, but the glass remained whole in all of them, and Neil took himself into the kitchen to try to find some tougher tape. Andie stood, assessed the collapsed box, and, deciding that it was past its best, went to find a replacement. When Neil came back into the sitting room, he stopped dead still, for there did not seem to be a way of competing with the thickened atmosphere.

Winnie was no longer kneeling, but standing by the window. She had left behind her the two broken frames, the arms of wood lying neatly in a pile with the two panes of glass stacked out of harm's reach on the bureau. The woman's head was bathed in weak sunlight and tipped downwards, her hands gripping the photo which had survived the smashing of its display. She was so completely still, studying the image, that Neil's curiosity began to outweigh the need to match her immobility. In the past two weeks they had tried, without any real awkwardness, to piece together their individual lives from the moment Neil had been born, and it had worked well enough. Speaking about the past had been quite a safe topic, as it had not required any decisions to be made. However, Winnie was most definitely reacting to something she had just seen, and Neil had walked in on it. Well, he had seen every photograph in this house, so whatever it was, he could help her with it. Time to have a contemporary conversation.

"What have you got there, then?" asked Neil, twirling the roll of tape in his hand.

Winnie did not seem startled by his voice, but she did look up at him with the wildest expression he had seen on her face. He glanced at the photo.

"Oh, hell, look at that one. I think I had some idea that I could ignore what was happening by getting my hair chopped and a professional shave."

Winnie seemed to be holding her breath, but in the next moment, her eyes flickered and she shook her head, not following his meaning.

"That," said Neil, finally removing the photograph from her hands, "was my fortieth birthday party."

If anything, the image was too dark to qualify as a memento, the dim lighting removing a lot of the clarity, but the subjects were close enough to recognise. Neil did indeed look younger than his party suggested, especially since the two men flanking him were about twenty years his senior. Standing in front of the three of them were Kate and a third stranger. She had a drumstick in her hand and was laughing, pointing the stick at Neil's smooth chin. Her companion held its twin loosely at his side and was smiling at her joke, whatever that joke might be. The flash had lit up only their faces, the crowd and the hall's interior disappearing into the background. Winnie was not interested in the background.

"Are these your friends?"

Neil looked again, more closely, at the people on show.

"Actually, they were the band. Kate insisted that a ceilidh was the only way to celebrate in style."

Winnie nodded, but dared not take the photograph back from him for fear that he would see how badly her hands were shaking. There were things to consider here. Things that could not be unsaid after the event, but more than that, there were her own feelings to acknowledge.

"It's not a bad one," Neil declared, holding it nearer to the window, "although I wouldn't have thought it merited a frame. Anyway, would you like it?"

"You know," Winnie croaked, "I bet Kate would appreciate it even more. It looks like a happy memory."

Shrugging, he moved away. "No doubt. She has some sort of obsession with photos. Likes to keep those memories close, I guess."

As Neil gathered together the arms of the frame and began to assess the best course of action, Winnie looked around at the empty room. She had harboured many desires in her lifetime and apparently was still finding things, even at her age, to wish for. At that moment, she wished for Rose's possessions to be sitting in their proper places and for the room to be warmed by the old lady's presence, instead of merely the stove. She wanted to share the incredible feeling inside her, to ask her how the whole situation had come about. To ask her who had taken the photo, and what had made her decide to frame a pretty mediocre attempt at capturing a moment. Winnie looked again at where the coloured image lay and tried to convince herself that she was mistaken, that she was looking for something which was not there. Yet she had not gone looking for anything. She had been wrapping ornaments.

Andie, delighted to find a sturdier, plastic container under the kitchen sink, came humming into the room and began to repack the rest of the spilled items, unaware that Winnie was no longer doing anything other than watching the pair of them at work. When Andie herself picked up the unframed photo, she hooted out loud.

"Oh, that was such a great night!" she cried, moving to Neil's side. "We should have another ceilidh, the girls would love it."

"Who took the photograph?" Winnie could not help herself.

Neil was about to answer, then looked at Andie for help. She shrugged and laughed.

"Not a clue," she replied. "David maybe? Or Rose."

Winnie smiled and turned away. She desperately needed some air, some space where she could breathe at the pace her body wished her to, without raising any alarms.

"Gosh," she announced, moving towards the kitchen, "it's warm in here. I should definitely invest in a Canadian stove. The wind fairly howls over the Cheviots some days."

Outside, Winnie wandered round to the front of the house and found a sunny spot, just to the right of the three wooden steps. She stopped then, leaning against the porch rail and letting her breath catch as it pleased. This was almost beyond belief, certainly beyond her comprehension, and yet somehow it felt joyous. There was pure joy in the knowledge that photographic evidence existed of a moment in time– a very significant moment in time– when Rose had made a connection and decided it was important enough to photograph and frame. Winnie grinned, remembering how whip smart Rose had always been, how tuned in she was to certain aspects of people, how she had initially recognised Ian and James as her brothers, from their facial expressions alone. Maybe she had even been gifted. She certainly had the gift of timing, deciding to make her presence felt one last time, in the shape of a poorly taped-up box. Winnie was still grinning when Neil joined her. Somehow, with the skill of a craftsman, he had fitted the broken frame back together and held it out to her.

"Kate has thousands of photos," he said, placing it in her hands. "You keep this one. It's got the date written on the back. I thought it could act like the tattoo on your wrist."

The smile Neil gave Winnie was tinged with embarrassment, probably at his own sentimental words. Or perhaps he feared her reaction. Whatever it was, she took the photograph and looked closely at the faces once again. There could be no more doubt; truly there had never really been any at all.

"It was Rose's writing, so I guess she was the photographer," stated Neil. "Maybe she liked it because somebody had finally cleaned up the hair on my chin."

"Maybe that was it," agreed Winnie and without thinking, touched Neil's face. He did not quite recoil, but she instantly pulled her hand away in any case. "I'm sorry."

"You're okay," the man replied and took a step back. Then, "Hey, got things to do."

"Thank you," said Winnie, holding up her gift, and had never meant the words more.

As he began to walk towards the back door, he called over his shoulder. "Oh, it also says 'Neil, Kate and Ned Patterson.' I guess he was one of the band members."

"I guess so," smiled Winnie, watching him bow his head to negotiate the door frame and disappear inside. She took in a breath and exhaled the words softly. "I guess he was the drummer."